MAPS IN A MIRROR

Volume One

MAPS IN A MIRROR

Volume One

The Short Fiction of Orson Scott Card

Orson Scott Card

A Legend Book

Arrow Books Limited
20 Vauxhall Bridge Road, London SW1V 2SA

An imprint of the Random Century Group

London Melbourne Sydney Auckland
Johannesburg and agencies throughout
the world

First published in the UK by Legend, 1991

This Legend edition 1992

1 3 5 7 9 10 8 6 4 2

© Orson Scott Card 1990

Phototypeset by Intype, London

Printed and bound in Great Britain by
Cox & Wyman Ltd, Reading, Berkshire

ISBN 0 09 988470 4

To Charlie Ben,
who can fly

Contents

THE HANGED MAN
Tales of Dread

FLUX
Tales of Human Futures

BOOK 1

THE HANGED MAN

TALES OF DREAD

INTRODUCTION

I can't watch horror or suspense movies in the theater. I've tried—but the tension becomes too much for me. The screen is too large, the figures are too real. I always end up having to get up, walk out, go home. It's more than I can bear.

You know where I end up watching those movies? At home. On cable TV. That little screen is so much *safer*. The familiar scenes of my home surround it. And when it gets too tense, I can flip away, watch reruns of *Dick Van Dyke* or *Green Acres* or some utterly lame depression-era movie until I calm down enough to flip back and see how things turned out.

That's how I watched *Aliens* and *The Terminator*—I never have watched them beginning-to-end. I realize that by doing this I'm subverting the filmmaker's art, which is linear. But then, my TV's remote control has turned viewing into a participatory art. I can now perform my own recutting on films that are too upsetting for my taste. For me, *Lethal Weapon* is much more pleasurable when intercut with fragments of *Wild and Beautiful on Ibiza* and *Life on Earth*.

Which brings us to the most potent tool of storytellers. Fear. And not just fear, but dread. *Dread* is the first and the strongest of the three kinds of fear.

It is that tension, that waiting that comes when you know there is something to fear but you have not yet identified what it is. The fear that comes when you first realize that your spouse should have been home an hour ago; when you hear a strange sound in the baby's bedroom; when you realize that a window you are sure you closed is now open, the curtains billowing, and you're alone in the house.

Terror only comes when you see the thing you're afraid of. The intruder is coming at you with a knife. The headlights coming toward you are clearly in your lane. The klansmen have emerged from the bushes and one of them is holding a rope. This is when all the muscles of your body, except perhaps the sphincters, tauten and you stand rigid; or you scream; or you run. There is a frenzy to this moment, a climactic power—but it is the power of release, not the power of tension. And bad as it is, it is better than dread in this respect: Now, at least, you know the face of the thing you fear. You know its borders, its dimensions. You know what to expect.

Horror is the weakest of all. After the fearful thing has happened, you see its remainder, its relics. The grisly, hacked-up corpse. Your emotions range from nausea to pity for the victim. And even your pity is tinged with revulsion and disgust; ultimately you reject the scene and deny its humanity; with repetition, horror loses its ability to move you and, to some degree, dehumanizes the victim and therefore dehumanizes you. As the sonderkommandos in the death camps learned, after you move enough naked murdered corpses, it stops making you want to weep or puke. You just do it. They've stopped being people to you.

This is why I am depressed by the fact that contemporary storytellers of fear have moved almost exclusively toward horror and away from dread. The slasher movies almost don't bother anymore with creating the sympathy for character that is required to fill an audience with dread. The moments of terror are no longer terrifying because we empathize with the victim, but are rather fascinating because we want to see what creative new method of mayhem the writer and art director have come up with. Ah— murder by shish-ka-bob! Oh, cool—the monster poked the guy's eye out from *inside* his head!

Obsessed with the desire to film the unfilmable, the makers of horror flicks now routinely show the unspeakable, in the process dehumanizing their audience by turning human suffering into pornographically escalating "entertainment." This is bad enough, but to my regret, too many writers of the fiction of fear are doing the same thing. They failed to learn the real lesson of Stephen King's success. It isn't the icky stuff that makes King's stories work. It's how much he makes you care about his characters before the icky stuff ever happens. And his best books are the ones like *The Dead Zone* and *The Stand* in which not that much horror ever happens at all. Rather the stories are suffused with dread leading up to cathartic moments of terror and pain. Most important, the suffering that characters go through *means something*.

That is the artistry of fear. To make the audience so empathize with a character that we fear what he fears, for his reasons. We don't stand outside, looking at a gory slime cover him or staring at his gaping wounds. We stand inside him, anticipating the terrible things that might or will happen. Anybody

5

can hack a fictional corpse. Only a storyteller can make you hope the character will live.

So: I don't write horror stories. True, bad things happen to my characters. Sometimes terrible things. But I don't show it to you in living color. I don't have to. I don't *want* to. Because, caught up in dread, you'll imagine far worse things happening than I could ever think up to show you myself.

EUMENIDES IN THE FOURTH FLOOR LAVATORY

Living in a fourth-floor walkup was part of his revenge, as if to say to Alice, "Throw me out of the house, will you? Then I'll live in squalor in a Bronx tenement, where the toilet is shared by four apartments! My shirts will go unironed, my tie will be perpetually awry. *See what you've done to me?*"

But when he told Alice about the apartment, she only laughed bitterly and said, "Not anymore, Howard. I won't play those games with you. You win every damn time."

She pretended not to care about him anymore, but Howard knew better. He knew people, knew what they wanted, and Alice wanted *him*. It was his strongest card in their relationship—that she wanted him more than he wanted her. He thought of this often: at work in the offices of Humboldt and Breinhardt, Designers; at lunch in a cheap lunchroom (part of the punishment); on the subway home to his tenement (Alice had kept the Lincoln Continental). He thought and thought about how much she wanted him. But he kept remembering what she had said the day she threw him out: If you ever come near Rhiannon again I'll kill you.

He could not remember why she had said that. Could not remember and did not try to remember because that line of thinking made him uncomfortable and one thing Howard insisted on being was comfortable with himself. Other people could spend hours and days of their lives chasing after some accommodation with themselves, but Howard was accommodated. Well adjusted. At ease. I'm OK, I'm OK, I'm OK. Hell with you. "If you let them make you feel uncomfortable," Howard would often say, "you give them a handle on you and they can run your life." Howard could find other people's handles, but they could never find Howard's.

It was not yet winter but cold as hell at three A.M. when Howard got home from Stu's party. A must attend party, if you wished to get ahead at Humboldt and Breinhardt. Stu's ugly wife tried to be tempting, but Howard had played innocent and made her feel so uncomfortable that she dropped the matter. Howard paid careful attention to office gossip and knew that several earlier departures from the company had got caught with, so to speak, their pants down. Not that Howard's pants were an impenetrable barrier. He got Dolores from the front office into the bedroom and accused her of making life miserable for him. "In little ways," he insisted. "I know you don't mean to, but you've got to stop."

"What ways?" Dolores asked, incredulous yet (because she honestly tried to make other people happy) uncomfortable.

"Surely you knew how attracted I am to you."

"No. That hasn't—that hasn't even crossed my mind."

Howard looked tongue-tied, embarrassed. He actually was neither. "Then—well, then, I was—I was wrong, I'm sorry, I thought you were doing it deliberately—"

"Doing what?"

"Snub—snubbing me—never mind, it sounds adolescent, just little things, hell, Dolores, I had a stupid schoolboy crush—"

"Howard, I didn't even know I was hurting you."

"God, how insensitive," Howard said, sounding even more hurt.

"Oh, Howard, do I mean that much to you?"

Howard made a little whimpering noise that meant everything she wanted it to mean. She looked uncomfortable. She'd do anything to get back to feeling right with herself again. She was so uncomfortable that they spent a rather nice half hour making each other feel comfortable again. No one else in the office had been able to get to Dolores. But Howard could get to anybody.

He walked up the stairs to his apartment feeling very, very satisfied. Don't need you, Alice, he said to himself. Don't need nobody, and nobody's who I've got. He was still mumbling the little ditty to himself as he went into the communal bathroom and turned on the light.

He heard a gurgling sound from the toilet stall, a hissing sound. Had someone been in there with the light off? Howard went into the toilet stall and saw nobody. Then looked closer and saw a baby, probably about two months old, lying in the toilet bowl. Its nose and eyes were barely above the water; it looked terrified, its legs and hips and stomach were down the drain. Someone had obviously hoped to kill it by drowning—it was inconceivable to Howard that anyone could be so moronic as to think it would fit down the drain.

For a moment he thought of leaving it there, with the big-city temptation to mind one's own business even when to do so would be an atrocity. Saving this baby would mean inconvenience: calling the police, taking care of the child in his apartment, perhaps even headlines, certainly a night of filling out reports. Howard was tired. Howard wanted to go to bed.

But he remembered Alice saying, "You aren't even human, Howard. You're a goddam selfish monster." I am not a monster, he answered silently, and reached down into the toilet bowl to pull the child out.

The baby was firmly jammed in—whoever had tried to kill it had meant to catch it tight. Howard felt a brief surge of genuine indignation that anyone could think to solve his problems by killing an innocent child. But thinking of crimes committed on children was something Howard was determined not to do, and besides, at that moment he suddenly acquired other things to think about.

As the child clutched at Howard's arm, he noticed the baby's fingers were fused together into flipper-like flaps of bone and skin at the end of the arm. Yet the flippers gripped his arms with an unusual strength as, with two hands deep in the toilet bowl, Howard tried to pull the baby free.

At last, with a gush, the child came up and the water finished its flushing action. The legs, too, were fused into a single limb that was hideously twisted at the end. The child was male; the genitals, larger than normal, were skewed off to one side. And Howard noticed that where the feet should be were two more flippers, and near the tips were red spots that looked like putrefying sores. The child cried, a savage mewling that reminded Howard of a dog he had seen in its death throes. (Howard refused to be reminded that it had been he who killed the dog by throwing it out in the street in front of a passing car, just to watch the driver swerve; the driver hadn't swerved.)

Even the hideously deformed have a right to live, Howard thought, but now, holding the child in his arms, he felt a revulsion that translated into sympathy for whoever, probably the parents, had tried to kill the creature. The child shifted its grip on him, and where the flippers had been Howard felt a sharp, stinging pain that quickly turned to agony as it was exposed to the air. Several huge, gaping sores on his arm were already running with blood and pus.

It took a moment for Howard to connect the sores with the child, and by then the leg flippers were already pressed against his stomach, and the arm flippers already gripped his chest. The sores on the child's flippers were not sores; they were powerful suction devices that gripped Howard's skin so tightly that it ripped away when the contact was broken. He tried to pry the child off, but no sooner was one flipper free than it found a new place to hold even as Howard struggled to break the grip of another.

What had begun as an act of charity had now become an intense struggle. This was not a child, Howard realized. Children could not hang on so tightly, and the creature had teeth that snapped at his hands and arms whenever they came near enough. A human face, certainly, but not a human being. Howard threw himself against the wall, hoping to stun the creature so it would drop away.

11

It only clung tighter, and the sores where it hung on him hurt more. But at last Howard pried and scraped it off by levering it against the edge of the toilet stall. It dropped to the ground, and Howard backed quickly away, on fire with the pain of a dozen or more stinging wounds.

It had to be a nightmare. In the middle of the night, in a bathroom lighted by a single bulb, with a travesty of humanity writhing on the floor, Howard could not believe that it had any reality.

Could it be a mutation that had somehow lived? Yet the thing had far more purpose, far more control of its body that any human infant. The baby slithered across the floor as Howard, in pain from the wounds on his body, watched in a panic of indecision. The baby reached the wall and cast a flipper onto it. The suction held and the baby began to inch its way straight up the wall. As it climbed, it defecated, a thin drool of green tracing down the wall behind it. Howard looked at the slime following the infant up the wall, looked at the pus-covered sores on his arms.

What if the animal, whatever it was, did not die soon of its terrible deformity? What if it lived? What if it were found, taken to a hospital, cared for? What if it became an adult?

It reached the ceiling and made the turn, clinging tightly to the plaster, not falling off as it hung upside down and inched across toward the light bulb.

The thing was trying to get directly over Howard, and the defecation was still dripping. Loathing overcame fear, and Howard reached up, took hold of the baby from the back, and, using his full weight, was finally able to pry it off the ceiling. It writhed and twisted in his hands, trying to get the suction

12

cups on him, but Howard resisted with all his strength and was able to get the baby, this time headfirst, into the toilet bowl. He held it there until the bubbles stopped and it was blue. Then he went back to his apartment for a knife. Whatever the creature was, it had to disappear from the face of the earth. It had to die, and there had to be no sign left that could hint that Howard had killed it.

He found the knife quickly, but paused for a few moments to put something on his wounds. They stung bitterly, but in a while they felt better. Howard took off his shirt; thought a moment and took off all his clothes, then put on his bathrobe and took a towel with him as he returned to the bathroom. He didn't want to get any blood on his clothes.

But when he got to the bathroom, the child was not in the toilet. Howard was alarmed. Had someone found it drowning? Had they, perhaps, seen him leaving the bathroom—or worse, returning with his knife? He looked around the bathroom. There was nothing. He stepped back into the hall. No one. He stood a moment in the doorway, wondering what could have happened.

Then a weight dropped onto his head and shoulders from above, and he felt the suction flippers tugging at his face, at his head. He almost screamed. But he didn't want to arouse anyone. Somehow the child had not drowned after all, had crawled out of the toilet, and had waited over the door for Howard to return.

Once again the struggle resumed, and once again Howard pried the flippers away with the help of the toilet stall, though this time he was hampered by the fact that the child was behind and above him. It was exhausting work. He had to set down the knife so

13

he could use both hands, and another dozen wounds stung bitterly by the time he had the child on the floor. As long as the child lay on it stomach, Howard could seize it from behind. He took it by the neck with one hand and picked up the knife with the other. He carried both to the toilet.

He had to flush twice to handle the flow of blood and pus. Howard wondered if the child was infected with some disease—the white fluid was thick and at least as great in volume as the blood. Then he flushed seven more times to take the pieces of the creature down the drain. Even after death, the suction pads clung tightly to the porcelain; Howard pried them off with the knife.

Eventually, the child was completely gone. Howard was panting with the exertion, nauseated at the stench and horror of what he had done. He remembered the smell of his dog's guts after the car hit it, and he threw up everything he had eaten at the party. Got the party out of his system, felt cleaner; took a shower, felt cleaner still. When he was through, he made sure the bathroom showed no sign of his ordeal.

Then he went to bed.

It wasn't easy to sleep. He was too keyed up. He couldn't take out of his mind the thought that he had committed murder (not murder, not murder, simply the elimination of something too foul to be alive). He tried thinking of a dozen, a hundred other things. Projects at work—but the designs kept showing flippers. His children—but their faces turned to the intense face of the struggling monster he had killed. Alice—ah, but Alice was harder to think of than the creature.

At last he slept, and dreamed, and in his dream

remembered his father, who had died when he was ten. Howard did not remember any of his standard reminiscences. No long walks with his father, no basketball in the driveway, no fishing trips. Those things had happened, but tonight, because of the struggle with the monster, Howard remembered darker things that he had long been able to keep hidden from himself.

"We can't afford to get you a ten-speed bike, Howie. Not until the strike is over."

"I know, Dad. You can't help it." Swallow bravely. "And I don't mind. When all the guys go riding around after school, I'll just stay home and get ahead on my homework."

"Lots of boys don't have ten-speed bikes, Howie."

Howie shrugged, and turned away to hide the tears in his eyes. "Sure, lot of them. Hey, Dad, don't you worry about me. Howie can take care of himself."

Such courage. Such strength. He had got a ten-speed within a week. In his dream, Howard finally made a connection he had never been able to admit to himself before. His father had a rather elaborate ham radio setup in the garage. But about that time he had become tired of it, he said, and he sold it off and did a lot more work in the yard and looked bored as hell until the strike was over and he went back to work and got killed in an accident in the rolling mill.

Howard's dream ended madly, with him riding piggy-back on his father's shoulders as the monster had ridden on *him*, tonight—and in his hand was a knife, and he was stabbing his father again and again in the throat.

15

He awoke in early morning light, before his alarm rang, sobbing weakly and whimpering, "I killed him, I killed him, I killed him."

And then he drifted upward out of sleep and saw the time. Six-thirty. "A dream," he said. And the dream had woken him early, too early, with a headache and sore eyes from crying. The pillow was soaked. "A hell of a lousy way to start the day," he mumbled. And, as was his habit, he got up and went to the window and opened the curtain.

On the glass, suction cups clinging tightly, was the child.

It was pressed close, as if by sucking very tightly it would be able to slither through the glass without breaking it. Far below were the honks of early morning traffic, the roar of passing trucks: but the child seemed oblivious to its height far above the street, with no ledge to break its fall. Indeed, there seemed little chance it would fall. The eyes looked closely, piercingly at Howard.

Howard had been prepared to pretend that the night before had been another terribly realistic nightmare.

He stepped back from the glass, watched the child in fascination. It lifted a flipper, planted it higher, pulled itself up to a new position where it could stare at Howard eye to eye. And then, slowly and methodically, it began beating on the glass with its head.

The landlord was not generous with upkeep on the building. The glass was thin, and Howard knew that the child would not give up until it had broken through the glass so it could get to Howard.

He began to shake. His throat tightened. He was terribly afraid. Last night had been no dream. The

16

fact that the child was here today was proof of that. Yet he had cut the child into small pieces. It could not possibly be alive. The glass shook and rattled with every blow the child's head struck.

The glass slivered in a starburst from where the child had hit it. The creature was coming in. And Howard picked up the room's one chair and threw it at the child, threw it at the window. Glass shattered and the sun dazzled on the fragments as they exploded outward like a glistening halo around the child and the chair.

Howard ran to the window, looked out, looked down and watched as the child landed brutally on the top of a large truck. The body seemed to smear as it hit, and fragments of the chair and shreds of glass danced around the child and bounced down into the street and the sidewalk.

The truck didn't stop moving; it carried the broken body and the shards of glass and the pool of blood on up the street, and Howard ran to the bed, knelt beside it, buried his face in the blanket, and tried to regain control of himself. He had been seen. The people in the street had looked up and seen him in the window. Last night he had gone to great lengths to avoid discovery, but today discovery was impossible to avoid. He was ruined. And yet he could not, could never have let the child come into the room.

Footsteps on the stairs. Stamping up the corridor. Pounding on the door. "Open up! Hey in there!"

If I'm quiet long enough, they'll go away, he said to himself, knowing it was a lie. He must get up, must answer the door. But he could not bring himself to admit that he ever had to leave the safety of his bed.

17

"Hey, you son-of-a-bitch—" The imprecations went on but Howard could not move until, suddenly, it occurred to him that the child could be under the bed, and as he thought of it he could feel the tip of the flipper touching his thigh, stroking and ready to fasten itself—

Howard leaped to his feet and rushed for the door. He flung it wide, for even if it was the police come to arrest him, they could protect him from the monster that was haunting him.

It was not a policeman at the door. It was the man on the first floor who collected rent. "You son-of-a-bitch irresponsible pig-kisser!" the man shouted, his toupee only approximately in place. "That chair could have hit somebody! That window's expensive! Out! Get out of here, right now, I want you out of this place, I don't care how the hell drunk you are—"

"There was—there was this thing on the window, this creature—"

The man looked at him coldly, but his eyes danced with anger. No, not anger. Fear. Howard realized the man was afraid of him.

'This is a decent place," the man said softly. "You can take your creatures and your booze and your pink stinking elephants and that's a hundred bucks for the window, a hundred bucks right now, and you can get out of here in an hour, an hour, you hear? Or I'm calling the police, you hear?"

"I hear." He heard. The man left when Howard counted out five twenties. The man seemed careful to avoid touching Howard's hands, as if Howard had become, somehow, repulsive. Well, he had. To himself, if to no one else. He closed the door as soon as the man was gone. He packed the few

18

belongings he had brought to the apartment in two suitcases and went downstairs and called a cab and rode to work. The cabby looked at him sourly, and wouldn't talk. It was fine with Howard, if only the driver hadn't kept looking at him through the mirror—nervously, as if he was afraid of what Howard might do or try. I won't try anything, Howard said to himself, I'm a decent man. Howard tipped the cabby well and then gave him twenty to take his bags to his house in Queens, where Alice could damn well keep them for a while. Howard was through with the tenement—that one or any other.

Obviously it had been a nightmare, last night and this morning. The monster was only visible to him, Howard decided. Only the chair and the glass had fallen from the fourth floor, or the manager would have noticed.

Except that the baby had landed on the truck, and might have been real, and might be discovered in New Jersey or Pennsylvania later today.

Couldn't be real. He had killed it last night and it was whole again this morning. A nightmare. I didn't really kill anybody, he insisted. (Except the dog. Except Father, said a new, ugly voice in the back of his mind.)

Work. Draw lines on paper, answer phone calls, dictate letters, keep your mind off your nightmares, off your family, off the mess your life is turning into. "Hell of a good party last night." Yeah, it was, wasn't it? "How are you today, Howard?" Feel fine, Dolores, fine—thanks to you. "Got the roughs on the IBM thing?" Nearly, nearly. Give me another twenty minutes. "Howard, you don't look well." Had a rough night. The party, you know.

He kept drawing on the blotter on his desk instead

of going to the drawing table and producing real work. He doodled out faces. Alice's face, looking stern and terrible. The face of Stu's ugly wife. Dolores's face, looking sweet and yielding and stupid. And Rhiannon's face.

But with his daughter Rhiannon, he couldn't stop with the face.

His hand started to tremble when he saw what he had drawn. He ripped the sheet off the blotter, crumpled it, and reached under the desk to drop it in the wastebasket. The basket lurched, and flippers snaked out to seize his hand in an iron grip.

Howard screamed, tried to pull his hand away. The child came with it, the leg flippers grabbing Howard's right leg. The suction pad stung, bringing back the memory of all the pain last night. He scraped the child off against a filing cabinet, then ran for the door, which was already opening as several of his co-workers tumbled into his office demanding, "What is it! What's wrong! Why did you scream like that!"

Howard led them gingerly over to where the child should be. Nothing. Just an overturned wastebasket, Howard's chair capsized on the floor. But Howard's window was open, and he could not remember opening it. "Howard, what is it? Are you tired, Howard? What's wrong?"

I don't feel well. I don't feel well at all.

Dolores put her arm around him, led him out of the room. "Howard, I'm worried about you."

I'm worried, too.

"Can I take you home? I have my car in the garage downstairs. Can I take you home?"

Where's home? Don't have a home, Dolores.

20

"My home, then. I have an apartment, you need to lie down and rest. Let me take you home."

Dolores's apartment was decorated in early Holly Hobby, and when she put records on the stereo it was old Carpenters and recent Captain and Tennille. Dolores led him to the bed, gently undressed him, and then, because he reached out to her, undressed herself and made love to him before she went back to work. She was naively eager. She whispered in his ear that he was only the second man she had ever loved, the first in five years. Her inept lovemaking was so sincere it made him want to cry.

When she was gone he did cry, because she thought she meant something to him and she did not.

Why am I crying? he asked himself. Why should I care? It's not my fault she let me get a handle on her . . .

Sitting on the dresser in a curiously adult posture was the child, carelessly playing with itself as it watched Howard intently. "No," Howard said, pulling himself up to the head of the bed. "You don't exist," he said. "No one's ever seen you but me." The child gave no sign of understanding. It just rolled over and began to slither down the front of the dresser.

Howard reached for his clothes, took them out of the bedroom. He put them on in the living room as he watched the door. Sure enough, the child crept along the carpet to the living room; but Howard was dressed by then, and he left.

He walked the streets for three hours. He was coldly rational at first. Logical. The creature does not exist. There is no reason to believe in it.

But bit by bit his rationality was worn away by

21

constant flickers of the creature at the edges of his vision. On a bench, peering over the back at him; in a shop window; staring from the cab of a milk truck. Howard walked faster and faster, not caring where he went, trying to keep some intelligent process going on in his mind, and failing utterly as he saw the child, saw it clearly dangling from a traffic signal.

What made it even worse was that occasionally a passerby, violating the unwritten law that New Yorkers are forbidden to look at each other, would gaze at him, shudder, and look away. A short European-looking woman crossed herself. A group of teenagers looking for trouble weren't looking for him—they grew silent, let him pass in silence, and in silence watched him out of sight.

They may not be able to see the child, Howard realized, but they see something.

And as he grew less and less coherent in the ramblings of his mind, memories began flashing on and off, his life passing before his eyes like a drowning man is supposed to see, only, he realized, if a drowning man saw this he would gulp at the water, breathe it deeply just to end the visions. They were memories he had been unable to find for years; memories he would never have wanted to find.

His poor, confused mother, who was so eager to be a good parent that she read everything. Her precocious son Howard read it, too, and understood it better. Nothing she tried ever worked. And he accused her several times of being too demanding, of not demanding enough; of not giving him enough love, of drowning him in phony affection; of trying to take over with his friends, of not liking his friends enough. Until he had badgered and tortured the woman until she was timid every time she spoke to him, careful and longwinded and she phrased everything in such a way that it wouldn't offend, and while now and then he made her feel wonderful by giving her a hug and saying, "Have I got a wonderful Mom," there were far more times when he put a patient look on his face and said, "That again, Mom? I thought we went over that years ago." A failure as a parent, that's what you are, he reminded her again and again, though not in so many words, and she nodded and believed and died inside with every contact they had. He got everything he wanted from her.

And Vaughn Robles, who was just a little bit smarter than Howard and Howard wanted very badly to be valedictorian and so Vaughn and Howard became best friends and Vaughn would do anything for Howard and whenever Vaughn got a better grade than Howard he could not help but notice that Howard was hurt, that Howard wondered if he was really worth anything at all. "Am I really worth anything at all, Vaughn? No matter how well I do, there's always someone ahead of me, and I guess it's just that before my father died he told me and told me, Howie, be better than your Dad. Be the top. And I promised him I'd be the top but hell, Vaughn, I'm just not cut out for it —" and once he even cried. Vaughn was proud of himself as he sat there and listened to Howard give the valedictory address at high school graduation. What were a few grades, compared to a true friendship? Howard got a scholarship and went away to college and he and Vaughn almost never saw each other again.

And the teacher he provoked into hitting him and losing his job; and the football player who snubbed

23

him and Howard quietly spread the rumor that the fellow was gay and he was obstracized from the team and finally quit; and the beautiful girls he stole from their boyfriends just to prove that he could do it and the friendships he destroyed just because he didn't like being excluded and the marriages he wrecked and the co-workers he undercut and he walked along the street with tears streaming down his face, wondering where all these memories had come from and why, after such a long time in hiding, they had come out now. Yet he knew the answer. The answer was slipping behind doorways, climbing lightpoles as he passed, waving obscene flippers at him from the sidewalk almost under his feet.

And slowly, inexorably, the memories wound their way from the distant past through a hundred tawdry exploitations because he could find people's weak spots without even trying until finally memory came to the one place where he knew it could not, could not ever go.

He remembered Rhiannon.

Born fourteen years ago. Smiled early, walked early, almost never cried. A loving child from the start, and therefore easy prey for Howard. Oh, Alice was a bitch in her own right—Howard wasn't the only bad parent in the family. But it was Howard who manipulated Rhiannon most. "Daddy's feelings are hurt, Sweetheart," and Rhiannon's eyes would grow wide, and she'd be sorry, and whatever Daddy wanted, Rhiannon would do. But this was normal, this was part of the pattern, this would have fit easily into all his life before, except for last month.

And even now, after a day of grief at his own life, Howard could not face it. Could not but did. He unwillingly remembered walking by Rhiannon's

24

almost-closed door, seeing just a flash of cloth moving quickly. He opened the door on impulse, just on impulse, as Rhiannon took off her brassiere and looked at herself in the mirror. Howard had never thought of his daughter with desire, not until that moment, but once the desire formed Howard had no strategy, no pattern in his mind to stop him from trying to get what he wanted. He was *uncomfortable*, and so he stepped into the room and closed the door behind him and Rhiannon knew no way to say no to her father. When Alice opened the door Rhiannon was crying softly, and Alice looked and after a moment Alice screamed and screamed and Howard got up from the bed and tried to smooth it all over but Rhiannon was still crying and Alice was still screaming, kicking at his crotch, beating him, raking at his face, spitting at him, telling him he was a monster, a monster, until at last he was able to flee the room and the house and, until now, the memory.

He screamed now as he had not screamed then, and threw himself against a plate-glass window, weeping loudly as the blood gushed from a dozen glass cuts on his right arm, which had gone through the window. One large piece of glass stayed embedded in his forearm. He deliberately scraped his arm against the wall to drive the glass deeper. But the pain in his arm was no match for the pain in his mind, and he felt nothing.

They rushed him to the hospital, thinking to save his life, but the doctor was surprised to discover that for all the blood there were only superficial wounds, not dangerous at all. "I don't know why you didn't reach a vein or an artery," the doctor said. "I think the glass went everywhere it could possibly go without causing any important damage."

After the medical doctor, of course, there was the psychiatrist, but there were many suicidals at the hospital and Howard was not the dangerous kind. "I was insane for a moment, Doctor, that's all. I don't want to die, I didn't want to die then, I'm all right now. You can send me home." And the psychiatrist let him go home. They bandaged his arm. They did not know that his real relief was that nowhere in the hospital did he see the small, naked, child-shaped creature. He had purged himself. He was free.

Howard was taken home in an ambulance, and they wheeled him into the house and lifted him from the stretcher to the bed. Through it all Alice hardly said a word except to direct them to the bedroom. Howard lay still on the bed as she stood over him, the two of them alone for the first time since he left the house a month ago.

"It was kind of you," Howard said softly, "to let me come back."

"They said there wasn't room enough to keep you, but you needed to be watched and taken care of for a few weeks. So lucky me, I get to watch you." Her voice was a low monotone, but the acid dripped from every word. It stung.

"You were right, Alice," Howard said.

"Right about what? That marrying you was the worst mistake of my life? No, Howard. *Meeting* you was my worst mistake."

Howard began to cry. Real tears that welled up from places in him that had once been deep but that now rested painfully close to the surface. "I've been a monster, Alice. I haven't had any control over

26

myself. What I did to Rhiannon—Alice, I wanted to die, I wanted to die!"

Alice's face was twisted and bitter. "And I wanted you to, Howard. I have never been so disappointed as when the doctor called and said you'd be all right. You'll never be all right, Howard, you'll always be—"

"Let him be, Mother."

Rhiannon stood in the doorway.

"Don't come in, Rhiannon," Alice said.

Rhiannon came in. "Daddy, it's all right."

"What she means," Alice said, "is that we've checked her and she isn't pregnant. No little monster is going to be born."

Rhiannon didn't look at her mother, just gazed with wide eyes at her father. "You didn't need to—hurt yourself, Daddy. I forgive you. People lose control sometimes. And it was as much my fault as yours, it really was, you don't need to feel bad, Father."

It was too much for Howard. He cried out, shouted his confession, how he had manipulated her all his life, how he was an utterly selfish and rotten parent, and when it was over Rhiannon came to her father and laid her head on his chest and said, softly, "Father, it's all right. We are who we are. We've done what we've done. But it's all right now. I forgive you."

When Rhiannon left, Alice said, "You don't deserve her."

I know.

"I was going to sleep on the couch, but that would be stupid. Wouldn't it, Howard?"

I deserve to be left alone, like a leper.

"You misunderstand, Howard. I need to stay here

27

to make sure you don't do anything else. To yourself or to anyone."

Yes. Yes, please. I can't be trusted.

"Don't wallow in it, Howard. Don't enjoy it. Don't make yourself even more disgusting than you were before."

All right.

They were drifting off to sleep when Alice said, "Oh, when the doctor called he wondered if I knew what had caused those sores all over your arms and chest."

But Howard was asleep, and didn't hear her. Alseep with no dreams at all, the sleep of peace, the sleep of having been forgiven, of being clean. It hadn't taken that much, after all. Now that it was over, it was easy. He felt as if a great weight had been taken from him.

He felt as if something heavy was lying on his legs. He awoke, sweating even though the room was not hot. He heard breathing. And it was not Alice's low-pitched, slow breath, it was quick and high and hard, as if the breather had been exerting himself.

Itself.

Themselves.

One of them lay across his legs, the flippers plucking at the blanket. The other two lay on either side, their eyes wide and intent, creeping slowly toward where his face emerged from the sheets.

Howard was puzzled. "I thought you'd be gone," he said to the children. "You're supposed to be gone now."

Alice stirred at the sound of his voice, mumbled in her sleep.

He saw more of them stirring in the gloomy corners of the room, another writhing slowly along the top of the dresser, another inching up the wall toward the ceiling.

"I don't need you anymore," he said, his voice oddly high-pitched.

Alice started breathing irregularly, mumbling, "What? What?"

And Howard said nothing more, just lay there in the sheets, watching the creatures carefully but not daring to make a sound for fear Alice would wake up. He was terribly afraid she would wake up and not see the creatures, which would prove, once and for all, that he had lost his mind.

He was even more afraid, however, that when she awoke she *would* see them. That was the one unbearable thought, yet he thought it continuously as they relentlessly approached with nothing at all in their eyes, not even hate, not even anger, not even contempt. We are with you, they seemed to be saying, we will be with you from now on. We will be with you, Howard, forever.

And Alice rolled over and opened her eyes.

QUIETUS

It came to him suddenly, a moment of blackness as he sat working late at his desk. It was as quick as an eye-blink, but before the darkness the papers on his desk had seemed terribly important, and afterward he stared at them blankly, wondering what they were and then realizing that he didn't really give a damn what they were and he ought to be going home now.

Ought definitely to be going home now. And C. Mark Tapworth of CMT Enterprises, Inc., arose from his desk without finishing all the work that was on it, the first time he had done such a thing in the twelve years it had taken him to bring the company from nothing to a multi-million-dollar-a-year business. Vaguely it occurred to him that he was not acting normally, but he didn't really care, it didn't really matter to him a bit whether any more people bought—bought—

And for a few seconds C. Mark Tapworth could not remember what it was that his company made.

It frightened him. It reminded him that his father and his uncles had all died of strokes. It reminded him of his mother's senility at the fairly young age of sixty-eight. It reminded him of something he had always known and never quite believed, that he was mortal and that all the works of all his days would trivialize gradually until his death, at which time his life would be his only act, the forgotten stone whose fall had set off ripples in the lake that would in time reach the shore having made, after all, no difference.

I'm tired, he decided. MaryJo is right. I need a rest.

But he was not the resting kind, not until that moment standing by his desk when again the blackness came, this time a jog in his mind and he remembered nothing, saw nothing, heard nothing, was falling interminably through nothingness.

Then, mercifully, the world returned to him and he stood trembling, regretting now the many, many nights he had stayed far too late, the many hours he had not spent with MaryJo, had left her alone in their large but childless house; and he imagined her waiting for him forever, a lonely woman dwarfed by the huge living room, waiting patiently for a husband who would, who must, who always had come home.

Is it my heart? Or a stroke? he wondered. Whatever it was, it was enough that he saw the end of the world lurking in the darkness that had visited him, and like the prophet returning from the mount things that once had mattered overmuch mattered not at all, and things he had long postponed now silently importuned him. He felt a terrible urgency that there was something he must do before—

Before what? He would not let himself answer. He just walked out through the large room full of ambitious younger men and women trying to impress him by working later than he; noticed but did not care that they were visibly relieved at their reprieve from another endless night. He walked out into the night and got in his car and drove home through

31

a thin mist of rain that made the world retreat a comfortable distance from the windows of his car.

The children must be upstairs, he realized. No one ran to greet him at the door. The children, a boy and a girl half his height and with twice his energy, were admirable creatures who ran down stairs as if they were skiing, who could no more hold completely still than a hummingbird in midair. He could hear their footsteps upstairs, running lightly across the floor. They hadn't come to greet him at the door because their lives, after all, had more important things in them than mere fathers. He smiled, set down his attaché case, and went to the kitchen.

MaryJo looked harried, upset. He recognized the signals instantly—she had cried earlier today.

"What's wrong?"

"Nothing," she said, because she always said Nothing. He knew that in a moment she would tell him. She always told him everything, which had sometimes made him impatient. Now as she moved silently back and forth from counter to counter, from cupboard to stove, making another perfect dinner, he realized that she was not going to tell him. It made him uncomfortable. He began to try to guess.

"You work too hard," he said. "I've offered to get a maid or a cook. We can certainly afford them."

MaryJo only smiled thinly. "I don't want anyone else mucking around in the kitchen," she said. "I thought we dropped that subject years ago. Did you — did you have a hard day at the office?"

Mark almost told her about his strange lapses of memory, but caught himself. This would have to be led up to gradually. MaryJo would not be able to

32

cope with it, not in the state she was already in. "Not too hard. Finished up early."

"I know," she said. "I'm glad."

She didn't sound glad. It irritated him a little. Hurt his feelings. But instead of going off to nurse his wounds, he merely noticed his emotions as if he were a dispassionate observer. He saw himself: important self-made man, yet at home a little boy who can be hurt, not even by a word, but by a short pause of indecision. Sensitive, sensitive, and he was amused at himself: for a moment he almost saw himself standing a few inches away, could observe even the bemused expression on his own face.

"Excuse me," MaryJo said, and she opened a cupboard door as he stepped out of the way. She pulled out a pressure cooker. "We're out of potato flakes," she said. "Have to do it the primitive way." She dropped the peeled potatoes into the pan.

"The children are awfully quiet today," he said. "Do you know what they're doing?"

MaryJo looked at him with a bewildered expression.

"They didn't come meet me at the door. Not that I mind. They're busy with their own concerns, I know."

"Mark," MaryJo said.

"All right, you see right through me so easily. But I was only a little hurt. I want to look through today's mail." He wandered out of the kitchen. He was vaguely aware that behind him MaryJo had started to cry again. He did not let it worry him much. She cried easily and often.

He wandered into the living room, and the furniture surprised him. He had expected to see the green sofa and chair that he had bought from Deseret

33

Industries, and the size of the living room and the tasteful antiques looked utterly wrong. Then his mind did a quick turn and he remembered that the old green sofa and chair were fifteen years ago, when he and MaryJo had first married. Why did I expect to see them? he wondered, and he worried again; worried also because he had come into the living room expecting to find the mail, even though for years MaryJo had put it on his desk every day.

He went into his study and picked up the mail and started sorting through it until he noticed out of the corner of his eye that something large and dark and massive was blocking the lower half of one of the windows. He looked. It was a coffin, a rather plain one, sitting on a rolling table from a mortuary.

"MaryJo," he called. "MaryJo."

She came into the study, looking afraid. "Yes?"

"Why is there a coffin in my study?" he asked.

"Coffin?" she asked.

"By the window, MaryJo. How did it get here?'

She looked disturbed. "Please don't touch it," she said.

"Why not?"

"I can't stand seeing you touch it. I told them they could leave it here for a few hours. But now it looks like it has to stay all night." The idea of the coffin staying in the house any longer was obviously repugnant to her.

"*Who* left it here? And why us? It's not as if we're in the market. Or do they sell these at parties now, like Tupperware?"

"The bishop called and asked me—asked me to let the mortuary people leave it here for the funeral tomorrow. He said nobody could get away to unlock

34

the church and so could we take it here for a few
hours—"

It occurred to him that the mortuary would not
have parted with a funeral-bound coffin unless it
were full.

"MaryJo, is there a body in this?"

She nodded, and a tear slipped over her lower
eyelid. He was aghast. He let himself show it. "They
left a corpse in a coffin here in the house with you
all day? With the kids?"

She buried her face in her hands and ran from the
room, ran upstairs.

Mark did not follow her. He stood there and
regarded the coffin with distaste. At least they had
the good sense to close it. But a coffin! He went
to the telephone at his desk, dialed the bishop's
number.

"He isn't here." The bishop's wife sounded irritated at his call.

"He has to get this body out of my office and out
of my house tonight. This is a terrible imposition."

"I don't know where to reach him. He's a doctor,
you know, Brother Tapworth. He's at the hospital.
Operating. There's no way I can contact him for
something like this."

"So what am I supposed to do?"

She got surprisingly emotional about it. "Do what
you want! Push the coffin out in the street if you
want! It'll just be one more hurt to the poor man!"

"Which brings me to another question. Who is
he, and why isn't his family—"

"He doesn't have a family, Brother Tapworth.
And he doesn't have any money. I'm sure he regrets
dying in our ward, but we just thought that even
though he had no friends in the world someone

35

might offer him a little kindness on his way out of it."

Her intensity was irresistible, and Mark recognized the hopelessness of getting rid of the box that night. "As long as it's gone tomorrow," he said. A few amenities, and the conversation ended. Mark sat in his chair staring angrily at the coffin. He had come home worried about his health. And found a coffin to greet him when he came. Well, at least it explained why poor MaryJo had been so upset. He heard the children quarreling upstairs. Well, let MaryJo handle it. Their problems would take her mind off this box, anyway.

And so he sat and stared at the coffin for two hours, and had no dinner, and did not particularly notice when MaryJo came downstairs and took the burnt potatoes out of the pressure cooker and threw the entire dinner away and lay down on the sofa in the living room and wept. He watched the patterns of the grain of the coffin, as subtle as flames, winding along the wood. He remembered having taken naps at the age of five in a makeshift bedroom behind a plywood partition in his parents' small home. The wood grain there had been his way of passing the empty sleepless hours. In those days he had been able to see shapes: clouds and faces and battles and monsters. But on the coffin, the wood grain looked more complex and yet far more simple. a road map leading upward to the lid. An engineering drawing describing the decomposition of the body. A graph at the foot of the patient's bed, saying nothing to the patient but speaking death into the trained physician's mind. Mark wondered, briefly, about the bishop, who was even now operating on someone

36

who might very well end up in just such a box as this.

And finally his eyes hurt and he looked at the clock and felt guilty about having spent so long closed off in his study on one of his few nights home early from the office. He meant to get up and find MaryJo and take her up to bed. But instead he got up and went to the coffin and ran his hands along the wood. It felt like glass, because the varnish was so thick and smooth. It was as if the living wood had to be kept away, protected from the touch of a hand. But the wood was not alive, was it? It was being put into the ground also to decompose. The varnish might keep it alive longer. He thought whimsically of what it would be like to varnish a corpse, to preserve it. The Egyptians would have nothing on us then, he thought.

"Don't," said a husky voice from the door. It was MaryJo, her eyes red-rimmed, her face looking slept in.

"Don't what?" Mark asked her. She didn't answer, just glanced down at his hands. To his surprise, Mark noticed that his thumbs were under the lip of the coffin lid, as if to lift it.

"I wasn't going to open it," he said.

"Come upstairs," MaryJo said.

"Are the children asleep?"

He had asked the question innocently, but her face was immediately twisted with pain and grief and anger.

"Children?" she asked. "What is this? And why tonight?"

He leaned against the coffin in surprise. The wheeled table moved slightly.

"We don't have any children," she said.

And Mark remembered with horror that she was right. On the second miscarriage, the doctor had tied her tubes because any further pregnancies would risk her life. There were no children, none at all, and it had devastated her for years; it was only through Mark's great patience and utter dependability that she had been able to stay out of the hospital. Yet when he came home tonight—he tried to remember what he had heard when he came home. Surely he had heard the children running back and forth upstairs. Surely—

"I haven't been well," he said.

"If it was a joke, it was sick."

"It wasn't a joke—it was—" But again he couldn't, at least didn't tell her about the strange memory lapses at the office, even though this was even more proof that something was wrong. He had never had any children in his home, their brothers and sisters had all been discreetly warned not to bring children around poor MaryJo, who was quite distraught to be—the Old Testament word?—barren.

And he had talked about having children all evening.

"Honey, I'm sorry," he said, trying to put his whole heart into the apology.

"So am I," she answered, and went upstairs.

Surely she isn't angry at me, Mark thought. Surely she realizes something is wrong. Surely she'll forgive me.

But as he climbed the stairs after her, taking off his shirt as he did, he again heard the voice of a child.

"I want a drink, Mommy." The voice was plaintive, with the sort of whine only possible to a child who is comfortable and sure of love. Mark turned at the landing in time to see MaryJo passing the top of the stairs on the way to the children's bedroom, a glass of water in her hand. He thought nothing of it. The children always wanted extra attention at bedtime.

The children. The children, of course there were children. This was the urgency he had felt in the office, the reason he had to get home. They had always wanted children and so there *were* children. C. Mark Tapworth always got what he set his heart on.

"Asleep at last," MaryJo said wearily when she came into the room.

Despite her weariness, however, she kissed him good night in the way that told him she wanted to make love. He had never worried much about sex. Let the readers of *Reader's Digest* worry about how to make their sex lives fuller and richer, he always said. As for him, sex was good, but not the best thing in his life; just one of the ways that he and MaryJo responded to each other. Yet tonight he was disturbed, worried. Not because he could not perform, for he had never been troubled by even temporary impotence except when he had a fever and didn't feel like sex anyway. What bothered him was that he didn't exactly care.

He didn't *not* care, either. He was just going through the motions as he had a thousand times before, and this time, suddenly, it all seemed so silly, so redolent of petting in the backseat of a car. He felt embarrassed that he should get so excited over a little stroking. So he was almost relieved when one of the children cried out. Usually he would say to ignore the cry, would insist on continuing the

39

lovemaking. But this time he pulled away, put on a robe, went into the other room to quiet the child down.

There was no other room.

Not in this house. He had, in his mind, been heading for their hopeful room filled with crib, changing table, dresser, mobiles, cheerful wallpaper—but that room had been years ago, in the small house in Sandy, not here in the home in Federal Heights with its magnificent view of Salt Lake City, its beautiful shape and decoration that spoke of taste and shouted of wealth and whispered faintly of loneliness and grief. He leaned against a wall. There were no children. He could still hear the child's cry ringing in his mind.

MaryJo stood in the doorway to their bedroom, naked but holding her nightgown in front her. "Mark," she said. "I'm afraid."

"So am I," he answered.

But she asked him no questions, and he put on his pajamas and they went to bed and as he lay there in darkness listening to his wife's faintly rasping breath he realized that it didn't really matter as much as it ought. He was losing his mind, but he didn't much care. He thought of praying about it, but he had given up praying years ago, though of course it wouldn't do to let anyone else know about his loss of faith, not in a city where it's good business to be an active Mormon. There'd be no help from God on this one, he knew. And not much help from MaryJo, either, for instead of being strong as she usually was in an emergency, this time she would be, as she said, afraid.

"Well, so am I," Mark said to himself. He reached over and stroked his wife's shadowy cheek, realized

40

that there were some creases near the eye, understood that what made her afraid was not his specific
ailment, odd as it was, but the fact that it was a
hint of aging, of senility, of imminent separation.
He remembered the box downstairs, like death
appointed to watch for him until at last he consented
to go. He briefly resented them for bringing death
to his home, for so indecently imposing on them;
and then he ceased to care at all. Not about the box,
not about his strange lapses of memory, not about
anything.

I am at peace, he realized as he drifted off to
sleep. I am at peace, and it's not all that pleasant.

"Mark," said MaryJo, shaking him awake. "Mark,
you overslept."

Mark opened his eyes, mumbled something so the
shaking would stop, then rolled over to go back to
sleep.

"Mark," MaryJo insisted.

"I'm tired," he said in protest.

"I know you are," she said. "So I didn't wake you
any sooner. But they just called. There's something
of an emergency or something—"

"They can't flush the toilet without someone holding their hands."

"I wish you wouldn't be crude, Mark," MaryJo
said. "I sent the children off to school without letting
them wake you by kissing you good-bye. They were
very upset."

"Good children."

"Mark, they're expecting you at the office."

Mark closed his eyes and spoke in measured
tones. "You can tell them and tell them I'll come in
when I damn well feel like it and if they can't cope

41

with the problem themselves I'll fire them all as incompetents."

MaryJo was silent for a moment. "Mark, I can't say that."

"Word for word. I'm tired. I need a rest. My mind is doing funny things to me." And with that Mark remembered all the illusions of the day before, including the illusion of having children.

"There aren't any children," he said.

Her eyes grew wide. "What do you mean?"

He almost shouted at her, demanded to know what was going on, why she didn't just tell him the truth for a moment. But the lethargy and disinterest clamped down and he said nothing, just rolled back over and looked at the curtains as they drifted in and out with the air conditioning. Soon MaryJo left him, and he heard the sound of machinery starting up downstairs. The washer, the dryer, the dishwasher, the garbage disposer: it seemed that all the machines were going at once. He had never heard the sounds before—MaryJo never ran them in the evenings or on weekends, when he was home.

At noon he finally got up, but he didn't feel like showering and shaving, though any other day he would have felt dirty and uncomfortable until those rituals were done with. He just put on his robe and went downstairs. He planned to go in to breakfast, but instead he went into his study and opened the lid of the coffin.

It took him a bit of preparation, of course. There was some pacing back and forth before the coffin, and much stroking of the wood, but finally he put his thumbs under the lid and lifted.

The corpse looked stiff and awkward. A man, not particularly old, not particularly young. Hair of a determinedly average color. Except for the grayness of the skin color the body looked completely natural and so utterly average that Mark felt sure he might have seen the man a million times without remembering he had seen him at all. Yet he was unmistakably dead, not because of the cheap satin lining the coffin rather slackly, but because of the hunch of the shoulders, the jut of the chin. The man was not comfortable.

He smelled of embalming fluid.

Mark was holding the lid open with one hand, leaning on the coffin with the other. He was trembling. Yet he felt no excitement, no fear. The trembling was coming from his body, not from anything he could find within his thoughts. The trembling was because it was cold.

There was a soft sound or absence of sound at the door. He turned around abruptly. The lid dropped closed behind him. MaryJo was standing in the door, wearing a frilly housedress, her eyes wide with horror.

In that moment years fell away and to Mark she was twenty, a shy and somewhat awkward girl who was forever being surprised by the way the world actually worked. He waited for her to say, "But Mark, you cheated him." She had said it only once, but ever since then he had heard the words in his mind whenever he was closing a deal. It was the closest thing to a conscience he had in his business dealings. It was enough to get him a reputation as a very honest man.

"Mark," she said softly, as if struggling to keep control of herself, "Mark, I couldn't go on without you."

She sounded as if she were afraid something

43

terrible was going to happen to him, and her hands were shaking. He took a step toward her. She lifted her hands, came to him, clung to him, and cried in a high whimper into his shoulder. "I couldn't. I just couldn't."

"You don't have to," he said, puzzled.

"I'm just not," she said between gentle sobs, "the kind of person who can live alone."

"But even if I, even if something happened to me, MaryJo, you'd have the—" He was going to say the children. Something was wrong with that, though, wasn't there? They loved no one better in the world than their children; no parents had ever been happier than they had been when their two were born. Yet he couldn't say it.

"I'd have what?" MaryJo asked. "Oh, Mark, I'd have nothing."

And then Mark remembered again (what's happening to me!) that they were childless, that to MaryJo, who was old-fashioned enough to regard motherhood as the main purpose for her existence, the fact that they had no hope of children was God's condemnation of her. The only thing that had pulled her through after the operation was Mark, was her fussing over his meaningless and sometimes invented problems at the office or telling him endlessly the events of her lonely days. It was as if he were her anchor to reality, and only he kept her from going adrift in the eddies of her own fears. No wonder the poor girl (for at such times Mark could not think of her as completely adult) was distraught as she thought of Mark's death, and the damned coffin in the house did no good at all.

But I'm in no position to cope with this, Mark thought. I'm falling apart, I'm not only forgetting things, I'm remembering things that didn't happen. And what if I died? What if I suddenly had a stroke like my father had and died on the way to the hospital? What would happen to MaryJo?

She'd never lack for money. Between the business and the insurance, even the house would be paid off, with enough money to live like a queen on the interest. But would the insurance company arrange for someone to hold her patiently while she cried out her fears? Would they provide someone for her to waken in the middle of the night because of the nameless terrors that haunted her?

Her sobs turned into frantic hiccoughs and her fingers dug more deeply into his back through the soft fabric of his robe. See how she clings to me, he thought. She'll never let me go, he thought, and then the blackness came again and again he was falling backward into nothing and again he did not care about anything. Did not even know there was anything to care about.

Except for the fingers pressing into his back and the weight he held in his arms. I do not mind losing the world, he thought. I do not mind losing even my memories of the past. But these fingers. This woman. I cannot lay this burden down because there is no one who can pick it up again. If I mislay her she is lost.

And yet he longed for the darkness, resented her need that held him. Surely there is a way out of this, he thought. Surely a balance between two hungers that leaves both satisfied. But still the hands held him. All the world was silent and the silence was peace except for the sharp, insistent fingers and he cried out in frustration and the sound was still ringing in the room when he opened his eyes and saw MaryJo standing against a wall, leaning against the wall, looking at him in terror.

"What's wrong?" she whispered.

"I'm losing," he answered. But he could not remember what he had thought to win.

And at that moment a door slammed in the house and Amy came running with little loud feet through the kitchen and into the study, flinging herself on her mother and bellowing about the day at school and the dog that chased her for the second time and how the teacher told her she was the *best* reader in the second grade but Darrel had spilled milk on her and could she have a sandwich because she had dropped hers and stepped on it accidentally at lunch—

MaryJo looked at Mark cheerfully and winked and laughed. "Sounds like Amy's had a busy day, doesn't it, Mark?"

Mark could not smile. He just nodded as MaryJo straightened Amy's disheveled clothing and led her toward the kitchen.

"MaryJo," Mark said. "There's something I have to talk to you about."

"Can it wait?" MaryJo asked, not even pausing. Mark heard the cupboard door opening, heard the lid come off the peanut butter jar, heard Amy giggle and say, "Mommy, not so *thick*."

Mark didn't understand why he was so confused and terrified. Amy had had a sandwich after school ever since she had started going—even as an infant she had had seven meals a day, and never gained an ounce of fat. It wasn't what was happening in the kitchen that was bothering him, couldn't be. Yet he could not stop himself from crying out, "MaryJo! MaryJo, come here!"

"Is Daddy mad?" he heard Amy ask softly.

"No," MaryJo answered, and she bustled back into the room and impatiently said, "What's wrong, dear?"

"I just need—just need to have you in here for a minute."

"Really, Mark, that's not your style, is it? Amy needs to have a lot of attention right after school, it's the way she is. I wish you wouldn't stay home from work with nothing to do, Mark, you become quite impossible around the house." She smiled to show that she was only half serious and left again to go back to Amy.

For a moment Mark felt a terrible stab of jealousy that MaryJo was far more sensitive to Amy's needs than to his.

But that jealousy passed quickly, like the memory of the pain of MaryJo's fingers pressing into his back, and with a tremendous feeling of relief Mark didn't care about anything at all, and he turned around to the coffin, which fascinated him, and he opened the lid again and looked inside. It was as if the poor man had no face at all, Mark realized. As if death stole faces from people and made them anonymous even to themselves.

He ran his fingers back and forth across the satin and it felt cool and inviting. The rest of the room, the rest of the world receded into deep background. Only Mark and the coffin and the corpse remained and Mark felt very tired and very hot, as if life itself were a terrible friction making heat within him, and he took off his robe and pajamas and awkwardly climbed on a chair and stepped over the edge into the coffin and knelt and then lay down. There was no other corpse to share the slight space with him;

47

nothing between his body and the cold satin, and as he lay on it it didn't get any warmer because at last the friction was slowing, was cooling, and he reached up and pulled down the lid and the world was dark and silent and there was no odor and no taste and no feel but the cold of the sheets.

"Why is the lid closed?" asked little Amy, holding her mother's hand.

"Because it's not the body we must remember," MaryJo said softly, with careful control, "but the way Daddy always was. We must remember him happy and laughing and loving us."

Amy looked puzzled. "But I remember he spanked me."

MaryJo nodded, smiling, something she had not done recently. "It's all right to remember that, too," MaryJo said, and then she took her daughter from the coffin back into the living room, where Amy, not realizing yet the terrible loss she had sustained, laughed and climbed on Grandpa.

David, his face serious and tear-stained because he did understand, came and put his hand in his mother's hand and held tightly to her. "We'll be fine," he said.

"Yes," MaryJo answered. "I think so."

And her mother whispered in her ear, "I don't know how you can stand it so bravely, my dear."

Tears came to MaryJo's eyes. "I'm not brave at all," she whispered back. "But the children. They depend on me so much. I can't let go when they're leaning on me."

"How terrible it would be," her mother said, nodding wisely, "if you had no children."

*

Inside the coffin, his last need fulfilled, Mark Tapworth heard it all, but could not hold it in his mind, for in his mind there was space or time for only one thought; consent. Everlasting consent to his life, to his death, to the world, and to the everlasting absence of the world. For now there were children.

Deep Breathing Exercises

If Dale Yorgason weren't so easily distracted, he might never have noticed the breathing. But he was on his way upstairs to change clothes, noticed the headline on the paper, and got deflected; instead of climbing the stairs, he sat on them and began to read. He could not even concentrate on that, however. He began to hear all the sounds of the house. Brian, their two-year-old son, was upstairs, breathing heavily in sleep. Colly, his wife, was in the kitchen, kneading bread and also breathing heavily.

Their breath was exactly in unison. Brian's rasping breath upstairs, thick with the mucus of a child's sleep; Colly's deep breaths as she labored with the dough. It set Dale to thinking, the newspapers forgotten. He wondered how often people did that— breathed perfectly together for minutes on end. He began to wonder about coincidence.

And then, because he was easily distracted, he remembered that he had to change his clothes and went upstairs. When he came down in his jeans and sweatshirt, ready for a good game of outdoor basketball now that it was spring, Colly called to him. "I'm out of cinnamon, Dale!"

"I'll get it on the way home!"

"I need it *now*!" Colly called.

"We have two cars!" Dale yelled back, then closed the door. He briefly felt bad about not helping her out, but reminded himself that he was already running late and it wouldn't hurt her to take Brian with her and get outside the house; she never seemed to get out of the house anymore.

His team of friends from Allways Home Products, Inc., won the game, and he came home deliciously sweaty. No one was there. The bread dough had risen impossibly, was spread all over the counter and dropping in large chunks onto the floor. Colly had obviously been gone too long. He wondered what could have delayed her.

Then came the phone call from the police, and he did not have to wonder anymore. Colly had a habit of inadvertently running stop signs.

The funeral was well attended because Dale had a large family and was well liked at the office. He sat between his own parents and Colly's parents. The speakers droned on, and Dale, easily distracted, kept thinking of the fact that of all the mourners there, only a few were there in private grief. Only a few had actually known Colly, who preferred to avoid office functions and social gatherings; who stayed home with Brian most of the time being a perfect housewife and reading books and being, in the end, solitary. Most of the people at the funeral had come for Dale's sake, to comfort him. Am I comforted? he asked himself. Not by my friends— they had little to say, were awkward and embarrassed. Only his father had had the right instinct, just embracing him and then talking about everything except Dale's wife and son who were dead, so mangled in the incident that the coffin was never

51

opened for anyone. There was talk of the fishing in Lake Superior this summer; talk of the bastards at Continental Hardware who thought that the 65-year retirement rule ought to apply to the president of the company; talk of nothing at all. But it was good enough. It distracted Dale from his grief.

Now, however, he wondered whether he had really been a good husband for Colly. Had she really been happy, cooped up in the house all day? He had tried to get her out, get to meet people, and she had resisted. But in the end, as he wondered whether he knew her at all, he could not find an answer, not one he was sure of. And Brian—he had not known Brian at all. The boy was smart and quick, speaking in sentences when other children were still struggling with single words; but what had he and Dale ever had to talk about? All Brian's companionship had been with his mother; all Colly's companionship had been with Brian. In a way it was like their breathing—the last time Dale had heard them breathe—in unison, as if even the rhythms of their bodies were together. It pleased Dale somehow to think that they had drawn their last breath together, too, the unison continuing to the grave; now they would be lowered into the earth in perfect unison, sharing a coffin as they had shared every day since Brian's birth.

Dale's grief swept over him again, surprising him because he had thought he had cried as much as he possible could, and now he discovered there were more tears waiting to flow. He was not sure whether he was crying because of the empty house he would come home to, or because he had always been somewhat closed off from his family; was the coffin, after all, just an expression of the way their relationship had always been? It was not a productive line of thought, and Dale let himself be distracted. He let himself notice that his parents were breathing together.

Their breaths were soft, hard to hear. But Dale heard, and looked at them, watched their chests rise and fall together. It unnerved him—was unison breathing more common than he had thought? He listened for others, but Colly's parents were not breathing together, and certainly Dale's breaths were at his own rhythm. Then Dale's mother looked at him, smiled, and nodded to him in an attempt at silent communication. Dale was not good at silent communication; meaningful pauses and knowing looks always left him baffled. They always made him want to check his fly. Another distraction, and he did not think of breathing again.

Until at the airport, when the plane was an hour late in arriving because of technical difficulties in Los Angeles. There was not much to talk to his parents about; even his father's chatter failed him, and they sat in silence most of the time, as did most of the other passengers. Even a stewardess and the pilot sat near them, waiting silently for the plane to arrive.

It was in one of the deeper silences that Dale noticed that his father and the pilot were both swinging their crossed legs in unison. Then he listened, and realized there was a strong sound in the gate waiting area, a rhythmic soughing of many of the passengers inhaling and exhaling together. Dale's mother and father, the pilot, the stewardess, several other passengers, all were breathing together. It unnerved him. How could this be? Brian and Colly had been mother and son; Dale's parents had been together for years. But why should half the people in the waiting area breathe together?

He pointed it out to his father.

"Kind of strange, but I think you're right," his father said, rather delighted with the odd event. Dale's father loved odd events.

And then the rhythm broke, and the plane taxied close to the windows, and the crowd stirred and got ready to board, even though the actual boarding was surely half an hour off.

The plane broke apart at landing. About half the people in the airplane survived. However, the entire crew and several passengers, including Dale's parents, were killed when the plane hit the ground.

It was then that Dale realized that the breathing was not a result of coincidence, or the people's closeness during their lives. It was a messenger of death; they breathed together *because* they were going to draw their last breath together. He said nothing about this thought to anyone else, but whenever he got distracted from other things, he tended to speculate on this. It was better than dwelling on the fact that he, a man to whom family had been very important, was now completely without family; that the only people with whom he was completely himself, completely at ease, were gone, and there was no more ease for him in the world. Much better to wonder whether his knowledge might be used to save lives. After all, he often thought, reasoning in a circular pattern that never seemed to end, if I notice this again, I should be able to alert someone, to warn someone, to save their lives. Yet if I were going to save their lives, would they then breathe in unison? If my parents had been warned, and changed flights, he thought, they wouldn't have died, and therefore wouldn't have breathed together, and so I wouldn't have been able to warn them, and so they *wouldn't* have changed flights, and so they *would* have died, and so they *would* have breathed in unison, and so I would have noticed and warned them. . . .

More than anything that had ever passed through his mind before, this thought engaged him, and he was not easily distracted from it. It began to hurt his work; he slowed down, made mistakes, because he concentrated only on breathing, listening constantly to the secretaries and other executives in his company, waiting for the fatal moment when they would breathe in unison.

He was eating alone in a restaurant when he heard it again. The sighs of breath came all together, from every table near him. It took him a few moments to be sure; then he leaped from the table and walked briskly outside. He did not stop to pay, for the breathing was still in unison at every table to the door of the restaurant.

The maître d', predictably, was annoyed at his leaving without paying, and called out to him. Dale did not answer. "Wait! You didn't pay!" cried the man, following Dale out into the street.

Dale did not know how far he had to go for safety from whatever danger faced everyone in the restaurant; he ended up having no choice in the matter. The maître d' stopped him on the sidewalk, only a few doors down from the restaurant, tried to pull him back toward the place, Dale resisting all the way.

"You can't leave without paying! What do you think you're doing?"

"I can't go back," Dale shouted. "I'll pay you!

I'll pay you right here!" And he fumbled in his wallet for the money as a huge explosion knocked him and the maître d' to the ground. Flame erupted from the restaurant, and people screamed as the building began crumbling from the force of the explosion. It was impossible that anyone still inside the building could be alive.

The maître d', his eyes wide with horror, stood up as Dale did, and looked at him with dawning understanding. "You knew!" the maître d' said. "You knew!"

Dale was acquitted at the trial—phone calls from a radical group and the purchase of a large quantity of explosives in several states led to indictment and conviction of someone else. But at the trial enough was said to convince Dale and several pyschiatrists that something was seriously wrong with him. He was voluntarily committed to an institution, where Dr. Howard Rumming spent hours in conversation with Dale, trying to understand his madness, his fixation on breathing as a sign of coming death.

"I'm sane in every other way, aren't I, Doctor?" Dale asked, again and again.

And repeatedly the doctor answered, "What is sanity? Who has it? How can *I* know?"

Dale soon found that the mental hospital was not an unpleasant place to be. It was a private institution, and a lot of money had gone into it; most of the people there were voluntary commitments, which meant that conditions had to remain excellent. It was one of the things that made Dale grateful for his father's wealth. In the hospital he was safe; the only contact with the outside world was on the television. Gradually, meeting people and becoming

56

attached to them in the hospital, he began to relax, to lose his obsession with breathing, to stop listening quite so intently for the sound of inhalation and exhalation, the way that different people's breathing rhythms fit together. Gradually he began to be his old, distractable self.

"I'm nearly cured, Doctor," Dale announced one day in the middle of a game of backgammon.

The doctor sighed. "I know it, Dale. I have to admit it—I'm disappointed. Not in your cure, you understand. It's just that you've been a breath of fresh air, you should pardon the expression." They both laughed a little. "I get so tired of middle-aged women with fashionable nervous breakdowns."

Dale was gammoned—the dice were all against him. But he took it well, knowing that next time he was quite likely to win handily—he usually did. Then he and Dr. Rumming got up from their table and walked toward the front of the recreation room, where the television program had been interrupted by a special news bulletin. The people around the television looked disturbed; news was never allowed on the hospital television, and only a bulletin like this could creep in. Dr. Rumming intended to turn it off immediately, but then heard the words being said.

". . . from satellites fully capable of destroying every major city in the United States. The President was furnished with a list of fifty-four cities targeted by the orbiting missiles. One of these, said the communique, will be destroyed immediately to show that the threat is serious and will be carried out. Civil defense authorities have been notified, and citizens of the fifty-four cities will be on standby for immediate evacuation." There followed the normal parade of special reports and deep background, but the reporters were all afraid.

Dale's mind could not stay on the program, however, because he was distracted by something far more compelling. Every person in the room was breathing in perfect unison, including Dale. He tried to break out of the rhythm, and couldn't.

It's just my fear, Dale thought. Just the broadcast, making me think that I hear the breathing.

A Denver newsman came on the air then, overriding the network broadcast. "Denver, ladies and gentlemen, is one of the targeted cities. The city has asked us to inform you that orderly evacuation is to begin immediately. Obey all traffic laws, and drive east from the city, if you live in the following neighborhoods. . . ."

Then the newsman stopped, and, breathing heavily, listened to something coming through his earphone.

The newsman was breathing in perfect unison with all the people in the room.

"Dale," Dr. Rumming said.

Dale only breathed, feeling death poised above him in the sky.

"Dale, can you hear the breathing?"

Dale heard the breathing.

The newsman spoke again. "Denver is definitely the target. The missiles have already been launched. Please leave immediately. Do not stop for any reason. It is estimated that we have less than—less than three minutes. My God," he said, and got up from his chair, breathing heavily, running out of the range of the camera. No one turned any equipment off in the station—the tube kept on showing the local news set, the empty chairs, the tables, the weather map.

"We can't get out in time,' Dr. Rumming said to the inmates in the room. "We're near the center of Denver. Our only hope is to lie on the floor. Try to get under tables and chairs as much as possible." The inmates, terrified, complied with the voice of authority.

"So much for my cure," Dale said, his voice trembling. Rumming managed a half-smile. They lay together in the middle of the floor, leaving the furniture for everyone else because they knew that the furniture would do no good at all.

"You definitely don't belong here," Rumming told him. "I never met a saner man in all my life."

Dale was distracted, however. Instead of his impending death he thought of Colly and Brian in their coffin. He imagined the earth being swept away in a huge wind, and the coffin being ashed immediately in the white explosion from the sky. The barrier is coming down at last, Dale thought, and I will be with them as completely as it is possible to be. He thought of Brian learning to walk, crying when he fell; he remembered Colly saying, "Don't pick him up every time he cries, or he'll just learn that crying gets results." And so for three days Dale had listened to Brian cry and cry, and never lifted a hand to help the boy. Brian learned to walk quite well, and quickly. But now, suddenly, Dale felt again that irresistible impulse to pick him up, to put his pathetically red and weeping face on his shoulder, to say, That's all right, Daddy's holding you.

"That's all right, Daddy's holding you," Dale said aloud, softly. Then there was a flash of white so bright that it could be seen as easily through the walls as through the window, for there were no walls, and all the breath was drawn out of their bodies at once, their voices robbed from them so suddenly that they all involuntarily shouted and then, forever, were silent. Their shout was taken up in a violent wind that swept the sound, wrung from every throat in perfect unison, upward into the clouds forming over what had once been Denver.

And in the last moment, as the shout was drawn from his lungs and the heat took his eyes out of his face, Dale realized that despite all his foreknowledge, the only life he had ever saved was that of a maître d'hôtel, whose life, to Dale, didn't mean a thing.

FAT FARM

The receptionist was surprised that he was back so soon.

"Why, Mr Barth, how glad I am to see you," she said.

"Surprised, you mean," Barth answered. His voice rumbled from the rolls of fat under his chin.

"Delighted."

"How long has it been?" Barth asked.

"Three years. How time flies."

The receptionist smiled, but Barth saw the awe and revulsion on her face as she glanced over his immense body. In her job she saw fat people every day. But Barth knew he was unusual. He was proud of being unusual.

"Back to the fat farm," he said, laughing.

The effort of laughing made him short of breath, and he gasped for air as she pushed a button and said, "Mr Barth is back."

He did not bother to look for a chair. No chair could hold him. He did lean against a wall, however. Standing was a labor he preferred to avoid.

Yet it was not shortness of breath or exhaustion at the slightest effort that had brought him back to Anderson's Fitness Center. He had often been fat before, and he rather relished the sensation of bulk, the impression he made as crowds parted for him. He pitied those who could only be slightly fat—short people, who were not able to bear the weight. At well over two meters, Barth could get gloriously fat, stunningly fat. He owned thirty wardrobes and took delight in changing from one to another as his belly and buttocks and thighs grew. At times he felt that if he grew large enough, he could take over the world, be the world. At the dinner table he was a conqueror to rival Genghis Khan.

It was not his fatness, then, that had brought him in. It was that at last the fat was interfering with his other pleasures. The girl he had been with the night before had tried and tried, but he was incapable—a sign that it was time to renew, refresh, reduce.

"I am a man of pleasure," he wheezed to the receptionist, whose name he never bothered to learn. She smiled back.

"Mr Anderson will be here in a moment."

"Isn't it ironic," he said, "that a man such as I, who is capable of fulfilling every one of his desires, is never satisfied!" He gasped with laughter again. "Why haven't we ever slept together?" he asked.

She looked at him, irritation crossing her face. "You always ask that, Mr Barth, on your way in. But you never ask it on your way out."

True enough. When he was on his way out of the Anderson Fitness Center, she never seemed as attractive as she had on his way in.

Anderson came in, effusively handsome, gushingly warm, taking Barth's fleshy hand in his and pumping it with enthusiasm.

"One of my best customers," he said.

"The usual," Barth said.

"Of course," Anderson answered. "But the price *has* gone up."

"If you ever go out of business," Barth said, following Anderson into the inner rooms, "give me plenty of warning. I only let myself go this much because I know you're here."

"Oh," Anderson chuckled. "We'll never go out of business."

"I have no doubt you could support your whole organization on what you charge *me*."

"You're paying for much more than the simple service we perform. You're also paying for privacy. Our, shall we say, lack of government intervention."

"How many of the bastards do you bribe?"

"Very few, very few. Partly because so many high officials also need our service."

"No doubt."

"It isn't just weight gains that bring people to us, you know. It's cancer and aging and accidental disfigurement. You'd be surprised to learn who has had our service."

Barth doubted that he would. The couch was ready for him, immense and soft and angled so that it would be easy for him to get up again.

"Damn near got married this time," Barth said, by way of conversation.

Anderson turned to him in surprise.

"But you didn't?"

"Of course not. Started getting fat, and she couldn't cope."

"Did you tell her?"

"That I was getting fat? It was obvious."

"About us, I mean."

"I'm not a fool."

Anderson looked relieved. "Can't have rumors

63

getting around among the thin and young, you know."

"Still, I think I'll look her up again, afterward. She did things to me a woman shouldn't be able to do. And I thought I was jaded."

Anderson placed a tight-fitting rubber cap over Barth's head.

"Think your key thought," Anderson reminded him.

Key thought. At first that had been such a comfort, to make sure that not one iota of his memory would be lost. Now it was boring, almost juvenile. Key thought. Do you have your own Captain Aardvark secret decoder ring? Be the first on your block. The only thing Barth had been the first on his block to do was reach puberty. He had also been the first on his block to reach one hundred fifty kilos.

How many times have I been here? he wondered as the tingling in his scalp began. *This is the eighth time. Eight times, and my fortune is larger than ever, the kind of wealth that takes on a life on its own. I can keep this up forever*, he thought, with relish. Forever at the supper table with neither worries nor restraints. "It's dangerous to gain so much weight," Lynette had said. "Heart attacks, you know." But the only things that Barth worried about were hemorrhoids and impotence. The former was a nuisance, but the latter made life unbearable and drove him back to Anderson.

Key thought. What else? Lynette, standing naked on the edge of the cliff with the wind blowing. She was courting death, and he admired her for it, almost hoped that she would find it. She despised safety precautions. Like clothing, they were restrictions to be cast aside. She had once talked him into playing

64

tag with her on a construction site, racing along the girders in the darkness, until the police came and made them leave. That had been when Barth was still thin from his last time at Anderson's. But it was not Lynette on the girders that he held in his mind. It was Lynette, fragile and beautiful Lynette, daring the wind to snatch her from the cliff and break up her body on the rocks by the river.

Even that, Barth thought, *would be a kind of pleasure. A new kind of pleasure, to taste a grief so magnificently, so admirably earned.*

And then the tingling in his head stopped. Anderson came back in.

"Already?" Barth asked.

"We've streamlined the process." Anderson carefully peeled the cap from Barth's head, helped the immense man lift himself from the couch.

"I can't understand why it's illegal," Barth said. "Such a simple thing."

"Oh, there are reasons. Population control, that sort of thing. This is a kind of immortality, you know. But it's mostly the repugnance most people feel. They can't face the thought. You're a man of rare courage."

But it was not courage, Barth knew. It was pleasure. He eagerly anticipated seeing, and they did not make him wait.

"Mr Barth, meet Mr Barth."

It nearly broke his heart to see his own body young and strong and beautiful again, as it never had been the first time through his life. It was unquestionably himself, however, that they led into the room. Except that the belly was firm, the thighs well muscled but slender enough that they did not

65

meet, even at the crotch. They brought him in naked, of course. Barth insisted on it.

He tried to remember the last time. Then *he* had been the one coming from the learning room, emerging to see the immense fat man that all his memories told him was himself. Barth remembered that it had been a double pleasure, to see the mountain he had made of himself, yet to view it from inside this beautiful young body.

"Come here," Barth said, his own voice arousing echoes of the last time, when it had been the other Barth who had said it. And just as that other had done the last time, he touched the naked young Barth, stroked the smooth and lovely skin, and finally embraced him.

And the young Barth embraced him back, for that was the way of it. No one loved Barth as much as Barth did, thin or fat, young or old. Life was a celebration of Barth; the sight of himself was his strongest nostalgia.

"What did I think of?" Barth asked.

The young Barth smiled into his eyes. "Lynette," he said. "Naked on a cliff. The wind blowing. And the thought of her thrown to her death."

"Will you go back to her?" Barth asked his young self eagerly.

"Perhaps. Or to someone like her." And Barth saw with delight that the mere thought of it had aroused his young self more than a little.

"He'll do," Barth said, and Anderson handed him the simple papers to sign—papers that would never be seen in a court of law because they attested to Barth's own compliance in and initiation of an act that was second only to murder in the lawbooks of every state.

"That's it, then," Anderson said, turning from the fat Barth to the young, thin one. "You're Mr Barth now, in control of his wealth and his life. Your clothing is in the next room."

"I know where it is," the young Barth said with a smile, and his footsteps were buoyant as he left the room. He would dress quickly and leave the Fitness Center briskly, hardly noticing the rather plain-looking receptionist, except to take note of her wistful look after him, a tall, slender, beautiful man who had, only moments before, been lying mindless in storage, waiting to be given a mind and a memory, waiting for a fat man to move out of the way so he could fill his space.

In the memory room Barth sat on the edge of the couch, looking at the door, and then realized, with surprise, that he had no idea what came next.

"My memories run out here," Barth said to Anderson. "The agreement was—what was the agreement?"

"The agreement was tender care of you until you passed away."

"Ah, yes."

"The agreement isn't worth a damn thing," Anderson said, smiling.

Barth looked at him with surprise. "What do you mean?"

"There are two options, Barth. A needle within the next fifteen minutes. Or employment."

"What are you talking about?"

"You didn't think we'd waste time and effort feeding you the ridiculous amounts of food you require, did you?"

Barth felt himself sink inside. This was not what he had expected, though he had not honestly

expected anything. Barth was not the kind to antici-
pate trouble. Life had never given him much
trouble.

"A needle?"

"Cyanide, if you insist, though we'd rather be able
to vivisect you and get as many useful body parts as
we can. Your body's still fairly young. We can get
incredible amounts of money for your pelvis and
your glands, but they have to be taken from you
alive."

"What are you talking about? This isn't what we
agreed."

"I agreed to nothing with *you*, my friend," Anderson said, smiling. "I agreed with Barth. And Barth
just left the room."

"Call him back! I insist—"

"Barth doesn't give a damn what happens to you."

And he knew that it was true.

"You said something about employment."

"Indeed."

"What kind of employment?"

Anderson shook his head. "It all depends," he
said.

"On what?"

"On what kind of work turns up. There are several
assignments every year that must be performed by
a living human being, for which no volunteer can
be found. No person, not even a criminal, can be
compelled to do them."

"And I?"

"Will do them. Or one of them, rather, since you
rarely get a second job."

"How can you do this? I'm a human being!"

Anderson shook his head. "The law says that
there is only one possible Barth in all the world.

And you aren't it. You're just a number. And a letter. The letter *H*."

"Why *H*?"

"Because you're such a disgusting glutton, my friend. Even our first customers haven't got past *C* yet."

Anderson left then, and Barth was alone in the room. Why hadn't he anticipated this? *Of course, of course*, he shouted to himself now. Of course they wouldn't keep him pleasantly alive. He wanted to get up and try to run. But walking was difficult for him; running would be impossible. He sat there, his belly pressing heavily on his thighs, which were spread wide by the fat. He stood, with great effort, and could only waddle because his legs were so far apart, so constrained in their movement.

This has happened every time, Barth thought. *Every damn time I've walked out of this place young and thin, I've left behind someone like me, and they've had their way, haven't they?* His hands trembled badly.

He wondered what he had decided before and knew immediately that there was no decision to make at all. Some fat people might hate themselves and choose death for the sake of having a thin version of themselves live on. But not Barth. Barth could never choose to cause himself any pain. And to obliterate even an illegal, clandestine version of himself—impossible. Whatever else he might be, he was still Barth. The man who walked out of the memory room a few minutes before had not taken over Barth's identity. He had only duplicated it. *They've stolen my soul with mirrors*, Barth told himself. *I have to get it back*.

"Anderson!" Barth shouted. "Anderson! I've made up my mind."

It was not Anderson who entered, of course. Barth would never see Anderson again. It would have been too tempting to try to kill him.

"Get to work, H!" the old man shouted from the other side of the field.

Barth leaned on his hoe a moment more, then got back to work, scraping weeds from between the potato plants. The calluses on his hands had long since shaped themselves to fit the wooden handle, and his muscles knew how to perform the work without Barth's having to think about it at all. Yet that made the labor no easier. When he first realized that they meant him to be a potato farmer, he had asked, "Is this my assignment? Is this *all*?" And they had laughed and told him no. "It's just preparation," they said, "to get you in shape." So for two years he had worked in the potato fields, and now he began to doubt that they would ever come back, that the potatoes would ever end.

The old man was watching, he knew. His gaze always burned worse than the sun. The old man was watching, and if Barth rested too long or too often, the old man would come to him, whip in hand, to scar him deeply, to hurt him to the soul.

He dug into the ground, chopping at a stubborn plant whose root seemed to cling to the foundation of the world. "Come up, damn you," he muttered. He thought his arms were too weak to strike harder, but he struck harder anyway. The root split, and the impact shattered him to the bone.

He was naked and brown to the point of blackness from the sun. The flesh hung loosely on him in

70

great folds, a memory of the mountain he had been. Under the loose skin, however, he was tight and hard. It might have given him pleasure, for every muscle had been earned by hard labor and the pain of the lash. But there was no pleasure in it. The price was too high.

I'll kill myself, he often thought and thought again now with his arms trembling with exhaustion. *I'll kill myself so they can't use my body and can't use my soul.*

But he would never kill himself. Even now, Barth was incapable of ending it.

The farm he worked on was unfenced, but the time he had gotten away he had walked and walked and walked for three days and had not once seen any sign of human habitation other than an occasional jeep track in the sagebrush-and-grass desert. Then they found him and brought him back, weary and despairing, and forced him to finish a day's work in the field before letting him rest. And even then the lash had bitten deep, the old man laying it on with a relish that spoke of sadism or a deep, personal hatred.

But why should the old man hate me? Barth wondered. *I don't know him.* He finally decided that it was because he had been so fat, so obviously soft, while the old man was wiry to the point of being gaunt, his face pinched by years of exposure to the sunlight. Yet the old man's hatred had not diminished as the months went by and the fat melted away in the sweat and sunlight of the potato field.

A sharp sting across his back, the sound of slapping leather on skin, and then an excruciating pain deep in his muscles. He had paused too long. The old man had come to him.

The old man said nothing. Just raised the lash again, ready to strike. Barth lifted the hoe out of the ground, to start work again. It occurred to him, as it had a hundred times before, that the hoe could reach as far as the whip, with as good effect. But, as a hundred times before, Barth looked into the old man's eyes, and what he saw there, while he did not understand it, was enough to stop him. He could not strike back. He could only endure.

The lash did not fall again. Instead he and the old man just looked at each other. The sun burned where blood was coming from his back. Flies buzzed near him. He did not bother to brush them away.

Finally the old man broke the silence.

"H," he said.

Barth did not answer. Just waited.

"They've come for you. First job," said the old man.

First job. It took Barth a moment to realize the implications. The end of the potato fields. The end of the sunlight. The end of the old man with the whip. The end of the loneliness or, at least, of the boredom.

"Thank God," Barth said. His throat was dry.

"Go wash," the old man said.

Barth carried the hoe back to the shed. He remembered how heavy the hoe had seemed when he first arrived. How ten minutes in the sunlight had made him faint. Yet they had revived him in the field, and the old man had said, "Carry it back." So he had carried back the heavy, heavy hoe, feeling for all the world like Christ bearing his cross. Soon enough the others had gone, and the old man and he had been alone together, but the ritual with the hoe never changed. They got to the shed, and the old man carefully took the hoe from him and locked it away, so that Barth couldn't get it in the night and kill him with it.

And then into the house, where Barth bathed painfully and the old man put an excruciating disinfectant on his back. Barth had long since given up on the idea of an anesthetic. It wasn't in the old man's nature to use an anesthetic.

Clean clothes. A few minutes' wait. And then the helicopter. A young, businesslike man emerged from it, looking unfamiliar in detail but very familiar in general. He was an echo of all the businesslike young men and women who had dealt with him before. The young man came to him, unsmiling, and said, "H?"

Barth nodded. It was the only name they used for him.

"You have an assignment."

"What is it?" Barth asked.

The young man did not answer. The old man, behind him whispered, "They'll tell you soon enough. And then you'll wish you were back here, H. They'll tell you, and you'll pray for the potato fields."

But Barth doubted it. In two years there had not been a moment's pleasure. The food was hideous, and there was never enough. There were no women, and he was usually too tired to amuse himself. Just pain and labor and loneliness, all excruciating. He would leave that now. Anything would be better, anything at all.

"Whatever they assign you, though," the old man said, "it can't be any worse than my assignment."

Barth would have asked him what his assignment had been, but there was nothing in the old man's

73

voice that invited the question, and there was nothing in their relationship in the past that would allow the question to be asked. Instead, they stood in silence as the young man reached into the helicopter and helped a man get out. An immensely fat man, stark-naked and white as the flesh of a potato, looking petrified. The old man strode purposefully toward him.

"Hello, I," the old man said.

"My name's Barth," the fat man answered, petulantly. The old man struck him hard across the mouth, hard enough that the tender lip split and blood dripped from where his teeth had cut into the skin.

"I," said the old man. "Your name is I."

The fat man nodded pitiably, but Barth—H—felt no pity for him. Two years this time. Only two damnable years and he was already in this condition. Barth could vaguely remember being proud of the mountain he had made of himself. But now he felt only contempt. Only a desire to go to the fat man, to scream in his face, "Why did you do it! Why did you let it happen again!"

It would have meant nothing. To I, as to H, it was the first time, the first betrayal. There had been no others in his memory.

Barth watched as the old man put a hoe in the fat man's hands and drove him out into the field. Two more young men got out of the helicopter. Barth knew what they would do, could almost see them helping the old man for a few days, until I finally learned the hopelessness of resistance and delay.

But Barth did not get to watch the replay of his own torture of two years before. The young man who had first emerged from the copter now led him

74

to it, put him in a seat by a window, and sat beside him. The pilot speeded up the engines, and the copter began to rise.

"The bastard," Barth said, looking out the window at the old man as he slapped I across the face brutally.

The young man chuckled. Then he told Barth his assignment.

Barth clung to the window, looking out, feeling his life slip away from him even as the ground receded slowly. "I can't do it."

"There are worse assignments," the young man said.

Barth did not believe it.

"If I live," he said, "if I live, I want to come back here."

"Love it that much?"

"To kill him."

The young man looked at him blankly.

"The old man," Barth explained, then realized that the young man was ultimately incapable of understanding anything. He looked back out the window. The old man looked very small next to the huge lump of white flesh beside him. Barth felt a terrible loathing for I. A terrible despair in knowing that nothing could possibly be learned, that again and again his selves would replay this hideous scenario.

Somewhere, the man who would be J was dancing, was playing polo, was seducing and perverting and being delighted by every woman and boy and, God knows, sheep that he could find; somewhere the man who would be J dined.

I bent immensely in the sunlight and tried, clumsily, to use the hoe. Then, losing his balance, he fell over into the dirt, writhing. The old man raised his whip.

The helicopter turned then, so that Barth could see nothing but sky from his window. He never saw the whip fall. But he imagined the whip falling. Imagined and relished it, longed to feel the heaviness of the blow flowing from his own arm. *Hit him again!* he cried out inside himself. *Hit him for me!* And inside himself he made the whip fall a dozen times more.

"What are you thinking?" the young man asked, smiling, as if he knew the punch line of a joke.

"I was thinking," Barth said, "that the old man can't possibly hate him as much as I do."

Apparently that was the punch line. The young man laughed uproariously. Barth did not understand the joke, but somehow he was certain that he was the butt of it. He wanted to strike out but dared not.

Perhaps the young man saw the tension in Barth's body, or perhaps he merely wanted to explain. He stopped laughing but could not repress his smile, which penetrated Barth far more deeply than the laugh.

"But don't you see?" the young man asked. "Don't you know who the old man is?"

Barth didn't know.

"What do you think we did with A?" And the young man laughed again.

There are worse assignments than mine, Barth realized. And the worst of all would be to spend day after day, month after month, supervising that contemptible animal that he could not deny was himself.

The scar on his back bled a little, and the blood stuck to the seat when it dried.

CLOSING THE TIMELID

Gemini lay back in his cushioned chair and slid the box over his head. It was pitch black inside, except the light coming from down around his shoulders.

"All right, I'm pulling us over," said Orion. Gemini braced himself. He heard the clicking of a switch (or someone's teeth clicking shut in surprise?) and the timelid closed down on him, shut out the light, and green and orange and another, nameless color beyond purple danced at the edges of his eyes.

And he stood, abruptly, in the thick grass at the side of a road. A branch full of leaves brushed heavily against his back with the breeze. He moved forward, looking for—

The road, just as Orion had said. About a minute to wait, then.

Gemini slid awkwardly down the embankment, covering his hands with dirt. To his surprise it was moist and soft, clinging. He had expected it to be hard. That's what you get for believing pictures in the encyclopedia, he thought. And the ground gave gently under his feet.

He glanced behind him. Two furrows down the bank showed his path. I have a mark in this world after all, he thought. It'll make no difference, but there is a sign of me in this time when men could still leave signs.

Then dazzling lights far up the road. The truck was coming. Gemini sniffed the air. He couldn't smell anything—and yet the books all stressed how smelly gasoline engines had been. Perhaps it was too far.

Then the lights swerved away. The curve. In a moment it would be here, turning just the wrong way on the curving mountain road until it would be too late.

Gemini stepped out into the road, a shiver of anticipation running through him. Oh, he had been under the timelid several times before. Like everyone, he had seen the major events. Michelangelo doing the Sistine Chapel. Handel writing the *Messiah* (everyone strictly forbidden to hum *any* tunes). The premiere performance of *Love's Labour's Lost*. And a few offbeat things that his hobby of history had sent him to: the assassination of John F. Kennedy, a politician; the meeting between Lorenzo d'Medici and the King of Naples; Jeanne d'Arc's death by fire—grisly.

And now, at last, to experience in the past something he was utterly unable to live through in the present.

Death.

And the truck careened around the corner, the lights sweeping the far embankment and then swerving in, brilliantly lighting Gemini for one instant before he leaped up and in, toward the glass (how horrified the face of the driver, how bright the lights, how harsh the metal) and then agony. Ah, agony in a tearing that made him feel, for the first time, every particle of his body as it screamed in pain. Bones

79

shouting as they splintered like old wood under a sledgehammer. Flesh and fat slithering like jelly up and down and sideways. Blood skittering madly over the surface of the truck. Eyes popping open as the brain and skull crushed forward, demanding to be let through, let by, let fly. No no no no no, cried Gemini inside the last fragment of his mind. No no no no no, make it stop!

And green and orange and more-than-purple dazzled the sides of his vision. A twist of his insides, a shudder of his mind, and he was back, snatched from death by the inexorable mathematics of the timelid. He felt his whole, unmarred body rushing back, felt every particle, yes, as clearly as when it had been hit by the truck, but now with pleasure—pleasure so complete that he didn't even notice the mere orgasm his body added to the general symphony of joy.

The timelid lifted. The box was slid back. And Gemini lay gasping, sweating, yet laughing and crying and longing to sing.

What was it like? The others asked eagerly, crowding around. What is it like, what is it, is it like—

"It's like nothing. It's." Gemini had no words. "It's like everything God promised the righteous and Satan promised the sinners rolled into one." He tried to explain about the delicious agony, the joy passing all joys, the—

"Is it better than fairy dust?" asked one man, young and shy, and Gemini realized that the reason he was so retiring was that he was undoubtedly dusting tonight.

"After this," Gemini said, "dusting is no better than going to the bathroom."

80

Everyone laughed, chattered, volunteered to be next ("Orion knows how to throw a party"), as Gemini left the chair and the timelid and found Orion a few meters away at the controls.

"Did you like the ride?" Orion asked, smiling gently at his friend.

Gemini shook his head. "Never again," he said.

Orion looked disturbed for a moment, worried. "That bad for you?"

"Not bad. Strong. I'll never forget it, I've never felt so—alive, Orion. Who would have thought it. Death being so—"

"Bright," Orion said, supplying the word. His hair hung loosely and clean over his forehead—he shook it out of his eyes. "The second time is better. You have more time to appreciate the dying."

Gemini shook his head. "Once is enough for me. Life will never be bland again." He laughed. "Well, time for somebody else, yes?"

Harmony had already lain down on the chair. She had removed her clothing, much to the titillation of the other party-goers, saying, "I want nothing between me and the cold metal." Orion made her wait, though, while he corrected the setting. While he worked, Gemini thought of a question. "How many times have you done this, Orion?"

"Often enough," the man answered, studying the holographic model of the timeclip. And Gemini wondered then if death could not, perhaps, be as addictive as fairy dust, or cresting, or pitching in.

Rod Bingley finally brought the truck to a halt, gasping back the shock and horror. The eyes were still resting there in the gore on the windshield. Only they seemed real. The rest was road-splashing, mud flipped by the weather and the tires.

Rod flung open the door and ran around the front of the truck, hoping to do—what? There was no hope that the man was alive. But perhaps some identification. A nuthouse freak, turned loose in weird white clothes to wander the mountain roads? But there was no hospital near here.

And there was no body on the front of his truck.

He ran his hand across the shiny metal, the clean windshield. A few bugs on the grill.

Had this dent in the metal been there before? Rod couldn't remember. He looked all around the truck. Not a sign of anything. Had he imagined it?

He must have. But it seemed so real. And he hadn't drunk anything, hadn't taken any uppers—no trucker in his right mind *ever* took stay-awakes. He shook his head. He felt creepy. *Watched*. He glanced back over his shoulder. Nothing but the trees bending slightly in the wind. Not even an animal. Some moths already gathering in the headlights. That's all.

Ashamed of himself for being afraid at nothing, he nevertheless jumped into the cab quickly and slammed the door shut behind him and locked it. The key turned in the starter. And he had to force himself to look up through that windshield. He half-expected to see those eyes again.

The windshield was clear. And because he had a deadline to meet, he pressed on. The road curved away infinitely before him.

He drove more quickly, determined to get back to civilization before he had another hallucination.

And as he rounded a curve, his lights sweeping the trees on the far side of the road, he thought he glimpsed a flash of white to the right, in the middle of the road.

The lights caught her just before the truck did, a beautiful girl, naked and voluptuous and eager. Madly eager, standing there, legs broadly apart, arms wide. She dipped, then jumped up as the truck caught her, even as Rod smashed his foot into the brake, swerved the truck to the side. Because he swerved she ended up, not centered, but caught on the left side, directly in front of Rod, one of her arms flapping crazily around the edge of the cab, the hand rapping on the glass of the side window. She, too, splashed.

Rod whimpered as the truck again came to a halt. The hand had dropped loosely down to the woman's side, so it no longer blocked the door. Rod got out quickly, swung himself around the open door, and touched her.

Body warm. Hand real. He touched the buttock nearest him. It gave softly, sweetly, but under it Rod could feel that the pelvis was shattered. And then the body slopped free of the front of the truck, slid to the oil-and-gravel surface of the road and disappeared.

Rod took it calmly for a moment. She fell from the front of the truck, and then there was nothing there. Except a faint (and new, definitely new!) crack in the windshield, there was no sign of her.

Rodney screamed.

The sound echoed from the cliff on the other side of the chasm. The trees seemed to swell the sound, making it louder among the trunks. An owl hooted back.

And finally, Rod got back into the truck and drove again, slowly, but erratically, wondering what, please God tell me what the hell's the matter with my mind.

Harmony rolled off the couch, panting and shuddering violently.

"Is it better than sex?" one of the men asked her. One who had doubtless tried, but failed, to get into her bed.

"It *is* sex," she answered. "But it's better than sex with *you*."

Everyone laughed. What a wonderful party. Who could top this? The would-be hosts and hostesses despaired, even as they clamored for a chance at the timelid.

But the crambox opened then, buzzing with the police override. "We're busted!" somebody shrieked gaily, and everyone laughed and clapped.

The policeman was young, and she seemed unused to the forceshield, walking awkwardly as she stepped into the middle of the happy room.

"Orion Overweed?" she asked, looking around.

"I," answered Orion, from where he sat at the controls, looking wary, Gemini beside him.

"Officer Mercy Manwool, Los Angeles Timesquad."

"Oh no," somebody muttered.

"You have no jurisdiction here," Orion said.

"We have a reciprocal enforcement agreement with the Canadian Chronospot Corporation. And we have reason to believe you are interfering with timetracks in the eighth decade of the twentieth century." She smiled curtly. "We have witnessed two suicides, and by making a careful check of your recent use of your private timelid, we have found several others. Apparently, you have a new way to pass the time, Mr Overweed."

Orion shrugged. "It's merely a passing fancy. But I am not interfering with timetracks."

She walked over to the controls and reached unerringly for the coldswitch. Orion immediately snagged her wrist with his hand. Gemini was surprised to see how the muscles of his forearm bulged with strength. Had he been playing some kind of *sport*? It would be just like Orion, of course, behaving like one of the lower orders—

"A warrant," Orion said.

She withdrew her arm. "I have an official complaint from the Timesquad's observation team. That is sufficient. I must interrupt your activity."

"According to law," Orion said, "you must show cause. Nothing we have done tonight will in any way change history."

"That truck is not robot-driven," she said, her voice growing strident. "There's a man in there. You are changing his life."

Orion only laughed. "Your observers haven't done their homework. I have. Look."

He turned to the control and played a speeded-up sequence, focused always on the shadow image of a truck speeding down a mountain road. The truck made turn after turn, and since the hologram was centered perpetually on the truck, it made the surrounding scenery dance past in a jerky rush, swinging left and right, up and down as the truck banked for turns or struck bumps.

And then, near the bottom of the chasm, between mountains, the truck got on a long, slow curve that led across the river on a slender bridge.

But the bridge wasn't there.

And the truck, unable to stop, skidded and swerved off the end of the truncated road, hung in the air over the chasm, then toppled, tumbled, banging against first this side, then that side of the ravine. It wedged between two outcroppings of rock more than ten meters above the water. The cab of the truck was crushed completely.

"He dies," Orion said. "Which means that anything we do with him before his death and after his last possible contact with another human being is legal. According to the code."

The policeman turned red with anger.

"I saw your little games with airplanes and sinking ships. But this is cruelty, Mr Overweed."

"Cruelty to a dead man is, by definition, not cruelty. I don't change history. And Mr Rodney Bingley is dead, has been for more than four centuries. I am doing no harm to any living man. And you owe me an apology."

Officer Mercy Manwool shook her head. "I think you're as bad as the Romans, who threw people into circuses to be torn by lions—"

"I know about the Romans," Orion said coldly, "and I know whom they threw. In this case, however, I am throwing my friends. And retrieving them very safely through the full retrieval and reassembly feature of the Hamburger Safety Device built inextricably into every timelid. And you owe me an apology."

She drew herself erect. "The Los Angeles Timesquad officially apologizes for making improper allegations about the activities of Orion Overweed."

Orion grinned. "Not exactly heartfelt, but I accept it. And while you're here, may I offer you a drink?"

"Nonalcoholic," she said instantly, and then

looked away from him at Gemini, who was watching her with sad but intent eyes. Orion went for glasses and to try to find something nonalcoholic in the house.

"You performed superbly," Gemini said.

"And you, Gemini," she said softly (voicelessly), "were the first subject to travel."

Gemini shrugged. "Nobody said anything about my not taking part."

She turned her back on him. Orion came back with the drink. He laughed. "Coca Cola," he said. "I had to import it all the way from Brazil. They still drink it there, you know. Original recipe." She took it and drank.

Orion sat back at the controls.

"Next!" he shouted, and a man and woman jumped on the couch together, laughing as the others slid the box over their heads.

Rod had lost count. At first he had tried to count the curves. Then the white lines in the road, until a new asphalt surface covered them. Then stars. But the only number that stuck in his head was nine.

9

NINE

Oh God, he prayed silently, what is happening to me, what is happening to me, change this night, let me wake up, whatever is happening to me make it *stop*.

A gray-haired man was standing beside the road, urinating. Rod slowed to a crawl. Slowed until he was barely moving. Crept past the man so slowly that if he had even twitched Rod could have stopped the truck. But the gray-haired man only finished, dropped his robe, and waved gaily to Rod. At that moment Rod heaved a sigh of relief and sped up.

Dropped his robe. The man was wearing a robe. Except for this gory night men did not wear *robes*. And at that moment he caught through his side mirror the white flash of the man throwing himself under the rear tires. Rod slammed on the brake and leaned his head against the steering wheel and wept loud, wracking sobs that shook the whole cab, that set the truck rocking slightly on its heavy-duty springs.

For in every death Rod saw the face of his wife after the traffic accident (not my fault!) that had killed her instantly and yet left Rod to walk away from the wreck without a scratch on him.

I was not supposed to live, he thought at the time, and thought now. I was not supposed to live, and now God is telling me that I am a murderer with my wheels and my motor and my steering wheel.

And he looked up from the wheel.

Orion was still laughing at Hector's account of how he fooled the truck driver into speeding up.

"He thought I was conking into the bushes at the side of the road!" he howled again, and Orion burst into a fresh peal of laughter at his friend.

"And then a backflip into the road under his tires! How I wish I could see it!" Orion shouted. The other guests were laughing, too. Except Gemini and Officer Manwool.

"You can see it, of course," Manwool said softly.

Her words penetrated through the noise, and Orion shook his head. "Only on the holo. And that's not very good, not a good image at all."

"It'll do," she said.

And Gemini, behind Orion, murmured, "Why not, Orry?"

The sound of the old term of endearment was startling to Orion, but oddly comforting. Did Gemini, then, treasure those memories as Orion did? Orion turned slowly, looked into Gemini's sad, deep eyes. "Would you like to see it on the holo?" he asked.

Gemini only smiled. Or rather, twitched his lips into that momentary piece of a smile that Orion knew from so many years before (only forty years, but forty years was back into my childhood, when I was only thirty and Gemini was—what?—fifteen. Helot to my Spartan; Slav to my Hun) and Orion smiled back. His fingers danced over the controls.

Many of the guests gathered around, although others, bored with the coming and going in the time-lid, however extravagant it might be as a party entertainment ("Enough energy to light all of Mexico for an hour," said the one with the giddy laugh who had already promised her body to four men and a woman and was now giving it to another who would not wait), occupied themselves with something decadent and delightful and distracting in the darker corners of the room.

The holo flashed on. The truck crept slowly down the road, its holographic image flickering.

"Why does it do that?" someone asked, and Orion answered mechanically, "There aren't as many chronons as there are photons, and they have a lot more area to cover."

And then the image of a man flickering by the side of the road. Everyone laughed as they realized it was Hector, conking away with all his heart. Then another laugh as he dropped his robe and waved.

The truck sped up, and then a backflip by the man-figure, under the wheels. The body flopped under the doubled back tires, then lay limp and shattered in the road as the truck came to a stop only a few meters ahead. A few moments later, the body disappeared.

"Brilliantly done, Hector!" Orion shouted again. "Better than you told it!" Everyone applauded in agreement, and Orion reached over to flip off the holo. But Officer Manwool stopped him.

"Don't turn it off, Mr Overweed," she said. "Freeze it, and move the image."

Orion looked at her for a moment, then shrugged and did as she said. He expanded the view, so that the truck shrank. And then he suddenly stiffened, as did the guests close enough and interested enough to notice. Not more than ten meters in front of the truck was the ravine, where the broken bridge waited.

"He can see it," somebody gasped. And Officer Manwool slipped a lovecord around Orion's wrist, pulled it taut, and fastened the loose end to her workbelt.

"Orion Overweed, you're under arrest. That man can see the ravine. He will not die. He was brought to a stop in plenty of time to notice the certain death ahead of him. He will live—with a knowledge of whatever he saw tonight. And already you have altered the future, the present, and all the past from his time until the present."

And for the first time in all his life, Orion realized that he had reason to be afraid.

"But that's a capital offense," he said lamely.

"I only wish it included torture," Officer Manwool

said heatedly, "the kind of torture you put that poor truck driver through!"

And then she started to pull Orion out of the room.

Rod Bingley lifted his eyes from the steering wheel and stared uncomprehendingly at the road ahead. The truck's light illuminated the road clearly for many meters. And for five seconds or thirty minutes or some other length of time that was both brief and infinite he did not understand what it meant.

He got out of the cab and walked to the edge of the ravine, looking down. For a few minutes he felt relieved.

Then he walked back to the truck and counted the wounds in the cab. The dents on the grill and the smooth metal. Three cracks in the windshield.

He walked back to where the man had been urinating. Sure enough, though there was no urine, there was an indentation in the ground where the hot liquid had struck, speckles in the dirt where it had splashed.

And in the fresh asphalt, laid, surely, that morning (but then why no warning signs on the bridge? Perhaps the wind tonight blew them over), his tire tracks showed clearly. Except for a manwidth stretch where the left rear tires had left no print at all.

And Rodney remembered the dead, smashed faces, especially the bright and livid eyes among the blood and broken bone. They all looked like Rachel to him. Rachel who had wanted him to—to what? Couldn't even remember the dreams anymore?

He got back into the cab and gripped the steering wheel. His head spun and ached, but he felt himself on the verge of a marvelous conclusion, a simple answer to all of this. There was evidence, yes even though the bodies were gone, there was evidence that he had hit those people. He had not imagined it.

They must, then, be (he stumbled over the word, even in his mind, laughed at himself as he concluded:) angels. Jesus sent them, he knew it, as his mother had taught him, destroying angels teaching him the death that he had brought to his wife while daring, himself, to walk away scatheless.

It was time to even up the debt.

He started the engine and drove, slowly, deliberately toward the end of the road. And as the front tires bumped off and a sickening moment passed when he feared that the truck would be too heavy for the driving wheels to push along the ground, he clasped his hands in front of his face and prayed, aloud: "Forward!"

And then the truck slid forward, tipped downward, hung in the air, and fell. His body pressed into the back of the truck. His clasped hands struck his face. He meant to say, "Into thy hands I commend my spirit," but instead he screamed, "No no no no no," in an infinite negation of death that, after all, didn't do a bit of good once he was committed into the gentle, unyielding hands of the ravine. They clasped and enfolded him, pressed him tightly, closed his eyes and pillowed his head between the gas tank and the granite.

"Wait," Gemini said.

"Why the hell should we?" Officer Manwool said, stopping at the door with Orion following docilely on the end of the lovecord. Orion, too, stopped, and looked at the policeman with the adoring expression all lovecord captives wore.

"Give the man a break," Gemini said.

"He doesn't deserve one," she said. "And neither do you."

"I say give the man a break. At least wait for the proof."

She snorted. "What more proof does he need, Gemini? A signed statement from Rodney Bingley that Orion Overweed is a bloody hitler?"

Gemini smiled and spread his hands. "We didn't actually *see* what Rodney did next, did we? Maybe he was struck by lightning two hours later, before he saw anybody—I mean, you're required to show that damage did happen. And I don't feel any change to the present—"

"You know that changes aren't felt. They aren't even known, since we wouldn't remember anything other than how things actually happened!"

"At least," Gemini said, "watch what happens and see whom Rodney tells."

So she led Orion back to the controls, and at her instructions Orion lovingly started the holo moving again.

And they all watched as Rodney Bingley walked to the edge of the ravine, then walked back to the truck, drove it to the edge and over into the chasm, and died on the rocks.

As it happened, Hector hooted in joy. "He died after all! Orion didn't change a damned thing, not one damned thing!"

Manwool turned on him in disgust. "You make me sick," she said.

"The man's dead," Hector said in glee. "So get

93

that stupid string off Orion or I'll sue for a writ of—"

"Go pucker in a corner," she said, and several of the women pretended to be shocked. Manwool loosened the lovecord and slid it off Orion's wrist. Immediately he turned on her, snarling. "Get out of here! Get out! Get out!"

He followed her to the door of the crambox. Gemini was not the only one who wondered if he would hit her. But Orion kept his control, and she left unharmed.

Orion stumbled back from the crambox rubbing his arms as if with soap, as if trying to scrape them clean from contact with the lovecord. "That thing ought to be outlawed. I actually loved her. I actually loved that stinking, bloody, son-of-a-bitching cop!" And he shuddered so violently that several of the guests laughed and the spell was broken.

Orion managed a smile and the guests went back to amusing themselves. With the sensitivity that even the insensitive and jaded sometimes exhibit, they left him alone with Gemini at the controls of the timelid.

Gemini reached out and brushed a strand of hair out of Orion's eyes. "Get a comb someday," he said. Orion smiled and gently stroked Gemini's hand. Gemini slowly removed his hand from Orion's reach. "Sorry, Orry," Gemini said, "but not any-more."

Orion pretended to shrug. "I know," he said. "Not even for old times' sake." He laughed softly. "That stupid string made me love her. They shouldn't even do that to criminals."

He played with the controls of the holo, which was still on. The image zoomed in; the cab of the truck grew larger and larger. The chronons were too scattered and the image began to blur and fade. Orion stopped it.

By ducking slightly and looking through a window into the cab, Orion and Gemini could see the exact place where the outcropping of rock crushed Rod Bingley's head against the gas tank. Details, of course, were indecipherable.

"I wonder," Orion finally said, "if it's any different."

"What's any different?" Gemini asked.

"Death. If it's any different when you don't wake up right afterward."

A silence.

Then the sound of Gemini's soft laughter.

"What's funny?" Orion asked.

"You," the younger man answered. "Only one thing left that you haven't tried, isn't there?"

"How could I do it?" Orion asked, half-seriously (only half?). "They'd only clone me back."

"Simple enough," Gemini said. "All you need is a friend who's willing to turn off the machine while you're on the far end. Nothing is left. And you can take care of the actual suicide yourself."

"Suicide," Orion said with a smile. "Trust you to use the policeman's term."

And that night, as the other guests slept off the alcohol in beds or other convenient places, Orion lay on the chair and pulled the box over his head. And with Gemini's last kiss on his cheek and Gemini's left hand on the controls, Orion said, "All right. Pull me over."

After a few minutes Gemini was alone in the room. He did not even pause to reflect before he went to the breaker box and shut off all the power for a critical few seconds. Then he returned, sat alone in the room with the disconnected machine and the empty chair. The crambox soon buzzed with the police override, and Mercy Manwool stepped out. She went straight to Gemini, embraced him. He kissed her, hard.

"Done?" she asked.

He nodded.

"The bastard didn't deserve to live," she said.

Gemini shook his head. "You didn't get your justice, my dear Mercy."

"Isn't he dead?"

"Oh yes, that. Well, it's what he wanted, you know. I told him what I planned. And he asked me to do it."

She looked at him angrily. "You would. And then tell *me* about it, so I wouldn't get any joy out of this at all." Gemini only shrugged.

Manwool turned away from him, walked to the timelid. She ran her fingers along the box. Then she detached her laser from her belt and slowly melted the timelid until it was a mass of hot plastic on a metal stand. The few metal components had even melted a little, bending to be just a little out of shape.

"Screw the past anyway," she said. "Why can't it stay where it belongs?"

FREEWAY GAMES

Except for Donner Pass, everything on the road between San Francisco and Salt Lake City was boring. Stanley had driven the road a dozen deadly times until he was sure he knew Nevada by heart: an endless road winding among hills covered with sagebrush. "When God got through making scenery," Stanley often said, "there was a lot of land left over in Nevada, and God said, 'Aw, to hell with it,' and that's where Nevada's been ever since."

Today Stanley was relaxed, there was no rush for him to get back to Salt Lake, and so, to ease the boredom, he began playing freeway games.

He played Blue Angels first. On the upslope of the Sierra Nevadas he found two cars riding side by side at fifty miles an hour. He pulled his Datsun 260Z into formation beside them. At fifty miles an hour they cruised along, blocking all the lanes of the freeway. Traffic began piling up behind them.

The game was successful—the other two drivers got into the spirit of the thing. When the middle car drifted forward, Stanley eased back to stay even with the driver on the right, so that they drove down the freeway in an arrowhead formation. They made diagonals, funnels; danced around each other for half an hour; and whenever one of them pulled slightly ahead, the frantically angry drivers behind them jockeyed behind the leading car.

Finally, Stanley tired of the game, despite the fun of the honks and flashing lights behind them. He honked twice, and waved jauntily to the driver beside him, then pressed on the accelerator and leaped forward at seventy miles an hour, soon dropping back to sixty as dozens of other cars, their drivers trying to make up for lost time (or trying to compensate for long confinement), passed by going much faster. Many paused to drive beside him, honking, glaring, and making obscene gestures. Stanley grinned at them all.

He got bored again east of Reno.

This time he decided to play Follow. A yellow AM Hornet was just ahead of him on the highway, going fifty-eight to sixty miles per hour. A good speed. Stanley settled in behind the car, about three lengths behind, and followed. The driver was a woman, with dark hair that danced in the erratic wind that came through her open windows. Stanley wondered how long it would take her to notice that she was being followed.

Two songs on the radio (Stanley's measure of time while traveling), and halfway through a commercial for hair spray—and she began to pull away. Stanley prided himself on quick reflexes. She didn't even gain a car length; even when she reached seventy, he stayed behind her.

He hummed along with an old Billy Joel song even as the Reno radio station began to fade. He hunted for another station, but found only country and western, which he loathed. So in silence he followed as the woman in the Hornet slowed down.

She went thirty miles an hour, and still he didn't

pass. Stanley chuckled. At this point, he was sure she was imagining the worst. A rapist, a thief, a kidnapper, determined to destroy her. She kept on looking in her rearview mirror.

"Don't worry, little lady," Stanley said, "I'm just a Salt Lake City boy who's having fun." She slowed down to twenty, and he stayed behind her; she sped up abruptly until she was going fifty, but her Hornet couldn't possibly out-accelerate his Z.

"I made forty thousand dollars for the company," he sang in the silence of his car, "and that's six thousand dollars for me."

The Hornet came up behind a truck that was having trouble getting up a hill. There was a passing lane, but the Hornet didn't use it at first, hoping, apparently, that Stanley would pass. Stanley didn't pass. So the Hornet pulled out, got even with the nose of the truck, then rode parallel with the truck all the rest of the way up the hill.

"Ah," Stanley said, "playing Blue Angels with the Pacific Intermountain Express." He followed her closely.

At the top of the hill, the passing lane ended. At the last possible moment the Hornet pulled in front of the truck—and stayed only a few yards ahead of it. There was no room for Stanley, and now on a two-lane road a car was coming straight at him.

"What a bitch!" Stanley mumbled. In a split second, because when angry Stanley doesn't like to give in, he decided that she wasn't going to outsmart *him*. He nosed into the space between the Hornet and the truck anyway.

There wasn't room. The truck driver leaned on his horn and braked; the woman, afraid, pulled forward. Stanley got out of the way just as the oncoming car, its driver a father with a wife and several rowdy children looking petrified at the accident that had nearly happened, passed on the left.

"Think you're smart, don't you, bitch? But Stanley Howard's feeling rich." Nonsense, nonsense, but it sounded good and he sang it in several keys as he followed the woman, who was now going a steady sixty-five, two car-lengths behind. The Hornet had Utah plates—she was going to be on that road a long time.

Stanley's mind wandered. From thoughts of Utah plates to a memory of eating at Alioto's and on to his critical decision that no matter how close you put Alioto's to the wharf, the fish there wasn't any better than the fish at Bratten's in Salt Lake. He decided that he would have to eat there soon, to make sure his impression was correct; he wondered whether he should bother taking Liz out again, since she so obviously wasn't interested; speculated on whether Genevieve would say yes if he asked her.

And the Hornet wasn't in front of him anymore.

He was only going forty-five, and the PIE truck was catching up to him on a straight section of the road. There were curves into a mountain pass up ahead—she must have gone faster when he wasn't noticing. But he sped up, sped even faster, and didn't see her. She must have pulled off somewhere, and Stanley chuckled to think of her panting, her heart beating fast, as she watched Stanley drive on by. What a relief that must have been, Stanley thought. Poor lady. What a nasty game. And he giggled with delight, silently, his chest and stomach shaking but making no sound.

He stopped for gas in Elko, had a package of cupcakes from the vending machine in the gas station, and was leaning on his car when he watched the Hornet go by. He waved, but the woman didn't see him. He did notice, however, that she pulled into an Amoco station not far up the road.

It was just a whim. I'm taking this too far, he thought, even as he waited in his car for her to pull out of the gas station. She pulled out. For just a moment Stanley hesitated, decided not to go on with the chase, then pulled out and drove along the main street of Elko a few blocks behind the Hornet. The woman stopped at a light. When it turned green, Stanley was right behind her. He saw her look in her rearview mirror again, stiffen; her eyes were afraid.

"Don't worry, lady," he said. "I'm not following you this time. Just going my own sweet way home."

The woman abruptly, without signalling, pulled into a parking place. Stanley calmly drove on. "See?" he said. "Not following. Not following."

A few miles outside Elko, he pulled off the road. He knew why he was waiting. He denied it to himself. Just resting, he told himself. Just sitting here because I'm in no hurry to get back to Salt Lake City. But it was hot and uncomfortable, and with the car stopped, there wasn't the slightest breeze coming through the windows of the Z. This is stupid, he told himself. Why persecute the poor woman anymore? he asked himself. Why the hell am I still sitting here?

He was still sitting there when she passed him. She saw him. She sped up. Stanley put the car in gear, drove out into the road from the shoulder, caught up with her quickly, and settled in behind her. "I am a shithead," he announced to himself. "I am the meanest asshole on the highway. I ought to

101

be shot." He meant it. But he stayed behind her, cursing himself all the way.

In the silence of his car (the noise of the wind did not count as sound; the engine noise was silent to his accustomed ears), he recited the speeds as they drove. "Fifty-five, sixty, sixty-five on a curve, are we out of our minds, young lady? Seventy—ah, ho, now, look for a Nevada state trooper anywhere along here." They took curves at ridiculous speeds; she stopped abruptly occasionally; always Stanley's reflexes were quick, and he stayed a few car lengths behind her.

"I really am a nice person, young lady," he said to the woman in the car, who was pretty, he realized as he remembered the face he saw when she passed him back in Elko. "If you met me in Salt Lake City, you'd like me. I might ask you out for a date sometime. And if you aren't some tight-assed little Mormon girl we might get it on. You know? I'm a nice person."

She was pretty, and as he drove along behind her ("What? Eighty-five? I never thought a Hornet could go eighty-five"), he began to fantasize. He imagined her running out of gas, panicking because now, on some lonely stretch of road, she would be at the mercy of the crazy man following her. But in his fantasy, when he stopped it was she who had a gun, she who was in control of the situation. She held the gun on him, forced him to give her his car keys, and then she made him strip, took his clothes and stuffed them in the back of the Z, and took off in his car. "It's you that's dangerous, lady," he said. He replayed the fantasy several times, and each time she spent more time with him before she left him

102

naked by the road with an out-of-gas Hornet and horny as hell.

Stanley realized the direction his fantasies had taken him. "I've been too lonely too long," he said. "Too lonely too long, and Liz won't unzip anything without a license." The word *lonely* made him laugh, thinking of tacky poetry. He sang: "Bury me not on the lone prairie where the coyotes howl and wind blows free."

For hours he followed the woman. By now he was sure she realized it was a game. By now she must know he meant no harm. He had done nothing to try to get her to pull over. He was just tagging along. "Like a friendly dog," he said. "Arf. Woof. Growrrr." And he fantasized again until suddenly the lights of Wendover were dazzling, and he realized it was dark. He switched on his lights. When he did, the Hornet sped up, its taillights bright for a moment, then ordinary among the lights and signs saying that this was the last chance to lose money before getting to Utah.

Just inside Wendover, a police car was pulled to the side of the road, its lights flashing. Some poor sap caught speeding. Stanley expected the woman to be smart, to pull over behind the policeman, while Stanley moved on over the border, out of Nevada jurisdiction.

The Hornet, however, went right by the policeman, sped up, in fact, and Stanley was puzzled for a moment. Was the woman crazy? She must be scared out of her wits by now, and here was a chance for relief and rescue, and she ignored it. Of course, Stanley reasoned, as he followed the Hornet out of Wendover and down to the long straight stretch of the highway over the Salt Flats, of course she didn't stop. Poor lady was so conscious of having broken the law speeding that she was *afraid* of cops.

Crazy. People do crazy things under pressure, Stanley decided.

The highway stretched out straight into the blackness. No moon. Some starlight, but there were no landmarks on either side of the road, and so the cars barreled on as if in a tunnel, with only a hypnotic line to the left and headlights behind and taillights ahead.

How much gas would the tank of a Hornet hold? The Salt Flats went a long way before the first gas station, and what with daylight saving time it must be ten-thirty, eleven o'clock, maybe only ten, but some of those gas stations would be closing up now. Stanley's Z could get home to Salt Lake with gas to spare after a fill-up in Elko, but the Hornet might run out of gas.

Stanley remembered his daydreams of the afternoon and now translated them into night, into her panic in the darkness, the gun flashing in his headlights. This lady was armed and dangerous. She was carrying drugs into Utah, and thought he was from the mob. She probably thought he was planning to get her on the lonely Salt Flats, miles from anywhere. She was probably checking the clip of her gun.

Eight-five, said the speedometer.

"Going pretty fast, lady," he said.

Ninety, said the speedometer.

Of course, Stanley realized. She *is* running out of gas. She wants to get going as fast as she can, outrun me, but at least have enough momentum to coast when she runs out.

Nonsense, thought Stanley. It's dark, and the poor

lady is scared out of her wits. I've got to stop this. This is dangerous. It's dark and it's dangerous and this stupid game has gone on for four hundred miles. I never meant it to go on this long.

Stanley passed the road signs that told him, habituated as he was to this drive, that the first big curve was coming up. A lot of people unfamiliar with the Salt Flats thought it went straight as an arrow all the way. But there was a curve where there was no reason to have a curve, before the mountains, before anything. And in typical Utah Highway Department fashion, the Curve sign was posted right in the middle of the turn. Instinctively, Stanley slowed down.

The woman in the Hornet did not.

In his headlights Stanley saw the Hornet slide off the road. He screeched on his brakes; as he went past, he saw the Hornet bounce on its nose, flip over and bounce on its tail, then topple back and land flat on the roof. For a moment the car lay there. Stanley got his car stopped, looked back over his shoulder. The Hornet erupted in flames.

Stanley stayed there for only a minute or so, gasping, shuddering. In horror. In horror, he insisted to himself, saying, "What have I done! My God, what have I done," but knowing even as he pretended to be appalled that he was having an orgasm, that the shuddering of his body was the most powerful ejaculation he had ever had, that he had been trying to get up the Hornet's ass all the way from Reno and finally, finally, he had come.

He drove on. He drove for twenty minutes and came to a gas station with a pay phone. He got out of the car stiffly, his pants sticky and wet, and fumbled in his sticky pocket for a sticky dime, which he put in the phone. He dialed the emergency number.

"I—I passed a car on the Salt Flats. In flames. About fifteen miles before this Chevron station. Flames."

He hung up. He drove on. A few minutes later he saw a patrol car, lights whirling, speeding past going the other way. From Salt Lake City out into the desert. And still later he saw an ambulance and a fire truck go by. Stanley gripped the wheel tightly. They would know. They would see his skid marks. Someone would tell about the Z that was following the Hornet from Reno until the woman in the Hornet died in Utah.

But even as he worried, he knew that no one would know. He hadn't touched her. There wasn't a mark on his car.

The highway turned into a six-lane street with motels and shabby diners on either side. He went under the freeway, over the railroad tracks, and followed North Temple street up to Second Avenue, the school on the left, the Slow signs, everything normal, everything as he had left it, everything as it always had been when he came home from a long trip. To L Street, to the Chateau LeMans apartments; he parked in the underground garage, got out. All the doors opened to his key. His room was undisturbed.

What the hell do I expect? he asked himself. Sirens heading my way? Five detectives in my living room waiting to grill me?

The woman, the woman had died. He tried to feel terrible. But all that he could remember, all that was important in his mind, was the shuddering of his body, the feeling that the orgasm would never

106

end. There was nothing. Nothing like that in the world.

He went to sleep quickly, slept easily. Murderer? he asked himself as he drifted off.

But the word was taken by his mind and driven into a part of his memory where Stanley could not retrieve it. Can't live with that. Can't live with that. And so he didn't.

Stanley found himself avoiding looking at the paper the next morning, and so he forced himself to look. It wasn't front page news. It was buried back in the local news section. Her name was Alix Humphreys. She was twenty-two and single, working as a secretary to some law firm. Her picture showed her as a young, attractive girl.

"The driver apparently fell asleep at the wheel, according to police investigators. The vehicle was going faster than eighty miles per hour when the mishap occurred."

Mishap.

Hell of a word for the flames.

Yet, Stanley went to work just as he always did, flirted with the secretaries just as he always did, and even drove his car, just as he always did, carefully and politely on the road.

It wasn't long, however, before he began playing freeway games again. On his way up to Logan, he played Follow, and a woman in a Honda Civic smashed head-on into a pickup truck as she foolishly tried to pass a semitruck at the crest of a hill in Sardine Canyon. The police reports didn't mention (and no one knew) that she was trying to get away from a Datsun 260Z that had relentlessly followed her for eighty miles. Her name was Donna Weeks, and she had two children and a husband who had been expecting her back in Logan that evening. They couldn't get all her body out of the car.

On a hop over to Denver, a seventeen-year-old skier went out of control on a snowy road, her VW smashing into a mountain, bouncing off, and tumbling down a cliff. One of the skis on the back of her bug, incredibly enough, was unbroken. The other was splintered into kindling. Her head went through the windshield. Her body didn't.

The roads between Cameron trading post and Page, Arizona, were the worst in the world. It surprised no one when an eighteen-year-old blond model from Phoenix was killed when she smashed into the back of a van parked beside the road. She had been going more than a hundred miles an hour, which her friends said did not surprise them, she had always sped, especially when driving at night. A child in the van was killed in his sleep, and the family was hospitalized. There was no mention of a Datsun with Utah plates.

And Stanley began to remember more often. There wasn't room in the secret places of his mind to hold all of this. He clipped their faces out of the paper. He dreamed of them at night. In his dreams they always threatened him, always deserved the end they got. Every dream ended with orgasm. But never as strong a convulsion as the ecstacy when the collision came on the highway.

Check. And mate.

Aim, and fire.

Eighteen, seven, twenty-three, hike.

Games, all games, and the moment of truth.

"I'm sick." He sucked the end of his Bic four-color pen. "I need help."

The phone rang.

"Stan? It's Liz."

Hi, Liz.

"Stan, aren't you going to answer me?"

Go to hell, Liz.

"Stan, what kind of game is this? You don't call for nine months, and now you just sit there while I'm trying to talk to you?"

Come to bed, Liz.

"That *is* you, isn't it?"

"Yeah, it's me."

"Well, why didn't you answer me? Stan, you scared me. That really scared me."

"I'm sorry."

"Stan, what happened? Why haven't you called?"

"I needed you too much." Melodramatic, melodramatic. But true.

"Stan, I know. I was being a bitch."

"No, no, not really. I was being too demanding."

"Stan, I miss you. I want to be with you."

"I miss you, too, Liz. I've really needed you these last few months."

She droned on as Stanley sang silently, "Oh, bury me not on the lone prairie, where the coyotes howl—"

"Tonight? My apartment?"

"You mean you'll let me past the sacred chain lock?"

"Stanley. Don't be mean. I miss you."

"I'll be there."

"I love you."

"Me, too."

After this many months, Stanley was not sure, not sure at all. But Liz was a straw to grasp at. "I

109

drown," Stanley said. "I die. *Morior. Moriar. Mortuus sum.*"

Back when he had been dating Liz, back when they had been together, Stanley hadn't played these freeway games. Stanley hadn't watched these women die. Stanley hadn't had to hide from himself in his sleep. "*Caedo. Caedam. Cecidi.*"

Wrong, wrong. He had been dating Liz the first time. He had only stopped after—after. Liz had nothing to do with it. Nothing would help. "*Despero. Desperabo. Desperavi.*"

And because it was the last thing he wanted to do, he got up, got dressed, went out to his car, and drove out onto the freeway. He got behind a woman in a red Audi. And he followed her.

She was young, but she was a good driver. He tailed her from Sixth South to the place where the freeway forks, 1–15 continuing south, 1–80 veering east. She stayed in the right-hand lane until the last moment, then swerved across two lanes of traffic and got onto 1–80. Stanley did not think of letting her go. He, too, cut across traffic. A bus honked loudly; there was a screeching of brakes; Stanley's Z was on two wheels and he lost control; a lightpost loomed, then passed.

And Stanley was on 1–80, following a few hundred yards behind the Audi. He quickly closed the gap. This woman was smart, Stanley said to himself. "You're smart, lady. You won't let me get away with anything. Nobody today. Nobody today." He meant to say nobody dies today, and he knew that was what he was really saying (hoping; denying), but he did not let himself say it. He spoke as if a microphone hung over his head, recording his words for posterity.

The Audi wove through traffic, averaging seventy-five. Stanley followed close behind. Occasionally, a gap in the traffic closed before he could use it; he found another. But he was a dozen cars behind when she cut off and took the last exit before 1–80 plunged upward into Parley's Canyon. She was going south on 1–215, and Stanley followed, though he had to brake violently to make the tight curve that led from one freeway to the other.

She drove rapidly down 1–215 until it ended, turned into a narrow two-lane road winding along the foot of the mountain. As usual, a gravel truck was going thirty miles an hour, shambling along shedding stones like dandruff onto the road. The Audi pulled behind the gravel truck, and Stanley's Z pulled behind the Audi.

The woman was smart. She didn't try to pass. Not on that road.

When they reached the intersection with the road going up Big Cottonwood Canyon to the ski resorts (closed now in the spring, so there was no traffic), she seemed to be planning to turn right, to take Fort Union Boulevard back to the freeway. Instead, she turned left. But Stanley had been anticipating the move, and he turned left, too.

They were not far up the winding canyon road before it occurred to Stanley that this road led to nowhere. At Snowbird it was a dead end, a loop that turned around and headed back down. This woman, who had seemed so smart, was making a very stupid move.

And then he thought, I might catch her. He said, "I might catch you, girl. Better watch out."

What he would do if he caught her he wasn't sure.

She must have a gun. She must be armed, or she wouldn't be daring him like this.

She took the curves at ridiculous speeds, and Stanley was pressed to the limit of his driving skills to stay up with her. This was the most difficult game of Follow he had ever played. But it might end too quickly—on any of these curves she might smash up, might meet a car coming the other way. Be careful, he thought. Be careful, be careful, it's just a game, don't be afraid, don't panic.

Panic? The moment this woman had realized she was being followed, she had sped and dodged, leading him on a merry chase. None of the confusion the others had shown. This was a live one. When he caught her, she'd know what to do. She'd know. "*Veniebam. Veniam. Venies.*" He laughed at his joke.

Then he stopped laughing abruptly, swung the wheel hard to the right, jamming on the brake. He had seen just a flash of red going up a side road. Just a flash, but it was enough. This bitch in the red Audi thought she'd fool him. Thought she could ditch into a side road and he'd go on by.

He skidded in the gravel of the shoulder, but regained control and charged up the narrow dirt road. The Audi was stopped a few hundred yards from the entrance.

Stopped.

At last.

He pulled in behind her, even had his fingers on the door handle. But she had not meant to stop, apparently. She had only meant to pull out of sight till he went by. He had been too smart for her. He had seen. And now she was caught on a terribly lonely mountain road, still moist from the melting snow, with only trees around, in weather too warm for skiers, too cold for hikers. She had thought to trick him, and now he had trapped her.

She drove off. He followed. On the bumpy dirt road, twenty miles an hour was uncomfortably fast. She went thirty. His shocks were being shot to hell, but this was one that wouldn't get away. She wouldn't get away from Stanley. Her Audi was voluptuous with promises.

After interminable jolting progress up the side canyon, the mountains suddenly opened out into a small valley. The road, for a while, was flat, though certainly not straight. And the Audi sped up to forty incredible miles an hour. She wasn't giving up. And she was a damned good driver. But Stanley was a damned good driver, too. "I should quit now," he said to the invisible microphone in his car. But he didn't quit. He didn't quit and he didn't quit.

The road quit.

He came around a tree-lined curve and suddenly there was no road. Just a gap in the trees and, a few hundred yards away, the other side of a ravine. To the right, out of the corner of his eye, he saw where the road made a hairpin turn, saw the Audi stopped there, saw, he thought, a face looking at him in horror. And because of that face he turned to look, tried to look over his shoulder, desperate to see the face, desperate not to watch as the trees bent gracefully toward him and the rocks rose up and enlarged and engorged, and he impaled himself, himself and his Datsun 260Z on a rock that arched upward and shuddered as he swallowed its tip.

She sat in the Audi, shaking, her body heaving in great sobs of relief and shock at what had happened.

113

Relief and shock, yes. But by now she knew that the shuddering was more than that. It was also ecstacy.

This has to stop, she cried out silently to herself. Four, four, four. "Four is enough," she said, beating on the steering wheel. Then she got control of herself, and the orgasm passed except for the trembling in her thighs and occasional cramps, and she jockeyed the car until it was turned around, and she headed back down the canyon to Salt Lake City, where she was already an hour late.

A Sepulchre of Songs

She was losing her mind during the rain. For four weeks it came down nearly every day, and the people at the Millard County Rest Home didn't take any of the patients outside. It bothered them all, of course, and made life especially hellish for the nurses, everyone complaining to them constantly and demanding to be entertained.

Elaine didn't demand entertainment, however. She never seemed to demand much of anything. But the rain hurt her worse than anyone. Perhaps because she was only fifteen, the only child in an institution devoted to adult misery. More likely because she depended more than most on the hours spent outside; certainly she took more pleasure from them. They would lift her into her chair, prop her up with pillows so her body would stay straight, and then race down the corridor to the glass doors, Elaine calling, "Faster, faster," as they pushed her until finally they were outside. They told me she never really said anything out there. Just sat quietly in her chair on the lawn, watching everything. And then later in the day they would wheel her back in.

I often saw her being wheeled in—early, because I was there, though she never complained about my visits' cutting into her hours outside. As I watched

115

her being pushed toward the rest home, she would smile at me so exuberantly that my mind invented arms for her, waving madly to match her childishly delighted face; I imagined legs pumping, imagined her running across the grass, breasting the air like great waves. But there were the pillows where arms should be, keeping her from falling to the side, and the belt around her middle kept her from pitching forward, since she had no legs to balance with.

It rained four weeks, and I nearly lost her.

My job was one of the worst in the state, touring six rest homes in as many counties, visiting each of them every week. I "did therapy" wherever the rest home administrators thought therapy was needed. I never figured out how they decided—all the patients were mad to one degree or another, most with the helpless insanity of age, the rest with the anguish of the invalid and the crippled.

You don't end up as a state-employed therapist if you had much ability in college. I sometimes pretend that I didn't distinguish myself in graduate school because I marched to a different drummer. But I didn't. As one kind professor gently and brutally told me, I wasn't cut out for science. But I was sure cut out for the art of therapy. Ever since I comforted my mother during her final year of cancer I had believed I had a knack for helping people get straight in their minds. I was everybody's confidant.

Somehow I had never supposed, though, that I would end up trying to help the hopeless in a part of the state where even the healthy didn't have much to live for. Yet that's all I had the credentials for, and when I (so maturely) told myself I was over the initial disappointment, I made the best of it.

Elaine was the best of it.

116

"Raining raining raining," was the greeting I got when I visited her on the third day of the wet spell.

"Don't I know it?" I said. "My hair's soaking wet."

"Wish mine was," Elaine answered.

"No, you don't. You'd get sick."

"Not me," she said.

"Well, Mr. Woodbury told me you're depressed. I'm supposed to make you happy."

"Make it stop raining."

"Do I look like God?"

"I thought maybe you were in disguise. *I'm* in disguise," she said. It was one of our regular games. "I'm really a large Texas armadillo who was granted one wish. I wished to be a human being. But there wasn't enough of the armadillo to make a full human being, so here I am." She smiled. I smiled back.

Actually, she had been five years old when an oil truck exploded right in front of her parents' car, killing both of them and blowing her arms and legs right off. That she survived was a miracle. That she had to keep on living was unimaginable cruelty. That she managed to be a reasonably happy person, a favorite of the nurses—that I don't understand in the least. Maybe it was because she had nothing else to do. There aren't many ways that a person with no arms or legs can kill herself.

"I want to go outside," she said, turning her head away from me to look out the window.

Outside wasn't much. A few trees, a lawn, and beyond that a fence, not to keep the inmates in but to keep out the seamier residents of a rather seamy town. But there were low hills in the distance, and the birds usually seemed cheerful. Now, of course, the rain had driven both birds and hills into hiding.

117

There was no wind, and so the trees didn't even sway. The rain just came straight down.

"Outer space is like the rain," she said. "It sounds like that there, just a low drizzling sound in the background of everything."

"Not really," I said. "There's no sound out there at all."

"How do *you* know?" she asked.

"There's no air. Can't be any sound without air."

She looked at me scornfully. "Just as I thought. You don't *really* know. You've never *been* there, have you?"

"Are you trying to pick a fight?"

She started to answer, caught herself, and nodded. "Damned rain."

"At least you don't have to drive in it," I said. But her eyes got wistful, and I knew I had taken the banter too far. "Hey," I said. "First clear day I'll take you out driving."

"It's hormones," she said.

"What's hormones?"

"I'm fifteen. It always bothered me when I had to stay in. But I want to scream. My muscles are all bunched up, my stomach is all tight. I want to go outside and *scream*. It's hormones."

"What about your friends?" I asked.

"Are you kidding? They're all out there, playing in the rain."

"*All* of them?"

"Except Grunty, of course. He'd dissolve."

"And where's Grunty?"

"In the freezer, of course."

"Someday the nurses are going to mistake him for ice cream and serve him to the guests."

She didn't smile. She just nodded, and I knew that I wasn't getting anywhere. She really was depressed.

I asked her whether she wanted something.

"No pills," she said. "They make me sleep all the time."

"If I gave you uppers, it would make you climb the walls."

"Neat trick," she said.

"It's that strong. So do you want something to take your mind off the rain and these four ugly yellow walls?"

She shook her head. "I'm trying not to sleep."

"Why not?"

She just shook her head again. "Can't sleep. Can't let myself sleep too much."

I asked again.

"Because," she said, "I might not wake up." She said it rather sternly, and I knew I shouldn't ask anymore. She didn't often get impatient with me, but I knew this time I was coming perilously close to overstaying my welcome.

"Got to go," I said. "You *will* wake up." And then I left, and I didn't see her for a week, and to tell the truth I didn't think of her much that week, what with the rain and a suicide in Ford County that really got to me, since she was fairly young and had a lot to live for, in my opinion. She disagreed and won the argument the hard way.

Weekends I live in a trailer in Piedmont. I live alone. The place is spotlessly clean because cleaning is something I do religiously. Besides, I tell myself, I might want to bring a woman home with me one night. Some nights I even do, and some nights I even enjoy it, but I always get restless and irritable when they start trying to get me to change my work schedule or take them along to the motels I live in or, once only, get the trailer-park manager to let them into my trailer when I'm gone. To keep things cozy for me. I'm not interested in "cozy." This is probably because of my mother's death; her cancer and my responsibilities as housekeeper for my father probably explain why I am a neat housekeeper. Therapist, therap thyself. The days passed in rain and highways and depressing people depressed out of their minds; the nights passed in television and sandwiches and motel bedsheets at state expense; and then it was time to go to the Millard County Rest Home again, where Elaine was waiting. It was then that I thought of her and realized that the rain had been going on for more than a week, and the poor girl must be almost out of her mind. I bought a cassette of Copland conducting Copland. She insisted on cassettes, because they stopped. Eight-tracks went on and on until she couldn't think.

"Where have you been?" she demanded.

"Locked in a cage by a cruel duke in Transylvania. It was only four feet high, suspended over a pond filled with crocodiles. I got out by picking the lock with my teeth. Luckily, the crocodiles weren't hungry. Where have *you* been?"

"I mean it. Don't you keep a schedule?"

"I'm right on my schedule, Elaine. This is Wednesday. I was here last Wednesday. This year Christmas falls on a Wednesday, and I'll be here on Christmas."

"It feels like a year."

"Only ten months. Till Christmas. Elaine, you aren't being any fun."

She wasn't in the mood for fun. There were tears in her eyes. "I can't stand much more," she said.

"I'm sorry."

"I'm afraid."

And she *was* afraid. Her voice trembled.

"At night, and in the daytime, whenever I sleep. I'm just the right size."

"For what?"

"What do you mean?"

"You said you were just the right size."

"I did? Oh, I don't know what I meant. I'm going crazy. That's what you're here for, isn't it? To keep me sane. It's the rain. I can't do anything, I can't see anything, and all I can hear most of the time is the hissing of the rain."

"Like outer space," I said, remembering what she had said the last time.

She apparently didn't remember our discussion. She looked startled. "How did you know?" she asked.

"You told me."

"There isn't any sound in outer space," she said.

"Oh," I answered.

"There's no air out there."

"I knew that."

"Then why did you say, 'Oh, of course'? The engines. You can hear them all over the ship. It's a drone, all the time. That's just like the rain. Only after a while you can't hear it anymore. It becomes like silence. Anansa told me."

Another imaginary friend. Her file said she had kept her imaginary friends long after most children give them up. That was why I had first been assigned to see her, to get rid of the friends. Grunty, the ice pig; Howard, the boy who beat up everybody; Sue

121

Ann, who would bring her dolls and play with them for her, making them do what Elaine said for them to do; Fuchsia, who lived among the flowers and was only inches high. There were others. After a few sessions with her I saw that she knew that they weren't real. But they passed time for her. They stepped outside her body and did things she could never do. I felt they did her no harm at all, and destroying that imaginary world for her would only make her lonelier and more unhappy. She was sane, that was certain. And yet I kept seeing her, not entirely because I liked her so much. Partly because I wondered whether she had been pretending when she told me she knew her friends weren't real. Anansa was a new one.

"Who's Anansa?"

"Oh, you don't want to know." She didn't want to talk about her; that was obvious.

"I want to know."

She turned away. "I can't make you go away, but I wish you would. When you get nosy."

"It's my job."

"Job!" She sounded contemptuous. "I see all of you, running around on your healthy legs, doing all your *jobs*."

What could I say to her? "It's how we stay alive," I said. "I do my best."

Then she got a strange look on her face; *I've got a secret*, she seemed to say, *and I want you to pry it out of me*. "Maybe I can get a job, too."

"Maybe," I said. I tried to think of something she could do.

"There's always music," she said.

I misunderstood. "There aren't many instruments

122

you can play. That's the way it is." Dose of reality and all that.

"Don't be stupid."

"Okay. Never again."

"I meant that there's always the music. On my job."

"And what job is this?"

"Wouldn't you like to know?" she said, rolling her eyes mysteriously and turning toward the window. I imagined her as a normal fifteen-year-old. Ordinarily I would have interpreted this as flirting. But there was something else under all this. A feeling of desperation. She was right. I really would like to know. I made a rather logical guess. I put together the two secrets she was trying to get me to figure out today.

"What kind of job is Anansa going to give you?"

She looked at me, startled. "So it's true then."

"What's true?"

"It's so frightening. I keep telling myself it's a dream. But it isn't, is it?"

"What, Anansa?"

"You think she's just one of my friends, don't you. But they're not in my dreams, not like this. Anansa—"

"What about Anansa?"

"She sings to me. In my sleep."

My trained psychologist's mind immediately conjured up mother figures. "Of course," I said.

"She's in space, and she sings to me. You wouldn't believe the songs."

It reminded me. I pulled out the cassette I had bought for her.

"Thank you," she said.

"You're welcome. Want to hear it?"

123

She nodded. I put it on the cassette player. *Appalachian Spring*. She moved her head to the music. I imagined her as a dancer. She felt the music very well.

But after a few minutes she stopped moving and started to cry.

"It's not the same," she said.

"You've heard it before?"

"Turn it off. Turn it *off*!"

I turned it off. "Sorry," I said. "Thought you'd like it."

"Guilt, nothing but guilt," she said. "You always feel guilty, don't you?"

"Pretty nearly always," I admitted cheerfully. A lot of my parents threw psychological jargon in my face. Or soap-opera language.

"*I'm* sorry," she said. "It's just—it's just not the music. Not *the* music. Now that I've heard it, everything is so dark compared to it. Like the rain, all gray and heavy and dim, as if the composer is trying to see the hills but the rain is always in the way. For a few minutes I thought he was getting it right."

"Anansa's music?"

She nodded. "I know you don't believe me. But I hear her when I'm asleep. She tells me that's the only time she can communicate with me. It's not talking. It's all her songs. She's out there, in her starship, singing. And at night I hear her."

"Why you?"

"You mean, Why only me?" She laughed. "Because of what I am. You told me yourself. Because I can't run around, I live in my imagination. She says that the threads between minds are very thin and hard to hold. But mine she can hold, because I live completely in my mind. She holds on

124

to me. When I go to sleep, I can't escape her now anymore at all."

"Escape? I thought you liked her."

"I don't know what I like. I like—I like the music. But Anansa wants me. She wants to have me—she wants to give me a job."

"What's the singing like?" When she said *job*, she trembled and closed up; I referred back to something that she had been willing to talk about, to keep the floundering conversation going.

"It's not like anything. She's there in space, and it's black, just the humming of the engines like the sound of rain, and she reaches into the dust out there and draws in the songs. She reaches out her— out her fingers, or her ears, I don't know; it isn't clear. She reaches out and draws in the dust and the songs and turns them into the music that I hear. It's powerful. She says it's her songs that drive her between the stars."

"Is she alone?"

Elaine nodded. "She wants me."

"Wants you. How can she have you, with you here and her out there?"

Elaine licked her lips. "I don't want to talk about it," she said in a way that told me she was on the verge of telling me.

"I wish you would. I really wish you'd tell me."

"She says—she says that she can take me. She says that if I can learn the songs, she can pull me out of my body and take me there and give me arms and legs and fingers and I can run and dance and—"

She broke down, crying.

I patted her on the only place that she permitted, her soft little belly. She refused to be hugged. I had tried it years before, and she had screamed at me to stop it. One of the nurses told me it was because her mother had always hugged her, and Elaine wanted to hug back. And couldn't.

"It's a lovely dream, Elaine."

"It's a terrible dream. Don't you see? I'll be like *her*."

"And what's she like?"

"She's the ship. She's the starship. And she wants me with her, to be the starship with her. And sing our way through space together for thousands and thousands of years."

"It's just a dream. Elaine. You don't have to be afraid of it."

"They did it to her. They cut off her arms and legs and put her into the machines."

"But no one's going to put you into a machine."

"I want to go outside," she said.

"You can't. It's raining."

"Damn the rain."

"I do, every day."

"I'm not joking! She pulls me all the time now, even when I'm awake. She keeps pulling at me and making me fall asleep, and she sings to me, and I feel her pulling and pulling. If I could just go outside, I could hold on. I feel like I could hold on, if I could just—"

"Hey, relax. Let me give you a—"

"No! I don't want to sleep!"

"Listen, Elaine. It's just a dream. You can't let it get to you like this. It's just the rain keeping you here. It makes you sleepy, and so you keep dreaming this. But don't fight it. It's a beautiful dream in a way. Why not go with it?"

She looked at me with terror in her eyes.

"You don't mean that. You don't want me to go."

"No. Of course I don't want you to go anywhere. But you won't, don't you see? It's a dream, floating out there between the stars—"

"She's not floating. She's ramming her way through space so fast it makes me dizzy whenever she shows me."

"Then be dizzy. Think of it as your mind finding a way for you to run."

"You don't understand, Mr. Therapist. I thought you'd understand."

"I'm trying to."

"If I go with her, then I'll be dead."

I asked her nurse, "Who's been reading to her?"

"We all do, and volunteers from town. They like her. She always has someone to read to her."

"You'd better supervise them more carefully. Somebody's been putting ideas in her head. About spaceships and dust and singing between the stars. It's scared her pretty bad."

The nurse frowned. "We approve everything they read. She's been reading that kind of thing for years. It's never done her any harm before. Why now?"

"The rain, I guess. Cooped up in here, she's losing touch with reality."

The nurse nodded sympathetically and said, "I know. When she's asleep, she's doing the strangest things now."

"Like what? What kind of things?"

"Oh, singing these horrible songs."

"What are the words?"

"There aren't any words. She just sort of hums. Only the melodies are awful. Not even like music. And her voice gets funny and raspy. She's com-

127

pletely asleep. She sleeps a lot now. Mercifully, I think. She's always gotten impatient when she can't go outside."

The nurse obviously liked Elaine. It would be hard not to feel sorry for her, but Elaine insisted on being liked, and people liked her, those that could get over the horrible flatness of the sheets all around her trunk. "Listen," I said. "Can we bundle her up or something? Get her outside in spite of the rain?"

The nurse shook her head. "It isn't just the rain. It's cold out there. And the explosion that made her like she is—it messed her up inside. She isn't put together right. She doesn't have the strength to fight off any kind of disease at all. You understand—there's a good chance that exposure to that kind of weather would kill her eventually. And I won't take a chance on that."

"I'm going to be visiting her more often, then," I said. "As often as I can. She's got something going on in her head that's scaring half to death. She thinks she's going to die."

"Oh, the poor darling," the nurse said. "Why would she think that?"

"Doesn't matter. One of her imaginary friends may be getting out of hand."

"I thought you said they were harmless."

"They were."

When I left the Millard County Rest Home that night, I stopped back in Elaine's room. She was asleep, and I heard her song. It was eerie. I could hear, now and then, themes from the bit of Copland music she had listened to. But it was distorted, and most of the music was unrecognizable—wasn't even music. Her voice was high and strange, and then suddenly it would change, would become low and

128

raspy, and for a moment I clearly heard in her voice the sound of a vast engine coming through walls of metal, carried on slender metal rods, the sound of a great roar being swallowed up by a vast cushion of nothing. I pictured Elaine with wires coming out of her shoulders and hips, with her head encased in metal and her eyes closed in sleep, like her imaginary Anansa, piloting the starship as if it were her own body. I could see that this would be attractive to Elaine, in a way. After all, she hadn't been born this way. She had memories of running and playing, memories of feeding herself and dressing herself, perhaps even of learning to read, of sounding out the words as her fingers touched each letter. Even the false arms of a spaceship would be something to fill the great void.

Children's centers are not inside their bodies; their centers are outside, at the point where the fingers of the left hand and the fingers of the right hand meet. What they touch is where they live; what they see is their self. And Elaine had lost herself in an explosion before she had the chance to move inside. With this strange dream of Anansa she was getting a self back.

But a repellent self, for all that. I walked in and sat by Elaine's bed, listening to her sing. Her body moved slightly, her back arching a little with the melody. High and light; low and rasping. The sounds alternated, and I wondered what they meant. What was going on inside her to make this music come out?

If I go with her, then I'll be dead.

Of course she was afraid. I looked at the lump of flesh that filled the bed shapelessly below where her head emerged from the covers. I tried to change my perspective, to see her body as she saw it, from above. It almost disappeared then, with the fore-shortening and the height of her ribs making her stomach and hint of hips vanish into insignificance. Yet this was all she had, and if she believed—and certainly she seemed to—that surrendering to the fantasy of Anansa would mean the death of this pitiful body, is death any less frightening to those who have not been able to fully live? I doubt it. At least for Elaine, what life she had lived had been joyful. She would not willingly trade it for a life of music and metal arms, locked in her own mind.

Except for the rain. Except that nothing was so real to her as the outside, as the trees and birds and distant hills, and as the breeze touching her with a violence she permitted to no living person. And with that reality, the good part of her life, cut off from her by the rain, how long could she hold out against the incessant pulling of Anansa and her promise of arms and legs and eternal song?

I reached up, on a whim, and very gently lifted her eyelids.

Her eyes remained open, staring at the ceiling, not blinking.

I closed her eyes, and they remained closed.

I turned her head, and it stayed turned. She did not wake up. Just kept singing as if I had done nothing to her at all.

Catatonia, or the beginning of catalepsy. *She's losing her mind*, I thought, *and if I don't bring her back, keep her here somehow, Anansa will win, and the rest home will be caring for a lump of mindless flesh for the next however many years they can keep this remnant of Elaine alive.*

"I'll be back on Saturday," I told the administrator.

"Why so soon?"

"Elaine is going through a crisis of some kind," I explained. An imaginary woman from space wants to carry her off—that I didn't say. "Have the nurses keep her awake as much as they can. Read to her, play with her, talk to her. Her normal hours at night are enough. Avoid naps."

"Why?"

"I'm afraid for her, that's all. She could go catatonic on us at any time, I think. Her sleeping isn't normal. I want to have her watched all the time."

"This is really serious?"

"This is really serious."

On Friday it looked as if the clouds were breaking, but after only a few minutes of sunshine a huge new bank of clouds swept down from the northwest, and it was worse than before. I finished my work rather carelessly, stopping a sentence in the middle several times. One of my patients was annoyed with me. She squinted at me. "You're not paid to think about your woman troubles when you're talking to me." I apologized and tried to pay attention. She was a talker; my attention always wandered. But she was right in a way. I couldn't stop thinking of Elaine. And my patient's saying that about woman troubles must have triggered something in my mind. After all, my relationship with Elaine was the longest and closest I had had with a woman in many years. If you could think of Elaine as a woman.

On Saturday I drove back to Millard County and found the nurses rather distraught. They didn't realize how much she was sleeping until they tried to stop her, they all said. She was dozing off for two or three naps in the mornings, even more in the afternoons. She went to sleep at night at seven-thirty and slept at least twelve hours. "Singing all the time. It's awful. Even at night she keeps it up. Singing and singing."

But she was awake when I went in to see her.

"I stayed awake for you."

"Thanks," I said.

"A Saturday visit. I must really be going bonkers."

"Actually, no. But I don't like how sleepy you are."

She smiled wanly. "It isn't my idea."

I think my smile was more cheerful than hers. "And I think it's all in your head."

"Think what you like, Doctor."

"I'm not a doctor. My degree says I'm a master."

"How deep is the water outside?"

"Deep?"

"All this rain. Surely it's enough to keep a few dozen arks afloat. Is God destroying the world?"

"Unfortunately, no. Though He has killed the engines on a few cars that went a little fast through the puddles."

"How long would it have to rain to fill up the world?"

"The world is round. It would all drip off the bottom."

She laughed. It was good to hear her laugh, but it ended too abruptly, and she looked at me fearfully. "I'm going, you know."

"You are?"

"I'm just the right size. She's measured me, and I'll fit perfectly. She has just the place for me. It's a good place, where I can hear the music of the dust for myself, and learn to sing it. I'd have the directional engines."

I shook my head. "Grunty the ice pig was cute. This isn't cute, Elaine."

"Did I ever say I thought Anansa was cute? Grunty the ice pig was real, you know. My father made him out of crushed ice for a luau. He melted before they got the pig out of the ground. I don't make my friends up."

"Fuchsia the flower girl?"

"My mother would pinch blossoms off the fuchsia by our front door. We played with them like dolls in the grass."

"But not Anansa."

"Anansa came into my mind when I was asleep. She found me. I didn't make her up."

"Don't you see, Elaine, that's how the real hallucinations come? They feel like reality."

She shook her head. "I know all that. I've had the nurses read me psychology books. Anansa is— Anansa is other. She couldn't come out of my head. She's something else. She's real. I've heard her music. It isn't plain, like Copland. It isn't false."

"Elaine, when you were asleep on Wednesday, you were becoming catatonic."

"I know."

"You know?"

"I felt you touch me. I felt you turn my head. I wanted to speak to you, to say good-bye. But she was singing, don't you see? She was singing. And now she lets me sing along. When I sing with her, I can feel myself travel out, like a spider along a single thread, out into the place where she is. Into the darkness. It's lonely there, and black, and cold, but

I know that at the end of the thread there she'll be, a friend for me forever."

"You're frightening me, Elaine."

"There aren't any trees on her starship, you know. That's how I stay here. I think of the trees and the hills and the birds and the grass and the wind, and how I'd lose all of that. She gets angry at me, and a little hurt. But it keeps me here. Except now I can hardly remember the trees at all. I try to remember, and it's like trying to remember the face of my mother. I can remember her dress and her hair, but her face is gone forever. Even when I look at a picture, it's a stranger. The trees are strangers to me now."

I stroked her forehead. At first she pulled her head away, then slid it back.

"I'm sorry," she said. "I usually don't like people to touch me there."

"I won't," I said.

"No, go ahead. I don't mind."

So I stroked her forehead again. It was cool and dry, and she lifted her head almost imperceptibly, to receive my touch. Involuntarily I thought of what the old woman had said the day before. *Woman troubles*. I was touching Elaine, and I thought of making love to her. I immediately put the thought out of my mind.

"Hold me here," she said. "Don't let me go. I want to go so badly. But I'm not meant for that. I'm just the right size, but not the right shape. Those aren't my arms. I know what my arms felt like."

"I'll hold you if I can. But you have to help."

"No drugs. The drugs pull my mind away from my body. If you give me drugs, I'll die."

"Then what can I do?"

"Just keep me here, any way you can."

Then we talked about nonsense, because we had been so serious, and it was as if she weren't having any problems at all. We got on to the subject of the church meetings.

"I didn't know you were religious," I said.

"I'm not. But what else is there to do on Sunday? They sing hymns, and I sing with them. Last Sunday there was a sermon that really got to me. The preachers talked about Christ in the sepulcher. About Him being there three days before the angel came to let Him go. I've been thinking about that, what it must have been like for Him, locked in a cave in the darkness, completely alone."

"Depressing."

"Not really. It must have been exhilarating for Him, in a way. If it was true, you know. To lie there on that stone bed, saying to Himself, 'They thought I was dead, but I'm here. I'm not dead.' "

"You make Him sound smug."

"Sure. Why not? I wonder if I'd feel like that, if I were with Anansa."

Anansa again.

"I can see what you're thinking. You're thinking, 'Anansa again.' "

"Yeah," I said. "I wish you'd erase her and go back to some more harmless friends."

Suddenly her face went angry and fierce.

"You can believe what you like. Just leave me alone."

I tried to apologize, but she wouldn't have any of it. She insisted on believing in this star woman. Finally I left, redoubling my cautions against letting her sleep. The nurses looked worried, too. They could see the change as easily as I could.

135

That night, because I was in Millard on a week-end, I called up Belinda. She wasn't married or anything at the moment. She came to my motel. We had dinner, made love, and watched television. She watched television, that is. I lay on the bed, thinking. And so when the test pattern came on and Belinda at last got up, beery and passionate, my mind was still on Elaine. As Belinda kissed and tickled me and whispered stupidity in my ear, I imagined myself without arms and legs. I lay there, moving only my head.

"What's the matter, you don't want to?"

I shook off the mood. No need to disappoint Belinda—I was the one who had called *her*. I had a responsibility. Not much of one, though. That was what was nagging at me. I made love to Belinda slowly and carefully, but with my eyes closed. I kept superimposing Elaine's face on Belinda's. Woman troubles. Even though Belinda's fingers played up and down my back, I thought I was making love to Elaine. And the stumps of arms and legs didn't revolt me as much as I would have thought. Instead, I only felt sad. A deep sense of tragedy, of loss, as if Elaine were dead and I could have saved her, like the prince in all the fairy tales; a kiss, so symbolic, and the princess awakens and lives happily ever after. And I hadn't done it. I had failed her. When we were finished, I cried.

"Oh, you poor sweetheart," Belinda said, her voice rich with sympathy. "What's wrong—you don't have to tell me." She cradled me for a while, and at last I went to sleep with my head pressed against her breasts. She thought I needed her. I suppose that, briefly, I did.

I did not go back to Elaine on Sunday as I had planned. I spent the entire day almost going. Instead of walking out the door, I sat and watched the incredible array of terrible Sunday morning television. And when I finally did go out, fully intending to go to the rest home and see how she was doing, I ended up driving, luggage in the back of the car, to my trailer, where I went inside and again sat down and watched television.

Why couldn't I go to her?

Just keep me here, she had said. Any way you can, she had said.

And I thought I knew the way. That was the problem. In the back of my mind all this was much too real, and the fairy tales were wrong. The prince didn't wake her with a kiss. He wakened the princess with a promise. In his arms she would be safe forever. She awoke for the happily ever after. If she hadn't known it to be true, the princess would have preferred to sleep forever.

What was Elaine asking of me?

Why was I afraid of it?

Not my job. Unprofessional to get emotionally involved with a patient.

But then, when had I ever been a professional? I finally went to bed, wishing I had Belinda with me again, for whatever comfort she could bring. Why weren't all women like Belinda, soft and loving and undemanding?

Yet as I drifted off to sleep, it was Elaine I remembered, Elaine's face and hideous, reproachful stump of a body that followed me through all my dreams.

And she followed me when I was awake, through my regular rounds on Monday and Tuesday, and at last it was Wednesday, and still I was afraid to go

137

to the Millard County Rest Home. I didn't get there until afternoon. Late afternoon, and the rain was coming down as hard as ever, and there were lakes of standing water in the fields, torrents rushing through the unprepared gutters of the town.

"You're late," the administrator said.

"Rain," I answered, and he nodded. But he looked worried.

"We hoped you'd come yesterday, but we couldn't reach you anywhere. It's Elaine."

And I knew that my delay had served its damnable purpose, exactly as I expected. "She hasn't woken up since Monday morning. she just lies there, singing. We've got her on an IV. She's asleep."

She was indeed asleep. I sent the others out of the room.

"Elaine," I said.

Nothing.

I called her name again, several times. I touched her, rocked her head back and forth. Her head stayed wherever I placed it. And the song went on, softly, high and then low, pure and then gravelly. I covered her mouth. She sang on, even with her mouth closed, as if nothing were the matter.

I pulled down her sheet and pushed a pin into her belly, then into the thin flesh at her collarbone. No response. I slapped her face. No response. She was gone. I saw her again, connected to a starship, only this time I understood better. It wasn't her body that was the right size, it was her mind. And it was her mind that had followed the slender spider's thread out to Anansa, who waited to give her a body.

A job.

Shock therapy? I imagined her already-deformed body leaping and arching as the electricity coursed

138

through her. It would accomplish nothing, except to torture unthinking flesh. Drugs! I couldn't think of any that could bring her back from where she had gone. In a way, I think, I even believed in Anansa, for the moment. I called her name. "Anansa, let her go. Let her come back to me. Please. I need her."

Why had I cried in Belinda's arms? Oh, yes. Because I had seen the princess and let her lie there unawakened, because the happily ever after was so damnably much work.

I did not do it in the fever of the first realization that I had lost her. It was no act of passion or sudden fear or grief. I sat beside her bed for hours, looking at her weak and helpless body, now so empty. I wished for her eyes to open on their own, for her to wake up and say, "Hey, would you believe the dream *I* had!" For her to say, "Fooled you, didn't I? It was really hard when you poked me with pins, but I fooled you."

But she hadn't fooled me.

And so, finally, not with passion but in despair, I stood up and leaned over her, leaned my hands on either side of her and pressed my cheek against hers and whispered in her ear. I promised her everything I could think of. I promised her no more rain forever. I promised her trees and flowers and hills and birds and the wind for as long as she liked. I promised to take her away from the rest home, to take her to see things she could only have dreamed of before.

And then at last, with my voice harsh from pleading with her, with her hair wet with my tears, I promised her the only thing that might bring her back. I promised her me. I promised her love forever, stronger than any songs Anansa could sing.

And it was then that the monstrous song fell silent. She did not awaken, but the song ended, and she moved on her own, her head rocked to the side, and she seemed to sleep normally, not catatonically. I waited by her bedside all night. I fell asleep in the chair, and one of the nurses covered me. I was still there when I was awakened in the morning by Elaine's voice.

"What a liar you are! It's still raining."

It was a feeling of power, to know that I had called someone back from places far darker than death. Her life was painful, and yet my promise of devotion was enough, apparently, to compensate. This was how I understood it, at least. This was what made me feel exhilarated, what kept me blind and deaf to what had really happened.

I was not the only one rejoicing. The nurses made a great fuss over her, and the administrator promised to write up a glowing report. "Publish," he said.

"It's too personal," I said. But in the back of my mind I was already trying to figure out a way to get the case into print, to gain something for my career. I was ashamed of myself for twisting what had been an honest, heartfelt commitment into personal advancement. But I couldn't ignore the sudden respect I was receiving from people to whom, only hours before, I had been merely ordinary.

"It's too personal," I repeated firmly. "I have no intention of publishing."

And to my disgust I found myself relishing the administrator's respect for that decision. There was no escape from my swelling self-satisfaction. Not as long as I stayed around those determined to give me cheap payoffs. Ever the wise psychologist, I returned to the only person who would give me gratitude instead of admiration. *The gratitude I had earned*, I thought. I went back to Elaine.

"Hi," she said. "I wondered where you had gone."

"Not far," I said. "Just visiting with the Nobel Prize committee."

"They want to reward you for bringing me here?"

"Oh, no. They had been planning to give me the award for having contacted a genuine alien being from outer space. Instead, I blew it and brought you back. They're quite upset."

She looked flustered. It wasn't like her to look flustered—usually she came back with another quip. "But what will they do to you?"

"Probably boil me in oil. That's the usual thing. Though, maybe they've found a way to boil me in solar energy. It's cheaper." A feeble joke. But she didn't get it.

"This isn't the way she said it was—she said it was—"

She. I tried to ignore the dull fear that suddenly churned in my stomach. *Be analytical*, I thought. *She could be anyone*.

"She said? Who said?" I asked.

Elaine fell silent. I reached out and touched her forehead. She was perspiring.

"What's wrong?" I asked. "You're upset."

"I should have known."

"Known what?"

She shook her head and turned away from me.

I knew what it was, I thought. I knew what it was, but we could surely cope. "Elaine," I said, "you aren't completely cured, are you? You haven't got rid of Anansa, have you? You don't have to hide it

141

from me. Sure, I would have loved to think you'd been completely cured, but that would have been too much of a miracle. Do I look like a miracle worker? We've just made progress, that's all. Brought you back from catalepsy. We'll free you of Anansa eventually."

Still she was silent, staring at the rain-gray window.

"You don't have to be embarrassed about pretending to be completely cured. It was very kind of you. It made me feel very good for a little while. But I'm a grown-up. I can cope with a little disappointment. Besides, you're awake, you're back, and that's all that matters." Grown-up, hell! I was terribly disappointed, and ashamed that I wasn't more sincere in what I was saying. No cure after all. No hero. No magic. No great achievement. Just a psychologist who was, after all, not extraordinary.

But I refused to pay too much attention to those feelings. Be a professional, I told myself. She needs your help.

"So don't go feeling guilty about it."

She turned back to face me, her eyes full. "Guilty?" She almost smiled. "Guilty." Her eyes did not leave my face, though I doubted she could see me well through the tears brimming her lashes.

"You tried to do the right thing," I said.

"Did I? Did I really?" She smiled bitterly. It was a strange smile for her, and for a terrible moment she no longer looked like my Elaine, my bright young patient. "I meant to stay with her," she said. "I wanted her with me, she was so alive, and when she finally joined herself to the ship, she sang and danced and swung her arms, and I said, 'This is what

142

I've needed; this is what I've craved all my centuries lost in the songs.' But then I heard *you*."

"Anansa," I said, realizing at that moment who was with me.

"I heard *you*, crying out to her. Do you think I made up my mind quickly? She heard you, but she wouldn't come. She wouldn't trade her new arms and legs for anything. They were so new. But I'd had them for long enough. What I'd never had was— you."

"Where is she?" I asked.

"Out there," she said. "She sings better than I ever did." She looked wistful for a moment, then smiled ruefully. "And I'm here. Only I made a bad bargain, didn't I? Because I didn't fool you. You won't want me, now. It's Elaine you want, and she's gone. I left her alone out there. She won't mind, not for a long time. But then—then she will. Then she'll know I cheated her."

The voice was Elaine's voice, the tragic little body her body. But now I knew I had not succeeded at all. Elaine was gone, in the infinite outer space where the mind hides to escape from itself. And in her place—Anansa. A stranger.

"You cheated her?" I said. "How did you cheat her?"

"It never changes. In a while you learn all the songs, and they never change. Nothing moves. You go on forever until all the stars fail, and yet nothing ever moves."

I moved my hand and put it to my hair. I was startled at my own trembling touch on my head.

"Oh, God," I said. They were just words, not a supplication.

"You hate me," she said.

143

Hate her? Hate my little, mad Elaine? Oh, no. I had another object for my hate. I hated the rain that had cut her off from all that kept her sane. I hated her parents for not leaving her home the day they let their car drive them on to death. But most of all I remembered my days of hiding from Elaine, my days of resisting her need, of pretending that I didn't remember her or think of her or need her, too. She must have wondered why I was so long in coming. Wondered and finally given up hope, finally realized that there was no one who would hold her. And so she left, and when I finally came, the only person waiting inside her body was Anansa, the imaginary friend who had come, terrifyingly, to life. I knew whom to hate. I thought I would cry. I even buried my face in the sheet where her leg would have been. But I did not cry. I just sat there, the sheet harsh against my face, hating myself.

Her voice was like a gentle hand, a pleading hand touching me. "I'd undo it if I could," she said. "But I can't. She's gone, and I'm here. I came because of you. I came to see the trees and the grass and the birds and your smile. The happily ever after. That was what she had lived for, you know, all she lived for. Please smile at me."

I felt warmth on my hair. I lifted my head. There was no rain in the window. Sunlight rose and fell on the wrinkles of the sheet.

"Let's go outside," I said.

"It stopped raining," she said.

"A bit late, isn't it?" I answered. But I smiled at her.

"You can call me Elaine," she said. "You won't tell, will you?"

I shook my head. No, I wouldn't tell. She was

safe enough. I wouldn't tell because then they would take her away to a place where psychiatrists reigned but did not know enough to rule. I imagined her confined among others who had also made their escape from reality and I knew that I couldn't tell anyone. I also knew I couldn't confess failure, not now.

Besides, I hadn't really completely failed. There was still hope. Elaine wasn't really gone. She was still there, hidden in her own mind, looking out through this imaginary person she had created to take her place. Someday I would find her and bring her home. After all, even Grunty the ice pig had melted.

I noticed that she was shaking her head. "You won't find her," she said. "You won't bring her home. I won't melt and disappear. She *is* gone and you couldn't have prevented it."

I smiled. "Elaine," I said.

And then I realized that she had answered thoughts I hadn't put into words.

"That's right," she said, "Let's be honest with each other. You might as well. You can't lie to me."

I shook my head. For a moment, in my confusion and despair, I had believed it all, believed that Anansa was real. But that was nonsense. Of course Elaine knew what I was thinking. She knew me better than I knew myself. "Let's go outside," I said. A failure and a cripple, out to enjoy the sunlight, which fell equally on the just and the unjustifiable.

"I don't mind," she said. "Whatever you want to believe. Elaine or Anansa. Maybe it's better if you still look for Elaine. Maybe it's better if you let me fool you after all."

The worst thing about the fantasies of the mentally

ill is that they're so damned consistent. They never let up. They never give you any rest.

"I'm Elaine," she said, smiling. "I'm Elaine, pretending to be Anansa. You love me. That's what I came for. You promised to bring me home, and you did. Take me outside. You made it stop raining for me. You did everything you promised, and I'm home again, and I promise I'll never leave you."

She hasn't left me. I come to see her every Wednesday as part of my work, and every Saturday and Sunday as the best part of my life. I take her driving with me sometimes, and we talk constantly, and I read to her and bring her books for the nurses to read to her. None of them know that she is still unwell—to them she's Elaine, happier than ever, pathetically delighted at every sight and sound and smell and taste and every texture that they touch against her cheek. Only *I* know that she believes she is not Elaine. Only I know that I have made no progress at all since then, that in moments of terrible honesty I call her Anansa, and she sadly answers me.

But in a way I'm content. Very little has changed between us, really. And after a few weeks I realized, with certainty, that she was happier now than she had ever been before. After all, she had the best of all possible worlds, for her. She could tell herself that the real Elaine was off in space somewhere, dancing and singing and hearing songs, with arms and legs at last, while the poor girl who was confined to the limbless body at the Millard County Rest Home was really an alien who was very, very happy to have even that limited body.

And as for me, I kept my commitment to her, and I'm happier for it. I'm still human—I still take

146

another woman into my bed from time to time. But Anansa doesn't mind. She even suggested it, only a few days after she woke up. "Go back to Belinda sometimes," she said. "Belinda loves you, too, you know. I won't mind at all." I still can't remember when I spoke to her of Belinda, but at least she didn't mind, and so there aren't really any discontentments in my life. Except.

Except that I'm not God. I would like to be God. I would make some changes.

When I go to the Millard County Rest Home, I never enter the building first. She is never in the building. I walk around the outside and look across the lawn by the trees. The wheelchair is always there; I can tell it from the others by the pillows, which glare white in the sunlight. I never call out. In a few moments she always sees me, and the nurses wheel her around and push the chair across the lawn.

She comes as she has come hundreds of times before. She plunges toward me, and I concentrate on watching her, so that my mind will not see my Elaine surrounded by blackness, plunging through space, gathering dust, gathering songs, leaping and dancing with her new arms and legs that she loves better than me. Instead I watch the wheelchair, watch the smile on her face. She is happy to see me, so delighted with the world outside that her body cannot contain her. And when my imagination will not be restrained, I am God for a moment. I see her running toward me, her arms waving. I give her a left hand, a right hand, delicate and strong; I put a long and girlish left leg on her, and one just as sturdy on the right.

And then, one by one, I take them all away.

Prior Restraint

I met Doc Murphy in a writing class taught by a mad Frenchman at the University of Utah in Salt Lake City. I had just quit my job as a coat-and-tie editor at a conservative family magazine, and I was having a little trouble getting used to being a slob student again. Of a shaggy lot, Doc was the shaggiest and I was prepared to be annoyed by him and ignore his opinions. But his opinions were not to be ignored. At first because of what he did to me. And then, at last, because of what had been done to him. It has shaped me; his past looms over me whenever I sit down to write.

Armand the teacher, who had not improved on his French accent by replacing it with Bostonian, looked puzzled as he held up my story before the class. "This is commercially viable," he said. "It is also crap. What else can I say?"

It was Doc who said it. Nail in one hand, hammer in the other, he crucified me and the story. Considering that I had already decided not to pay attention to him, and considering how arrogant I was in the lofty position of being the one student who had actually sold a novel, it is surprising to me that I listened to him. But underneath the almost angry attack on my work was something else: A basic

148

respect, I think, for what a good writer should be. And for that small hint in my work that a good writer might be hiding somewhere in me.

So I listened. And I learned. And gradually, as the Frenchman got crazier and crazier, I turned to Doc to learn how to write. Shaggy though he was, he had a far crisper mind than anyone I had ever known in a business suit.

We began to meet outside class. My wife had left me two years before, so I had plenty of free time and a pretty large rented house to sprawl in; we drank or read or talked, in front of a fire or over Doc's convincing veal parmesan or out chopping down an insidious vine that wanted to take over the world starting in my backyard. For the first time since Denae had gone I felt at home in my house— Doc seemed to know by instinct what parts of the house held the wrong memories, and he soon balanced them by making me feel comfortable in them again.

Or uncomfortable. Doc didn't always say nice things.

"I can see why your wife left you," he said once.

"You don't think I'm good in bed, either?" (This was a joke—neither Doc nor I had any unusual sexual predilections.)

"You have a neanderthal way of dealing with people, that's all. If they aren't going where you want them to go, club 'em a good one and drag 'em away."

It was irritating. I didn't like thinking about my wife. We had only been married three years, and not good years either, but in my own way I had loved her and I missed her a great deal and I hadn't wanted her to go when she left. I didn't like having my nose rubbed in it. "I don't recall clubbing *you*."

He just smiled. And, of course, I immediately thought back over the conversation and realized that he was right. I hated his goddam smile.

"OK," I said, "you're the one with long hair in the land of the last surviving crew cuts. Tell me why you like 'Swap' Morris."

"I don't like Morris. I think Morris is a whore selling someone else's freedom to win votes."

And I *was* confused, then. I had been excoriating good old "Swap" Morris, Davis County Commissioner, for having fired the head librarian in the county because she had dared to stock a "pornographic" book despite his objections. Morris showed every sign of being illiterate, fascist, and extremely popular, and I would gladly have hit the horse at his lynching.

"So you don't like Morris either—what did I say wrong?"

"Censorship is never excusable for any reason, says you."

"You *like* censorship?"

And then the half-serious banter turned completely serious. Suddenly he wouldn't look at me. Suddenly he only had eyes for the fire, and I saw the flames dancing in tears resting on his lower eyelids, and I realized again that with Doc I was out of my depth completely.

"No," he said. "No, I don't *like* it."

And then a lot of silence until he finally drank two full glasses of wine, just like that, and went out to drive home; he lived up Emigration Canyon at the end of a winding, narrow road, and I was afraid he was too drunk, but he only said to me at the door, "I'm not drunk. It takes half a gallon of wine just to get up to normal after an hour with you, you're so damn sober."

One weekend he even took me to work with him. Doc made his living in Nevada. We left Salt Lake City on Friday afternoon and drove to Wendover, the first town over the border. I expected him to be an employer of the casino we stopped at. But he didn't punch in, just left his name with a guy; and then he sat in a corner with me and waited.

"Don't you have to work?" I asked.

"I'm working," he said.

"I used to work just the same way, but I got fired."

"I've got to wait my turn for a table. I told you I made my living with poker."

And it finally dawned on me that he was a free-lance professional—a player—a cardshark.

There were four guys named Doc there that night. Doc Murphy was the third one called to a table. He played quietly, and lost steadily but lightly for two hours. Then, suddenly, in four hands he made back everything he had lost and added nearly fifteen hundred dollars to it. Then he made his apologies after a decent number of losing hands and we drove back to Salt Lake.

"Usually I have to play again on Saturday night," he told me. Then he grinned. "Tonight I was lucky. There was an idiot who thought he knew poker."

I remembered the old saw: Never eat at a place called Mom's, never play poker with a man named Doc, and never sleep with a woman who's got more troubles than you. Pure truth. Doc memorized the deck, knew all the odds by heart, and it was a rare poker face that Doc couldn't eventually see through.

151

At the end of the quarter, though, it finally dawned on me that in all the time we were in class together, I had never see one of his own stories. He hadn't written a damn thing. And there was his grade on the bulletin board—A.

I talked to Armand.

"Oh, Doc writes," he assured me. "Better than you do, and you got an A. God knows how, you don't have the talent for it."

"Why doesn't he turn it in for the rest of the class to read?"

Armand shrugged. "Why should he? Pearls before swine."

Still it irritated me. After watching Doc disembowel more than one writer, I didn't think it was fair that his own work was never put on the chopping block.

The next quarter he turned up in a graduate seminar with me, and I asked him. He laughed and told me to forget it. I laughed back and told him I wouldn't. I wanted to read his stuff. So the next week he gave me a three-page manuscript. It was an unfinished fragment of a story about a man who honestly thought his wife had left him even though he went home to find her there every night. It was one of the best writings I've ever read in my life. No matter how you measure it. The stuff was clear enough and exciting enough that any moron who likes Harold Robbins could have enjoyed it. But the style was rich enough and the matter of it deep enough even in a few pages that it made most other "great" writers look like chicken farmers. I reread the fragment five times just to make sure I got it all. The first time I had thought it was metaphorically about me. The third time I knew it was about God.

The fifth time I knew it was about everything that mattered, and I wanted to read more.

"Where's the rest?" I asked.

He shrugged. "That's it," he said.

"It doesn't feel finished."

"It isn't."

"Well, finish it! Doc, you could sell this anywhere, even the *New Yorker*. For them you probably don't even *have* to finish it."

"Even the *New Yorker*. Golly."

"I can't believe you think you're too good for anybody, Doc. Finish it. I want to know how it ends."

He shook his head. "That's all there is. That's all there ever will be."

And that was the end of the discussion.

But from time to time he'd show me another fragment. Always better than the one before. And in the meantime we became closer, not because he was such a good writer—I'm not so self-effacing I like hanging around with people who can write me under the table—but because he was Doc Murphy. We found every decent place to get a beer in Salt Lake City—not a particular time-consuming activity. We saw three good movies and another dozen that were so bad they were fun to watch. He taught me to play poker well enough that I broke even every weekend. He put up with my succession of girlfriends and prophesied that I would probably end up married again. "You're just weak willed enough to try to make a go of it," he cheerfully told me.

At last, when I had long since given up asking, he told me why he never finished anything.

I was two and a half beers down, and he was drinking a hideous mix of Tab and tomato juice that

153

he drank whenever he wanted to punish himself for his sins, on the theory that it was even worse than the Hindu practice of drinking your own piss. I had just got a story back from a magazine I had been sure would buy it. I was thinking of giving it up. He laughed at me.

"I'm serious," I said.

"Nobody who's any good at all needs to give up writing."

"Look who's talking. The king of the determined writers." He looked angry. "You're a paraplegic making fun of a one-legged man," he said.

"I'm sick of it."

"Quit then. Makes no difference. Leave the field to the hacks. You're probably hack, too."

Doc hadn't been drinking anything to make him surly, not drunk-surly, anyway. "Hey, Doc, I'm asking for encouragement."

"If you need encouragement, you don't deserve it. There's only one way a good writer can be stopped."

"Don't tell me you have a selective writer's block. Against endings."

"Writer's block? Jesus, I've never been blocked in my life. Blocks are what happen when you're not good enough to write the thing you know you have to write."

I was getting angry. 'And *you*, of course, are always good enough."

He leaned forward, looked at me in the eyes. "I'm the best writer in the English language."

"I'll give you this much. You're the best who never finished anything."

"I finish everything," he said. "I finish everything, beloved friend, and then I burn all but the first three pages. I finish a story a week, sometimes. I've

154

written three complete novels, four plays. I even did a screenplay. It would've made millions of dollars and been a classic."

"Says who?"

"Says—never mind who says. It was bought, it was cast, it was ready for filming. It had a budget of thirty million. The studio believed in it. Only intelligent thing I've ever heard of them doing."

I couldn't believe it. "You're joking."

"If I'm joking, who's laughing? It's true."

I'd never seen him looked so poisoned. It was true, if I knew Doc Murphy, and I think I did. Do. "Why?" I asked.

"The Censorship Board."

"What? There's no such thing in America."

He laughed. "Not full-time anyway."

"Who the hell is the Censorship Board?"

He told me:

When I was twenty-two I lived on a rural road in Oregon, he said, outside of Portland. Mailboxes out on the road. I was writing, I was a playwright, I thought there'd be a career in that; I was just starting to try fiction. I went out one morning after the mailman had gone by. It was drizzling slightly. But I didn't much care. There was an envelope there from my Hollywood agent. It was a contract. Not an option—a sale. A hundred thousand dollars. It had just occurred to me that I was getting wet and I ought to go in when two men came out of the bushes—yeah, I know, I guess they go for dramatic entrances. They were in business suits. God, I hate men who wear business suits. The one guy just held out his hand. He said, "Give it to me now and save yourself a lot of trouble." Give it to him? I told him what I thought of his suggestion. They looked like

155

the mafia, or like a comic parody of the mafia, actually.

They were about the same height, and they seemed almost to be the same person, right down to a duplicate glint of fierceness in the eyes; but then I realized that my first impression had been deceptive. One was blond, one dark-haired; the blond had a slightly receding chin that gave his face a meek look from the nose down; the dark one had once had a bad skin problem and his neck was tree-ish, giving him an air of stupidity, as if a face had been pasted on the front of the neck with no room for a head at all. Not mafia at all. Ordinary people.

Except the eyes. The glint in the eyes was not false, and that was what had made me see them wrong at first. Those eyes had seen people weep, and had cared, and had hurt them again anyway. It's a look that human eyes should never have.

"It's just the *contract*, for Christ's sake," I told them, but the dark one with acne scars only told me again to hand it over.

By now, though, my first fear had passed; they weren't armed, and so I might be able to get rid of them without violence. I started back to the house. They followed me.

"What do you want my contract for?" I asked.

"That film will never be made," says Meek, the blond one with the missing chin. "We won't allow it to be made."

I'm thinking who writes their dialogue for them, do they crib it from Fenimore Cooper? "Their hundred thousand dollars says they want to try. I want them to."

"You'll never get the money, Murphy. And this

156

contract and the screenplay will pass out of existence within the next four days. I promise you that."

I ask him, "What are you, a critic?"

"Close enough."

By now I was inside the door and they were on the other side of the threshold. I should have closed the door, probably, but I'm a gambler. I had to stay in this time because I had to know what kind of hand they had. "Plan to take it by force?" I asked.

"By inevitability," Tree says. And then he says, "You see, Mr. Murphy, you're a dangerous man; with your IBM Self-Correcting Selective II typewriter that has a sluggish return so that you sometimes get letters printed a few spaces in from the end. With your father who once said to you, 'Billy, to tell you the honest-to-God truth, I don't know if I'm your father or not. I wasn't the only guy your Mom had been seeing when I married her, so I really don't give a damn if you live or die.' "

He had it right down. *Word for word*, what my father told me when I was four years old. I'd never told anybody. And he had it word for word.

CIA, Jesus. That's pathetic.

No, they weren't CIA. They just wanted to make sure that I didn't write. Or rather, that I didn't publish.

I told them I wasn't interested in their suggestions. And I was right—they weren't muscle types. I closed the door and they just went away.

And then the next day as I was driving my old Galaxy along the road, under the speed limit, a boy on a bicycle came right out in front of me. I didn't even have a chance to brake. One second he wasn't there, and the next second he was. I hit him. The bicycle went under the car, but he mostly came up

157

the top. His foot stuck in the bumper, jammed in by the bike. The rest of him slid up over the hood, pulling his hip apart and separating his spine in three places. The hood ornament disemboweled him and the blood flowed up the windshield like a heavy rainstorm, so that I couldn't see anything except his face, which was pressed up against the glass with the eyes open. He died on the spot, of course. And I wanted to.

He had been playing Martians or something with his brother. The brother was standing there near the road with a plastic ray gun in his hand and a stupid look on his face. His mother came out of the house screaming. I was screaming, too. There were two neighbors who saw the whole thing. One of them called the cops and ambulance. The other one tried to control the mother and keep her from killing me. I don't remember where I was going. All I remember is that the car had taken an unusually long time starting that morning. Another minute and a half, I think—a long time, to start a car. If it had started up just like usual, I wouldn't have hit the kid. I kept thinking that—it was all just a coincidence that I happened to be coming by just at that moment. A half-second sooner and he would have seen me and swerved. A half-second later and I would have seen him. Just coincidence. The only reason the boy's father didn't kill me when he came home ten minutes later was because I was crying so damn hard. It never went to court because the neighbors testified that I hadn't a chance to stop, and the police investigator determined that I hadn't been speeding. Not even negligence. Just terrible, terrible chance.

I read the article in the paper. The boy was only nine, but he was taking special classes at school and was very bright, a good kid, ran a paper route and always took care of his brothers and sisters. A real tear-jerker for the consumption of the subscribers. I thought of killing myself. And then the men in the business suits came back. They had four copies of my script, my screenplay. Four copies is all I had ever made—the original was in my file.

"You see, Mr. Murphy, we have every copy of the screenplay. You will give us the original."

I wasn't in the mood for this. I started closing the door.

"You have so much taste," I said. I didn't care how they got the script, not then. I just wanted to find a way to sleep until when I woke up the boy would still be alive.

They pushed the door open and came in. "You see, Mr. Murphy, until we altered your car yesterday, your path and the boy's never did intersect. We had to try four times to get the timing right, but we finally made it. It's the nice thing about time travel. If you blow it, you can always go back and get it right the next time."

I couldn't believe anyone would want to take credit for the boy's death. "What for?" I asked.

And they told me. Seems the boy was even more talented than anyone thought. He was going to grows up and be a writer. A journalist and critic. And he was going to cause a lot of problems for a particular government some forty years down the line. He was especially going to write three books that would change the whole way of thinking of a large number of people. The wrong way.

"We're all writers ourselves," Meek says to me. "It shouldn't surprise you that we take our writing very seriously. More seriously than you do. Writers, the good writers, can change people. And some of the changes aren't very good. By killing that boy yesterday, you see, you stopped a bloody civil war some sixty years from now. We've already checked and there are some unpleasant side effects, but nothing that can't be coped with. Saved seven million lives. You shouldn't feel bad about it."

I remembered the things they had known about me. Things that nobody could have known. I felt stupid because I began to believe they might be for real. I felt afraid because they were calm when they talked of the boy's death. I asked, "Where do I come in? Why me?"

"Oh, it's simple. You're a very good writer. Destined to be the best of your age. Fiction. And this screenplay. In three hundred years they're going to compare you to Shakespeare and the poor old bard will lose. The trouble is, Murphy, you're a godawful hedonist and a pessimist to boot, and if we can just keep you from publishing anything, the whole artistic mood of two centuries will be brightened considerably. Not to mention the prevention of a famine in seventy years. History makes strange connections, Murphy, and you're at the heart of a lot of suffering. If you never publish, the world will be a much better place for everyone."

You weren't there, you didn't hear them. You didn't see them, sitting on my couch, legs crossed, nodding, gesturing like they were saying the most natural thing in the world. From them I learned how to write genuine insanity. Not somebody frothing at the mouth; just somebody sitting there like a good friend, saying impossible things, cruel things, and smiling and getting excited and—Jesus, you don't know. Because I believed them. They knew, you see. And they were *too* insane, even a madman could have come up with a better hoax than that. And I'm making it sound as if I believed them logically, but I didn't, I don't think I can persuade you, either, but trust me—if I know when a man is bluffing or telling the truth, and I do, these two were not bluffing. A child had died, and they knew how many times I had turned the key in the ignition. And there was truth in those terrible eyes when Meek said, "If you willingly refrain from publishing, you will be allowed to live. If you refuse, then you will die within three days. Another writer will kill you—accidentally, of course. We only have authority to work through authors."

I asked them why. The answer made me laugh. It seems they were from the Authors' Guild. "It's a matter of responsibility. If you refuse to take responsibility for the future consequences of your acts, we'll have to give the responsibility to somebody else."

And so I asked them why they didn't just kill me in the first place instead of wasting time talking to me.

It was Tree who answered, and the bastard was crying, and he says to me, "Because we love you. We love everything you write. We've learned everything we know about writing from you. And we'll lose if you die."

They tried to console me by telling me what good company I was in. Thomas Hardy—they made him give up novels and stick to poetry which nobody read and so it was safe. Meek tells me, "Hemingway decided to kill himself instead of waiting for us to do it. And there are some others who only had to refrain from writing a particular book. It hurt them, but Fitzgerald was still able to have a decent career with the other books he could write, and Perelman gave it to us in laughs, since he couldn't be allowed to write his real work. We only bother with great writers. Bad writers aren't a threat to anybody."

We struck a sort of bargain. I could go on writing. But after I had finished everything, I had to burn it. All but the first three pages. "If you finish it at all," says Meek, "we'll have a copy of it here. There's a library here that—uh, I guess the easiest way to say it is that it exists outside time. You'll be published, in a way. Just not in your own time. Not for about eight hundred years. But at least you can write. There are others who have to keep their pens completely still. It breaks our hearts, you know."

I knew all about broken hearts, yes sir, I knew all about it. I burned all but the first three pages.

There's only one reason for a writer to quit writing, and that's when the Censorship Board gets to him. Anybody else who quits is just a gold-plated jackass. "Swap" Morris doesn't even know what real censorship is. It doesn't happen in libraries. It happens on the hoods of cars. So go on, become a real estate broker, sell insurance, follow Santa Claus and clean up the reindeer poo, I don't give a damn. But if you give up something that I will never have, I'm through with you. There's nothing in you for me.

So I write. And Doc reads it and tears it to pieces; everything except this. This he'll never see. This he'd probably kill me for, but what the hell? It'll never get published. No, no I'm too vain. You're reading it, aren't you? See how I put my ego on the line? If I'm really a good enough writer, if my work is important enough to change the world, then a

162

couple of guys in business suits will come make me a proposition I can't refuse, and you won't read this at all, but you are reading it, aren't you? Why am I doing this to myself? Maybe I'm hoping they'll come and give me an excuse to quit writing now, before I find out that I've already written as well as I'm ever going to. But here I thumb my nose at those goddam future critics and they ignore me, they tell exactly what my work is worth.

Or maybe not. Maybe I really *am* good, but my work just happens to have a positive effect, happens not to make any unpleasant waves in the future. Maybe I'm one of the lucky ones who can accomplish something powerful that doesn't need to be censored to protect the future.

Maybe pigs have wings.

THE CHANGED MAN AND THE KING OF WORDS

Once there was a man who loved his son more than life. Once there was a boy who loved his father more than death.

They are not the same story, not really. But I can't tell you one without telling you the other.

The man was Dr. Alvin Bevis, and the boy was his son, Joseph, and the only woman that either of them loved was Connie, who in 1977 married Alvin, with hope and joy, and in 1978 gave birth to Joe on the brink of death and adored them both accordingly. It was an affectionate family. This made it almost certain that they would come to grief.

Connie could have no more children after Joe. She shouldn't even have had *him*. Her doctor called her a damn fool for refusing to abort him in the fourth month when the problems began. "He'll be born retarded. You'll die in labor." To which she answered, "I'll have one child, or I won't believe I ever lived." In her seventh month they took Joe out of her, womb and all. He was scrawny and little, and the doctor told her to expect him to be mentally deficient and physically uncoordinated. Connie

164

nodded and ignored him. She was lucky. She had Joe, alive, and silently she said to any who pitied her, *I am more a woman than any of you barren ones who still have to worry about the phases of the moon.*

Neither Alvin nor Connie ever believed Joe would be retarded. And soon enough it was clear that he wasn't. He walked at eight months. He talked at twelve months. He had his alphabet at eighteen months. He could read at a second-grade level by the time he was three. He was inquisitive, demanding, independent, disobedient, and exquisitely beautiful, with a shock of copper-colored hair and a face as smooth and deep as a coldwater pool.

His parents watched him devour learning and were sometimes hard pressed to feed him with what he needed. *He will be a great man*, they both whispered to each other in the secret conversations of night. It made them proud; it made them afraid to know that his learning and his safety had, by chance or the grand design of things, been entrusted to them.

Out of all the variety the Bevises offered their son in the first few years of his life, Joe became obsessed with stories. He would bring books and insist that Connie or Alvin read to him, but if it was not a storybook, he quickly ran and got another, until at last they were reading a story. Then he sat imprisoned by the chain of events as the tale unfolded, saying nothing until the story was over. Again and again "Once upon a time," or "There once was a," or "One day the king sent out a proclamation," until Alvin and Connie had every storybook in the house practically memorized. Fairy tales were Joe's favorites, but as time passed, he graduated to movies and contemporary stories and even history.

The problem was not the thirst for tales, however. The conflict began because Joe had to live out his stories. He would get up in the morning and announce that Mommy was Mama Bear, Daddy was Papa Bear, and he was Baby Bear. When he was angry, he would be Goldilocks and run away. Other mornings Daddy would be Rumpelstiltskin, Mommy would be the Farmer's Daughter, and Joe would be the King. Joe was Hansel, Mommy was Gretel, and Alvin the Wicked Witch.

"Why can't I be Hansel's and Gretel's father?" Alvin asked. He resented being the Wicked Witch. Not that he thought it *meant* anything. He told himself it merely annoyed him to have his son constantly assigning him dialogue and action for the day's activities. Alvin never knew from one hour to the next who he was going to be in his own home.

After a time, mild annoyance gave way to open irritation; if it was a phase Joe was going through, it ought surely to have ended by now. Alvin finally suggested that the boy be taken to a child psychologist. The doctor said it was a phase.

"Which means that sooner or later he'll get over it?" Alvin asked. "Or that you just can't figure out what's going on?"

"Both," said the psychologist cheerfully. "You'll just have to live with it."

But Alvin did not like living with it. He wanted his son to call him Daddy. He *was* the father, after all. Why should he have to put up with his child, no matter how bright the boy was, assigning him silly roles to play whenever he came home? Alvin put his foot down. He refused to answer to any name but

Father. And after a little anger and a lot of repeated attempts, Joe finally stopped trying to get his father to play a part. Indeed, as far as Alvin knew, Joe entirely stopped acting out stories.

It was not so, of course. Joe simply acted them out with Connie after Alvin had gone for the day to cut up DNA and put it back together creatively. That was how Joe learned to hide things from his father. He wasn't *lying*; he was just biding his time. Joe was sure that if only he found good enough stories, Daddy would play again.

So when Daddy was home, Joe did not act out stories. Instead he and his father played number and word games, studied elementary Spanish as an introduction to Latin, plinked out simple programs on the Atari, and laughed and romped until Mommy came in and told her boys to calm down before the roof fell in on them. *This is being a father*, Alvin told himself. *I am a good father*. And it was true. It was true, even though every now and then Joe would ask his mother hopefully, "Do you think that Daddy will want to be in *this* story?"

"Daddy just doesn't like to pretend. He likes your stories, but not acting them out."

In 1983 Joe turned five and entered school; that same year Dr. Bevis created a bacterium that lived on acid precipitation and neutralized it. In 1987 Joe left school, because he knew more than any of his teachers; at precisely that time Dr. Bevis began earning royalties on commercial breeding of his bacterium for spot cleanup in acidized bodies of water. The university suddenly became terrified that he might retire and live on his income and take his name away from the school. So he was given a laboratory and twenty assistants and secretaries and an administrative assistant, and from then on Dr. Bevis could pretty well do what he liked with his time.

What he liked was to make sure the research was still going on as carefully and methodically as was proper and in directions that he approved of. Then he went home and became the faculty of one for his son's very private academy.

It was an idyllic time for Alvin.

It was hell for Joe.

Joe loved his father, mind you. Joe played at learning, and they had a wonderful time reading *The Praise of Folly* in the original Latin, duplicating great experiments and then devising experiments of their own—too many things to list. Enough to say that Alvin had never had a graduate student so quick to grasp new ideas, so eager to devise newer ones of his own. How could Alvin have known that Joe was starving to death before his eyes?

For with Father home, Joe and Mother could not play.

Before Alvin had taken him out of school Joe used to read books with his mother. All day at home she would read *Jane Eyre* and Joe would read it in school, hiding it behind copies of *Friends and Neighbors*. Homer. Chaucer. Shakespeare. Twain. Mitchell. Galsworthy. Elswyth Thane. And then in those precious hours after school let out and before Alvin came home from work they would be Ashley and Scarlett, Tibby and Julian, Huck and Jim, Walter and Griselde, Odysseus and Circe. Joe no longer assigned the parts the way he did when he was little. They both knew what book they were reading and they would live within the milieu of that book. Each had to guess from the other's behavior what role had been chosen that particular day; it was a triumphant moment when at last Connie would dare to venture Joe's name for the day, or Joe call Mother by hers. In all the years of playing the games never once did he choose to be the same person; never once did they fail to figure out what role the other played.

Now Alvin was home, and that game was over. No more stolen moments of reading during school. Father frowned on stories. History, yes; lies and poses, no. And so, while Alvin thought that joy had finally come, for Joe and Connie joy was dead.

Their life became one of allusion, dropping phrases to each other out of books, playing subtle characters without ever allowing themselves to utter the other's name. So perfectly did they perform that Alvin never knew what was happening. Just now and then he'd realize that something was going on that he didn't understand.

"What sort of weather is this for January?" Alvin said one day looking out the window at heavy rain.

"Fine," said Joe, and then thinking of "The Merchant's Tale," he smiled at his mother. "In May we climb trees."

"What?" Alvin asked. "What does that have to do with anything?"

"I just like tree climbing."

"It all depends," said Connie, "on whether the sun dazzles your eyes."

When Connie left the room, Joe asked an innocuous question about teleology, and Alvin put the previous exchange completely out of his mind.

Or rather tried to put it out of his mind. He was no fool. Though Joe and Connie were very subtle, Alvin gradually realized he did not speak the native language of his own home. He was well enough read to catch a reference or two. Turning into swine. Sprinkling dust. "Frankly, I don't give a damn." Remarks that didn't quite fit into the conversation, phrases that seemed strangely resonant. And as he grew more aware of his wife's and his son's private language, the more isolated he felt. His lessons with Joe began to seem not exciting but hollow, as if they were both acting a role. Taking parts in a story. The story of the loving father-teacher and the dutiful, brilliant student-son. It had been the best time of Alvin's life, better than any life he had created in the lab, but that was when he had believed it. Now it was just a play. His son's real life was somewhere else.

I didn't like playing the parts he gave me, years ago, Alvin thought. *Does he like playing the part that I gave him?*

"You've gone as far as I can take you," Alvin said at breakfast one day, "in everything, except biology of course. So I'll guide your studies in biology, and for everything else I'm hiring advanced graduate students in various fields at the university. A different one each day."

Joe's eyes went deep and distant. "You won't be my teacher anymore?"

"Can't teach you what I don't know," Alvin said. And he went back to the lab. Went back and with delicate cruelty tore apart a dozen cells and made them into something other than themselves, whether they would or not.

Back at home, Joe and Connie looked at each other in puzzlement. Joe was thirteen. He was getting tall and felt shy and awkward before his mother. They had been three years without stories together. With Father there, they had played at being prisoners, passing messages under the guard's very nose. Now there was no guard, and without the need for secrecy there was no message anymore. Joe took to going outside and reading or playing obsessively at the computer; more doors were locked in the Bevis home than had ever been locked before.

Joe dreamed terrifying, gentle nightmares, dreamed of the same thing, over and over; the setting was different, but always the story was the same. He dreamed of being on a boat, and the gunwale began to crumble wherever he touched it, and he tried to warn his parents, but they wouldn't listen, they leaned, it broke away under their hands, and they fell into the sea, drowning. He dreamed that he was bound up in a web, tied like a spider's victim, but the spider never, never, never came to taste of him, left him there to desiccate in helpless bondage, though he cried out and struggled. How could he explain such dreams to his parents? He remembered Joseph in Genesis, who spoke too much of dreams; remembered Cassandra; remembered Iocaste, who thought to slay her child for fear of oracles. *I am caught up in a story*, Joe thought, *from which I cannot escape. Each change is a fall; each fall tears me from myself. If I cannot be the people of the tales, who am I then?*

Life was normal enough for all that. Breakfast lunch dinner, sleep wake sleep, work earn spend own, use break fix. All the cycles of ordinary life played out despite the shadow of inevitable ends. One day Alvin and his son were in a bookstore, the Gryphon, which had the complete Penguin Classics. Alvin was browsing through the titles to see what might be of some use when he noticed Joe was no longer following him.

His son, all the slender five feet nine inches of him, was standing half the store away bent in avid concentration over something on the counter. Alvin felt a terrible yearning for his son. He was so beautiful and yet somehow in these dozen and one years of Joe's life, Alvin had lost him. Now Joe was nearing manhood and very soon it would be too late. *When did he cease to be mine?* Alvin wondered. *When did he become so much his mother's son? Why must he be as beautiful as she and yet have the mind he has? He is Apollo*, Alvin said to himself.

And in that moment he knew what he had lost. By calling his son Apollo he had told himself what he had taken from his son. A connection between stories the child acted out and his knowledge of who he was. The connection was so real it was almost tangible and yet Alvin could not put it into words, could not bear the knowledge and so and so and so.

Just as he was sure he had the truth of things it slipped away. Without words his memory could not hold it, lost the understanding the moment it came. *I knew it all and I have already forgotten.* Angry at himself, Alvin strode to his son and and realized that Joe was not doing anything intelligent at all. He had a deck of tarot cards spread before him. He was doing a reading.

"Cross my palm with silver," said Alvin. He thought he was making a joke but his anger spoke too loudly in his voice. Joe looked up with shame on his face. Alvin cringed inside himself. *Just by speaking to you I wound you.* Alvin wanted to apologize but he had no strategy for that so he tried to

172

affirm that it had been a joke by making another. "Discovering the secrets of the universe?"

Joe half-smiled and quickly gathered up the cards and put them away.

"No," Alvin said. "No, you were interested: you don't have to put them away."

"It's just nonsense," Joe said.

You're lying, Alvin thought.

"All the meanings are so vague they could fit just about anything." Joe laughed mirthlessly.

"You looked pretty interested."

'I was just, you know, wondering how to program a computer for this, wondering whether I could do a program that would make it make some sense. Not just the random fall of the cards, you know. A way to make it respond to who a person really is. Cut through all the—"

"Yes?"

"Just wondering."

"Cut through all the—?"

"Stories we tell ourselves. All the lies that we believe about ourselves. About who we really are."

Something didn't ring true in the boy's words, Alvin knew. Something was wrong. And because in Alvin's world nothing could long exist unexplained he decided the boy seemed awkward because his father made him ashamed of his own curiosity. *I am ashamed that I have made you ashamed*, Alvin thought. *So I will buy you the cards*.

"I'll buy the cards. And the book you were looking at."

"No, Dad," said Joe.

"No, it's all right. Why not? Play around with the computer. See if you can turn this nonsense into something. What the hell, you might come up with some good graphics and sell the program for a bundle." Alvin laughed. So did Joe. Even Joe's *laugh* was a lie.

What Alvin didn't know was this: Joe was not ashamed. Joe was merely afraid. For he had laid out the cards as the book instructed, but he had not needed the explanations, had not needed the names of the faces. He had known their names at once, had known their faces. It was Creon who held the sword and the scales. Ophelia, naked, wreathed in green, with man and falcon, bull and lion around. Ophelia who danced in her madness. And I was once the boy with the starflower in the sixth cup, giving to my child-mother, when gifts were possible between us. The cards were not dice, they were names, and he laid them out in stories, drawing them in order from the deck in a pattern that he knew was largely the story of his life. All the names that he had borne were in these cards, and all the shapes of past and future dwelt here, waiting to be dealt. It was this that frightened him. He had been deprived of stories for so long, his own story of father, mother, son was so fragile now that he was madly grasping at anything; Father mocked, but Joe looked at the story of the cards, and he believed. *I do not want to take these home. It puts myself wrapped in a silk in my own hands*. "Please don't," he said to his father.

But Alvin, who knew better, bought them anyway, hoping to please his son.

Joe stayed away from the cards for a whole day. He had only touched them the once; surely he need not toy with this fear again. It was irrational, mere wish fulfillment, Joe told himself. *The cards mean nothing. They are not to be feared. I can touch them and learn no truth from them*. And yet all his rationalism, all his certainty that the cards were meaningless, were, he knew, merely lies he was telling to persuade himself to try the cards again, and this time seriously.

"What did you bring *those* home for?" Mother asked in the other room.

Father said nothing. Joe knew from the silence that Father did not want to make any explanation that might be overheard.

"They're silly," said Mother. "I thought you were a scientist and a skeptic. I thought you didn't believe in things like this."

"It was just a lark," Father lied. "I bought them for Joe to plink around with. He's thinking of doing a computer program to make the cards respond somehow to people's personalities. The boy has a right to play now and then."

And in the family room, where the toy computer sat mute on the shelf, Joe tried not to think of Odysseus walking away from the eight cups, treading the lip of the ocean's basin, his back turned to the wine. *Forty-eight kilobytes and two little disks. This isn't computer enough for what I mean to do*, Joe thought. *I will not do it, of course. But with Father's computer from his office upstairs, with the hard disk and the right type of interface, perhaps there is space and time enough for all the operations. Of course I will not do it. I do not care to do it. I do not dare to do it.*

At two in the morning he got up from his bed, where he could not sleep, went downstairs, and began to program the graphics of the tarot deck upon the screen. But in each picture he made changes, for he knew that the artist, gifted as he was, had made mistakes. Had not understood that the Page of Cups was a buffoon with a giant phallus, from which flowed the sea. Had not known that the Queen of Swords was a statue and it was her throne that was alive, an angel groaning in agony at the stone burden she had to bear. The child at the Gate of Ten Stars was being eaten by the old man's dogs. The man hanging upside down with crossed legs and peace upon his face, he wore no halo; his hair was afire. And the Queen of Pentacles had just given birth to a bloody star, whose father was not the King of Pentacles, that poor cuckold.

And as the pictures and their stories came to him, he began to hear the echoes of all the other stories he had read. Cassandra, Queen of Swords, flung her bladed words, and people batted them out of the air like flies, when if they had only caught them and used them, they would not have met the future unarmed. For a moment Odysseus bound to the mast was the Hanged Man; in the right circumstances. Macbeth could show up in the ever-trusting Page of Cups, or crush himself under the ambitious Queen of Pentacles, Queen of Coins if she crossed him. The cards held tales of power, tales of pain, in the invisible threads that bound them to one another. Invisible threads, but Joe knew they were there, and he had to make the pictures right, make the program right, so that he could find true stories when he read the cards.

Through the night he labored until each picture was right: the job was only begun when he fell asleep at last. His parents were worried on finding him there in the morning, but they hadn't the heart to waken him. When he awoke, he was alone in the house, and he began again immediately, drawing the cards on the TV screen, storing them in the computer's memory; as for his own memory, he needed no help to recall them all, for he knew their names and their stories and was beginning to understand how their names changed every time they came together.

By evening it was done, along with a brief randomizer program that dealt the cards. The pictures were right. The names were right. But this time when the computer spread the cards before him— This is you, this covers you, this crosses you—it was meaningless. The computer could not do what hands could do. It could not understand and unconsciously deal the cards. It was not a randomizer program that was needed at all, for the shuffling of the tarot was not done by chance.

"May I tinker with your computer?" Joe asked.

"The hard disk?" Father looked doubtful. "I don't want you to open it, Joe. I don't want to try to come up with another ten thousand dollars this week if something goes wrong." Behind his words was a worry: *This business with the tarot cards has gone far enough, and I'm sorry I bought them for you, and I don't want you to use the computer, especially if it would make this obsession any stronger.*

"Just an interface, Father. You don't use the parallel port anyway, and I can put it back afterward."

"The Atari and the hard disk aren't even compatible."

"I know," said Joe.

But in the end there really couldn't be much argument. Joe knew computers better than Alvin did, and they both knew that what Joe took apart, Joe could put together. It took days of tinkering with hardware and plinking at the program. During that time Joe did nothing else. In the beginning he tried to distract himself. At lunch he told Mother about books they ought to read; at dinner he spoke to Father about Newton and Einstein until Alvin had to remind him that he was a biologist, not a mathematician. No one was fooled by these attempts at breaking the obsession. The tarot program drew Joe back after every meal, after every interruption, until at last he began to refuse meals and ignore the interruptions entirely.

"You have to eat. You can't die for this silly game," said Mother.

Joe said nothing. She set a sandwich by him, and he ate some of it.

"Joe, this has gone far enough. Get yourself under control," said Father.

Joe didn't look up. "I'm under control," he said, and he went on working.

After six days Alvin came and stood between Joe and the television set. "This nonsense will end now," Alvin said. "You are behaving like a boy with serious problems. The most obvious cure is to disconnect the computer, which I will do if you do not stop working on this absurd program at once. We try to give you freedom, Joe, but when you do this to us and to yourself, then—"

"That's all right," said Joe. "I've mostly finished it anyway." He got up and went to bed and slept for fourteen hours.

Alvin was relieved. "I thought he was losing his mind."

Connie was more worried than ever. "What do you think he'll do if it doesn't work?"

"Work? How could it work? Work at what? Cross my palm with silver and I'll tell your future."

"Haven't you been *listening* to him?"

"He hasn't said a word in days."

"He believes in what he's doing. He thinks his program will tell the truth."

Alvin laughed. "Maybe your doctor, what's-his-name, maybe he was right. Maybe there was brain damage after all."

Connie looked at him in horror. "God, Alvin."

"A joke, for Christ's sake."

"It wasn't funny."

They didn't talk about it, but in the middle of the night, at different times, each of them got up and went into Joe's room to look at him in his sleep.

Who are you? Connie asked silently. *What are you going to do if this project of yours is a failure? What are you going to do if it succeeds?*

Alvin, however, just nodded. He refused to be worried. Phases and stages of life. Children go through times of madness as they grow.

Be a lunatic thirteen-year-old, Joe, if you must. You'll return to reality soon enough. You're my son, and I know that you'll prefer reality in the long run.

The next evening Joe insisted that his father help him test the program. "It won't work on me," Alvin said. "I don't believe in it. It's like faith healing and taking vitamin C for colds. It never works on skeptics."

Connie stood small near the refrigerator. Alvin noticed the way she seemed to retreat from the conversation.

"Did you try it?" Alvin asked her.

She nodded.

"Mom did it four times for me," Joe said gravely.

"Couldn't get it right the first time?" Father asked. It was a joke.

179

"Got it right every time," Joe said.

Alvin looked at Connie. She met his gaze at first, but then looked away in—what? Fear? Shame? Embarrassment? Alvin couldn't tell. But he sensed that something painful had happened while he was at work. "Should I do it?" Alvin asked her.

"No," Connie whispered.

"Please," Joe said. "How can I test it if you won't help? I can't tell if it's right or wrong unless I know the people doing it."

"What kind of fortune-teller are you?" Alvin asked. "You're supposed to be able to tell the future of strangers."

"I don't tell the future," Joe said. "The program just tells the truth."

"Ah, truth!" said Alvin. "Truth about what?"

"Who you really are."

"Am I in disguise?"

"It tells your names. It tells your story. Ask Mother if it doesn't."

"Joe," Alvin said, "I'll play this little game with you. But don't expect me to regard it as *true*. I'll do almost anything for you, Joe, but I won't lie for you."

"I know."

"Just so you understand."

"I understand."

Alvin sat down at the keyboard. From the kitchen came a sound like the whine a cringing hound makes, back in its throat. It was Connie, and she was terrified. Her fear, whatever caused it, was contagious. Alvin shuddered and then ridiculed himself for letting this upset him. He was in control, and it was absurd to be afraid. He wouldn't be snowed by his own son.

"What do I do?"

180

"Just type things in."

"What things?"

"Whatever comes to mind."

"Words? Numbers? How do I know what to write it you don't tell me?"

"It doesn't matter what you write. Just so you write whatever you feel like writing."

I don't feel like writing anything, Alvin thought. *I don't feel like humoring this nonsense another moment.* But he could not say so, not to Joe; he had to be the patient father, giving this absurdity a fair chance. He began to come up with numbers, with words. But after a few moments there was no randomness, no free association in his choice. It was not in Alvin's nature to let chance guide his choices. Instead he began reciting on the keyboard the long strings of genetic-code information on his most recent bacterial subjects, fragments of names, fragments of numeric data, progressing in order through the DNA. He knew as he did it that he was cheating his son, that Joe wanted something of himself. But he told himself, *What could be more a part of me than something I made?*

"Enough?" he asked Joe.

Joe shrugged. "Do you think it is?"

"I could have done five words and you would have been satisfied?"

"If you think you're through, you're through," Joe said quietly.

"Oh, you're very good at this," Alvin said. "Even the hocus-pocus."

"You're through then?"

"Yes."

Joe started the program running. He leaned back and waited. He could sense his father's impatience, and he found himself relishing the wait. The whirring and clicking of the disk drive. And then the cards began appearing on the screen. This is you. This covers you. This crosses you. This is above you, below you, before you, behind you. Your foundation and your house, your death and your name. Joe waited for what had come before, what had come so predictably, the stories that had flooded upon him when he read for his mother and for himself a dozen times before. But the stories did not come. Because the cards were the same. Over and over again, the King of Swords.

Joe looked at it and understood at once. Father had lied. Father had consciously controlled his input, had ordered it in some way that told the cards that they were being forced. The program had not failed. Father simply would not be read. The King of Swords, by himself, was power, as all the Kings were power. The King of Pentacles was the power of money, the power of the bribe. The King of Wands was the power of life, the power to make new. The King of Cups was the power of negation and obliteration, the power of murder and sleep. And the King of Swords was the power of words that others would believe. Swords could say, "I will kill you," and be believed, and so be obeyed. Swords could say, "I love you," and be believed, and so be adored. Swords could lie. And all his father had given him was lies. What Alvin didn't know was that even the choice of lies told the truth.

"Edmund," said Joe. Edmund was the lying bastard in *King Lear*.

"What?" asked Father.

"We are only what nature makes us. And nothing more."

"You're getting this from the cards?"

Joe looked at his father, expressing nothing.

"It's all the same card," said Alvin.

"I know," said Joe.

"What's this supposed to be?"

"A waste of time," said Joe. Then he got up and walked out of the room.

Alvin sat there, looking at the little tarot cards laid out on the screen. As he watched, the display changed, each card in turn being surrounded by a thin line and then blown up large, nearly filling the screen. The King of Swords every time. With the point of his sword coming out of his mouth, and his hands clutching at his groin. *Surely*, Alvin thought, *that was not what was drawn on the Waite deck*.

Connie stood near the kitchen doorway, leaning on the refrigerator. "And that's all?" she asked.

"Should there be more?" Alvin asked.

"God," she said.

"What happened with you?"

"Nothing," she said, walking calmly out of the room. Alvin heard her rush up the stairs. And he wondered how things got out of control like this.

Alvin could not make up his mind how to feel about his son's project. It was silly, and Alvin wanted nothing to do with it, wished he'd never bought the cards for him. For days on end Alvin would stay at the laboratory until late at night and rush back again in the morning without so much as eating breakfast with his family. Then, exhausted from lack of sleep, he would get up late, come downstairs, and pretend for the whole day that nothing unusual was going on. On such days he discussed Joe's readings with him, or his own genetic experiments; sometimes, when the artificial cheer had been maintained long enough to be believed, Alvin would even discuss Joe's tarot program. It was at such times that Alvin offered to provide Joe with introductions, to get him better computers to work with, to advise him on the strategy of development and publication. Afterward Alvin always regretted having helped Joe, because what Joe was doing was a shameful waste of a brilliant mind. It also did not make Joe love him any more.

Yet as time passed, Alvin realized that other people were taking Joe seriously. A group of psychologists administered batteries of tests to hundreds of subjects—who had also put random data into Joe's program. When Joe interpreted the tarot readouts for these people, the correlation was statistically significant. Joe himself rejected those results, because the psychological tests were probably invalid measurements themselves. More important to him was the months of work in clinics, doing readings with people the doctors knew intimately. Even the most skeptical of the participating psychologists had to admit that Joe knew things about people that he could not possibly know. And most of the psychologists said openly that Joe not only confirmed much that they already knew but also provided brilliant new insights. "It's like stepping into my patient's mind," one of them told Alvin.

"My son is brilliant, Dr. Fryer, and I want him to succeed, but surely this mumbo jumbo can't be more than luck."

Dr. Fryer only smiled and took a sip of wine. "Joe tells me that you have never submitted to the test yourself."

Alvin almost argued, but it was true. He never

had *submitted*, even though he went through the motions. "I've seen it in action," Alvin said.

"Have you? Have you seen his results with someone you know well?"

Alvin shook his head, then smiled. "I figured that since I didn't believe in it, it wouldn't work around me."

"It isn't magic."

"It isn't science, either," said Alvin.

"No, you're right. Not science at all. But just because it isn't science doesn't mean it isn't true."

"Either it's science or it isn't."

"What a clear world you live in," said Dr. Fryer. "All the lines neatly drawn. We've run double-blind tests on his program, Dr. Bevis. Without knowing it, he has analyzed data taken from the same patient on different days, under different circumstances: the patient has even been given different instructions in some of the samples so that it wasn't random. And you know what happened?"

Alvin knew but did not say so.

"Not only did his program read substantially the same for all the different random inputs for the same patient, but the program also spotted the ringers. Easily. And then it turned out that the ringers were a consistent result for the woman who wrote the test we happened to use for the non-random input. Even when it shouldn't have worked, it worked."

"Very impressive," said Alvin, sounding as unimpressed as he could.

"It *is* impressive."

"I don't know about that," said Alvin, "So the cards are consistent. How do we know that they *mean* anything, or that what they mean is *true*?"

"Hasn't it occurred to you that your *son* is why it's true?"

Alvin tapped his spoon on the tablecloth, providing a muffled rhythm.

"Your son's computer program objectifies random input. But only your son can read it. To me that says that it's his *mind* that makes his method work, not his program. If we could figure out what's going on inside your son's head, Dr. Bevis, then his method would be science. Until then it's an art. But whether it is art or science, he tells the truth."

"Forgive me for what might seem a slight to your profession," said Alvin, "but how in God's name do *you* know whether what he says is true?"

Dr. Fryer smiled and cocked his head. "Because I can't conceive of it being wrong. We can't test his interpretations the way we tested his program. I've tried to find objective tests. For instance, whether his findings agree with my notes. But my notes mean nothing, because until your son reads my patients, I really don't understand them. And after he reads them, I can't conceive of any other view of them. Before you dismiss me as hopelessly subjective, remember please, Dr. Bevis, that I have every reason to fear and fight against your son's work. It undoes everything that I have believed in. It undermines my own life's work. And Joe is just like you. He doesn't think psychology is a science, either. Forgive *me* for what might seem a slight to your son, but he is troubled and cold and difficult to work with. I don't like him much. So why do I believe him?"

"That's your problem, isn't it?"

"On the contrary, Dr. Bevis. Everyone who's seen

what Joe does, believes it. Except for you. I think
that most definitely makes it *your* problem."

Dr. Fryer was wrong. Not everyone believed Joe.

"No," said Connie.

"No what?" asked Alvin. It was breakfast. Joe
hadn't come downstairs yet. Alvin and Connie
hadn't said a word since "Here's the eggs" and
"Thanks."

Connie was drawing paths with her fork through
the yolk stains on her plate. "Don't do another reading with Joe."

"I wasn't planning on it."

"Dr. Fryer told you to believe it, didn't he?" She
put her fork down.

"But I didn't believe Dr. Fryer."

Connie got up from the table and began washing
the dishes. Alvin watched her as she rattled the
plates to make as much noise as possible. Nothing
was normal anymore. Connie was angry as she
washed the dishes. There was a dishwasher, but she
was scrubbing everything by hand. Nothing was as
it should be. Alvin tried to figure out why he felt
such dread.

"You will do a reading with Joe," said Connie,
"*because* you don't believe Dr. Fryer. You always
insist on verifying everything for yourself. If you
believe, you must question your belief. If you doubt,
you doubt your own disbelief. Am I not right?"

"No." *Yes*.

"And I'm telling you this once to have faith in
your doubt. There is no truth whatever in his God-
damned tarot."

In all these years of marriage, Alvin could not
remember Connie using such coarse language. But

187

then she hadn't said *god-damn*; she had said God-*damned*, with all the theological overtones.

"I mean," she went on, filling the silence. "I mean how can anyone take this seriously? The card he calls Strength—a woman closing a lion's mouth, yes, fine, but then he makes up a God-*damned* story about it, how the lion wanted her baby and she *fed it to him*." She looked at Alvin with fear. "It's sick, isn't it?"

"He said that?"

"And the Devil, forcing the lovers to stay together. He's supposed to be the firstborn child, chaining Adam and Eve together. That's why Io-caste and Laios tried to kill Oedipus. Because they hated each other, and the baby would force them to stay together. But then they stayed together anyway because of shame at what they had done to an innocent child. And then they told everyone that asinine lie about the oracle and her prophecy."

"He's read too many books."

Connie trembled. "If he does a reading of you, I'm afraid of what will happen."

"If he feeds me crap like that, Connie, I'll just bite my lip. No fights, I promise."

She touched his chest. Not his shirt, his chest. It felt as if her finger burned right through the cloth. "I'm not worried that you'll fight," she said. "I'm afraid that you'll believe him."

"Why would I believe him?"

"We don't live in the Tower, Alvin!"

"Of course we don't."

"I'm not Iocaste, Alvin!"

"Of course you aren't."

"Don't believe him. Don't believe anything he says."

"Connie, don't get so upset." Again: "Why should I believe him?"

She shook her head and walked out of the room. The water was still running in the sink. She hadn't said a word. But her answer rang in the room as if she had spoken: "Because it's true."

Alvin tried to sort it out for hours. Oedipus and Iocaste. Adam, Eve, and the Devil. The mother feeding her baby to the lion. As Dr. Fryer had said, it isn't the cards, it isn't the program, it's Joe. Joe and the stories in his head. Is there a story in the world that Joe hasn't read? All the tales that man has told himself, all the visions of the world, and Joe knew them. Knew and believed them. Joe the repository of all. the world's lies, and now he was telling the lies back, and they believed him, every one of them believed him.

No matter how hard Alvin tried to treat this non-sense with the contempt it deserved, one thing kept coming back to him. Joe's program had known that Alvin was lying, that Alvin was playing games, not telling the truth. Joe's program was valid at least that far. *If his method can pass that negative test, how can I call myself a scientist if I disbelieve it before I've given it the* positive test *as well?*

That night while Joe was watching M*A*S*H reruns, Alvin came into the family room to talk to him. It always startled Alvin to see his son watching normal television shows, especially old ones from Alvin's own youth. The same boy who had read *Ulysses* and made sense of it without reading a single commentary, and he was laughing out loud at the television.

It was only after he had sat beside his son and

watched for a while that Alvin realized that Joe was not laughing at the places where the laugh track did. He was not laughing at the jokes. He was laughing at Hawkeye himself.

"What was so funny?" asked Alvin.

"Hawkeye," said Joe.

"He was being serious."

"I know," said Joe. "But he's so sure he's *right*, and everybody believes him. Don't you think that's funny?"

As a matter of fact, no, I don't. "I want to give it another try, Joe," said Alvin.

Even though it was an abrupt change of subject, Joe understood at once, as if he had long been waiting for his father to speak. They got into the car, and Alvin drove them to the university. The computer people immediately make one of the full-color terminals available. This time Alvin allowed himself to be truly random, not thinking at all about what he was choosing, avoiding any meaning as he typed. When he was sick of typing, he looked at Joe for permission to be through. Joe shrugged. Alvin entered one more set of letters and then said, "Done."

Alvin entered a single command that told the computer to start analyzing the input, and father and son sat together to watch the story unfold.

After a seemingly eternal wait, in which neither of them said a word, a picture of a card appeared on the screen.

"This is you," said Joe. It was the King of Swords.

"What does it mean?" asked Alvin.

"Very little by itself."

"Why is the sword coming out of his mouth?"

"Because he kills by the words of his mouth."

Father nodded. "And why is he holding his crotch?"

"I don't know."

"I thought you knew," said Father.

"I don't know until I see the other cards." Joe pressed the return key, and a new card almost completely covered the old one. A thin blue line appeared around it, and then it was blown up to fill the screen. It was Judgment, an angel blowing a trumpet, awakening the dead, who were gray with corruption, standing in their graves. "This covers you," said Joe.

"What does it mean?"

"It's how you spend your life. Judging the dead."

"Like God? You're saying I think I'm God?"

"It's what you do, Father," said Joe. "You judge everything. You're a scientist. I can't help what the cards say."

"I study life."

"You break life down into its pieces. Then you make your judgment. Only when it's all in fragments like the flesh of the dead."

Alvin tried to hear anger or bitterness in Joe's voice, but Joe was calm, matter-of-fact, for all the world like a doctor with a good bedside manner. Or like a historian telling the simple truth.

Joe pressed the key, and on the small display another card appeared, again on top of the first two, but horizontally. "This crosses you," said Joe. And the card was outlined in blue, and zoomed close. It was the Devil.

"What does it mean, crossing me?"

"Your enemy, your obstacle. The son of Laios and Iocaste."

Alvin remembered that Connie had mentioned

191

Iocaste. "How similar is this to what you told Connie?" he asked.

Joe looked at him impassively. "How can I know after only three cards?"

Alvin waved him to go on.

A card above. "This crowns you." The Two of Wands, a man holding the world in his hands, staring off into the distance, with two small saplings growing out of the stone parapet beside him. "The crown is what you think you are, the story you tell yourself about yourself. Lifegiver, the God of Genesis, the Prince whose kiss awakens Sleeping Beauty and Snow White."

A card below. "This is beneath you, what you most fear to become." A man lying on the ground, ten swords piercing him in a row. He did not bleed.

"I've never lain awake at night afraid that someone would stab me to death."

Joe looked at him placidly. "But, Father, I told you, swords are words as often as not. What you fear is death at the hands of storytellers. According to the cards, you're the sort of man who would have killed the messenger who brought bad news."

According to the cards, or according to you? But Alvin held his anger and said nothing.

A card to the right. "This is behind you, the story of your past." A man in a sword-studded boat, poling the craft upstream, a woman and child sitting bowed in front of him. "Hansel and Gretel sent into the sea in a leaky boat."

"It doesn't look like a brother and sister," said Alvin. "It looks like a mother and child."

"Ah," said Joe. A card to the left. "This is before you, where you know your course will lead." A

192

sarcophagus with a knight sculpted in stone upon it, a bird resting on his head.

Death, thought Alvin. Always a safe prediction. And yet not safe at all. The cards themselves seemed malevolent. They all depicted situations that cried out with agony or fear. That was the gimmick, Alvin decided. Potent enough pictures will seem to be important whether they really mean anything or not. Heavy with meaning like a pregnant woman, they can be made to bear anything.

"It isn't death," said Joe.

Alvin was startled to have his thoughts so appropriately interrupted.

"It's a monument after you're dead. With your words engraved on it and above it. Blind Homer. Jesus. Mahomet. To have your words read like scripture."

And for the first time Alvin was genuinely frightened by what his son had found. Not that this future frightened him. Hadn't he forbidden himself to hope for it, he wanted it so much? No, what he feared was the way he felt himself say, silently, *Yes, yes, this is True. I will not be flattered into belief*, he said to himself. But underneath every layer of doubt that he built between himself and the cards he believed. Whatever Joe told him, he would believe, and so he denied belief now, not because of disbelief but because he was afraid. Perhaps that was why he had doubted from the start.

Next the computer placed a card in the lower right-hand corner. "This is your house." It was the Tower, broken by lightning, a man and woman falling from it, surrounded by tears of flame.

A card directly above it. "This answers you." A man under a tree, beside a stream, with a hand coming from a small cloud, giving him a cup. "Elijah by the brook, and the ravens feed him."

And above that a man walking away from a stack of eight cups, with a pole and traveling cloak. The pole is a wand, with leaves growing from it. The cups are arranged so that a space is left where a ninth cup had been. "This saves you."

And then, at the top of the vertical file of four cards, Death. "This ends it." A bishop, a woman, and a child kneeling before Death on a horse. The horse is trampling the corpse of a man who had been a king. Beside the man lie his crown and a golden sword. In the distance a ship is foundering in a swift river. The sun is rising between pillars in the east. And Death holds a leafy wand in his hand, with a sheaf of wheat bound to it at the top. A banner of life over the corpse of the king. "This ends it," said Joe definitively.

Alvin waited, looking at the cards, waiting for Joe to explain it. But Joe did not explain. He just gazed at the monitor and then suddenly got to his feet. "Thank you, Father," he said. "It's all clear now."

"To you it's clear," Alvin said.

"Yes," said Joe. "Thank you very much for not lying this time." Then Joe made as if to leave.

"Hey, wait," Alvin said. "Aren't you going to explain it to me?"

"No," said Joe.

"Why not?"

"You wouldn't believe me."

Alvin was not about to admit to anyone, least of all himself, that he did believe. "I still want to know. I'm curious. Can't I be curious?"

Joe studied his father's face. "I told Mother, and she hasn't spoken a natural word to me since."

So it was not just Alvin's imagination. The tarot program had driven a wedge between Connie and Joe. He'd been right. "I'll speak a natural word or two every day, I promise," Alvin said.

"That's what I'm afraid of," Joe said.

"Son," Alvin said. "Dr. Fryer told me that the stories you tell, the way you put things together, is the closest thing to truth about people that he's ever heard. Even if I don't believe it, don't I have the right to hear the truth?"

"I don't know if it *is* the truth. Or if there is such a thing."

"There is. The way things *are*, that's truth."

"But how *are* things, with people? What causes me to feel the way I do or act the way I do? Hormones? Parents? Social patterns? All the causes or purposes of all our acts are just stories we tell ourselves, stories we believe or disbelieve, changing all the time. But still we live, still we act, and all those acts have *some* kind of cause. The patterns all fit together into a web that connects everyone who's ever lived with everyone else. And every new person changes the web, adds to it, changes the connections, makes it all different. That's what I find with this program, how you believe you fit into the web."

"Not how I *really* fit?"

Joe shrugged. "How can I know? How can I measure it? I discover the stories that you believe most secretly, the stories that control your acts. But the very telling of the story changes the way you believe. Moves some things into the open, changes who you *are*. I undo my work by doing it."

"Then undo your work with me, and tell me the truth."

"I don't want to."

"Why not?"

"Because I'm in your story."

Alvin spoke then more honestly than he ever meant to. "Then for God's sake tell me the story, because I don't know who the hell you are."

Joe walked back to his chair and sat down. "I am Goneril and Regan, because you made me act out the lie that you needed to hear. I am Oedipus, because you pinned my ankles together and left me exposed on the hillside to save your own future."

"I have loved you more than life."

"You were always afraid of me, Father. Like Lear, afraid that I wouldn't care for you when I was still vigorous and you were enfeebled by age. Like Laios, terrified that my power would overshadow you. So you took *control*; you put me out of my place."

"I gave years to educating you—"

"Educating me in order to make me forever your shadow, your student. When the only thing that I really loved was the one thing that would free me from you—all the stories."

"Damnable stupid fiction."

"No more stupid than the fiction *you* believe. Your story of little cells and DNA, your story that there is such a thing as reality that can be objectively perceived. God, what an idea, to see with inhuman eyes, without interpretation. That's exactly how stones see, without interpretation, because without interpretation there isn't any *sight*."

"I think I know that much at least," Alvin said, trying to feel as contemptuous as he sounded. "I never said I was objective."

"*Scientific* was the word. What could be verified was scientific. That was all that you would ever let me study, what could be verified. The trouble is, Father, that nothing in the world that matters at all is verifiable. What makes us who we are is forever tenuous, fragile, the web of a spider eaten and remade every day. I can never see out of your eyes. Yet I can never see any other way than through the eyes of every storyteller who ever taught me how to see. That was what you did to me, Father. You forbade me to hear any storyteller but you. It was *your* reality I had to surrender to. *Your* fiction I had to believe."

Alvin felt his past slipping out from under him. "If I had known those games of make-believe were so important to you, I wouldn't have—"

'You knew they were that important to me," Joe said coldly. "Why else would you have bothered to forbid me? But my mother dipped me into the water, all but my heel, and I got all the power you tried to keep from me. You see, Mother was not Griselde. She wouldn't kill her children for her husband's sake. When you exiled me, you exiled her. We lived the stories together as long as we were free."

"What do you mean?"

"Until you came home to teach me. We were free until then. We acted out all the stories that we could. Without you."

It conjured for Alvin the ridiculous image of Connie playing Goldilocks and the Three Bears day after day for years. He laughed in spite of himself, laughed sharply, for only a moment.

Joe took the laugh all wrong. Or perhaps took it exactly right. He took his father by the wrist and gripped him so tightly that Alvin grew afraid. Joe was stronger than Alvin had thought. "Grendel feels the touch of Beowulf on his hand," Joe whispered, "and he thinks, Perhaps I should have stayed at home tonight. Perhaps I am not hungry after all."

Alvin tried for a moment to pull his arm away but could not. *What have I done to you, Joe?* he shouted inside himself. Then he relaxed his arm and surrendered to the tale. "Tell me my story from the cards," he said. "Please."

Without letting go of his father's arm, Joe began. "You are Lear, and your kingdom is great. Your whole life is shaped so that you will live forever in stone, in memory. Your dream is to create life. You thought I would be such life, as malleable as the little worlds you make from DNA. But from the moment I was born you were afraid of me. I couldn't be taken apart and recombined like all your little animals. And you were afraid that I would steal the swords from your sepulchre. You were afraid that you would live on as Joseph Bevis's father, instead of me forever being Alvin Bevis's son."

"I was jealous of my child," said Alvin, trying to sound skeptical.

"Like the father rat that devours his babies because he knows that someday they will challenge his supremacy, yes. It's the oldest pattern in the world, a tale older than teeth."

"Go on, this is quite fascinating." *I refuse to care*.

"All the storytellers know how this tale ends. Every time a father tries to change the future by controlling his children, it ends the same. Either the children lie, like Goneril and Regan, and pretend to be what he made them, or the children tell the truth, like Cordelia, and the father casts them out. I tried to tell the truth, but then together Mother and I lied to you. It was so much easier, and it kept me alive. She was Grim the Fisher, and she saved me alive."

198

Iocaste and Laios and Oedipus. "I see where this is going," Alvin said. "I thought you were bright enough not to believe in that Freudian nonsense about the Oedipus complex."

"Freud thought he was telling the story of all mankind when he was only telling his own. Just because the story of Oedipus isn't true for everyone doesn't mean that it isn't true for me. But don't worry, Father. I don't have to kill you in the forest in order to take possession of your throne."

"I'm not worried.' It was a lie. It was a truthful understatement.

'Laios died only because he would not let his son pass along the road."

"Pass along any road you please."

"And I am the Devil. You and Mother were in Eden until I came. Because of me you were cast out. And now you're in hell."

"How neatly it all fits."

"For you to achieve your dream, you had to kill me with your story. When I lay there with your blades in my back, only then could you be sure that your sepulchre was safe. When you exiled me in a boat I could not live in, only then could you be safe, you thought. But I am the Horn Child, and the boat bore me quickly across the sea to my true kingdom."

"This isn't anything coming from the computer," said Alvin. "This is just you being a normal resentful teenager. Just a phase that everyone goes through."

Joe's grip on Alvin's arm only tightened. "I didn't die, I didn't wither, I have my power now, and you're not safe. Your house is broken, and you and Mother are being thrown from it to your destruction, and you know it. Why did you come to me, except that you knew you were being destroyed?"

Again Alvin tried to find a way to fend off Joe's story with ridicule. This time he could not. Joe had pierced through shield and armor and cloven him, neck to heart. "In the name of God, Joe, how do we end it all?" He barely kept from shouting.

Joe relaxed his grip on Alvin's arm at last. The blood began to flow again, painfully; Alvin fancied he could measure it passing through his calibrated arteries.

"Two ways," said Joe. "There is one way you can save yourself."

Alvin looked at the cards on the screen. "Exile."

"Just leave. Just go away for a while. Let us alone for a while. Let me pass you by, stop trying to rule, stop trying to force your story on me, and then after a while we can see what's changed."

"Oh, excellent. A son divorcing his father. Not too likely."

"Or death. As the deliverer. As the fulfillment of your dream. If you die now, you defeat me. As Laios destroyed Oedipus at last."

Alvin stood up to leave. "This is rank melodrama. Nobody's going to die because of this."

"Then why can't you stop trembling?" asked Joe.

"Because I'm angry, that's why," Alvin said. "I'm angry at the way you choose to look at me. I love you more than any other father I know loves his son, and this is the way you choose to view it. How sharper than a serpent's tooth—"

"How sharper than a serpent's tooth it is to have a thankless child. Away, away!"

"Lear, isn't it? You gave me the script, and now I'm saying the goddamn lines."

Joe smiled a strange, sphinxlike smile. "It's a good exit line, though, isn't it?"

"Joe, I'm not going to leave, and I'm not going to drop dead, either. You've told me a lot. Like you said, not the truth, not *reality*, but the way you see things. That helps, to know how you see things."

Joe shook his head in despair. "Father, you don't understand. It was *you* who put those cards up on the screen. Not I. My reading is completely different. Completely different, but no better."

"If I'm the King of Swords, who are you?"

"The Hanged Man," Joe said.

Alvin shook his head. "What an ugly world you choose to live in."

"Not neat and pretty like yours, not bound about by rules the way yours is. Laws and principles, theories and hypotheses, may they cover your eyes and keep you happy."

"Joe, I think you need help," said Alvin.

"Don't we all," said Joe.

"So do I. A family counselor maybe. I think we need outside help."

"I've told you what you can do."

'I'm not going to run away from this, Joe, no matter how much you want me to."

"You already have. You've been running away for months. These are *your* cards, Father, not mine."

"Joe, I want to help you out of this—unhappiness."

Joe frowned. "Father, don't you understand? The Hanged Man is smiling. The Hanged Man has won."

Alvin did not go home. He couldn't face Connie right now, did not want to try to explain what he felt about what Joe had told him. So he went to the laboratory and lost himself for a time in reading records of what was happening with the different subject organisms. Some good results. If it all held up, Alvin Bevis would have taken mankind a long way toward being able to read the DNA chain. There was a Nobel in it. More important still, there was real change. *I will have changed the world*, he thought. And then there came into his mind the picture of the man holding the world in his hands, looking off into the distance. The Two of Wands. His dream. Joe was right about that. Right about Alvin's longing for a monument to last forever.

And in a moment of unusual clarity Alvin saw that Joe was right about everything. Wasn't Alvin even now doing just what the cards called for him to do to save himself, going into hiding with the Eight of Cups? His house was breaking down, all was being undone, and he was setting out on a long journey that would lead him to solitude. Greatness, but solitude.

There was one card that Joe hadn't worked into his story, however. The Four of Cups. "This answers you," he had said. The hand of God coming from a cloud. Elijah by the brook. *If God were to whisper to me, what would He say?*

He would say, Alvin thought, that there is something profoundly wrong, something circular in all that Joe has done. He has synthesized things that no other mind in the world could have brought together meaningfully. He is, as Dr. Fryer said, touching on the borders of Truth. But, by God, there is something wrong, something he has overlooked. Not a *mistake*, exactly. Simply a place where Joe has not put two true things together in his own life: Stories make us who we are: the tarot program identifies the stories we believe: by hearing the tale of the tarot, we have changed who we are: therefore—

202

Therefore, no one knows how much of Joe's tarot story is believed because it is true, and how much becomes true because it is believed. Joe is not a scientist. Joe is a tale-teller. But the gifted, powerful teller of tales soon lives in the world he has created, for as more and more people believe him, his tales become true.

We do not have to be the family of Laios. I do not have to play at being Lear. I can say no to this story, and make it false. Not that Joe could tell any other story, because this is the one that he believes. But I can change what he believes by changing what the cards say, and I can change what the cards say by being someone else.

King of Swords. Imposing my will on others, making them live in the world that my words created. And now my son, too, doing the same. But I can change, and so can he, and then perhaps his brilliance, his insights can shape a better world than the sick one he is making us live in.

And as he grew more excited, Alvin felt himself fill with light, as if the cup had poured into him from the cloud. He believed, in fact, that he had already changed. That he was already something other than what Joe said he was.

The telephone rang. Rang twice, three times, before Alvin reached out to answer it. It was Connie.

"Alvin?" she asked in a small voice.

"Connie," he said.

"Alvin, Joe called me." She sounded lost, distant.

"Did he? Don't worry, Connie, everything's going to be fine."

"Oh, I know," Connie said. "I finally figured it out. It's the thing that Helen never figured out. It's

203

the thing that Iocaste never had the guts to do. Enid knew it, though, Enid could do it. I love you, Alvin." She hung up.

Alvin sat with his hand on the phone for thirty seconds. That's how long it took him to realize that Connie sounded *sleepy*. That Connie was trying to change the cards, too. By killing herself.

All the way home in the car, Alvin was afraid that he was going crazy. He kept warning himself to drive carefully, not to take chances. He wouldn't be able to save Connie if he had an accident on the way. And then there would come a voice that sounded like Joe's, whispering, That's the story you tell yourself, but the truth is you're driving slowly and carefully, hoping she will die so everything will be simple again. It's the best solution. Connie has solved it all, and you're being *slow* so she can succeed, but telling yourself you're being *careful* so you can live with yourself after she's dead.

No, said Alvin again and again, pushing on the accelerator, weaving through the traffic, then forcing himself to slow down, not to kill himself to save two seconds. Sleeping pills weren't *that* fast. And maybe he was wrong; maybe she hadn't taken pills. Or maybe he was thinking that in order to slow himself down so that Connie would die and everything would be simple again—

Shut up, he told himself. *Just get there*, he told himself.

He got there, fumbled with the key, and burst inside. "Connie!" he shouted.

Joe was standing in the archway between the kitchen and the family room.

"It's all right," Joe said. "I got here when she was

on the phone to you. I forced her to vomit, and most of the pills hadn't even dissolved yet."

"She's awake?"

"More or less."

Joe stepped aside, and Alvin walked into the family room. Connie sat on a chair, looking catatonic. But as he came nearer, she turned away, which at once hurt him and relieved him. At least she was not hopelessly insane. So it was not too late for change.

"Joe," Alvin said, still looking at Connie. "I've been thinking. About the reading."

Joe stood behind him, saying nothing.

"I believe it. You told the truth. The whole thing, just as you said."

Still Joe did not answer. *Well, what can he say, anyway?* Alvin asked himself. *Nothing. At least he's listening.* "Joe, you told the truth. I really screwed up the family. I've had to have the whole thing my way, and it really screwed things up. Do you hear me, Connie? I'm telling both of you, I agree with Joe about the past. But not the future. There's nothing magical about those cards. They don't tell the future. They just tell the outcome of the pattern, the way things will end if the pattern isn't changed. But we can change it, don't you see? That's what Connie was trying to do with the pills, change the way things turn out. Well, *I'm* the one who can really change, by changing me. Can you see that? I'm changed already. As if I drank from the cup that came to me out of the cloud, Joe. I don't have to control things the way I did. It's all going to be better now. We can build up from, up from—"

The ashes, those were the next words. But they were the wrong words, Alvin could sense that. All

205

his words were wrong. It had seemed true in the lab, when he thought of it; now it sounded dishonest. Desperate. Ashes in his mouth. He turned around to Joe. His son was not listening silently. Joe's face was contorted with rage, his hands trembling, tears streaming down his cheeks.

As soon as Alvin looked at him, Joe screamed at him. "You can't just let it be, can you! You have to do it again and again and again, don't you!"

Oh, I see, Alvin thought. *By wanting to change things, I was just making them more the same. Trying to control the world they live in. I didn't think it through well enough. God played a dirty trick on me, giving me that cup from the cloud.*

"I'm sorry," Alvin said.

"No!" Joe shouted. "There's nothing you can say!"

"You're right," Alvin said, trying to calm Joe. "I should just have—"

"Don't say *anything*!" Joe screamed, his face red.

"I won't, I won't," said Alvin. "I won't say another—"

"*Nothing! Nothing! Nothing!*"

"I'm just agreeing with you, that's—"

Joe lunged forward and screamed it in his father's face. "God damn you, don't talk at all!"

"I see," said Alvin, suddenly realizing. "I see—as long as I try to put it in words, I'm forcing my view of things on the rest of you, and if I—"

There were no words left for Joe to say. He had tried every word he knew that might silence his father, but none would. Where words fail, there remains the act. The only thing close at hand was a heavy glass dish on the side table. Joe did not mean to grab it, did not mean to strike his father across the head with it. He only meant his father to be still. But all his incantations had failed, and still his father spoke, still his father stood in the way, refusing to let him pass, and so he smashed him across the head with the glass dish.

But it was the dish that broke, not his father's head. And the fragment of glass in Joe's hand kept right on going after the blow, followed through with the stroke, and the sharp edge of the glass cut neatly through the fleshy, bloody, windy part of Alvin's throat. All the way through, severing the carotid artery, the veins, and above all the trachea, so that no more air flowed through Alvin's larynx. Alvin was wordless as he fell backward, spraying blood from his throat, clutching at the pieces of glass embedded in the side of his face.

"Uh-oh," said Connie in a high and childish voice.

Alvin lay on his back on the floor, his head propped up on the front edge of the couch. He felt a terrible throbbing in his throat and a strange silence in his ears where the blood no longer flowed. He had not known how noisy the blood in the head could be, until now, and now he could not tell anyone. He could only lie there, not moving, not turning his head, watching.

He watched as Connie stared at his throat and slowly tore at her hair; he watched as Joe carefully and methodically pushed the bloody piece of glass into his right eye and then into his left. *I see now*, said Alvin silently. *Sorry I didn't understand before. You found the answer to the riddle that devoured us, my Oedipus. I'm just not good at riddles, I'm afraid.*

Memories of My Head

Even with the evidence before you, I'm sure you will not believe my account of my own suicide. Or rather, you'll believe that I wrote it, but not that I wrote it after the fact. You'll assume that I wrote this letter in advance, perhaps not yet sure that I would squeeze the shotgun between my knees, then balance a ruler against the trigger, pressing downward with a surprisingly steady hand until the hammer fell, the powder exploded, and a tumult of small shot at close range blew my head off, embedding brain, bone, skin and a few carbonized strands of hair in the ceiling and wall behind me. But I assure you that I did not write in anticipation, or as an oblique threat, or for any other purpose than to report to you, after I did it, why the deed was done.

You must already have found my raggedly decapitated body seated at my rolltop desk in the darkest corner of the basement where my only source of light is the old pole lamp that no longer went with the decor when the living room was redecorated. But picture me, not as you found me, still and lifeless, but rather as I am at this moment, with my left hand neatly holding the paper. My right hand moves smoothly across the page, reaching up now and then to dip the quill in the blood that has pooled in the ragged mass of muscles, veins, and stumpy bone between my shoulders.

Why do I, being dead, bother to write to you now? If I didn't choose to write before I killed myself, perhaps I should have abided by that decision after death; but it was not until I had actually carried out my plan that I finally had something to say to you. And having something to say, writing became my only choice, since ordinary diction is beyond one who lacks larynx, mouth, lips, tongue, and teeth. All my tools of articulation have been shredded and embedded in the plasterboard. I have achieved utter speechlessness.

Do you marvel that I continue to move my arms and hands after my head is gone? I'm not surprised: My brain has been disconnected from my body for many years. All my actions long since became habits. Stimuli would pass from nerves to spinal cord and rise no further. You would greet me in the morning or lob your comments at me for hours in the night and I would utter my customary responses without these exchanges provoking a single thought in my mind. I scarcely remember being alive for the last years—or, rather, I remember being alive, but can't distinguish one day from another, one Christmas from any other Christmas, one word you said from any other word you might have said. Your voice has become a drone, and as for my own voice, I haven't listened to a thing I said since the last time I humiliated myself before you, causing you to curl your lip in distaste and turn over the next three cards in your solitaire game. Nor can I remember which of the many lip-curlings and card-turnings in my memory was the particular one that coincided with my last self-debasement before you. Now my habitual body continues as it has for all these years, writing this memoir of my suicide as one last, complex, involuntary twitching of the muscles in my arm and hand and fingers.

I'm sure you have detected the inconsistency. You have always been able to evade my desperate attempts at conveying meaning. You simply wait until you can catch some seeming contradiction in my words, then use it as a pretext to refuse to listen to anything else I say because I am not being logical, and therefore am not rational, and you refuse to speak to someone who is not being rational. The inconsistency you have noticed is: If I am completely a creature of habit, how is it that I committed suicide in the first place, since that is a new and therefore non-customary behavior?

But you see, this is no inconsistency at all. You have schooled me in all the arts of self-destruction. Just as the left hand will sympathetically learn some measure of a skill practiced only with the right, so I have made such a strong habit of subsuming my own identity in yours that it was almost a reflex finally to perform the physical annihilation of myself.

Indeed, it is merely the culmination of long custom that when I made the most powerful statement of my life, my most dazzling performance, my finest hundredth of a second, in that very moment I lost my eyes and so will not be able to witness the response of my audience. I write to you, but you will not write or speak to me, or if you do, I shall not have eyes to read or ears to hear you. Will you scream? (Will someone else find me, and will *that* person scream? But it *must* be you.) I imagine disgust, perhaps. Kneeling, retching on the old rug that was all we could afford to use in my basement corner.

And later, who will peel the ceiling plaster? Rip out the wallboard? And when the wall has been stripped down to the studs, what will be done with those large slabs of drywall that have been plowed with shot and sown with bits of my brain and skull? Will there be fragments of drywall buried with me in my grave? Will they even be displayed in the open coffin, neatly broken up and piled where my head used to be? It would be appropriate, I think, since a significant percentage of my corpse is there, not attached to the rest of my body. And if some fragment of your precious house were buried with me, perhaps you would come occasionally to shed some tears on my grave.

I find that in death I am not free of worries. Being speechless means I cannot correct misinterpretations. What if someone says, "It wasn't suicide: The gun fell and discharged accidentally"? Or what if *murder* is supposed? Will some passing vagrant be apprehended? Suppose he heard the shot and came running, and then was found, holding the shotgun and gibbering at his own blood-covered hands; or, worse, going through my clothes and stealing the hundred-dollar bill I always carry on my person. (You remember how I always joked that I kept it as busfare in case I ever decided to leave you, until you forbade me to say it one more time or you would not be responsible for what you did to me. I have kept my silence on that subject ever since—have you noticed?—for I want you always to be responsible for what you do.)

The poor vagrant could not have administered first aid to me—I'm quite sure that nowhere in the Boy

Scout Handbook would he have read so much as a paragraph on caring for a person whose head has been torn away so thoroughly that there's not enough neck left to hold a tourniquet. And since the poor fellow couldn't help me, why shouldn't he help himself? I don't begrudge him the hundred dollars— I hereby bequeath him all the money and other valuables he can find on my person. You can't charge him with stealing what I freely give to him. I also hereby affirm that he did not kill me, and did not dip my drawing pen into the blood in the stump of my throat and then hold my hand, forming the letters that appear on the paper you are reading. You are also witness of this, for you recognize my handwriting. No one should be punished for my death who was not involved in causing it.

But my worst fear is not sympathetic dread for some unknown body-finding stranger, but rather that no one will discover me at all. Having fired the gun, I have now had sufficient time to write all these pages. Admittedly I have been writing with a large hand and much space between the lines, since in writing blindly I must be careful not to run words and lines together. But this does not change the fact that considerable time has elapsed since the unmissable sound of a shotgun firing. Surely some neighbor must have heard; surely the police have been summoned and even now are hurrying to investigate the anxious reports of a gunshot in our picture-book home. For all I know the sirens even now are sounding down the street, and curious neighbors have gathered on their lawns to see what sort of burden the police carry forth. But even when I wait for a few moments, my pen hovering over the page, I feel no vibration of heavy footfalls on the stairs.

No hands reach under my armpits to pull me away from the page. Therefore I conclude that there has been no phone call. No one has come, no one will come, unless you come, *until* you come.

Wouldn't it be ironic if you chose this day to leave me? Had I only waited until your customary homecoming hour, you would not have come, and instead of transplanting a cold rod of iron into my lap I could have walked through the house for the first time as if it were somewhat my own. As the night grew later and later, I would have become more certain you were not returning; how daring I would have been then! I might have kicked the shoes in their neat little rows on the closet floor. I might have jumbled up my drawers without dreading your lecture when you discovered it. I might have read the newspaper in the holy of holies, and when I needed to get up to answer a call of nature, I could have left the newspaper spread open on the coffee table instead of folding it neatly just as it came from the paperboy and when I came back there it would be, wide open, just as I left it, without a tapping foot and a scowl and a rosary of complaints about people who are unfit to live with civilized persons.

But you have not left me. I know it. You will return tonight. This will simply be one of the nights that you were detained at the office and if I were a productive human being I would know that there are times when one cannot simply drop one's work and come home because the clock has struck such an arbitrary hour as five. You will come in at seven or eight, after dark, and you will find the cat is not indoors, and you will begin to seethe with anger that I have left the cat outside long past its hour of exercise on the patio. But I couldn't very well kill myself with the cat in here, could I? How could I write you such a clear and eloquent missive as this, my sweet, with your beloved feline companion climbing all over my shoulders trying to lick at the blood that even now I use as ink? No, the cat had to remain outdoors, as you will see; I actually had a valid reason for having violated the rules of civilized living.

Cat or no cat, all the blood is gone and now I am using my ballpoint pen. Of course, I can't actually see whether the pen is out of ink. I remember the pen running out of ink, but it is the memory of many pens running out of ink many times, and I can't recall how recent was the most recent case of running-out-of-ink, and whether the most recent case of pen-buying was before or after it.

In fact it is the issue of memory that most troubles me. How is it that, headless, I remember anything at all? I understand that my fingers might know how to form the alphabet by reflex, but how is it that I remember how to spell these words, how has so much language survived within me, how can I cling to these thoughts long enough to write them down? Why do I have the shadowy memory of all that I am doing now, as if I had done it all before in some distant past?

I removed my head as brutally as possible, yet memory persists. This is especially ironic for, if I remember correctly, memory is what I most hoped to kill. Memory is a parasite that dwells within me, a mutant creature that has climbed up my spine and now perches atop my ragged neck, taunting me as it spins a sticky thread out of its own belly like a spider, then weaves it into shapes that harden in the air and become bone. I am being cheated; human bodies are not supposed to be able to regrow body parts that are any more complex than fingernails or hair, and here I can feel with my fingers that the bone has changed. My vertebrae are once again complete, and now the base of my skull has begun to form again.

How quickly? Too fast! And inside the bone grow softer things, the terrible small creature that once inhabited my head and refuses even now to die. This little knob at the top of my spine is a new limbic node; I recognize it, for when I squeeze it lightly with my fingers I feel strange passions, half-forgotten passions. Soon, though, such animality will be out of reach, for the tissues will swell outward to form a cerebellum, a folded gray cerebrum; and then the skull will close around it, sheathed in wrinkled flesh and scanty hair.

My undoing is undone, and far too quickly. What if my head is fully restored to my shoulders before you come home? Then you will find me in the basement with a bloody mess and no rational explanation for it. I can imagine you speaking of it to your friends. You can't leave me alone for a single hour, you poor thing, it's just a constant burden living with someone who is constantly making messes and then lying about them. Imagine, you'll say to them, a whole letter, so many pages, explaining how I killed myself—it would be funny if it weren't so sad.

You will expose me to the scorn of your friends; but that changes nothing. Truth is truth, even when it is ridiculed. Still, why should I provide entertainment for those wretched soulless creatures who live only to laugh at one whose shoe-latchets they are not fit to unlace? If you cannot find me headless, I refuse to let you know what I have done at all. You

215

will not read this account until some later day, after I finally succeed in dying and am embalmed. You'll find these pages taped on the bottom side of a drawer in my desk, where you will have looked, not because you hoped for some last word from me, but because you are searching for the hundred-dollar bill, which I will tape inside it.

And as for the blood and brains and bone embedded in the plasterboard, even that will not trouble you. I will scrub; I will sand; I will paint. You will come home to find the basement full of fumes and you will wear your martyr's face and take the paint away and send me to my room as if I were a child caught writing on the walls. You will have no notion of the agony I suffered in your absence, of the blood I shed solely in the hope of getting free of you. You will think this was a day like any other day. But I will know that on this day, this one day like the marker between B.C. and A.D., I found the courage to carry out an abrupt and terrible plan that I did not first submit for your approval.

Or has this, too, happened before? Will I, in the maze of memory, be unable to recall which of many head-explodings was the particular one that led me to write this message to you? Will I find, when I open the drawer, that on its underside there is already a thick sheaf of papers tied there around a single hundred-dollar bill? There is nothing new under the sun, said old Solomon in Ecclesiastes. Vanity of vanities; all is vanity. Nothing like that nonsense from King Lemuel at the end of Proverbs: Many daughters have done virtuously, but thou excellest them all.

Let her own works praise her in the gates, ha! I say let her own head festoon the walls.

Lost Boys

I've worried for a long time about whether to tell this story as fiction or fact. Telling it with made-up names would make it easier for some people to take. Easier for me, too. But to hide my own lost boy behind some phony made-up name would be like erasing him. So I'll tell it the way it happened, and to hell with whether it's easy for either of us.

Kristine and the kids and I moved to Greensboro on the first of March, 1983. I was happy enough about my job—I just wasn't sure I wanted a job at all. But the recession had the publishers all panicky, and nobody was coming up with advances large enough for me to take a decent amount of time writing a novel. I suppose I could whip out 75,000 words of junk fiction every month and publish them under a half dozen pseudonyms or something, but it seemed to Kristine and me that we'd do better in the long run if I got a job to ride out the recession. Besides, my Ph.D. was down the toilet. I'd been doing good work at Notre Dame, but when I had to take out a few weeks in the middle of a semester to finish *Hart's Hope*, the English Department was about as understanding as you'd expect from people who prefer their authors dead or domesticated. Can't feed your family? So sorry. You're a writer?

217

Ah, but not one that anyone's written a scholarly essay about. So long, boy-oh!

So sure, I was excited about my job, but moving to Greensboro also meant that I had failed. I had no way of knowing that my career as a fiction writer wasn't over. Maybe I'd be editing and writing books about computers for the rest of my life. Maybe fiction was just a phase I had to go through before I got a *real* job.

Greensboro was a beautiful town, especially to a family from the western desert. So many trees that even in winter you could hardly tell there was a town at all. Kristine and I fell in love with it at once. There were local problems, of course—people bragged about Greensboro's crime rate and talked about racial tension and what-not—but we'd just come from a depressed northern industrial town with race riots in the high schools, so to us this was Eden. There were rumors that several child disappearances were linked to some serial kidnapper, but this was the era when they started putting pictures of missing children on milk cartons—those stories were in every town.

It was hard to find decent housing for a price we could afford. I had to borrow from the company against my future earnings just to make the move. We ended up in the ugliest house on Chinqua Drive. You know the house—the one with cheap wood siding in a neighborhood of brick, the one-level rambler surrounded by split-level and two-stories. Old enough to be shabby, not old enough to be quaint. But it had a big fenced yard and enough bedrooms for all the kids and for my office, too—because we hadn't given up on my writing career, not yet, not completely.

218

The little kids—Geoffrey and Emily—thought the whole thing was really exciting, but Scotty, the oldest, he had a little trouble with it. He'd already had kindergarten and half of first grade at a really wonderful private school down the block from our house in South Bend. Now he was starting over in mid-year, losing all his friends. He had to ride a school bus with strangers. He resented the move from the start, and it didn't get better.

Of course, *I* wasn't the one who saw this. *I* was at work—and I very quickly learned that success at Compute! Books meant giving up a few little things like seeing your children. I had expected to edit books written by people who couldn't write. What astonished me was that I was editing books about computers written by people who could *program*. Not all of them, of course, but enough that I spent far more time rewriting programs so they made sense—so they even *ran*—than I did fixing up people's language. I'd get to work at 8:30 or 9:00, then work straight through till 9:30 or 10:30 at night. My meals were Three Musketeers bars and potato chips from the machine in the employee lounge. My exercise was typing. I met deadlines, but I was putting on a pound a week and my muscles were all atrophying and I saw my kids only in the mornings as I left for work.

Except Scotty. Because he left on the school bus at 6:45 and I rarely dragged out of bed until 7:30, during the week I never saw Scotty at all.

The whole burden of the family had fallen on Kristine. During my years as a freelancer from 1978 till 1983, we'd got used to a certain pattern of life, based on the fact that Daddy was *home*. She could duck out and run some errands, leaving the kids,

219

because I was home. If one of the kids was having discipline problems, I was there. Now if she had her hands full and needed something from the store; if the toilet clogged; if the xerox jammed, then she had to take care of it herself, somehow. She learned the joys of shopping with a cartful of kids. Add to this the fact that she was pregnant and sick half the time, and you can understand why sometimes I couldn't tell whether she was ready for sainthood or the funny farm.

The finer points of child-rearing just weren't within our reach at that time. She knew that Scotty wasn't adapting well at school, but what could she do? What could I do?

Scotty had never been the talker Geoffrey was— he spent a lot of time just keeping to himself. Now, though, it was getting extreme. He would answer in monosyllables, or not at all. Sullen. As if he were angry, and yet if he was, he didn't know it or wouldn't admit it. He'd get home, scribble out his homework (did they give homework when *I* was in first grade?), and then just mope around.

If he had done more reading, or even watched TV, then we wouldn't have worried so much. His little brother Geoffrey was already a compulsive reader at age five, and Scotty used to be. But now Scotty'd pick up a book and set it down again without reading it. He didn't even follow his mom around the house or anything. She'd see him sitting in the family room, go in and change the sheets on the beds, put away a load of clean clothes, and then come back in and find him sitting in the same place, his eyes open, staring at *nothing*.

I tried talking to him. Just the conversation you'd expect:

"Scotty, we know you didn't want to move. We had no choice."

"Sure. That's OK."

"You'll make new friends in due time."

"I know."

"Aren't you ever happy here?"

"I'm OK."

Yeah, right.

But we didn't have *time* to fix things up, don't you see? Maybe if we'd imagined this was the last year of Scotty's life, we'd have done more to right things, even if it meant losing the job. But you never know that sort of thing. You always find out when it's too late to change anything.

And when the school year ended, things *did* get better for a while.

For one thing, I saw Scotty in the mornings. For another thing, he didn't have to go to school with a bunch of kids who were either rotten to him or ignored him. And he didn't mope around the house all the time. Now he moped around outside.

At first Kristine thought he was playing with our other kids, the way he used to before school divided them. But gradually she began to realize that Geoffrey and Emily always played together, and Scotty almost never played with them. She'd see the younger kids with their squirtguns or running through the sprinklers or chasing the wild rabbit who lived in the neighborhood, but Scotty was never with them. Instead, he'd be poking a twig into the tentfly webs on the trees, or digging around at the open skirting around the bottom of the house that kept animals out of the crawl space. Once or twice a week he'd come in so dirty that Kristine had to heave him into the tub, but it didn't reassure her that Scotty was acting normally.

On July 28th, Kristine went to the hospital and gave birth to our fourth child. Charlie Ben was born having a seizure, and stayed in intensive care for the first weeks of his life as the doctors probed and poked and finally figured out that they didn't know what was wrong. It was several months later that somebody uttered the words "cerebral palsy," but our lives had already been transformed by then. Our whole focus was on the child in the greatest need— that's what you *do*, or so we thought. But how do you measure a child's need? How do you compare those needs and decide who deserves the most?

When we finally came up for air, we discovered that Scotty had made some friends. Kristine would be nursing Charlie Ben, and Scotty'd come in from outside and talk about how he'd been playing army with Nicky or how he and the guys had played pirate. At first she thought they were neighborhood kids, but then one day when he talked about building a fort in the grass (I didn't get many chances to mow), she happened to remember that she'd seen him building that fort all by himself. Then she got suspicious and started asking questions. Nicky who? I don't know, Mom. Just Nicky. Where does he live? Around. I don't know. Under the house.

In other words, imaginary friends.

How long had he known them? Nicky was the first, but now there were eight names—Nicky, Van, Roddy, Peter, Steve, Howard, Rusty, and David. Kristine and I had never heard of anybody having more than one imaginary friend.

"The kid's going to be more successful as a writer

than I am," I said. "Coming up with eight fantasies in the same series."

Kristine didn't think it was funny. "He's so *lonely*, Scott," she said. "I'm worried that he might go over the edge."

It *was* scary. But if he was going crazy, what then? We even tried taking him to a clinic, though I had no faith at all in psychologists. Their fictional explanations of human behavior seemed pretty lame, and their cure rate was a joke—a plumber or barber who performed at the same level as a psychotherapist would be out of business in a month. I took time off work to drive Scotty to the clinic every week during August, but Scotty didn't like it and the therapist told us nothing more than what we already knew—that Scotty was lonely and morose and a little bit resentful and a little bit afraid. The only difference was that she had fancier names for it. We were getting a vocabulary lesson when we needed help. The only thing that seemed to be helping was the therapy we came up with ourselves that summer. So we didn't make another appointment.

Our homegrown therapy consisted of keeping him from going outside. It happened that our landlord's father, who had lived in our house right before us, was painting the house that week, so that gave us an excuse. And I brought home a bunch of video games, ostensibly to review them for *Compute!*, but primarily to try to get Scotty involved in something that would turn his imagination away from these imaginary friends.

It worked. Sort of. He didn't complain about not going outside (but then, he never complained about anything), and he played the video games for hours a day. Kristine wasn't sure she loved *that*, but it was an improvement—or so we thought.

Once again, we were distracted and didn't pay much attention to Scotty for a while. We were having insect problems. One night Kristine's screaming woke me up. Now, you've got to realize that when Kristine screams, that means everything's pretty much OK. When something really terrible is going on, she gets cool and quiet and *handles* it. But when it's a little spider or a huge moth or a stain on a blouse, then she screams. I expected her to come back into the bedroom and tell me about this monstrous insect she had to hammer to death in the bathroom.

Only this time, she didn't stop screaming. So I got up to see what was going on. She heard me coming— I was up to 230 pounds by now, so I sounded like Custer's whole cavalry—and she called out, "Put your shoes on first!"

I turned on the light in the hall. It was hopping with crickets. I went back into my room and put on my shoes.

After enough crickets have bounced off your naked legs and squirmed around in your hands you stop wanting to puke—you just scoop them up and stuff them into a garbage bag. Later you can scrub yourself for six hours before you feel clean and have nightmares about little legs tickling you. But at the time your mind goes numb and you just do the job.

The infestation was coming out of the closet in the boys' room, where Scotty had the top bunk and Geoffrey slept on the bottom. There were a couple of crickets in Geoff's bed, but he didn't wake up even as we changed his top sheet and shook out his blanket. Nobody but us even saw the crickets. We found the crack in the back of the closet, sprayed Black Flag into it, and then stuffed it with an old sheet we were using for rags.

Then we showered, making jokes about how we could have used some seagulls to eat up our invasion of crickets, like the Mormon pioneers got in Salt Lake. Then we went back to sleep.

It wasn't just crickets, though. That morning in the kitchen Kristine called me again: There were dead June bugs about three inches deep in the window over the sink, all down at the bottom of the space between the regular glass and the storm window. I opened the window to vacuum them out, and the bug corpses spilled all over the kitchen counter. Each bug made a nasty little rattling sound as it went down the tube toward the vacuum filter.

The next day the window was three inches deep again, and the day after. Then it tapered off. Hot fun in the summertime.

We called the landlord to ask whether he'd help us pay for an exterminator. His answer was to send his father over with bug spray, which he pumped into the crawl space under the house with such gusto that we had to flee the house and drive around all that Saturday until a late afternoon thunderstorm blew away the stench or drowned it enough that we could stand to come back.

Anyway, what with that and Charlie's continuing problems, Kristine didn't notice what was happening with the video games at all. It was on a Sunday afternoon that I happened to be in the kitchen, drinking a Diet Coke, and heard Scotty laughing out loud in the family room.

That was such a rare sound in our house that I went and stood in the door to the family room, watching him play. It was a great little video game with terrific animation: Children in a sailing ship, battling pirates who kept trying to board, and shooting down giant birds that tried to nibble away the sail. It didn't look as mechanical as the usual video game, and one feature I really liked was the fact that the player wasn't alone—there were other computer-controlled children helping the player's figure to defeat the enemy.

"Come on, Sandy!" Scotty said. "Come on!" Whereupon one of the children on the screen stabbed the pirate leader through the heart, and the pirates fled.

I couldn't wait to see what scenario this game would move to then, but at that point Kristine called me to come and help her with Charlie. When I got back, Scotty was gone, and Geoffrey and Emily had a different game in the Atari.

Maybe it was that day, maybe later, that I asked Scotty what was the name of the game about children on a pirate ship. "It was just a game, Dad," he said.

"It's got to have a name."

"I don't know."

"How do you find the disk to put it in the machine?"

"I don't know." And he sat there staring past me and I gave up.

Summer ended. Scotty went back to school. Geoffrey started kindergarten, so they rode the bus together. Most important, things settled down with the newborn, Charlie—there wasn't a cure for cerebral palsy, but at least we knew the bounds of his condition. He wouldn't get *worse*, for instance. He also wouldn't get well. Maybe he'd talk and walk some day, and maybe he wouldn't. Our job was just to stimulate him enough that if it turned out he wasn't retarded, his mind would develop even though his body was so drastically limited. It was do-able. The fear was gone, and we could breathe again.

Then, in mid-October, my agent called to tell me that she'd pitched my Alvin Maker series to Tom Doherty at TOR Books, and Tom was offering enough of an advance that we could live. That plus the new contract for *Ender's Game*, and I realized that for us, at least, the recession was over. For a couple of weeks I stayed on at Compute! Books, primarily because I had so many projects going that I couldn't just leave them in the lurch. But then I looked at what the job was doing to my family and to my body, and I realized the price was too high. I gave two weeks' notice, figuring to wrap up the projects that only I knew about. In true paranoid fashion, they refused to accept the two weeks—they had me clean my desk out that afternoon. It left a bitter taste, to have them act so churlishly, but what the heck. I was free. I was home.

You could almost feel the relief. Geoffrey and Emily went right back to normal; I actually got acquainted with Charlie Ben; Christmas was coming (I start playing Christmas music when the leaves turn) and all was right with the world. Except Scotty. Always except Scotty.

It was then that I discovered a few things that I simply hadn't known. Scotty never played any of the video games I'd brought home from *Compute!* I knew that because when I gave the games back, Geoff and Em complained bitterly—but Scotty didn't even know what the missing games *were*. Most

227

important, that game about kids in a pirate ship wasn't there. Not in the games I took back, and not in the games that belonged to us. Yet Scotty was still playing it.

He was playing one night before he went to bed. I'd been working on *Ender's Game* all day, trying to finish it before Christmas. I came out of my office about the third time I heard Kristine say, "Scotty, go to bed *now*!"

For some reason, without yelling at the kids or beating them or anything, I've always been able to get them to obey when Kristine couldn't even get them to acknowledge her existence. Something about a fairly deep male voice—for instance, I could always sing insomniac Geoffrey to sleep as an infant when Kristine couldn't. So when I stood in the doorway and said, "Scotty, I think your mother asked you to go to bed," it was no surprise that he immediately reached up to turn off the computer.

"*I'll* turn it off," I said. "Go!"

He still reached for the switch.

"Go!" I said, using my deepest voice-of-God tones.

He got up and went, not looking at me.

I walked to the computer to turn it off, and saw the animated children, just like the ones I'd seen before. Only they weren't on a pirate ship, they were on an old steam locomotive that was speeding along a track. What a game, I thought. The single-sided Atari disks don't even hold a 100K, and here they've got two complete scenarios and all this animation and—

And there wasn't a disk in the disk drive.

That meant it was a game that you upload and then remove the disk, which meant it was completely

228

RAM resident, which meant all this quality animation fit into a mere 48K. I knew enough about game programming to regard that as something of a miracle.

I looked around for the disk. There wasn't one. So Scotty had put it away, thought I. Only I looked and looked and couldn't find any disk that I didn't already know.

I sat down to play the game—but now the children were gone. It was just a train. Just speeding along. And the elaborate background was gone. It was the plain blue screen behind the train. No tracks, either. And then no train. It just went blank, back to the ordinary blue. I touched the keyboard. The letters I typed appeared on the screen. It took a few carriage returns to realize what was happening—the Atari was in memo-pad mode. At first I thought it was a pretty terrific copy-protection scheme, to end the game by putting you into a mode where you couldn't access memory, couldn't do anything without turning off the machine, thus erasing the program code from RAM. But then I realized that a company that could produce a game so good, with such tight code, would surely have some kind of sign-off when the game ended. And why did it end? Scotty hadn't touched the computer after I told him to stop. I didn't touch it, either. Why did the children leave the screen? Why did the train disappear? There was no way the computer could "know" that Scotty was through playing, especially since the game *had* gone on for a while after he walked away.

Still, I didn't mention it to Kristine, not till after everything was over. She didn't know anything about computers then except how to boot up and

229

get WordStar on the Altos. It never occurred to her that there was anything weird about Scotty's game.

It was two weeks before Christmas when the insects came again. And they shouldn't have—it was too cold outside for them to be alive. The only thing we could figure was that the crawl space under our house stayed warmer or something. Anyway, we had another exciting night of cricket-bagging. The old sheet was still wadded up in the crack in the closet— they were coming from under the bathroom cabinet this time. And the next day it was daddy longlegs spiders in the bathtub instead of June bugs in the kitchen window.

"Just don't tell the landlord," I told Kristine. "I couldn't stand another day of that pesticide."

"It's probably the landlord's father *causing* it," Kristine told me. "Remember he was here painting when it happened the first time? And today he came and put up the Christmas lights."

We just lay there in bed chuckling over the absurdity of that notion. We had thought it was silly but kind of sweet to have the landlord's father insist on putting up Christmas lights for us in the first place. Scotty went out and watched him the whole time. It was the first time he'd ever seen lights put up along the edge of the roof—I have enough of a case of acrophobia that you couldn't get me on a ladder high enough to do the job, so our home always went undecorated except the tree lights you could see through the window. Still, Kristine and I are both suckers for Christmas kitsch. Heck, we even play the Carpenters' Christmas album. So we thought it was great that the landlord's father wanted to do that for us. "It was my house for so many years," he said. "My wife and I always had them. I don't think this house'd look *right* without lights."

He was such a nice old coot anyway. Slow, but still strong, a good steady worker. The lights were up in a couple of hours.

Christmas shopping. Doing Christmas cards. All that stuff. We were busy.

Then one morning, only about a week before Christmas, I guess, Kristine was reading the morning paper and she suddenly got all icy and calm—the way she does when something *really* is happening. "Scott, read this," she said.

"Just *tell* me," I said.

"This is an article about missing children in Greensboro."

I glanced at the headline: CHILDREN WHO WON'T BE HOME FOR CHRISTMAS. "I don't want to hear about it," I said. I can't read stories about child abuse or kidnappings. They make me crazy. I can't sleep afterward. It's always been that way.

"You've got to," she said. "Here are the names of the little boys who've been reported missing in the last three years. Russell DeVerge, Nicholas Tyler—"

"What are you getting at?"

"Nicky. Rusty. David. Roddy. Peter. Are these names ringing a bell with you?"

I usually don't remember names very well. "No."

"Steve, Howard, Van. The only one that doesn't fit is the last one, Alexander Booth. He disappeared this summer."

For some reason the way Kristine was telling me this was making me very upset. *She* was so agitated about it, and she wouldn't get to the point. "So *what*?" I demanded.

231

"Scotty's imaginary friends," she said.

"Come on," I said. But she went over them with me—she had written down all the names of his imaginary friends in our journal, back when the therapist asked us to keep a record of his behavior. The names matched up, or seemed to.

"Scotty must have read an earlier article," I said. "It must have made an impression on him. He's always been an empathetic kid. Maybe he started identifying with them because he felt—I don't know, like maybe he'd been abducted from South Bend and carried off to Greensboro." It sounded really plausible for a moment there—the same moment of plausibility that psychologists live on.

Kristine wasn't impressed. "This article says that it's the first time anybody's put all the names together in one place."

"Hype. Yellow journalism."

"Scott, he got *all* the names right."

"Except one."

"I'm so relieved."

But I wasn't. Because right then I remembered how I'd heard him talking during the pirate video game. Come on, Sandy. I told Kristine. Alexander, Sandy. It was as good a fit as Russell and Rusty. He hadn't matched a mere eight out of nine. He'd matched them all.

You can't put a name to all the fears a parent feels, but I can tell you that I've never felt any terror for myself that compares to the feeling you have when you watch your two-year-old run toward the street, or see your baby go into a seizure, or realize that somehow there's a connection between kidnappings and your child. I've never been on a plane seized by terrorists or had a gun pointed to my head or fallen off a cliff, so maybe there are worse fears. But then, I've been in a spin on a snowy freeway, and I've clung to the handles of my airplane seat while the plane bounced up and down in mid-air, and still those weren't like what I felt then, reading the whole article. Kids who just disappeared. Nobody saw anybody pick up the kids. Nobody saw anybody lurking around their houses. The kids just didn't come home from school, or played outside and never came in when they were called. Gone. And Scotty knew all their names. Scotty had played with them in his imagination. How did he know who they were? Why did he fixate on these lost boys?

We watched him, that last week before Christmas. We saw how distant he was. How he shied away, never let us touch him, never stayed with a conversation. He was aware of Christmas, but he never asked for anything, didn't seem excited, didn't want to go shopping. He didn't even seem to sleep. I'd come in when I was heading for bed—at one or two in the morning, long after he'd climbed up into his bunk—and he'd be lying there, all his covers off, his eyes wide open. His insomnia was even worse than Geoffrey's. And during the day, all Scotty wanted to do was play with the computer or hang around outside in the cold. Kristine and I didn't know what to do. Had we already lost him somehow?

We tried to involve him with the family. He wouldn't go Christmas shopping with us. We'd tell him to stay inside while we were gone, and then we'd find him outside anyway. I even unplugged the computer and hid all the disks and cartridges, but it was only Geoffrey and Emily who suffered—I still came into the room and found Scotty playing his impossible game.

233

He didn't ask for anything until Christmas Eve.

Kristine came into my office, where I was writing the scene where Ender finds his way out of the Giant's Drink problem. Maybe I was so fascinated with computer games for children in that book because of what Scotty was going through—maybe I was just trying to pretend that computer games made sense. Anyway, I still know the very sentence that was interrupted when she spoke to me from the door. So very calm. So very frightened.

"Scotty wants us to invite some of his friends in for Christmas Eve," she said.

"Do we have to set extra places for imaginary friends?" I asked.

"They're aren't imaginary," she said. "They're in the backyard, waiting."

"You're kidding,' I said. "It's *cold* out there. What kind of parents would let their kids go outside on Christmas Eve?"

She didn't say anything. I got up and we went to the back door together. I opened the door.

There were nine of them. Ranging in age, it looked like, from six to maybe ten. All boys. Some in shirt sleeves, some in coats, one in a swimsuit. I've got no memory for faces, but Kristine does. "They're the ones," she said softly, calmly, behind me. "That one's Van. I remembered him."

"Van?" I said.

He looked up at me. He took a timid step toward me.

I heard Scotty's voice behind me. "Can they come in, Dad? I told them you'd let them have Christmas Eve with us. That's what they miss the most."

I turned to him. "Scotty, these boys are all reported missing. Where have they been?"

234

"Under the house," he said.

I thought of the crawl space. I thought of how many times Scotty had come in covered with dirt last summer.

"How did they get there?" I asked.

"The old guy put them there," he said. "They said I shouldn't tell anybody or the old guy would get mad and they never wanted him to be mad at them again. Only I said it was OK, I could tell *you*."

"That's right," I said.

"The landlord's father," whispered Kristine.

I nodded.

"Only how could he keep them under there all this time? When does he feed them? When—"

She already knew that the old guy didn't feed them. I don't want you to think Kristine didn't guess that immediately. But it's the sort of thing you deny as long as you can, and even longer.

"They can come in," I told Scotty. I looked at Kristine. She nodded. I knew she would. You don't turn away lost children on Christmas Eve. Not even when they're dead.

Scotty smiled. What that meant to us—Scotty smiling. It had been so long. I don't think I really saw a smile like that since we moved to Greensboro. Then he called out to the boys. "It's OK! You can come in!"

Kristine held the door open, and I backed out of the way. They filed in, some of them smiling, some of them too shy to smile. "Go on into the living room," I said. Scotty led the way. Ushering them in, for all the world like a proud host in a magnificent new mansion. They sat around on the floor. There weren't many presents, just the ones from the kids; we don't put out the presents from the parents till

235

the kids are asleep. But the tree was there, lighted, with all our homemade decorations on it—even the old needlepoint decorations that Kristine made while lying in bed with desperate morning sickness when she was pregnant with Scotty, even the little puff-ball animals we glued together for that first Christmas tree in Scotty's life. Decorations older than he was. And not just the tree—the whole room was decorated with red and green tassels and little wooden villages and a stuffed Santa hippo beside a wicker sleigh and a large chimney-sweep nutcracker and anything else we hadn't been able to resist buying or making over the years.

We called in Geoffrey and Emily, and Kristine brought in Charlie Ben and held him on her lap while I told the stories of the birth of Christ—the shepherds and the wise men, and the one from the Book of Mormon about a day and a night and a day without darkness. And then I went on and told what Jesus lived for. About forgiveness for all the bad things we do.

"Everything?" asked one of the boys.

It was Scotty who answered. "No!" he said. "Not killing."

Kristine started to cry.

"That's right," I said. "In our church we believe that God doesn't forgive people who kill on purpose. And in the New Testament Jesus said that if anybody ever hurt a child, it would be better for him to tie a huge rock around his neck and jump into the sea and drown."

"Well, it *did* hurt, Daddy," said Scotty. "They never told me about that."

"It was a secret," said one of the boys. Nicky,

Kristine says, because she remembers names and faces.

"You should have told me," said Scotty. "I wouldn't have let him touch me."

That was when we knew, really knew, that it was too late to save him, that Scotty, too, was already dead.

"I'm sorry, Mommy," said Scotty. "You told me not to play with them anymore, but they were my friends, and I wanted to be with them." He looked down at his lap. "I can't even cry anymore. I used it all up."

It was more than he'd said to us since we moved to Greensboro in March. Amid all the turmoil of emotions I was feeling, there was this bitterness: All this year, all our worries, all our efforts to reach him, and yet nothing brought him to speak to us except death.

But I realized now it wasn't death. It was the fact that when he knocked, we opened the door, that when he asked, we let him and his friends come into our house that night. He had trusted us, despite all the distance between us during that year, and we didn't disappoint him. It was trust that brought us one last Christmas Eve with our boy.

But we didn't try to make sense of things that night. They were children, and needed what children long for on a night like that. Kristine and I told them Christmas stories and we told about Christmas traditions we'd heard of in other countries and other times, and gradually they warmed up until every one of the boys told all about his own family's Christmases. They were good memories. They laughed, they jabbered, they joked. Even though it was the most terrible of Christmases, it was also the best

237

Christmas of our lives, the one in which every scrap of memory is still precious to us, the perfect Christmas in which being together was the only gift that mattered. Even though Kristine and I don't talk about it directly now, we both remember it. And Geoffrey and Emily remember it, too. They call it "the Christmas when Scotty brought his friends." I don't think they ever really understood, and I'll be content if they never do.

Finally, though, Geoffrey and Emily were both asleep. I carried each of them to bed as Kristine talked to the boys, asking them to help us. To wait in our living room until the police came, so they could help us stop the old guy who stole them away from their families and their futures. They did. Long enough for the investigating officers to get there and see them, long enough for them to hear the story Scotty told.

Long enough for them to notify the parents. They came at once, frightened because the police had dared not tell them more over the phone than this: that they were needed in a matter concerning their lost boy. They came: with eager, frightened eyes they stood on our doorstep, while a policeman tried to help them understand. Investigators were bringing ruined bodies out from under our house—there was no hope. And yet if they came inside, they would see that cruel Providence was also kind, and *this* time there would be what so many other parents had longed for but never had: a chance to say good-bye. I will tell you nothing of the scenes of joy and heartbreak inside our home that night—those belong to other families, not to us.

Once their families came, once the words were spoken and the tears were shed, once the muddy bodies were laid on canvas on our lawn and properly identified from the scraps of clothing, then they brought the old man in handcuffs. He had our landlord and a sleepy lawyer with him, but when he saw the bodies on the lawn he brokenly confessed, and they recorded his confession. None of the parents actually had to look at him; none of the boys had to face him again.

But they knew. They knew that it was over, that no more families would be torn apart as theirs—as ours—had been. And so the boys, one by one, disappeared. They were there, and then they weren't there. With that the other parents left us, quiet with grief and awe that such a thing was possible, that out of horror had come one last night of mercy and of justice, both at once.

Scotty was the last to go. We sat alone with him in our living room, though by the lights and talking we were aware of the police still doing their work outside. Kristine and I remember clearly all that was said, but what mattered most to us was at the very end.

"I'm sorry I was so mad all the time last summer," Scotty said. "I knew it wasn't really your fault about moving and it was bad for me to be so angry but I just was."

For him to ask *our* forgiveness was more than we could bear. We were full of far deeper and more terrible regrets, we thought, as we poured out our remorse for all that we did or failed to do that might have saved his life. When we were spent and silent at last, he put it all in proportion for us. "That's OK. I'm just glad that you're not mad at me." And then he was gone.

We moved out that morning before daylight; good

239

friends took us in, and Geoffrey and Emily got to open the presents they had been looking forward to for so long. Kristine's and my parents all flew out from Utah and the people in our church joined us for the funeral. We gave no interviews to the press; neither did any of the other families. The police told only of the finding of the bodies and the confession. We didn't agree to it; it's as if everybody who knew the whole story also knew that it would be wrong to have it in headlines in the supermarket.

Things quieted down very quickly. Life went on. Most people don't even know we had a child before Geoffrey. It wasn't a secret. It was just too hard to tell. Yet, after all these years, I thought it *should* be told, if it could be done with dignity, and to people who might understand. Others should know how it's possible to find light shining even in the darkest place. How even as we learned of the most terrible grief of our lives, Kristine and I were able to rejoice in our last night with our firstborn son, and how together we gave a good Christmas to those lost boys, and they gave as much to us.

AFTERWORD

In August 1988 I brought this story to the Sycamore Hill Writers Workshop. That draft of the story included a disclaimer at the end, a statement that the story was fiction, that Geoffrey is my oldest child and that no landlord of mine has ever done us harm. The reaction of the other writers at the workshop ranged from annoyance to fury.

Karen Fowler put it most succinctly when she said, as best I can remember her words, "By telling this story in first person with so much detail from your own life, you've appropriated something that doesn't belong to you. You've pretended to feel the grief of a parent who has lost a child, and you don't have a right to feel that grief."

When she said that, I agreed with her. While this story had been rattling around in my imagination for years, I had only put it so firmly in first person the autumn before, at a Halloween party with the students of Watauga College at Appalachian State. Everybody was trading ghost stories that night, and so on a whim I tried out this one; on a whim I made it highly personal, partly because by telling true details from my own life I spared myself the effort of inventing a character, partly because ghost stories are most powerful when the audience half-believes they might be true. It worked better than any tale I'd ever told out loud, and so when it came time to write it down, I wrote it the same way.

Now, though, Karen Fowler's words made me see it in a different moral light, and I resolved to change it forthwith. Yet the moment I thought of revising the story, of stripping away the details of my own life and replacing them with those of a made-up character, I felt a sick dread inside. Some part of my mind was rebelling against what Karen said. No, it was saying, she's wrong, you *do* have a right to tell this story, to claim this grief.

I knew at that moment what this story was *really* about, why it had been so important to me. It wasn't a simple ghost story at all; I hadn't written it just for fun. I should have known—I never write anything just for fun. This story wasn't about a fictional eldest child named "Scotty." It was about my real-life youngest child, Charlie Ben.

Charlie, who in the five and a half years of his life

241

has never been able to speak a word to us. Charlie, who could not smile at us until he was a year old, who could not hug us until he was four, who still spends his days and nights in stillness, staying wherever we put him, able to wriggle but not to run, able to call out but not to speak, able to understand that he cannot do what his brother and sister do, but not to ask us why. In short, a child who is not dead and yet can barely taste life despite all our love and all our yearning.

Yet in all the years of Charlie's life, until that day at Sycamore Hill, I had never shed a single tear for him, never allowed myself to grieve. I had worn a mask of calm and acceptance so convincing that I had believed it myself. But the lies we live will always be confessed in the stories that we tell, and I am no exception. A story that I had fancied was a mere lark, a dalliance in the quaint old ghost-story tradition, was the most personal, painful story of my career—and, unconsciously, I had confessed as much by making it by far the most autobiographical of all my works.

Months later, I sat in a car in the snow at a cemetery in Utah, watching a man I dearly love as he stood, then knelt, then stood again at the grave of his eighteen-year-old daughter. I couldn't help but think of what Karen had said; truly I had no right to pretend that I was entitled to the awe and sympathy we give to those who have lost a child. And yet I knew that I couldn't leave this story untold, for that would also be a kind of lie. That was when I decided on this compromise: I would publish the story as I knew it had to be written, but then I would write this essay as an afterword, so that you would know exactly what was true and what was not true in it. Judge it as you will; this is the best that I know how to do.

Afterword

Authors have no more story ideas than anyone else. We all live through or hear about thousands of story ideas a day. Authors are simply more practiced at recognizing them as having the potential to become stories.

The real challenge is to move from the idea through the process of inventing the characters and their surroundings, structuring the tale, and discovering the narrative voice and the point of view, and finally writing it all down in a way that will be clear and effective for the reader. That's the part that separates people who wish they were writers or intend someday to write a book, and those of us who actually put the words down on paper and send them out in hope of finding an audience.

To the best of my memory, here are the origins of each of the stories in this book:

"EUMENIDES IN THE FOURTH FLOOR LAVATORY"

I was working at *The Ensign* magazine as an assistant editor and sometime staff writer. Jay A. Parry was copy editor there, as he had been at Brigham Young University Press, where my editorial career began.

In fact, Jay was the one who alerted me to the possibility of applying for a position at *The Ensign* and helped shepherd me through the process.

He and I and another editor, Lane Johnson, all had dreams of being writers. I had already had something of a career as a playwright, but when it came to prose fiction we were all new. We started taking lunch together down in the cafeteria of the LDS Church Office Building in Salt Lake City, riding the elevators down from the twenty-third floor, grabbing a quick salad, and then hunching over a table talking stories.

Naturally, when we actually wrote the stories down, we showed them to each other. In many ways we were the blind leading the blind—none of us had sold anything when we began. Yet we were all professional editors; we all worked in a daily mill of taking badly written articles, restructuring them, and then rewriting them smoothly and clearly. We might not have known how to sell fiction, but we certainly knew how to *write*. And we also knew how to see other people's work clearly and search for the soul of their story, in order to preserve that soul through any number of incarnations as text.

(Indeed, that may be the reason I have always been so skeptical of the whole contemporary critical scene, in which the text is regarded as some immutable miracle, to be worshiped or dissected as if it were the story itself. What anyone trained as an editor and rewriter knows is that the text is *not* the story—the text is merely one attempt to place the story inside the memory of the audience. The text can be replaced by an infinite number of other attempts. Some will be better than others, but no text will be "right" for all audiences, nor will any

245

one text be "perfect." The story exists only in the memory of the reader, as an altered version of the story intended (consciously or not) by the author. It is possible for the audience to create for themselves a better story than the author could ever have created in the text. Thus audiences have taken to their hearts miserably-written stories like *Tarzan of the Apes* by Edgar Rice Burroughs, because what they received transcended the text; while any number of beautifully written texts have been swallowed up without a trace, because the text, however lovely, did a miserable job of kindling a living story within the readers' memories.)

How other stories in this collection grew out of that friendship, those lunchtime meetings, will be recounted in their place. This story came rather late in that time. I had already left *The Ensign* magazine and was beginning my freelance career. I still had much contact with the *Ensign* staff because I was supposed to be finishing a project that I had not yet completed when I resigned my position as of 1 January 1978. In one conversation I had with Jay Parry, he mentioned a terrible dream he had had. "You can use it for a story if you want," he said. "I think there's a story in it, but it would be too terrible for me to write."

Jay lacks my vicious streak, you see; or perhaps it's just that he was already a father and I wasn't. I'm not altogether sure I could write this story after Kristine and I started having kids. At the time, though, Jay's nightmare image of a child with flipper arms drowning in a toilet seemed fascinating, even poignant.

I had recently read whatever story collection of Harlan Ellison's was current at the time, and I had

discerned a pattern in his toughest, meanest tales—
a sin-and-punishment motif in which terrible things
only seemed to happen to the most appropriate
people. It seemed obvious to me that the way to
develop this deformed baby into a story was to have
it come into the life of someone who deserved to be
confronted with a twisted child.

After my first draft, however, I submitted the
story to Francois Camoin, by then my teacher in
writing classes at the University of Utah. I had taken
writing classes before, and except for occasional
helpful comments had found that their primary value
was that they provided me with deadlines so I *had* to
produce stories. Francois was different—he actually
understood, not only how to write, but also how to
teach writing, a skill that is almost completely missing among teachers of creative writing in America
today. He didn't know everything—no one does—
but compared to what I knew at the time he might
as well have known everything! Even though I was
selling my science fiction quite regularly, I still didn't
understand, except in the vaguest way, why some of
my stories worked and others didn't. Francois
helped open up my own work to me, both its
strengths and weaknesses.

As a playwright I had learned that I have a tendency to write in epigrams; as one critical friend put
it, all my characters said words that were meant to
be carved in stone over the entrance of a public
building. That tendency toward clever didacticism
was still showing up in my fiction (and probably still
does). It was Francois who helped me understand
that while the events of the story should be clear—
what happened and why—the *meaning* of the story
should be subtle, arcane; it should be left lying about

247

for readers to discover, but never forced upon them. "This story is *about* guilt," said Francois. "In fact, the child, the tiny Fury, *is* guilt. When you have a word embodied in a story, the word itself should never appear. So don't ever say the word 'guilt' in this story."

I knew at once that he was right. It wasn't just a matter of removing the word, of course. It meant removing most sentences that had the word in it, and occasionally even whole paragraphs had to come out. It was a pleasurable process, though not without some pain—rather like peeling away dead skin after a bad sunburn. What was left was much stronger.

It appeared in a rather obscure place—Roy Torgeson's *Chrysalis* anthology series from Zebra books. But Terry Carr picked it up for his best-of-the-year fantasy anthology, so it got a little better exposure. My name is on it, but much of this story is owed to others: Jay, for the seminal image; Harlan, for the basic structure; and Francois, for the things that *aren't* in the text here printed.

"QUIETUS"

Like "Eumenides," this story began with someone else's nightmare. My wife woke up one morning upset by a strange lingering dream. We lived at the time in a rented Victorian house on J Street in the Avenues district of Salt Lake City. We were only a bit more than a block from the Emigration Ward LDS meetinghouse, where we attended church. In Kristine's dream, the bishop of our ward had called us up and told us that they were holding a funeral for a stranger the next day, but that tonight there was no place to keep the coffin. Would we be willing to let them bring it by and leave it in our living room until morning?

Kristine isn't in the habit of saying no to requests for help, even in her dreams, and so she agreed. She woke up from her dream just as she was opening the coffin lid.

That was all—a stranger's coffin in the living room. But I knew at once that there was a story in it, and what the story had to be. A coffin in your own living room can only have one body in it: your own. And so I sat down to write a story of a man who was haunting his own house without realizing it, until he finally opened the coffin and climbed in, accepting death.

What I *didn't* know when I started writing was *why* he was left outside his coffin for a while, and why he then reconciled himself to death. So I started writing as much of the story as I knew, hoping something would come to me. I told of the moment of his death in his office, though he didn't realize it was death; I wrote of his homecoming; but the ultimate meaning of the story came by accident. I can't remember now what my mistake was in the first draft. Something like this: During the office scene I had written that he had no children, but by the time I wrote his homecoming, I had forgotten his childlessness and had him hear children's voices or see their drawings on the refrigerator—or something to that effect. Only when I showed the first draft of the story's opening to Kristine did we (probably she) notice the contradiction.

It was one of those silly dumb authorial lapses that every writer commits. My first thought was simply to change one or the other reference so they were reconciled.

However, as I sat there, preparing to revise, I had an intuition that my "mistake" was no mistake at all, but rather my unconscious answer to the fundamental question in the story: Why couldn't he accept death at first? Instead of eliminating the contradiction, I enhanced it, switching back and forth. Now they have children, now they don't. He could not accept death until their childlessness was replaced with children.

If you want to get psychological about it, Kristine was pregnant with our first child at the time. My "mistake" may have been a traditional Freudian slip, revealing my ambivalence about entering onto the irrevocable step of having and raising children. What matters more, however, is not the personal source of the feeling, but what I learned about the process of writing: Trust your mistakes. Over and over again since then, I have found that when I do something "wrong" in an early draft of the story, I should not eliminate it immediately. I should instead explore it and see if there's some way that the mistake can be justified, amplified, made part of the story. I have come to believe that a storyteller's best work comes, not from his conscious plans, but from his impulses and errors. That is where his unconscious mind wells up to the surface. That is how stories become filled, not with what the writer believes that he believes, or thinks he ought to care about, but rather with what he believes without question and cares about most deeply. That is how a story acquires its truth.

"DEEP BREATHING EXERCISES"

The idea for this story came simply enough. My son, Geoffrey, was a born insomniac. It took him hours to fall asleep every night, and we learned that the most effective way to get him to sleep was for me to hold him and sing to him. (For some reason he responded more to a baritone than a mezzo-soprano.) This would continue until he was four or five years old; by that time I was spending a couple of hours a night lying by his bed, reading in the dim light from the hall while humming the tune to "Away in a Manger." When he was a baby, though, I stood in his room, rocking back and forth, singing nonsense songs that included tender lyrics like, "Go to sleep, you little creep, Daddy's about to die." Even when he finally seemed to have drifted off I learned that he was only faking, and if I laid him down too soon he'd immediately scream. I appreciate a call for an encore as much as the next guy, but enough is enough. Especially since Kristine was asleep in the other room. Most of the time I didn't begrudge her that—she would be up in the morning taking care of Geoffrey (always an early riser no matter how late he dropped off) while I slept in, so it all evened out. Still, there were many nights when I stood there, rocking back and forth, listening to both of them breathing during the breaks in my lullaby.

One night I realized that Geoffrey's breath on my shoulder was exactly in rhythm with my wife's breath as she slept in the other room. The two of them inhaling and exhaling in perfect unison. My mind immediately began to take the idea and wander with it. I thought: It doesn't matter how long Daddy stands here singing to the kid, the bond with his mother is always the strongest one, right down to the level of their breathing. Mother and child share the same breath so long together—it's no surprise that out of the womb the child still seeks to breathe

251

with her, to cling to the rhythms of his first and best home. From there my thoughts wandered to the fact that the unborn child is so tied to the mother that if she dies, he dies with her.

Before Geoffrey fell asleep, the story was written in my mind: Breathing in unison is a sign, not that people were born together, but that they were now irrevocably doomed to die together.

"FAT FARM"

My life can be viewed as one long struggle with my own body. I wasn't hopelessly uncoordinated as a kid. If I tried, I could swing a bat or get a ball through a hoop. And I suppose that if I had worked at it, I could have held my own in childhood athletics. But some are born nerds, some choose nerdhood, and some have nerdiness thrust upon them. I chose. I just didn't *care* about sports or physical games of any kind. As a child, given the choice, I would always rather read a book. Soon enough, however, I learned that this was a mistake. By the time I got to junior high, I realized that young male Americans are valued only for their contribution to athletic contests—or so it seemed to me. The result was that to avoid abuse, I avoided athletic situations.

Then, when I was about fifteen, I passed some sort of metabolic threshold. I had always been an outrageously skinny kid—you could count my ribs through my shirt. All of a sudden, though, without any change that I was aware of in my eating habits, I began to gain weight. Not a lot—just enough that I softened in the belly. Began to get that faintly pudgy wormlike look that is always so attractive and fashionable, especially in teenage boys. As the years passed, I gained a little more weight and began to discover that the abuse heaped upon nerds in childhood is nothing like the open, naked bigotry displayed toward adults who are overweight. People who would never dream of mocking a cripple or making racial or ethnic slurs feel no qualms about poking or pinching a fat person's midriff and making obscenely personal remarks. My hatred of such people was limitless. Some of my acquaintances in those days had no notion how close they came to immediate death.

The only thing that keeps fat people from striking back is that, in our hearts, most of us fear that our tormentors are right, that we somehow deserve their contempt, their utter despite for us as human beings. Their loathing for us is only surpassed by our loathing for ourselves.

I had my ups and downs. I weighed 220 pounds when I went on my LDS mission to Brazil in 1971. Through much walking and exercise, and relatively little eating (though Brazilian ice cream is exquisite), I came home two years later weighing 176 pounds. I looked and felt great. And the weight stayed off, mostly, for several years. I became almost athletic. My first two summers home, I operated a summer repertory theater at an outdoor amphitheater, the Castle, on the hill behind the state mental hospital. We weren't allowed to drive right up to the Castle, so at the beginning of every rehearsal we would walk up a switchback road. Within a few weeks I was in good enough shape that I was running up the steepest part of the hill right among the younger kids, and reaching the stage of the Castle without being out of breath. We had a piano that we stored in a metal box at the base of the amphitheater and carried—not rolled—up a stony walkway to the stage for rehearsals and performances of musicals (*Camelot*, *Man of La Mancha*, and my own *Father, Mother, Mother, and Mom*). Soon I was carrying one end of the piano alone. I reveled in the fact that my body could be slender and well-muscled, not wormlike at all.

But then I began my editorial career and my theatre company folded, leaving me with heavy debts. I spent every day then sedentary and tense, with a candy machine just around the corner. My only exercise was pushing quarters into the machine. By the time I got married in 1977 I was back up to 220 pounds. Freelance writing made things even worse. Whenever I needed a break, I'd get up, walk thirty feet into the kitchen, make some toast and pour some orange juice. All very healthy. And only about a billion calories a day. I was near 265 pounds when I wrote "Fat Farm." It was an exercise in self-loathing and desperate hope. I knew that I was capable of having a strong, healthy body, but lacked the discipline to create it for myself. I had actually gone through the experience of trading bodies—it just took me longer than it took the hero of the story. In a way, I suppose the story was a wish that someone would *make* me change.

Ironically, within a few months after writing "Fat Farm," our lives went through a transition. We were moving to a larger house. The first thing I did was take all my old thin clothes and give them away to charity. I knew that I would never be thin again. It was no longer an issue. I was going to be a fat person for the rest of my life. Orson Welles was my hero.

Then I began packing up our thousands of books and carrying and stacking the boxes. The exercise began to take up more and more of each day. I ate less and less, since I wasn't constantly looking for breaks from writing. By the time we got into our new place, I had dropped ten pounds. Just like that, without even trying.

So I kept it up. Eating little—I now followed a thousand-calorie balanced diet—and exercising more and more, within a year I was 185 pounds and was riding a bicycle many miles a day. And I stayed thin for several years. Not until I moved to North Carolina and got a sedentary job under extreme tension did I put the weight back on again. I sit here writing this with a current weight of 255 pounds. But that's down almost ten pounds from my holiday high, and I'm riding an exercise bike and enjoying the sensation of being hungry most of the time and— who knows?

In short, "Fat Farm" isn't fiction. It's my physical autobiography.

And it's no accident that the story ends with our hero set up to fulfill ugly violent assignments. The undercurrent of violence is real. I hereby warn all those who think it's all right to greet a friend by saying, "Put on a little weight, haven't you!" You would never dream of greeting a friend by saying, "Wow, that's quite an enormous pimple you've got on your nose there," or, "Can't you afford to buy clothes that look good or do you just have no taste?" If you did, you would expect to lose the friend. Well, be prepared. Some of us are about to run out of patience with your criminal boorishness. Someday one of you is going to glance down at our waistline, grin, and then—before you can utter one syllable of your offensive slur—we're going to break you into a pile of skinny little matchsticks. No jury of fat people would convict us.

"CLOSING THE TIMELID"

I think it was in a conversation with Jay and Lane that we began wondering what death might feel like. Maybe, after all our fear of it, the actual moment of death—not the injuries leading up to it, but the moment itself—was the most sublime pleasure imaginable. After a few months of letting this idea gel in the back of my mind, I hit on the device of using time travel as a way to let people experience death without dying.

Time travel is one of those all-purpose science fictional devices. You can do *anything* with it, depending on how you set up the rules. In this case, I made it so that the time-traveler's body *does* materialize in the past, and can be injured—but upon return the body is restored to its condition when it left, though still feeling whatever feelings it had just before the return. It's a fun exercise for science fiction writers, to think up new variations on the rules of time travel. Each variation opens up thousands of possible stories. That's why it's so discouraging to see how many time-travel stories use the same old tired clichés. These writers are like tourists with cameras. They don't actually come to experience a strange land. They just take snapshots of each other and move on. Snapshot science fiction might as well not be written. Why write a time-travel story if you don't think through the mechanics of your fantasy and find the implications of the particular rules of your time-travel device? As long as we're dealing in impossibilities, why not make them interesting and fresh?

But I digress. Being a preacher at heart, I found that with this story I had written a homily of hedonism as self-destruction. Absurd as these people may seem, their obsession with a perverse pleasure is no stranger than any other pleasure that seduces its seekers from the society of normal human beings. Drug users, homosexuals, corporate takeover artists, steroid-popping bodybuilders and athletes—all such groups have, at some time or another, constructed societies whose whole purpose is celebrating the single pleasure whose pursuit dominates their lives, while it separates them from the rest of the world, whose rules and norms they resent and despise. Furthermore, they pursue their pleasure at the constant risk of self-destruction. And then they wonder why so many other people look at them with something between horror and distaste.

"FREEWAY GAMES"

The origin of this idea is simple enough. I learned to drive a car only in my early twenties (the state of Utah required that you take driver's ed. before you could get a license, my high school didn't offer it, and I never had time to take it on my own), and so went through my aggressive teenage driving period when I was over twenty-one. Thus even as I went through my bouts of naked competitiveness and aggression on the highway, I was intellectually mature enough to recognize the madness of my behavior. And, rarely, that intellectual awareness curbed some of my stupidest impulses. For instance, long before freeway shootings in California, I realized that when

257

you flash your brights at some bozo you're taking your life in your hands. No, the way to punish a freeway offender was to do it passively. Follow them. Just—follow. Not tailgating. Just—following. If they squirt ahead in traffic, don't leap out to follow. Just work your way up until a few minutes later, there you are again, following. If they really deserve a scare, take a little bit of time out of your life and take their exit with them. Follow them along residential streets. Watch them panic.

I never actually went to that extreme—never actually followed somebody off the freeway. But I did follow a couple of bozos long enough that it clearly made them nervous; yet I never did anything aggressive enough to make them mad. They could never *really* be sure that they were being followed. It was the cruelest thing I can remember doing.

I thought for a while of writing a humor piece about freeway games—ways to pass the time while on long commutes. But when I showed my first draft to Kristine, she said, "That isn't funny, that's *horrible*." So I set it aside.

Later, taking a writing course from Francois Camoin, I decided to write a story that had no science fiction or fantasy element in it. While trying to think of something to write about, I hit on that "freeway games" essay and realized that when Kristine said it was horrible, I should have realized that she really meant that the idea was *horror*. A horror story with no monster except the human being behind the wheel. Somebody who didn't know when to stop. Who kept pushing and pushing until somebody died. In short, me—only out of control. So I wrote a story about a normal nice person who suddenly discovers one day that he's a monster after all.

258

I remember reading a spate of stories about human beings who had been cyborgized—their brains put into machinery so that moving an arm actually moved a cargo bay door and walking actually fired up a rocket engine, that sort of thing. It seemed that almost all of these stories—and a lot of robot and android stories as well—ended up being rewrites of "Pinocchio." They always wish they could be a real boy.

In years since then, the fashion has changed and more sf writers celebrate rather than regret the body mechanical. Still, at the time the issue interested me. Couldn't there be someone for whom a mechanical body would be liberating? So I wrote a story that juxtaposed two characters, one a pinocchio of a spaceship, a cyborg that wished for the sensations of real life; the other a hopelessly crippled human being, trapped in a body that can never *act*, longing for the power that would come from a mechanical replacement. They trade places, and both are happy.

A simple enough tale, but I couldn't tell it quite that way. Perhaps because I wanted it to be truer than a fantasy, I told the story from the point of view of a human observer who could never know whether a *real* trade had taken place or whether the story was just a fantasy that made life livable for a young girl with no arms or legs. Thus it became a story about the stories we tell ourselves that make it possible to live with *anything*.

All this was many years before my third son, Charlie, was born. I never really believed that someday I would have a child who lies on his bed except when we put him in a chair, who stays indoors unless we take him out. In some ways his condition is better than that of the heroine of "Sepulchre of Songs" — he has learned to grasp things and can manipulate his environment a little, since his limbs are not utterly useless. In some ways his condition is worse — so far he cannot speak, and so he is far more lonely, far more helpless than one who can at least have conversation with others. And sometimes when I hold him or sit and look at him, I think back to this story and realize that the fundamental truth of it is something quite unrelated to the issue of whether a powerful mechanical body would be preferable to a crippled one of flesh and bone.

The truth is this. The girl in the story brought joy and love into the lives of others, and when she left her body (however you interpret her leaving), she lost the power to do that. I would give almost anything to see my Charlie run; I wake up some mornings full of immeasurable joy because in the dream that is just fading Charlie spoke to me and I heard the words of his mouth; yet despite these longings I recognize something else: You don't measure whether a life is worth living except by measuring whether that life is giving any good to other people and receiving any joy from them. Plenty of folks with healthy bodies are walking minuses, subtracting from the joy of the world wherever they go, never able to receive much satisfaction either. But Charlie gives and receives many delights, and our family would be far poorer if he weren't a part of us. It teaches us something of goodness when we are able to earn his smile, his laughter. And nothing delights him more than when he earns our smiles, our praise, and our joy in his company. If some cyborg starship passed by, imaginary or otherwise, offering to trade bodies with my little boy, I would understand it if he chose to go. But I hope that he would not, and I would miss him terribly if he ever left.

"PRIOR RESTRAINT"

This story is a bit of whimsy, based in part on some thoughts about censorship and in part on the experience of knowing Doc Murdock, a fellow writing student in Francois Camoin's class. Doc really did support himself at times by gambling, though the last I heard he was making money hand-over-fist as a tech writer. Couldn't happen to a nicer guy.

I almost never consciously base characters on real people or stories on real events. Part of the reason is that the person involved will almost always be offended, unless you treat him as a completely romantic figure, the way I did with Doc Murdock. But the most important reason is that you don't really *know* any of the people you know in real life — that is, you never, ever, *ever* know *why* they do what they do. Even if they tell you why, that's no help because they never understand themselves the complete cause of anything they do. So when you try to follow a real person that you actually know, you will constantly run into vast areas of ignorance and misunderstanding. I find that I tell much more truthful and powerful stories when I work with fully fictional characters, because *them* I can know right down to the core, and am never hampered by thinking, "Oh, he'd never do that," or, worse yet, "I'd better not show him doing *that* or so-and-so will kill me."

And, in a way, "Prior Restraint" is proof that for me, at least, modeling characters on real people is a bad idea. Because, while I think the story is fun, it's also one of my shallower works. Scratch the surface and there's nothing there. It was never much deeper than the conscious idea.

By the way, this story was a *long* time making it into print. I wrote the first version of it very early in my career; Ben Bova rejected it, in part on the grounds that it's not a good idea to write stories about people writing stories, if only because it reminds the reader that he's reading a story. His advice was mostly right, though sometimes you *want* to remind readers they're reading. Still, I liked this idea, flaws and all, and so I sent it off to Charlie Ryan at *Galileo*. He accepted it—but then *Galileo* folded. Charlie wrote to me and offered to send the story back. I knew, however, that I wouldn't be able to sell it to Ben Bova or, probably, anybody else. So when Charlie suggested that he'd like to hang onto it in case someday he was able to restart *Galileo* or some other magazine, I agreed.

It was almost a decade later that a letter came out of the blue, telling me that Charlie was going to edit *Aboriginal SF*, and could he please use "Prior Restraint"? By then I was well aware of the relative weakness of the story, particularly considering the things I'd learned about storytelling since then. It might be a bit embarrassing to have such a primitive work come out now, in the midst of much more mature stories. But Charlie had taken the story back in the days when most editors didn't return my phone calls and some sent me insulting rejections; why shouldn't he profit from it now that things had changed? As long as the story wasn't too embarrassing. So I asked him to send me a copy and let me see if I still liked it.

I did. It wasn't a subtle piece, but it was still a decent idea and, with a bit of revision to get rid of my stylistic excesses from those days, I felt that it could be published without embarrassing me. I don't know whether to be chagrined or relieved that nobody seemed to be able to tell the difference — that nobody said, " 'Prior Restraint' feels like *early* Card." Maybe I haven't learned as much in the intervening years as I thought!

"THE CHANGED MAN AND THE KING OF WORDS"

The genesis of this story is easy enough. I was living in South Bend, Indiana, where I was working on a doctorate at Notre Dame. One of my professors was Ed Vasta, one of the great teachers that come along only a few times in one's life. We both loved Chaucer, and he was receptive to my quirky ideas about literature; he also wrote science fiction, so that there was another bond between us. One night I was at a party at his house. After an hour of everybody grousing about the stupidity of Hesburgh's choosing a high school teacher named Gerry Faust as the football coach, we got on the subject of tarot. Ed was a semi-believer — that is, he didn't really believe in any occult phenomena, but he did think that the cards provided a focus, a framework for bringing intuitive understanding into the open.

Kristine and I are both very uncomfortable around any occult dealings, partly because we are very uncomfortable with the sort of people who believe in the occult. But this was Ed Vasta, a very rational man, and so I consented to a reading. I remember thinking that the process was fascinating, precisely because nothing happened that could not be explained by Vasta's own personal knowledge of me; and yet the cards did provide a way of relating that previous knowledge together in surprising and illuminating patterns.

The experience led me to write a story, combining tarot with my then-new obsession with computers. The story itself is a cliché, a deliberately oedipal story by an author who thinks Freud's notion of an Oedipus complex is an utter crock. It's one of the few times that I've ever mechanically followed a symbolic structure, and for that reason it remains unsatisfying to me. What I really cared about were the ideas—the computer and the tarot cards—and I have since explored the interrelationship between storytelling computers and human beings in such works as my novels *Ender's Game* and *Speaker for the Dead*.

"MEMORIES OF MY HEAD"

This story began very recently when Lee Zacharias, my writing teacher at the University of North Carolina at Greensboro, mentioned that suicide stories were common enough among young writers that she despaired of ever seeing a good one. I remembered that when I was teaching at Elon College the semester before I had gotten enough of those suicide endings to make the pronouncement to my students that I hereby *forbade* them to end a story with suicide. It was a cop-out, said I—it was a confession that the writer had no idea how the story *really* ought to end.

Now, though, I was feeling a bit defiant. I had said that suicide stories were dumb, and now Lee was saying the same thing. Why not see if I could write one that was any good? And why not make it even more impossible by making it first person present tense, just because I detest present tense and have declared that first person is usually a bad choice?

The result is one of the strangest stories I've ever written. But I *like* it. I enjoyed using this epistolary form to tell the tale of a hideously malformed relationship between a couple who had lived together far longer than they had any reason to.

"LOST BOYS"

This story came with its own afterword. Let me only add that since its publication, it has been criticized somewhat for its supposed cheating—I promise at the beginning to tell the truth, and then I lie. I can only say that it is a long tradition in ghost stories to pretend to be telling the truth; part of the pleasure in the tale is to keep the reader wondering whether *this* time the story might not be real. The ghost stories *I've* enjoyed most and remember the best have been the ones told as if they were true and had really happened to the teller. I tip my hat to Jack McLaughlin, a wonderful grad student in the theater department at BYU, who spooked a whole bunch of us undergrad acting students with a really hair-raising poltergeist story that Actually Happened To Him.

I also enjoy the fact that criticisms of my story for violating expectations have all come from the more literary, "experimental" wing of the science fiction community. It seems that they love experimentation and literary flamboyance—but only if it follows the correct line. If somebody dares to do something that is *surprisingly* shocking instead of *predictably* shocking, well, fie on them. Thus do the radicals reveal their orthodoxy.

The fact remains that *Lost Boys* is the most autobiographical, personal, and painful story I've ever written. I wrote it in the absolutely only way *I* could have written it. So even if the manner of its writing is a literary crime, as these critics say, I can only answer, "So shoot me." I'm in the business of telling true stories as well as I possibly can. I've never yet found any of their rules that helped me tell a story better; and if I had followed their rules on this story, I never could have told it at all.

BOOK 2

FLUX

TALES OF HUMAN FUTURES

INTRODUCTION

Never mind the question of why anybody would ever become a writer at all. The sheer arrogance of thinking that other people ought to pay to read my words should be enough to mark all us writers as unfit for decent society. But then, few indeed are the communities that reward proper modesty and disdain those who thrust themselves into the limelight. All human societies hunger for storytellers, and those whose tales we like, we reward well. In the meantime, the storytellers are constantly reinventing and redefining their society. We are paid to bite the hand that feeds us. We are birds that keep tearing down and rebuilding every nest in the tree.

So never mind the question of why I became a writer. Instead let's ask an easy one. Why did I choose to write science fiction?

The glib answer is to say that I didn't. Some are born to science fiction, some choose science fiction, and some have science fiction thrust upon them. Surely I belong to the last category. I was a playwright by choice. Oh, I entered college as an archaeology major, but I soon discovered that being an archaeologist didn't mean being Thor Heyerdahl or Yigael Yadin. It meant sorting through eight billion potsherds. It meant moving a mountain with a teaspoon. In short, it meant work. Therefore it was not for me.

During the two semesters it took for me to make this personal discovery, I had already taken four theater classes for every archaeology class I signed up for, and it was in theater that I spent all my time. Because I attended Brigham Young High School, I was already involved with the BYU theater program before I officially started college. In fact, I had already been in a student production, and continued acting almost continuously through all my years at the university. I was no great shakes as an actor — too cerebral, not able to use my body well enough to look comfortable or right on stage. But I gave great cold readings at auditions, so I kept getting cast. And when I gave up on archaeology, it was theater that was there waiting for me. It was the first time I consciously made a decision based on autobiography. Instead of examining my feelings (which change hourly anyway) or making those ridiculous pro-and-con lists that always look so rational, I simply looked back at the last few years of my life and saw that the only thing I did that I really followed through on, the only thing I did over and over again regardless of whether it profited me in any way, was theater. So I changed majors, thereby determining much of my future.

One obvious result was that I lost my scholarship. I was at BYU on a full-ride presidential scholarship — tuition, books, housing. But I had to maintain a high grade point average, and while that was easy enough in academic subjects, it was devilishly hard in the subjective world of the arts. The matter hadn't come up before — presidential scholars hadn't ever gone into the arts before me. So there was no mechanism for dealing with the subjective grades that came out of theater. If I worked my tail off in an academic subject, I got an A. Period. No question. But I could work myself half to death on a play, do my very best, and still get a C because the teacher didn't agree with my interpretation or didn't like my blocking or just plain didn't like *me*, and who could argue? There was nothing quantifiable. So choosing the arts cost me money. It also taught me that you can never please a critic determined to detest your work. I had to choose my professors carefully, or reconcile myself to low grades. I did both.

But if I wasn't working for grades and I wasn't trying to change myself to fit professors' preconceived notions of what my work ought to be, what *was* I working for? The answer came to me gradually, but once I understood it I never wavered. I rejected the notion, put forth by one English professor, that one should write for oneself. Indeed, his own life was a clear refutation of his lofty sentiment that "I write for myself and God." In fact he spent half his life pressing his writings on anyone who would hold still long enough to read or listen. He showed me what I was already becoming aware of: Art is a dialogue with the audience. There is no reason to create art except to present it to other people; and you present it to other people in order to change them. The world must be changed by what I create, I decided, or it isn't worth doing.

Within a year of becoming a theater major, I was writing plays. I didn't plan it. Writing wasn't something I thought of as a career. In my family, writing was simply something that you *did*. My dad often bought *Writer's Digest*; I entered their contest a couple of times in my teens. But mostly I thought

271

of writing as coming up with skits or assemblies at school or roadshows at church (Mormons have a longstanding commitment to theater); it also meant that I could usually ace an essay exam if I knew even a little bit about the subject. It wasn't a *career*.

But as a fledgling director, I had run into the frustration of directing inadequate scripts. When I was assistant director of a college production of *Flowers for Algernon*, I finally got a professor—the director—to agree with me. The second act was terrible. I had read and loved the story, and so I was particularly frustrated by some bad choices made by the adapter. With the director's permission, I went home and rewrote the second act. We used my script.

About the same time (I think), I was taking a course in advanced interpretation, which included reader's theater. I loved the whole concept of stripping the stage and letting the actors, in plain clothes, with no sets and minimal movements, act out the story for the audience. As part of the course, I wrote an adaptation of Marjorie Kellogg's *Tell Me That You Love Me, Junie Moon*. I had loved the book, and my adaptation was (and still is) one of my best works, because it preserved both the story and the madcap flavor of the writing. I asked for permission to direct it. I was told that advanced interp wasn't a course for which students were allowed to direct. There was only *one* course undergraduates could take that allowed them to direct a play, and I had taken it and received a C, and that was that.

No it wasn't. My professor in that course, Preston Gledhill, was sympathetic, and so he arranged to bend the rules and I got my performance. Two nights in the Experimental Theater, doing reader's theater as it had never been done before. The audience laughed in all the right places. They sobbed at the end. The standing ovation was earned. The actors still remember, as I do, that it was something remarkable. I may have been using someone else's story, but that student production told me, for the first time, that I could produce a script and a performance that audiences would take into themselves. I had changed people.

Because of those two adaptations, I resolved to try playwriting in a more serious way. Charles Whitman, who was the favorite among us undergraduates in those days (the late 1960s), was also the playwriting teacher and a fervent advocate of Mormon theater. He thought that young Mormon theater people ought to be producing plays for their own people, and I agreed—and still agree, enough that I have never stopped producing Mormon art throughout my career, often allowing it to take precedence over my more visible (and lucrative) career in "the world." Taking Whitman's class opened the floodgates. I wrote dozens of plays. I tried my hand at realism, comedy, verse drama, vignettes, anything that would hold still long enough for me to write it. I adapted stories from Mormon history and the Book of Mormon; I took personal stories out of my life and my parents' lives; and through all this writing, I *still* thought of myself as primarily an actor and director.

I mean, just because I wrote a lot of plays didn't mean I *was* a playwright. I also designed costumes and did makeup and composed music and designed and built stage sets. The only reason I didn't do lighting was because of a healthy case of acrophobia. No, I wasn't a playwright, I was an all-around theater person. I didn't make the decision that I was a writer until one day I was sitting in the Theater Department office with a group—some meeting, I don't remember what—and a professor happened to say to me, "So you're going to be a playwright." I found something about his statement to be offensive. It flashed through my mind that I had already written a dozen plays that had been produced to sold-out houses. I was at least as much a writer as he was an actor or director or teacher—because I had done it to the satisfaction of an audience. So I answered, rather coldly, "I'm not *going* to be a playwright. I *am* a playwright."

A short while later, I happened to be sitting in on a class he was teaching, and he referred to that conversation in front of his class. "Some of you are going to be actors and some directors and some playwrights," he said. Then, pointing at me, he said, "Except for Scott Card, there, who already *is* a playwright." It was a great laugh line. The mockery I thought I heard in his words left me angry and frustrated. Later I would learn that he had intended his comments as a kind of respect; and we have worked together well on other projects. But I interpreted things then with the paranoia normal to "sensitive" adolescents, and took his words as a challenge. I brooded on them for days. Weeks. And at the end of that time, in my own mind I *was* a playwright, and all my other theatrical enterprises were secondary. I could succeed or fail at them without it making much difference—my future was tied to my writing.

Skip a few years now. Years in which I started a repertory theater company, which by some measures was a resounding success; but at the end of that time

I found myself $20,000 in debt on an annual income of about $5,000. My own scripts had been quite successful in the company, but some bad business decisions—*my* decisions, I must add—had made a good thing go sour. I folded the company, and probably should have declared personal and corporate bankruptcy, but instead decided to pay it all off.

How? My income as an editor at BYU Press would never be enough to make a dent in what I owed. I had to make money on the side. Doing what? The only thing I knew how to do was write, and because my plays were all aimed at the Mormon audience, there was no way that a script of mine would bring in that kind of money—not from royalties. There just weren't enough warm bodies with dollars in their pockets to bring me what I needed. I thought of writing plays for the New York audience, but that would be so chancy and require so much investment in time that I rejected it. Instead, I thought of writing fiction.

In a way, that was as scary as trying to write plays for the American audience at large. The difference was that with fiction, you find out much sooner whether you've failed. You can take years flogging a few scripts around in New York and regional theater and end up with nothing—no audience, no money, no future. But you can find yourself in exactly that condition after only a few months of mailing out fiction manuscripts.

And when considering what kind of fiction to write, science fiction was an easy choice. I wanted to start with short stories, and when it comes to short fiction, science fiction was then and is now the most open market there is. First, because the money is fairly low, the established novelists generally stay out of the short fiction market, making it more open to new names. Second, because science fiction thrives on strangeness, new writers are more welcome in this field than any other. True strangeness is the product of genius, but a good substitute is the strangeness inherent in every writer's unique voice, so that when a science fiction writer is both competent and new, he gives off the luster of an ersatz kind of genius, and the field welcomes him with open arms. (Others might say that the field chews you up, swallows you, and pukes you back, but that would be crude and unkind, and it doesn't *always* happen that way.)

So for purely commercial reasons, deep in debt, I chose science fiction. I was lucky enough that the second story I sent out sold after only a couple of tries (told about elsewhere) and went on to come in second for a Hugo and win me the Campbell Award for best new writer. So as long as people were paying me to write science fiction why should I stop?

That's the colorful, devil-may-care answer. It's also a crock.

Because during that whole time that I "was" a playwright, I was also writing science fiction. I had not yet written a play when at sixteen I first came up with the story idea that eventually became "Ender's Game." I was taking fiction-writing courses at BYU right along with my playwriting courses, and, although I had brains enough not to turn in sci-fi for class credit, my heart went into the Worthing stories I was already writing before my first play was produced. Like my plays, my stories were all written on narrow-ruled paper in spiral notebooks, and at first my mother typed them for me. Then I mailed them out and treasured the very kind rejection notes I got. Not many—only a couple of submissions, only a couple of rejections. But between rejections—and between plays—I worked on my fiction as assiduously as I ever worked on anything else in my life.

So now, glib answers aside, why science fiction? Why is it that, left to myself, the stories I am drawn to write are all science fiction and fantasy? It wasn't because sci-fi was all I read. On the contrary, while I went through several science fiction binges, during high school and college I usually read only the sci-fi and fantasy that were making the rounds. I read *Dune* when everybody read *Dune*; the same with *Lord of the Rings* and *Foundation* and *I Sing the Body Electric* and *Dandelion Wine*. At the same time, I was reading Hersey's *The Wall* and *White Lotus*, Ayn Rand's *Fountainhead*, Rod McKuen's *Stanyan Street and Other Sorrows*. Hell, I even read Khalil Gibran. I may not have dropped acid, but I wasn't totally cut off from my generation. (Fortunately, by the time *Jonathan Livingston Seagull* came out I had matured enough to recognize it immediately as drivel.) I never, not once, not for a moment, thought of myself as a "science fiction reader." Some science fiction books came to me like revelations, yes, but so did many other books—and none had anything like the influence on me that came from Shakespeare and Joseph Smith, the two writers who, more than any others, formed the way I think and write.

If I wasn't a science fiction reader, *per se*, why did my impulse toward storytelling come out in science fictional forms? I think it was the same reason that my playwriting impulses always expressed themselves in stories aimed at and arising from the Mormon audience. The possibility of the transcen-

277

dental is part of it. More important, though—for Mormonism is *not* a transcendental religion—is the fact that science fiction, like Mormonism, offered a vocabulary for rationalizing the transcendental. That is, within science fiction it is possible to find the meaning of life without resorting to Mystery. I detest Mystery (though I love mysteries); I think it is the name we put on our decision to stop trying to understand. From Joseph Smith I learned to reject any philosophy that requires you to swallow paradox as if it were profound; if it makes no sense, it's probably hogwash. Within the genre of science fiction, I could shuck off the shackles of realism and make up worlds in which the issues I cared about were clear and powerful. The tale could be told direct. It could be *about something*.

Since then I have learned ways to make more realistic fiction be *about something* as well—but not the ways my literature professors tried to teach me. The oblique methods used by contemporary American literateurs are bankrupt because they have forsaken the audience. But there are writers doing outside of science fiction the things that I thought, at the age of twenty-three, could only be done within it. I think of Olive Ann Burns's *Cold Sassy Tree* as the marker that informed me that all the so-called Mysteries could still be reached through stories that told of love and sex and death; the need to belong, the hungers of the body, and the search for individual worth; Community, Carnality, Identity. Ultimately, that triad is what all stories are about. The great stories are simply the ones that do it better for a particular audience at a particular place and time. So I'm gradually reaching out to write other stories, outside of both the Mormon and the science fiction communities. But the fact remains that it was in science fiction that I first found it possible to speak to non-Mormons about the things that mattered most to me. That's why I wrote science fiction, and write science fiction, and will write it for many years to come.

A Thousand Deaths

"You will make no speeches," said the prosecutor.

"I didn't expect they'd let me," Jerry Crove answered, affecting a confidence he didn't feel. The prosecutor was not hostile; he seemed more like a high school drama coach than a man who was seeking Jerry's death.

"They not only won't let you," the prosecutor said, "but if you try anything, it will go much worse for you. We have you cold, you know. We don't need anywhere near as much proof as we have."

"You haven't proved anything." "We've proved you knew about it," the prosecutor insisted mildly. "No point arguing now. Knowing about treason and not reporting it is exactly equal to committing treason."

Jerry shrugged and looked away.

The cell was bare concrete. The door was solid steel. The bed was a hammock hung from hooks on the wall. The toilet was a can with a removable plastic seat. There was no conceivable way to escape. Indeed, there was nothing that could conceivably occupy an intelligent person's mind for more than five minutes. In the three weeks he had been here, he had memorized every crack in the concrete, every bolt in the door. He had nothing to look at, except the prosecutor. Jerry reluctantly met the man's gaze.

"What do you say when the judge asks you how you plead to the charges?"

"Nolo contendere."

"Very good. It would be much nicer if you'd consent to say 'guilty'," the prosecutor said.

"I don't like the word."

"Just remember. Three cameras will be pointing at you. The trial will be broadcast live. To America, you represent all Americans. You must comport yourself with dignity, quietly accepting the fact that your complicity in the assassination of Peter Anderson—"

"Andreyevitch—"

"*Anderson* has brought you to the point of death, where all depends on the mercy of the court. And now I'll go have lunch. Tonight we'll see each other again. And remember. No speeches. Nothing embarrassing."

Jerry nodded. This was not the time to argue. He spent the afternoon practicing conjugations of Portuguese irregular verbs, wishing that somehow he could go back and undo the moment when he agreed to speak to the old man who had unfolded all the plans to assassinate Andreyevitch. "Now I must trust you," said the old man. "*Temos que confiar no senhor americano*. You love liberty, *né*?"

Love liberty? Who knew anymore? What was liberty? Being free to make a buck? The Russians had been smart enough to know that if they let Americans make money, they really didn't give a damn which language the government was speaking. And, in fact, the government spoke English anyway.

The propaganda that they had been feeding him

281

wasn't funny. It was too true. The United States had never been so peaceful. It was more prosperous than it had been since the Vietnam War boom thirty years before. And the lazy, complacent American people were going about business as usual, as if pictures of Lenin on buildings and billboards were just what they had always wanted.

I was no different, he reminded himself. I sent in my work application, complete with oath of allegiance. I accepted it meekly when they opted me out for a tutorial with a high Party official. I even taught his damnable little children for three years in Rio.

When I should have been writing plays.

But what do I write about? Why not a comedy— *The Yankee and the Commissar*, a load of laughs about a woman commissar who marries an American blue blood who manufactures typewriters. There are no women commissars, of course, but one must maintain the illusion of a free and equal society.

"Bruce, my dear," says the commissar in a thick but sexy Russian accent, "your typewriter company is suspiciously close to making a profit."

"And if it were running at a loss, you'd turn me in, yes, my little noodle?" (Riotous laughs from the Russians in the audience; the Americans are not amused, but then, they speak English fluently and don't need broad humor. Besides, the reviews are all approved by the Party, so we don't have to worry about the critics. Keep the Russians happy, and screw the American audience.) Dialogue continues:

"All for the sake of Mother Russia."

"Screw Mother Russia."

"Please do," says Natasha. "Regard me as her personal incarnation."

282

Oh, but the Russians do love onstage sex. Forbidden in Russia, of course, but Americans are *supposed* to be decadent.

I might as well have been a ride designer for Disneyland, Jerry thought. Might as well have written shtick for vaudeville. Might as well go stick my head in an oven. But with my luck, it would be electric.

He may have slept. He wasn't sure But the door opened, and he opened his eyes with no memory of having heard footsteps approach. The calm before the storm: and now, the storm.

The soldiers were young, but unSlavic. Slavish, but definitely American. Slaves to the Slavs. Put that in a protest poem sometime, he decided, if only there were someone who wanted to read a protest poem.

The young American soldiers (But the uniforms were wrong. I'm not old enough to remember the old ones, but these are not made for American bodies.) escorted him down corridors, up stairs, through doors, until they were outside and they put him into a heavily armored van. What did they think, he was part of a conspiracy and his fellows would come to save him? Didn't they know that a man in his position would have no friends by now?

Jerry had seen it at Yale. Dr. Swick had been very popular. Best damn professor in the department. He could take the worst drivel and turn it into a *play*, take terrible actors and make them look good, take apathetic audiences and make them, of all things, enthusiastic and hopeful. And then one day the police had broken into his home and found Swick with four actors putting on a play for a group of maybe a score of friends. What was it—*Who's Afraid*

283

of Virginia Woolf? Jerry remembered. A sad script. A despairing script. But a sharp one, nonetheless, one that showed despair as being an ugly, destructive thing, one that showed lies as suicide, one that, in short, made the audience feel that, by God, something was *wrong* with their lives, that the peace was illusion, that the prosperity was a fraud, that America's ambitions had been cut off and that so much that was good and proud was still undone—

And Jerry realized that he was weeping. The soldiers sitting across from him in the armored van were looking away. Jerry dried his eyes.

As soon as news got out that Swick was arrested, he was suddenly unknown. Everyone who had letters or memos or even class papers that bore his name destroyed them. His name disappeared from address books. His classes were empty as no one showed up. No one even hoping for a substitute, for the university suddenly had no record that there had ever been such a class, ever been such a professor. His house had gone up for sale, his wife had moved, and no one said good-bye. And then, more than a year later, the CBS news (which always showed official trials then) had shown ten minutes of Swick weeping and saying, "Nothing has ever been better for America than Communism. It was just a foolish, immature desire to prove myself by thumbing my nose at authority. It meant nothing. I was wrong. The Government's been kinder to me than I deserve." And so on. The words were silly. But as Jerry had sat, watching, he had been utterly convinced. However meaningless the words were, Swick's face was meaningful: he was utterly sincere.

The van stopped, and the doors in the back opened just as Jerry remembered that he had burned his copy of Swick's manual on playwriting. Burned it, but not until he had copied down all the major ideas. Whether Swick knew it or not, he had left something behind. But what will I leave behind? Jerry wondered. Two Russian children who now speak fluent English and whose father was blown up in their front yard right in front of them, his blood spattering their faces, because Jerry had neglected to warn him? What a legacy.

For a moment he was ashamed. A life is a life, no matter whose or how lived.

Then he remembered the night when Peter Andreyevitch (no—Anderson. Pretending to be American is fashionable nowadays, so long as everyone can tell at a glance that you're *really* Russian) had drunkenly sent for Jerry and demanded, as Jerry's employer (i.e., owner), that Jerry recite his poems to the guests at the party. Jerry had tried to laugh it off, but Peter was not that drunk: he insisted, and Jerry went upstairs and got his poems and came down and read them to a group of men who could not understand the poems, to a group of women who understood them and were merely amused. Little Andre said afterward, "The poems were good, Jerry," but Jerry felt like a virgin who had been raped and then given a two-dollar tip by the rapist.

In fact, Peter had given him a bonus. And Jerry had spent it.

Charlie Ridge, Jerry's defense attorney, met him just inside the doors of the court-house. "Jerry, old boy, looks like you're taking all this pretty well. Haven't even lost any weight."

"On a diet of pure starch, I've had to run around my cell all day just to stay thin." Laughter. Ha ho, what a fun time we're having. What jovial people we are.

"Listen, Jerry, you've got to do this right, you know. They have audience response measurements. They can judge how sincere you seem. You've got to really *mean* it."

"Wasn't there once a time when defense attorneys tried to get their clients off?" Jerry asked.

"Jerry, that kind of attitude isn't going to get you anywhere. These aren't the good old days when you could get off on a technicality and a lawyer could delay trial for five years. You're guilty as hell, and so if you cooperate, they won't do anything to you. They'll just deport you."

"What a pal," Jerry said. "With you on my side, I haven't a worry in the world."

"Exactly right," said Charlie. "And don't you forget it."

The courtroom was crowded with cameras. (Jerry had heard that in the old days of freedom of the press, cameras had often been barred from courtrooms. But then, in those days the defendant didn't usually testify and in those days the lawyers didn't both work from the same script. Still, there was the press, looking for all the world as if they thought they were free.)

Jerry had nothing to do for nearly half an hour. The audience (Are they paid? Jerry wondered. In America, they must be) filed in, and the show began at exactly eight o'clock. The judge came in looking impressive in his robes, and his voice was resonant and strong, like a father on television remonstrating his rebellious son. Everyone who spoke faced the camera with the red light on the top. And Jerry felt very tired.

He did not waver in his determination to try to turn this trial to his own advantage, but he seriously wondered what good it would do. And was it to his own advantage? They would certainly punish him more severely. Certainly they would be angry, would cut him off. But he had written his speech as if it were an impassioned climactic scene in a play (*Crove Against the Communists* or perhaps *Liberty's Last Cry*), and he the hero who would willingly give his life for the chance to instill a little bit of patriotism (a little bit of intelligence, who gives a damn about patriotism!) in the hearts and minds of the millions of Americans who would be watching.

"Gerald Nathan Crove, you have heard the charges against you. Please step forward and state your plea."

Jerry stood up and walked with, he hoped, dignity to the taped X on the floor where the prosecutor had insisted that he stand. He looked for the camera with the red light on. He stared into it intently, sincerely, and wondered if, after all, it wouldn't be better just to say *nolo contendere* or even *guilty* and have an easier time of it.

"Mr. Crove," intoned the judge, "America is watching. How do you plead?"

America was watching indeed. And Jerry opened his mouth and said not the Latin but the English he had rehearsed so often in his mind:

"There is a time for courage and a time for cowardice, a time when a man can give in to those who offer him leniency and a time when he must, instead, resist them for the sake of a higher goal. America was once a free nation. But as long as they pay our salaries, we seem content to be slaves! I plead not guilty, because any act that serves to weaken Russian domination of any nation in the world is a blow for all the things that make life worth living and against those to whom power is the only god worth worshiping!"

Ah. Eloquence. But in his rehearsals he had never dreamed he would get even this far, and yet they still showed no sign of stopping him. He looked away from the camera. He looked at the prosecutor, who was taking notes on a yellow pad. He looked at Charlie, and Charlie was resignedly shaking his head and putting his papers back in his briefcase. No one seemed to be particularly worried that Jerry was saying these things over live television. And the broadcasts *were* live—they had stressed that, that he must be careful to do everything correctly the first time because it was all live—

They were lying, of course. And Jerry stopped his speech and jammed his hands into his pockets, only to discover that the suit they had provided for him had no pockets (Save money by avoiding nonessentials, said the slogan), and his hands slid uselessly down his hips.

The prosecutor looked up in surprise when the judge cleared his throat. "Oh, I beg your pardon," he said. "The speeches usually go on much longer. I congratulate you, Mr. Crove, on your brevity."

Jerry nodded in mock acknowledgment, but he felt no mockery.

"We always have a dry run," said the prosecutor, "just to catch you last-chancers."

"Everyone knew that?"

"Well, everyone but you, of course, Mr. Crove. All right, everybody, you can go home now."

The audience arose and quietly shuffled out.

The prosecutor and Charlie got up and walked to

the bench. The judge was resting his chin on his hands, looking not at all fatherly now, just a little bored. "How much do you want?" the judge asked.

"Unlimited," said the prosecutor.

"Is he really that important?" Jerry might as well have not been there. "After all, they're doing the actual bombers in Brazil."

"Mr. Crove is an American," said the prosecutor, "who chose to let a Russian ambassador be assassinated."

"All right, all right," said the judge, and Jerry marveled that the man hadn't the slightest trace of a Russian accent.

"Gerald Nathan Crove, the court finds you guilty of murder and treason against the United States of America and its ally, the Union of Soviet Socialist Republics. Do you have anything to say before sentence is pronounced?"

"I just wondered," said Jerry, "why you all speak English."

"Because," said the prosecutor icily, "we are in America."

"Why do you even bother with trials?"

"To stop other imbeciles from trying what you did. He just wants to argue, Your Honor."

The judge slammed down his gavel. "The court sentences Gerald Nathan Crove to be put to death by every available method until such time as he convincingly apologizes for his action to the American people. Court stands adjourned. Lord in heaven, do I have a headache."

They wasted no time. At five o'clock in the morning, Jerry had barely fallen asleep. Perhaps they monitored this, because they promptly woke him up with

289

a brutal electric shock across the metal floor where Jerry was lying. Two guards—this time Russians—came in and stripped him and then dragged him to the execution chamber even though, had they let him, he would have walked.

The prosecutor was waiting. "I have been assigned your case," he said, "because you promise to be a challenge. Your psychological profile is interesting, Mr. Crove. You long to be a hero."

"I wasn't aware of that."

"You displayed it in the courtroom, Mr. Crove. You are no doubt aware—your middle name implies it—of the last words of the American Revolutionary War espionage agent named Nathan Hale. 'I regret that I have but one life to give for my country,' he said. You shall discover that he was mistaken. He should be very glad he had but one life.

"Since you were arrested several weeks ago in Rio de Janeiro, we have been growing a series of clones for you. Development is quite accelerated, but they have been kept in zero-sensation environments until the present. Their minds are blank.

"You are surely aware of somec, yes, Mr. Crove?"

Jerry nodded. The starship sleep drug.

"We don't need it in this case, of course. But the mind-taping technique we use on interstellar flights—that is quite useful. When we execute you, Mr. Crove, we shall be continuously taping your brain. All your memories will be rather indecorously dumped into the head of the first clone, who will immediately become *you*. However, he will clearly remember all your life up to and including the moment of death.

"It was so easy to be a hero in the old days, Mr.

Crove. Then you never knew for sure what death was like. It was compared to sleep, to great emotional pain, to quick departure of the soul from the body. None of these, of course, is particularly accurate."

Jerry was frightened. He had heard of multiple death before, of course—it was rumored to exist because of its deterrent value. "They resurrect you and kill you again and again," said the horror story, and now he knew that it was true. Or they wanted him to believe it was true.

What frightened Jerry was the way they planned to kill him. A noose hung from a hook in the ceiling. It could be raised and lowered, but there didn't seem to be the slightest provision for a quick, sharp drop to break his neck. Jerry had once almost choked to death on a salmon bone. The sensation of not being able to breathe terrified him.

"How can I get out of this?" Jerry asked, his palms sweating.

"The first one, not at all," said the prosecutor. "So you might as well be brave and use up your heroism this time around. Afterward we'll give you a screen test and see how convincing your repentance is. We're fair, you know. We try to avoid putting anyone through this unnecessarily. Please sit."

Jerry sat. A man in a lab coat put a metal helmet on his head. A few needles pricked into Jerry's scalp.

"Already," said the prosecutor, "your first clone is becoming aware. He already has all your memories. He is right now living through your panic—or shall we say your attempts at courage. Make sure you concentrate carefully on what is about to happen to you, Jerry. You want to make sure you remember every detail."

"Please," Jerry said.

"Buck up, my man," said the prosecutor with a grin. "You were wonderful in the courtroom. Let's have some of that noble resistance now."

Then the guards led him to the noose and put it around his neck, being careful not to dislodge the helmet. They pulled it tight and then tied his hands behind his back. The rope was rough on his neck. He waited, his neck tingling, for the sensation of being lifted in the air. He flexed his neck muscles, trying to keep them rigid, though he knew the effort would be useless. His knees grew weak, waiting for them to raise the rope.

The room was plain. There was nothing to see, and the prosecutor had left the room. There was, however, a mirror on a wall beside him. He could barely see into it without turning his entire body. He was sure it was an observation window. They would watch, of course.

Jerry needed to go to the bathroom.

Remember, he told himself, I won't really die. I'll be awake in the other room in just a moment.

But his body was not convinced. It didn't matter a bit that a new Jerry Crove would be ready to get up and walk away when this was over. *This* Jerry Crove would die.

"What are you waiting for?" he demanded, and as if that had been their cue the guards pulled the rope and lifted him into the air.

From the beginning it was worse than he had thought. The rope had an agonizingly tight grip on his neck; there was no question of resisting at all. The suffocation was nothing, at first. Like being under water holding your breath. But the rope itself was painful, and his neck hurt, and he wanted to cry out with the pain; but nothing could escape his throat.

Not at first.

There was some fumbling with the rope, and it jumped up and down as the guards tied it to the hook on the wall. Once Jerry's feet even touched the floor.

By the time the rope held still, however, the effects of the strangling were taking over and the pain was forgotten. The blood was pounding inside Jerry's head. His tongue felt thick. He could not shut his eyes. And now he wanted to breathe. He had to breathe. His body demanded a breath.

His body was not under control. Intellectually, he knew that he could not possibly reach the floor, knew that this death would be temporary, but right now his mind was not having much influence over his body. His legs kicked and struggled to reach the ground. His hands strained at the rope behind him. And all the exertion only made his eyes bulge more with the pressure of the blood that could not get past the rope; only made him need air more desperately.

There was no help for him, but now he tried to scream for help. The sound now escaped his throat — but at the cost of air. He felt as if his tongue were being pushed up into his nose. His kicking grew more violent, though every kick was agony. He spun on the rope; he caught a glimpse of himself in the mirror. His face was turning purple.

How long will it be? Surely not much longer!

But it was much longer.

If he had been underwater, holding his breath, he would now have given up and drowned.

If he had a gun and a free hand, he would kill himself now to end this agony and the sheer physical terror of being unable to breathe. But he had no gun, and there was no question of inhaling, and the blood throbbed in his head and made his eyes see everything in shades of red, and finally he saw nothing at all.

Saw nothing, except what was going through his mind, and that was a jumble, as if his consciousness were madly trying to make some arrangement that would eliminate the strangulation. He kept seeing himself in the creek behind his house, where he had fallen in when he was a child, and someone was throwing him a rope, but he couldn't and he couldn't and he couldn't catch it, and then suddenly it was around his neck and dragging him under.

Spots of black stabbed at his eyes. His body felt bloated, and then it erupted, his bowel and bladder and stomach ejecting all that they contained, except that his vomit was stopped at his throat, where it burned.

The shaking of his body turned into convulsive jerks and spasms, and for a moment Jerry felt himself reaching the welcome state of unconsciousness. Then, suddenly, he discovered that death is not so kind.

There is no such thing as slipping off quietly in your sleep. No such thing as being "killed immediately" or having death mercifully end the pain.

Death woke him from his unconsciousness, for perhaps a tenth of a second. But that tenth of a second was infinite, and in it he experienced the infinite agony of impending nonexistence. His life did not flash before his eyes. The lack of life instead exploded, and in his mind he experienced far greater pain and fear than anything he had felt from the mere hanging.

And then he died.

For an instant he hung in limbo, feeling and seeing nothing. Then a light stabbed at his eyes and soft foam peeled away from his skin and the prosecutor stood there, watching as he gasped and retched and clutched at his throat. It seemed incredible that he could now breathe, and if he had experienced only the strangling, he might now sigh with relief and say, "I've been through it once and now I'm not afraid of death." But the strangling was nothing. The strangling was a prelude. And he was afraid of death.

They forced him to come into the room where he had died. He saw his body hanging, black-faced, from the ceiling, the helmet still on the head, the tongue protruding.

"Cut it down," the prosecutor said, and for a moment Jerry waited for the guards to obey. Instead, a guard handed Jerry a knife.

With death still heavy in his mind, Jerry swung around and lunged at the prosecutor. But a guard caught his hand in an irresistible grip, and the other guard held a pistol pointed at Jerry's head.

"Do you want to die again so soon?" asked the prosecutor, and Jerry whimpered and took the knife and reached up to cut himself down from the noose. In order to reach above the knot, he had to stand close enough to the corpse to touch it. The stench was incredible. And the fact of death was unavoidable. Jerry trembled so badly he could hardly control the knife, but eventually the rope parted and the corpse slumped to the ground, knocking Jerry down as it fell. An arm lay across Jerry's legs. The face looked at Jerry eye-to-eye.

Jerry screamed.

"You see the camera?"

Jerry nodded, numbly.

"You will look at the camera and you will apologize for having done anything against the government that has brought peace to the earth."

Jerry nodded again, and the prosecutor said, "Roll it."

"Fellow Americans," Jerry said, "I'm sorry. I made a terrible mistake. I was wrong. There's nothing wrong with the Russians. I let an innocent man be killed. Forgive me. The government has been kinder to me than I deserve." And so on. For an hour Jerry babbled, insisting that he was craven, that he was guilty, that he was worthless, that the government was vying with God for respectability.

And when he was through, the prosecutor came back in, shaking his head.

"Mr. Crove, you can do better than that.

"Nobody in the audience believed you for one minute. Nobody in the test sample, not one person, believed that you were the least bit sincere. You still think the government ought to be deposed. And so we have to try the treatment again."

"Let me try to confess again."

"A screen test is a screen test, Mr. Crove. We have to give you a little more experience with death before we can permit you to have any involvement with life."

This time Jerry screamed right from the beginning. He made no attempt at all to bear it well. They hung him by the armpits over a long cylinder filled with boiling oil. They slowly lowered him. Death came when the oil was up to his chest—by then his legs had been completely cooked and the meat was falling off the bones in large chunks.

They made him come in and, when the oil had cooled enough to touch, fish out the pieces of his own corpse.

He wept all through his confession this time, but the test audience was completely unconvinced. "The man's a phony," they said. "He doesn't believe a word of what he's saying."

"We have a problem," said the prosecutor. "You seem so willing to cooperate after your death. But you have reservations. You aren't speaking from the heart. We'll have to help you again."

Jerry screamed and struck out at the prosecutor. When the guards had pulled him away (and the prosecutor was nursing an injured nose), Jerry shouted, "Of course I'm lying! No matter how often you kill me it won't change the fact that this is a government of fools by vicious, lying bastards!"

"On the contrary," said the prosecutor, trying to maintain his good manners and cheerful demeanor despite the blood pouring out of his nose, "if we kill you enough, you'll completely change your mind."

"You can't change the truth!"

"We've changed it for everyone else who's gone through this. And you are far from being the first who had to go to a third clone. But this time, Mr. Crove, do try to forget about being a hero."

They skinned him alive, arms and legs first, and then, finally, they castrated him and ripped the skin off his belly and chest. He died silently when they cut his larynx out—no, not silently. Just voiceless. He found that without a voice he could still whisper a scream that rang in his ears when he awoke and was forced to go in and carry his bloody corpse to the disposal room. He confessed again, and the audience was not convinced.

They slowly crushed him to death, and he had to scrub the blood out of the crusher when he awoke, but the audience only commented. "Who does the jerk think he's fooling?"

They disemboweled him and burned his guts in front of him. They infected him with rabies and let his death linger for two weeks. They crucified him and let exposure and thirst kill him. They dropped him a dozen times from the roof of a one-story building until he died.

Yet the audience knew that Jerry Crove had not repented.

"My God, Crove, how long do you think I can keep doing this?" asked the prosecutor. He did not seem cheerful. In fact, Jerry thought he looked almost desperate.

"Getting a little tough on you?" Jerry asked, grateful for the conversation because it meant there would be a few minutes between deaths.

"What kind of man do you think I am? We'll bring him back to life in a minute anyway, I tell myself, but I didn't get into this business in order to find new, hideous ways of killing people."

"You don't like it? And yet you have such a natural talent for it."

The prosecutor looked sharply at Crove. "Irony? Now you can joke? Doesn't death mean anything to you?"

Jerry did not answer, only tried to blink back the tears that these days came unbidden every few minutes.

"Crove, this is not cheap. Do you think it's cheap?

298

We've spent literally billions of rubles on you. And even with inflation, that's a hell of a lot of money."

"In a classless society there's no need for money."

"What is this, dammit! *Now* you're getting rebellious? *Now* you're trying to be a hero?"

"No."

"No wonder we've had to kill you eight times! You keep thinking up clever arguments against us!"

"I'm sorry. Heaven knows I'm sorry."

"I've asked to be released from this assignment. I obviously can't crack you."

"Crack me! As if I didn't long to be cracked."

"You're costing too much. There's a definite benefit in having criminals convincingly recant on television. But you're getting too expensive. The cost-benefit ratio is ridiculous now. There's a limit to how much we can spend on you."

"I have a way for you to save money."

"So do I. Convince the damned audience!"

"Next time you kill me, don't put a helmet on my head."

The prosecutor looked absolutely shocked. "That would be final. That would be capital punishment. We're a humane government. We never kill anybody permanently."

They shot him in the gut and let him bleed to death. They threw him from a cliff into the sea. They let a shark eat him alive. They hung him upside down so that just his head was under water, and when he finally got too tired to hold his head out of the water he drowned.

But through all this, Jerry had become more inured to the pain. His mind had finally learned that none of these deaths was permanent after all. And now when the moment of death came, though it was

299

still terrible, he endured it better. He screamed less. He approached death with greater calm. He even hastened the process, deliberately inhaling great draughts of water, deliberately wriggling to attract the shark. When they had the guards kick him to death he kept yelling, "Harder," until he couldn't yell anymore.

And finally when they set up a screen test, he fervently told the audience that the Russian government was the most terrifying empire the world had ever known, because this time they were efficient at keeping their power, because this time there was no outside for barbarians to come from, and because they had seduced the freest people in history into loving slavery. His speech was from the heart—he loathed the Russians and loved the memory that once there had been freedom and law and a measure of justice in America.

And the prosecutor came into the room ashen-faced.

"You bastard," he said.

"Oh. You mean the audience was live this time?"

"A hundred loyal citizens. And you corrupted all but three of them."

"Corrupted?"

"Convinced them."

Silence for a moment, and then the prosecutor sat down and buried his head in his hands.

"Going to lose your job?" Jerry asked.

"Of course."

"I'm sorry. You're good at it."

The prosecutor looked at him with loathing. "No one ever failed at this before. And I had never had to take anyone beyond a second death. You've died a dozen times, Crove, and you've got used to it."

"I didn't mean to."

"How did you do it?"

"I don't know."

"What kind of animal are you, Crove? Can't you make up a lie and *believe* it?"

Crove chuckled. (In the old days, at this level of amusement he would have laughed uproariously. But inured to death or not, he had scars. And he would never laugh loudly again.) "It was my business. As a playwright. The willing suspension of disbelief."

The door opened and a very important-looking man in a military uniform covered with medals came in, followed by four Russian soldiers. The prosecutor sighed and stood up. "Good-bye, Crove."

"Good-bye," Jerry said.

"You're a very strong man."

"So," said Jerry, "are you." And the prosecutor left.

The soldiers took Jerry out of the prison to a different place entirely. A large complex of buildings in Florida. Cape Canaveral. They were exiling him, Jerry realized.

"What's it like?" he asked the technician who was preparing him for the flight.

"Who knows?" the technician asked. "No one's ever come back. Hell, no one's ever arrived yet."

"After I sleep on somec, will I have any trouble waking up?"

"In the labs, here on earth, no. Out there, who knows?"

"But you think we'll live?"

"We send you to planets that look like they might be habitable. If they aren't, so sorry. You take your chances. The worst that can happen is you die."

"Is that all?" Jerry murmured.

"Now lie down and let me tape your brain."

Jerry lay down and the helmet, once again, recorded his thoughts. It was irresistible, of course: when you are conscious that your thoughts are being taped, Jerry realized, it is impossible not to try to think something important. As if you were performing. Only the audience would consist of just one person. Yourself when you woke up.

But he thought this: That this starship and the others that would be and had been sent out to colonize in prison worlds were not really what the Russians thought they were. True, the prisoners sent in the Gulag ships would be away from earth for centuries before they landed, and many or most of them would not survive. But some would survive.

I will survive, Jerry thought as the helmet picked up his brain pattern and transferred it to tape.

Out there the Russians are creating their own barbarians. I will be Attila the Hun. My child will be Mohammed. My grandchild will be Genghis Khan.

One of us, someday, will sack Rome.

Then the somec was injected, and it swept through him, taking consciousness with it, and Jerry realized with a shock of recognition that this, too, was death: but a welcome death, and he didn't mind. Because this time when he woke up he would be free.

He hummed cheerfully until he couldn't remember how to hum, and then they put his body with hundreds of others on a starship and pushed them all out into space, where they fell upward endlessly into the stars. Going home.

Clap Hands and Sing

On the screen the crippled man screamed at the lady, insisting that she must not run away. He waved a certificate. "I'm a registered rapist, dammit!" he cried. "Don't run so fast! You have to make allowances for the handicapped!" He ran after her with an odd, left-heavy lope. His enormous prosthetic phallus swung crazily, like a clumsy propeller that couldn't quite get started. The audience laughed madly. Must be a funny, funny scene!

Old Charlie sat slumped in his chair, feeling as casual and permanent as glacial debris. *I am here only by accident, but I'll never move.* He did not switch off the television set. The audience roared again with laughter. Canned or live? After more than eight decades of watching television, Charlie couldn't tell anymore. Not that the canned laughter had got any more real: It was the real laughter that had gone tinny, premeditated. As if the laughs were timed to come *now*, now matter what, and the poor actors could strain to get off their gags in time, but always they were just *this* much early, *that* much late.

"It's late," the television said, and Charlie started awake, vaguely surprised to see that the program had changed: Now it was a demonstration of a convenient electric breast pump to store up natural mother's milk for those times when you just can't be with baby. "It's late."

"Hello, Jock," Charlie said.

"Don't sleep in front of the television again, Charlie."

"Leave me alone, swine," Charlie said. And then: "Okay, turn it off."

He hadn't finished giving the order when the television flickered and went white, then settled down into its perpetual springtime scene that meant *off*. But in the flicker Charlie thought he saw—who? Name? From the distant past. A girl. Before the name came to him, there came another memory: a small hand resting lightly on his knee as they sat together, as light as a long-legged fly upon a stream. In his memory he did not turn to look at her; he was talking to others. But he knew just where she would be if he turned to look. Small, with mousy hair, and yet a face that was always the child Juliet. But that was not her name. Not Juliet, though she was Juliet's age in that memory. *I am Charlie*, he thought. *She is—Rachel*.

Rachel Carpenter. In the flicker on the screen hers was the face the random light had brought him, and so he remembered Rachel as he pulled his ancient body from the chair; thought of Rachel as he peeled the clothing from his frail skeleton, delicately, lest some rough motion strip away the wrinkled skin like cellophane.

And Jock, who of course did not switch himself off with the television, recited:

"An aged man is a paltry thing, a tattered coat upon a stick."

"Shut up," Charlie ordered.

"Unless Soul clap its hands."

"I said shut up!"

"And sing, and louder sing, for every tatter in its mortal dress."

"Are you finished?" Charlie asked. He knew Jock was finished. After all, Charlie had programmed him to recite—*it* to recite—just that fragment every night when his shorts hit the floor.

He stood naked in the middle of the room and thought of Rachel, whom he had not thought of in years. It was a trick of being old, that the room he was in now so easily vanished, and in its place a memory could take hold. *I've made my fortune from time machines*, he thought, *and now I discover that every aged person is his own time machine*. For now he stood naked. No, that was a trick of memory; memory had these damnable tricks. He was not naked. He only felt naked, as Rachel sat in the car beside him. Her voice—he had almost forgotten her voice—was soft. Even when she shouted, it got more whispery, so that if she shouted, it would have all the wind of the world in it and he wouldn't hear it at all, would only feel it cold on his naked skin. That was the voice she was using now, saying yes. I loved you when I was twelve, and when I was thirteen, and when I was fourteen, but when you got back from playing God in São Paulo, you didn't call me. All those letters, and then for three months you didn't call me and I knew that you thought I was just a child and I fell in love with—Name? Name gone. Fell in love with a *boy*, and ever since then you've been treating me like. Like. No, she'd never say *shit*, not in that voice. And take some of the anger out, that's right. Here are the words . . . here they come: You could have had me, Charlie, but

305

now all you can do is try to make me miserable. It's too late, the time's gone by, the time's over, so stop criticizing me. Leave me *alone*.

First to last, all in a capsule. The words are nothing, Charlie realized. A dozen women, not least his dear departed wife, had said exactly the same words to him since, and it had sounded just as maudlin, just as unpleasantly uninteresting every time. The difference was that when the others said it, Charlie felt himself insulated with a thousand layers of unconcern. But when Rachel said it to his memory, he stood naked in the middle of his room, a cold wind drying the parchment of his ancient skin.

"What's wrong?" asked Jock.

Oh, yes, dear computer, a change in the routine of the habitbound old man, and you suspect what, a heart attack? Incipient death? Extreme disorientation?

"A name," Charlie said. "Rachel Carpenter."

"Living or dead?"

Charlie winced again, as he winced every time Jock asked that question; yet it was an important one, and far too often the answer these days was Dead. "I don't know."

"Living and dead, I have two thousand four hundred eighty in the company archives alone."

"She was twelve when I was—twenty. Yes, twenty. And she lived then in Provo, Utah. Her father was a pianist. Maybe she became an actress when she grew up. She wanted to."

"Rachel Carpenter. Born 1959. Provo, Utah. Attended—"

"Don't show off, Jock. Was she ever married?"

"Thrice."

306

"And don't imitate my mannerisms. Is she still alive?"

"Died ten years ago."

Of course. Dead, of course. He tried to imagine her—where? "Where did she die?"

"Not pleasant."

"Tell me anyway. I'm feeling suicidal tonight."

"In a home for the mentally incapable."

It was not shocking; people often outlived their minds these days. But sad. For she had always been bright. Strange perhaps, but her thoughts always led to something worth the sometimes-convoluted path. He smiled even before he remembered what he was smiling at. Yes. Seeing through your knees. She had been playing Helen Keller in *The Miracle Worker*, and she told him how she had finally come to understand blindness. "It isn't seeing the red insides of your eyelids, I knew that. I knew it isn't even seeing black. It's like trying to see where you never had eyes at all. Seeing through your knees. No matter how hard you try, there just isn't any *vision* there." And she had liked him because he hadn't laughed. "I told my brother, and he laughed," she said. But Charlie had not laughed.

Charlie's affection for her had begun then, with a twelve-year-old girl who could never stay on the normal, intelligible track, but rather had to stumble her own way through a confusing underbrush that was thick and bright with flowers. "I think God stopped paying attention long ago," she said. "Any more than Michelangelo would want to watch them whitewash the Sistine Chapel."

And he knew that he would do it even before he knew what it was that he would do. She had ended in an institution, and he, with the best medical care that money could buy, stood naked in his room and remembered when passion still lurked behind the lattices of chastity and was more likely to lead to poems than to coitus.

You overtold story, he said to the wizened man who despised him from the mirror. You are only tempted because you're bored. Making excuses because you're cruel. Lustful because your dim old dong is long past the exercise.

And he heard the old bastard answer silently, You *will* do it, because you can. Of all the people in the world, *you* can.

And he thought he saw Rachel look back at him, bright with finding herself beautiful at fourteen, laughing at the vast joke of knowing she was admired by the very man who she, too, wanted. Laugh all you like, Charlie said to his vision of her. I was too kind to you then. I'm afraid I'll undo my youthful goodness now.

"I'm going back," he said aloud. "Find me a day."

"For what purpose?" Jock asked.

"My business."

"I have to know your purpose, or how can I find you a day?"

And so he had to name it. "I'm going to have her if I can."

Suddenly a small alarm sounded, and Jock's voice was replaced by another. "Warning. Illegal use of THIEF for possible present-altering manipulation of the past."

Charlie smiled. "Investigation has found that the alteration is acceptable. Clear." And the program release: "Byzantium."

"You're a son of a bitch," said Jock.

"Find me a day. A day when the damage will be least—when I can . . ."

"Twenty-eight October 1973."

That was after he got home from São Paulo, the contracts signed, already a capitalist before he was twenty-three. That was during the time when he had been afraid to call her, because she was only fourteen, for God's sake.

"What will it do to her, Jock?"

"How should I know?" Jock answered. "And what difference would it make to you?"

He looked in the mirror again. "A difference."

I won't do it, he told himself as he went to the THIEF that was his most ostentatious sign of wealth, a private THIEF in his own rooms. I won't do it, he decided again as he set the machine to wake him in twelve hours, whether he wished to return or not. Then he climbed into the couch and pulled the shroud over his head, despairing that even this, even doing it to *her*, was not beneath him. There was a time when he had automatically held back from doing a thing because he knew that it was wrong. *Oh, for that time!* he thought, but knew as he thought it that he was lying to himself. He had long since given up on right and wrong and settled for the much simpler standards of effective and ineffective, beneficial and detrimental.

He had gone in a THIEF before, had taken some of the standard trips into the past. Gone into the mind of an audience member at the first performance of Handel's *Messiah* and listened. The poor soul whose ears he used wouldn't remember a bit of it afterward. So the future would not be changed. That was safe, to sit in a hall and listen. He had been in the mind of a farmer resting under a tree

309

on a country lane as Wordsworth walked by and had hailed the poet and asked his name, and Wordsworth had smiled and been distant and cold, delighting in the countryside more than in those whose tillage made it beautiful. But those were legal trips— Charlie had done nothing that could alter the course of history.

This time, though. This time he would change Rachel's life. Not his own, of course. That would be impossible. But Rachel would not be blocked from remembering what happened. She would remember, and it would turn her from the path she was meant to take. Perhaps only a little. Perhaps not importantly. Perhaps just enough for her to dislike him a little sooner, or a little more. But too much to be legal, if he were caught.

He would not be caught. Not Charlie. Not the man who owned THIEF and therefore could have owned the world. It was all too bound up in secrecy. Too many agents had used his machines to attend the enemy's most private conferences. Too often the Attorney General had listened to the most perfect of wiretaps. Too often politicians who were willing to be in Charlie's debt had been given permission to lead their opponents into blunders that cost them votes. All far beyond what the law allowed; who would dare complain now if Charlie also bent the law to his own purpose?

No one but Charlie. *I can't do this to Rachel*, he thought. And then the THIEF carried him back and put him in his own mind, in his own body, on 28 October 1973, at ten o'clock, just as he was going to bed, weary because he had been wakened that morning by a six A.M. call from Brazil.

As always, there was the moment of resistance,

and then peace as his self of that time slipped into unconsciousness. Old Charlie took over and saw, not the past, but the now.

A moment before, he was standing before a mirror, looking at his withered, hanging face; now he realizes that this gazing into a mirror before going to bed is a lifelong habit. *I am Narcissus*, he tells himself, *an unbeautiful idolator at my own shrine*. But now he is not unbeautiful. At twenty-two, his body still has the depth of young skin. His belly is soft, for he is not athletic, but still there is a litheness to him that he will never have again. And now the vaguely remembered needs that had impelled him to this find a physical basis; what had been a dim memory has him on fire.

He will not be sleeping tonight, not soon. He dresses again, finding with surprise the quaint print shirts that once had been in style. The wide-cuffed pants. The shoes with inch-and-a-half heels. *Good God, I wore that!* he thinks, and then wears it. No questions from his family; he goes quietly downstairs and out to his car. The garage reeks of gasoline. It is a smell as nostalgic as lilacs and candlewax.

He still knows the way to Rachel's house, though he is surprised at the buildings that have not yet been built, which roads have not yet been paved, which intersections still don't have the lights he knows they'll have soon, should surely have already. He looks at his wristwatch; it must be a habit of the body he is in, for he hasn't worn a wristwatch in decades. The arm is tanned from Brazilian beaches, and it has no age spots, no purple veins drawing roadmaps under the skin. The time is ten-thirty. *She'll doubtless be in bed*.

He almost stops himself. Few things are left in his private catalog of sin, but surely this is one. He looks into himself and tries to find the will to resist his own desire solely because its fulfillment will hurt another person. He is out of practice—so far out of practice that he keeps losing track of the reason for resisting.

The lights are on, and her mother—Mrs. Carpenter, dowdy and delightful, scatterbrained in the most attractive way—her mother opens the door suspiciously until she recognizes him. "Charlie," she cries out.

"Is Rachel still up?"

"Give me a minute and she will be!"

And he waits, his stomach trembling with anticipation. *I am not a virgin*, he reminds himself, *but this body does not know that*. This body is alert, for it has not yet formed the habits of meaningless passion that Charlie knows far too well. At last she comes down the stairs. He hears her running on the hollow wooden steps, then stopping, coming slowly, denying the hurry. She turns the corner, looks at him.

She is in her bathrobe, a faded thing that he does not remember ever having seen her wear. Her hair is tousled, and her eyes show that she had been asleep.

"I didn't mean to wake you."

"I wasn't really asleep. The first ten minutes don't count anyway."

He smiles. Tears come to his eyes. Yes, he says silently. This is Rachel, yes. The narrow face; the skin so translucent that he can see into it like jade; the slender arms that gesture shyly, with accidental grace.

"I couldn't wait to see you."

"You've been home three days. I thought you'd phone."

He smiles. In fact he will not phone her for months. But he says, "I hate the telephone. I want to talk to you. Can you come out for a drive?"

"I have to ask my mother."

"She'll say yes."

She does say yes. She jokes and says that she trusts Charlie. And the Charlie she knows was trustworthy. *But not me*, Charlie thinks. You are putting your diamonds into the hands of a thief.

"Is it cold?" Rachel asks.

"Not in the car." And so she doesn't take a coat. It's all right. The night breeze isn't bad.

As soon as the door closes behind them, Charlie begins. He puts his arm around her waist. She does not pull away or take it with indifference. He has never done this before, because she's only fourteen, just a child, but she leans against him as they walk, as if she had done this a hundred times before. As always, she takes him by surprise.

"I've missed you," he says.

She smiled, and there are tears in her eyes. "I've missed you, too," she says.

They talk of nothing. It's just as well. Charlie does not remember much about the trip to Brazil, does not remember anything of what he's done in the three days since getting back. No problem, for she seems to want to talk only of tonight. They drive to the Castle, and he tells her its history. He feels an irony about it as he explains. She, after all, is the reason he knows the history. A few years from now she will be part of a theater company that revives the Castle as a public amphitheater. But now it is falling into ruin, a monument to the old WPA, a great castle with turrets and benches made of native stone. It is on the property of the state mental hospital, and so hardly anyone knows it's there. They are alone as they leave the car and walk up the crumbling steps to the flagstone stage.

She is entranced. She stands in the middle of the stage, facing the benches. He watches as she raises her hand, speech waiting at the verge of her lips. He remembers something. Yes, that is the gesture she made when she bade her nurse farewell in *Romeo and Juliet*. No, not *made*. Will make, rather. The gesture must already be in her, waiting for this stage to draw it out.

She turns to him and smiles because the place is strange and odd and does not belong in Provo, but it does belong to her. She should have been born in the Renaissance, Charlie says softly. She hears him. He must have spoken aloud. "You belong in an age when music was clean and soft and there was no makeup. No one would rival you then."

She only smiles at the conceit. "I missed you," she says.

He touches her cheek. She does not shy away. Her cheek presses into his hand, and he knows that she understands why he brought her here and what he means to do.

Her breasts are perfect but small, her buttocks are boyish and slender, and the only hair on her body is that which tumbles onto her shoulders, that which he must brush out of her face to kiss her again. "I love you," she whispers. "All my life I love you."

And it is exactly as he would have had it in a dream, except that the flesh is tangible, the ecstasy is real, and the breeze turns colder as she shyly dresses again. They say nothing more as he takes her home. Her mother has fallen asleep on the living room couch, a jumble of the *Daily Herald* piled around her feet. Only then does he remember that for her there will be a tomorrow, and on that tomorrow Charlie will not call. For three months Charlie will not call, and she'll hate him.

He tries to soften it. He tries by saying, "Some things can happen only once." It is the sort of thing he might then have said. But she only puts her finger on his lips and says, "I'll never forget." Then she turns and walks toward her mother, to waken her. She turns and motions for Charlie to leave, then smiles again and waves. He waves back and goes out of the door and drives home. He lies awake in this bed that feels like childhood to him, and he wishes it could have gone on forever like this. *It should have gone on like this*, he thinks. *She is no child. She* was *no child*, he should have thought, for THIEF was already transporting him home.

"What's wrong, Charlie?" Jock asked.

Charlie awoke. It had been hours since THIEF brought him back. It was the middle of the night, and Charlie realized that he had been crying in his sleep. "Nothing," he said.

"You're crying, Charlie. I've never seen you cry before."

"Go plug into a million volts, Jock. I had a dream."

"What dream?"

"I destroyed her."

"No, you didn't."

"It was a goddamned selfish thing to do."

"You'd do it again. But it didn't hurt her."

315

"She was only fourteen."

"No, she wasn't."

"I'm tired. I was asleep. Leave me alone."

"Charlie, remorse isn't your style."

Charlie pulled the blanket over his head, feeling petulant and wondering whether this childish act was another proof that he was retreating into senility after all.

"Charlie, let me tell you a bedtime story."

"I'll erase you."

"Once upon a time, ten years ago, an old woman named Rachel Carpenter petitioned for a day in her past. And it was a day *with* someone, and it was a day with *you*. So the routine circuits called me, as they always do when your name comes up, and I found her a day. She only wanted to visit, you see, only wanted to relive a good day. I was surprised, Charlie. I didn't know you ever had good days."

This program had been with Jock too long. It knew too well how to get under his skin.

"And in fact there were no days as good as she thought," Jock continued. "Only anticipation and disappointment. That's all you ever gave anybody, Charlie. Anticipation and disappointment."

"I can count on you."

"This woman was in a home for the mentally incapable. And so I gave her a day. Only instead of a day of disappointment, or promises she knew would never be fulfilled, I gave her a day of answers. I gave her a night of answers, Charlie."

"You couldn't know that I'd have you do this. You couldn't have known it ten years ago."

"That's all right, Charlie. Play along with me. You're dreaming anyway, aren't you?"

"And don't wake me up."

"So an old woman went back into a young girl's body on twenty-eight October 1973, and the young girl never knew what had happened; so it didn't change her life, don't you see?"

"It's a lie."

"No, it isn't. I can't lie, Charlie. You programmed me not to lie. Do you think I would have let you go back and *harm* her?"

"She was the same. She was as I remembered her."

"Her body was."

"She hadn't changed. She wasn't an old woman, Jock. She was a girl. She was a girl, Jock."

And Charlie thought of an old woman dying in an institution, surrounded by yellow walls and pale gray sheets and curtains. He imagined young Rachel inside that withered form, imprisoned in a body that would not move, trapped in a mind that could never again take her along her bright, mysterious trails.

"I flashed her picture on the television," Jock said.

And yet, Charlie thought, *how is it less bearable than that beautiful boy who wanted so badly to do the right thing that he did it all wrong, lost his chance, and now is caught in the sum of all his wrong turns? I got on the road they all wanted to take, and I reached the top, but it wasn't where I should have gone. I'm still that boy. I did not have to lie when I went home to her.*

"I know you pretty well, Charlie," Jock said. "I knew that you'd be enough of a bastard to go back. And enough of a human being to do it right when you got there. She came back happy. Charlie. She came back satisfied."

His night with a beloved child was a lie then; it

wasn't young Rachel any more than it was young Charlie. He looked for anger inside himself but couldn't find it. For a dead woman had given him a gift, and taken the one he offered, and it still tasted sweet.

"Time for sleep, Charlie. Go to sleep again. I just wanted you to know that there's no reason to feel any remorse for it. No reason to feel anything bad at all."

Charlie pulled the covers tight around his neck, unaware that he had begun that habit years ago, when the strange shadowy shapes hid in his closet and only the blanket could keep him safe. Pulled the covers high and tight, and closed his eyes, and felt her hand stroke him, felt her breast and hip and thigh, and heard her voice as breath against his cheek.

"O chestnut tree," Jock said, as he had been taught to say, ". . . great rooted blossomer,

"Are you the leaf, the blossom, or the bole?

"O body swayed to music, O brightening glance,

"How can we know the dancer from the dance?"

The audience applauded in his mind while he slipped into sleep, and he thought it remarkable that they sounded genuine. He pictured them smiling and nodding at the show. Smiling at the girl with her hand raised so; nodding at the man who paused forever, then came on stage.

Dogwalker

I was an innocent pedestrian. Only reason I got in this in the first place was I got a vertical way of thinking and Dogwalker thought I might be useful, which was true, and also he said I might enjoy myself, which was a prefabrication, since people done a lot more enjoying on me than I done on them.

When I say I think vertical, I mean to say I'm metaphysical, that is, simular, which is to say, I'm dead but my brain don't know it yet and my feet still move. I got popped at age nine just lying in my own bed when the goat next door shot at his lady and it went through the wall and into my head. Everybody went to look at them cause they made all the noise, so I was a quart low before anybody noticed I been poked.

They packed my head with supergoo and light pipe, but they didn't know which neutron was supposed to butt into the next so my alchemical brain got turned from rust to diamond. Goo Boy. The Crystal Kid.

From that bright electrical day I never grew another inch, anywhere. Bullet went nowhere near my gonadicals. Just turned off the puberty switch in my head. Saint Paul said he was a eunuch for Jesus, but who am I a eunuch for?

Worst thing about it is here I am near thirty and I still have to take barkeepers to court before they'll sell me beer. And it ain't hardly worth it even though the judge prints out in my favor and the barkeep pays the costs, because my corpse is so little I get toxed on six ounces and pass out pissing after twelve. I'm a lousy drinking buddy. Besides, anybody hangs out with me looks like a pederast.

No, I'm not trying to make you drippy-drop for me—I'm used to it, OK? Maybe the homecoming queen never showed me True Love in a four-point spread, but I got this knack that certain people find real handy and so I always made out. I dress good and I ride the worm and I don't pay much income tax. Because I am the Password Man. Give me five minutes with anybody's curriculum vitae, which is to say their autopsychoscopy, and nine times out of ten I'll spit out their password and get you into their most nasty sticky sweet secret files. Actually it's usually more like three times out of ten, but that's still a lot better odds than having a computer spend a year trying to push out fifteen characters to make just the right P-word, specially since after the third wrong try they string your phone number, freeze the target files, and call the dongs.

Oh, do I make you sick? A cute little boy like me, engaged in critical unspecified dispopulative behaviors? I may be half glass and four feet high, but I can simulate you better than your own mama, and the better I know you, the deeper my hooks. I not only know your password *now*, I can write a word on paper, seal it up, and then you go home and *change* your password and then open up what I

320

wrote and there it'll be, your *new* password, three times out of ten. I am *vertical*, and Dogwalker knowed it. Ten percent more supergoo and I wouldn't even be legally human, but I'm still under the line, which is more than I can say for a lot of people who are a hundred percent zoo inside their head.

Dogwalker comes to me one day at Carolina Circle, where I'm playing pinball standing on a stool. He didn't say nothing, just gave me a shove, so naturally he got my elbow in his balls. I get a lot of twelve-year-olds trying to shove me around at the arcades, so I'm used to teaching them lessons. Jack the Giant Killer. Hero of the fourth graders. I usually go for the stomach, only Dogwalker wasn't a twelve-year-old, so my elbow hit low.

I knew the second I hit him that this wasn't no kid. I didn't know Dogwalker from God, but he gots the look, you know, like he been hungry before, and he don't care what he eats these days.

Only he got no ice and he got no slice, just sits there on the floor with his back up against the Eat Shi'ite game, holding his boodle and looking at me like I was a baby he had to diaper. "I hope you're Goo Boy," he says, "cause if you ain't, I'm gonna give you back to your mama in three little tupperware bowls." He doesn't sound like he's making a threat, though. He sounds like he's chief weeper at his own funeral.

"You want to do business, use your mouth, not your hands," I says. Only I say it real apoplectic, which is the same as apologetic except you are also still pissed.

"Come with me," he says. "I got to go buy me a truss. You pay the tax out of your allowance."

321

So we went to Ivey's and stood around in children's wear while he made his pitch. "One P-word," he says, "only there can't be no mistake. If there's a mistake, a guy loses his job and maybe goes to jail."

So I told him no. Three chances in ten, that's the best I can do. No guarantees. My record speaks for itself, but nobody's perfect, and I ain't even close.

"Come on," he says, "you got to have ways to make sure, right? If you can do three times out of ten, what if you find out more about the guy? What if you meet him?"

"OK, maybe fifty-fifty."

"Look, we can't go back for seconds. So maybe you can't get it. But you do *know* when you ain't got it?"

"Maybe half the time when I'm wrong, I know I'm wrong."

"So we got three out of four that you'll know whether you got it?"

"No," says I. "Cause half the time when I'm right, I don't know I'm right."

"Shee-it," he says. "This is like doing business with my baby brother."

"You can't afford me anyway," I says. "I pull two dimes minimum, and you barely got breakfast on your gold card."

"I'm offering a cut."

"I don't want a cut. I want cash."

"Sure thing," he says. He looks around, real careful. As if they wired the sign that say Boys Briefs Sizes 10–12. "I got an inside man at Federal Coding," he says.

"That's nothing," I says. "I got a bug up the First

322

Lady's ass, and forty hours on tape of her breaking wind."

I got a mouth. I know I got a mouth. I especially know it when he jams my face into a pile of shorts and says, "Suck on this, Goo Boy."

I hate it when people push me around. And I know ways to make them stop. This time all I had to do was cry. Real loud, like he was hurting me. Everybody looks when a kid starts crying. "I'll be good." I kept saying it. "Don't hurt me no more! I'll be good."

"Shut up," he says. "Everybody's looking."

"Don't you ever shove me around again," I says. "I'm at least ten years older than you, and a hell of a lot more than ten years smarter. Now I'm leaving this store, and if I see you coming after me, I'll start screaming about how you zipped down and showed me the pope, and you'll get yourself a child-molesting tag so they pick you up every time some kid gets jollied within a hundred miles of Greensboro." I've done it before, and it works, and Dogwalker was no dummy. Last thing he needed was extra reasons for the dongs to bring him in for questioning. So I figured he'd tell me to get poked and that'd be the last of it.

Instead he says, "Goo Boy, I'm sorry, I'm too quick with my hands."

Even the goat who shot me never said he was sorry. My first thought was, what kind of sister is he, abjectifying right out like that. Then I reckoned I'd stick around and see what kind of man it is who emulsifies himself in front of a nine-year-old-looking kid. Not that I figured him to be purely sorrowful. He still wanted me to get the P-word for him, and he knew there wasn't nobody else to do it. But most street pugs aren't smart enough to tell the right lie under pressure. Right away I knew he wasn't your ordinary street hook or low arm, pugging cause they don't have the sense to stick with any kind of job. He had a deep face, which is to say his head was more than a hairball, by which I mean he had brains enough to put his hands in his pockets without seeking an audience with the pope. Right then was when I decided he was my kind of no-good lying son-of-a-bitch.

"What are you after at Federal Coding?" I asked him. "A record wipe?"

"Ten clear greens," he says. "Coded for unlimited international travel. The whole ID, just like a real person."

"The President has a green card," I says. "The Joint Chiefs have clean greens. But that's all. The U.S. Vice-President isn't even cleared for unlimited international travel."

"Yes he is," he says.

"Oh, yeah, you know everything."

"I need a P. My guy could do us reds and blues, but a clean green has to be done by a burr-oak rat two levels up. My guy knows how it's done."

"They won't just have it with a P-word," I says. "A guy who can make green cards, they're going to have his finger on it."

"I know how to get the finger," he says. "It takes the finger *and* the password."

"You take a guy's finger, he might report it. And even if you persuade him not to, somebody's gonna notice that it's gone."

"Latex," he says. "We'll get a mould. And don't start telling me how to do my part of the job. You get the P-words, I get fingers. You in?"

"Cash," I says.

"Twenty percent," says he.

"Twenty percent of pus."

"The inside guy gets twenty, the girl who brings me the finger, she gets twenty, and I damn well get forty."

"You can't just sell these things on the street, you know."

"They're worth a meg apiece," says he, "to certain buyers." By which he meant Orkish Crime, of course. Sell ten, and my twenty percent grows up to be two megs. Not enough to be rich, but enough to retire from public life and maybe even pay for some high-level medicals to sprout hair on my face. I got to admit that sounded good to me.

So we went into business. For a few hours he tried to do it without telling me the baroque rat's name, just giving me data he got from his guy at Federal Coding. But that was real stupid, giving me second-hand face like that, considering he needed me to be a hundred percent sure, and pretty soon he realized that and brought me in all the way. He hated telling me anything, because he couldn't stand to let go. Once I knew stuff on my own, what was to stop me from trying to go into business for myself? But unless he had another way to get the P-word, he had to get it from me, and for me to do it right, I had to know everything I could. Dogwalker's got a brain in his head, even if it is all biodegradable, and so he knows there's times when you got no choice but to trust somebody. When you just got to figure they'll do their best even when they're out of your sight.

He took me to his cheap condo on the old Guilford College campus, near the worm, which was real congenital for getting to Charlott or Winston or

325

Raleigh with no fuss. He didn't have no soft floor, just a bed, but it was a big one, so I didn't reckon he suffered. Maybe he bought it back in his old pimping days, I figured, back when he got his name, running a string of bitches with names like Spike and Bowser and Prince, real hydrant leg-lifters for the tweeze trade. I could see that he used to have money, and he didn't anymore. Lots of great clothes, tailor-tight fit, but shabby, out of sync. The really old ones, he tore all the wiring out, but you could still see where the diodes used to light up. We're talking neanderthal.

"Vanity, vanity, all is profanity," says I, while I'm holding out the sleeve of a camisa that used to light up like an airplane coming in for a landing.

"They're too comfortable to get rid of," he says. But there's a twist in his voice so I know he don't plan to fool nobody.

"Let this be a lesson to you," says I. "This is what happens when a walker don't walk."

"Walkers do steady work," says he. "But me, when business was good, it felt bad, and when business was bad, it felt good. You walk cats, maybe you can take some pride in it. But you walk dogs, and you know they're getting hurt every time—"

"They got built-in switch, they don't feel a thing. That's why the dongs don't touch you, walking dogs, cause nobody gets hurt."

"Yeah, so tell me, which is worse, somebody getting tweezed till they scream so some old honk can pop his pimple, or somebody getting half their brain replaced so when the old honk tweezes her she can't feel a thing? I had these women's bodies around me and I knew that they used to be people."

"You can be glass," say I, "and still be people."

326

He saw I was taking it personally. "Oh hey," says he, "you're under the line."

"So are dogs," says I.

"Yeah well," says he. "You watch a girl come back and tell about some of the things they done to her, and she's *laughing*, you draw your own line."

I look around his shabby place. "Your choice," says I.

"I wanted to feel clean," says he. "That don't mean I got to stay poor."

"So you're setting up this grope so you can return to the old days of peace and prosperity."

"Prosperity," says he. "What the hell kind of word is that? Why do you keep using words like that?"

"Cause I know them," says I.

"Well you *don't* know them," says he, "because half the time you get them wrong."

I showed him my best little-boy grin. "I know," says I. What I don't tell him is that the fun comes from the fact that almost nobody ever *knows* I'm using them wrong. Dogwalker's no ordinary pimp. But then the ordinary pimp doesn't bench himself halfway through the game because of a sprained moral qualm, by which I mean that Dogwalker had some stray diagonals in his head, and I began to think it might be fun to see where they all hooked up.

Anyway we got down to business. The target's name was Jesse H. Hunt, and I did a real job on him. The Crystal Kid really plugged in on this one. Dogwalker had about two pages of stuff—date of birth, place of birth, sex at birth (no changes since), education, employment history. It was like getting an armload of empty boxes. I just laughed at it.

"You got a jack to the city library?" I asked him, and he shows me the wall outlet. I plugged right in, visual onto my pocket sony, with my own little crystal head for ee-i-ee-i-oh. Not every goo-head can think clear enough to do this, you know, put out clean type just by thinking the right stuff out my left ear interface port.

I showed Dogwalker a little bit about research. Took me ten minutes. I know my way right through the Greensboro Public Library. I have P-words for every single librarian and I'm so ept that they don't even guess I'm stepping upstream through their access channels. From the Public Library you can get all the way into North Carolina Records Division in Raleigh, and from there you can jumble into federal personnel records anywhere in the country. Which meant that by nightfall on that most portentous day we had hardcopy of every document in Jesse H. Hunt's whole life, from his birth certificate and first grade report card to his medical history and security clearance reports when he first worked for the feds.

Dogwalker knew enough to be impressed. "If you can do all that," he says, "you might as well put his P-word straight out."

"No puedo, putz," says I as cheerful as can be. "Think of the fed as a castle. Personnel files are floating in the moat—there's a few alligators but I swim real good. Hot data is deep in the dungeon. You can get in there, but you can't get out clean. And P-words—P-words are kept up the queen's ass."

"No system is unbeatable," he says.

"Where'd you learn that, from graffiti in a toilet stall? If the P-word system was even a little bit breakable, Dogwalker, the gentlemen you plan to sell these cards to would already be inside looking out at us, and they wouldn't need to spend a meg to get clean greens from a street pug."

Trouble was that after impressing Dogwalker with all the stuff I could find out about Jesse H., I didn't know that much more than before. Oh, I could guess at some P-words, but that was all it was—guessing. I couldn't even pick a P most likely to succeed. Jesse was one ordinary dull rat. Regulation good grades in school, regulation good evaluations on the job, probably gave his wife regulation lube jobs on a weekly schedule.

"You don't really think your girl's going to get his finger," says I with sickening scorn.

"You don't know the girl," says he. "If we needed his flipper she'd get molds in five sizes."

"You don't know this guy," says I. "This is the straightest opie in Mayberry. I don't see him cheating on his wife."

"Trust me," says Dogwalker. "She'll get his finger so smooth he won't even know she took the mold."

I didn't believe him. I got a knack for knowing things about people, and Jesse H. wasn't faking. Unless he started faking when he was five, which is pretty unpopulated. He wasn't going to bounce the first pretty girl who made his zipper tight. Besides which he was smart. His career path showed that he was always in the right place. The right people always seemed to know his name. Which is to say he isn't the kind whose brain can't run if his jeans get hot. I said so.

"You're really a marching band," says Dogwalker. "You can't tell me his P-word, but you're obliquely sure that he's a limp or a wimp."

"Neither one," says I. "He's hard and straight. But a girl starts rubbing up to him, he isn't going to think it's because she heard that his crotch is cantilevered. He's going to figure she wants something, and he'll give her string till he finds out what."

He just grinned at me. "I got me the best Password Man in the Triass, didn't I? I got me a miracle worker named Goo-Boy, didn't I? The ice-brain they call Crystal Kid. I got him, didn't I?"

"Maybe," says I.

"I got him or kill him," he says, showing more teeth than a primate's supposed to have.

"You got me," says I. "But don't go thinking you can kill me."

He just laughs. "I got you and you're so good, you can bet I got me a girl who's at least as good at what she does."

"No such," says I.

"Tell me his P-word and then I'll be impressed."

"You want quick results? Then go ask him to give you his password himself."

Dogwalker isn't one of those guys who can hide it when he's mad. "I want quick results," he says. "And if I start thinking you can't deliver, I'll pull your tongue out of your head. Through your nose."

"Oh, that's good," says I. "I always do my best thinking when I'm being physically threatened by a client. You really know how to bring out the best in me."

"I don't want to bring out the best," he says. "I just want to bring out his password."

"I got to meet him first," says I.

He leans over me so I can smell his musk, which is to say I'm very olfactory and so I can tell you he reeked of testosterone, by which I mean ladies could

330

fill up with babies just from sniffing his sweat. "Meet him?" he asks me. "Why don't we just ask him to fill out a job application?"

"I've read all his job applications," says I.

"How's a glass-head like you going to meet Mr Fed?" says he. "I bet you're always getting invitations to the same parties as guys like him."

"I don't get invited to *grown-up* parties," says I. "But on the other hand, grown-ups don't pay much attention to sweet little kids like me."

He sighed. "You really have to meet him?"

"Unless fifty-fifty on a P-word is good enough odds for you."

All of a sudden he goes nova. Slaps a glass off the table and it breaks against the wall, and then he kicks the table over, and all the time I'm thinking about ways to get out of there unkilled. But it's me he's doing the show for, so there's no way I'm leaving, and he leans in close to me and screams in my face. "That's the last of your fifty-fifty and sixty-forty and three times in ten I want to hear about, Goo Boy, you hear me?"

And I'm talking real meek and sweet, cause this boy's twice my size and three times my weight and I don't exactly have no leverage. So I says to him, "I can't help talking in odds and percentages, Dogwalker, I'm vertical, remember? I've got glass channels in here, they spit out percentages as easy as other people sweat."

He slapped his hand against his own head. "This ain't exactly a sausage biscuit, either, but you know and I know that when you give me all them *ex*act numbers it's all guesswork anyhow. You don't know the odds on this beakrat anymore than I do."

"I don't know the odds on *him*, Walker, but I

331

know the odds on *me*. I'm sorry you don't like the way I sound so precise, but my crystal memory has every P-word I ever plumbed, which is to say I can give you exact to the third decimal percentages on when I hit it right on the first try after meeting the subject, and how many times I hit it right on the first try just from his curriculum vitae, and right now if I don't meet him and I go on just what I've got here you have a 48.838 percent chance I'll be right on my P-word first time and a 66.667 chance I'll be right with one out of three."

Well that took him down, which was fine I must say because he loosened up my sphincters with that glass-smashing table-tossing hot-breath-in-my-face routine he did. He stepped back and put his hands in his pockets and leaned against the wall. "Well I chose the right P-man, then, didn't I," he says, but he doesn't smile, no, he *says* the back-down words but his eyes don't back down, his eyes say don't try to flash my face because I see through you, I got most excellent inward shades all polarized to keep out your glitz and see you straight and clear. I never saw eyes like that before. Like he knew me. Nobody ever knew me, and I didn't think he *really* knew me either, but I didn't like him looking at me as if he *thought* he knew me cause the fact is *I* didn't know me all that well and it worried me to think he might know me better than I did, if you catch my drift.

"All I have to do is be a little lost boy in a store," I says.

"What if he isn't the kind who helps little lost boys?"

"Is he the kind who lets them cry?"

"I don't know. What if he is? What then? Think you can get away with meeting him a second time?"

"So the lost boy in the store won't work. I can crash my bicycle on his front lawn. I can try to sell him cable magazines."

But he was ahead of me already. "For the cable magazines he slams the door in your face, if he even comes to the door at all. For the bicycle crash, you're out of your little glass brain. I got my inside girl working on him right now, very complicated, because he's not the playing around kind, so she has to make this a real emotional come-on, like she's breaking up with a boyfriend and he's the only shoulder she can cry on, and his wife is so lucky to have a man like him. This much he can believe. But then suddenly he has this little boy crashing in his yard, and because he's paranoid, he begins to wonder if some weird rain isn't falling, right? I know he's paranoid because you don't get to his level in the fed without you know how to watch behind you and kill the enemy even before *they* know they're out to get you. So he even suspects, for one instant, that somebody's setting him up for something, and what does he do?"

I knew what Dogwalker was getting at now, and he was right, and so I let him have his victory and I let the words he wanted march out all in a row. "He changes all his passwords, all his habits, and watches over his shoulder all the time."

"And my little project turns into compost. No clean greens."

So I saw for the first time why this street boy, this ex-pimp, why he was the one to do this job. He wasn't vertical like me, and he didn't have the inside hook like his fed boy, and he didn't have bumps in his sweater so he couldn't do the girl part, but he had eyes in his elbows, ears in his knees, by which

I mean he noticed everything there was to notice and then he thought of new things that weren't even noticeable yet and noticed them. He earned his forty percent. And he earned part of my twenty, too.

Now while we waited around for the girl to fill Jesse's empty aching arms and get a finger off him, and while we were still working on how to get me to meet him slow and easy and sure, I spent a lot of time with Dogwalker. Not that he ever asked me, but I found myself looping his bus route every morning till he picked me up, or I'd be eating at Bojangle's when he came in to throw cajun chicken down into his ulcerated organs. I watched to make sure he didn't mind, cause I didn't want to piss the boy, having once beheld the majesty of his wrath, but if he wanted to shiver me he gave me no shiv.

Even after a few days, when the ghosts of the cold hard street started haunting us, he didn't shake me, and that includes when Bellbottom says to him, "Looks like you stopped walking dogs. Now you pimping little boys, right? Little catamites, we call you Catwalker now, that so? Or maybe you just keep him for private use, is that it? You be Boypoker now?" Well like I always said, someday somebody's going to kill Bellbottom just to flay him and use his skin for a convertible roof, but Dogwalker just waved and walked on by while I made little pissy bumps at Bell. Most people shake me right off when they start getting splashed on about liking little boys, but Doggy, he didn't say we were friends or nothing, but he didn't give me no Miami howdy, neither, which is to say I didn't find myself floating in the Bermuda Triangle with my ass pulled down around my ankles, by which I mean he wasn't ashamed to be seen with me on the street, which don't sound like a six-minute orgasm to you but to me it was like a breeze in August, I didn't ask for it and I don't trust it to last but as long as it's there I'm going to like it.

How I finally got to meet Jesse H. was dervish, the best I ever thought of. Which made me wonder why I never thought of it before, except that I never before had Dogwalker like a parrot saying "stupid idea" every time I thought of something. By the time I finally got a plan that he didn't say "stupid idea," I was almost drowned in the deepest light-holes of my lucidity. I mean I was going at a hundred watts by the time I satisfied him.

First we found out who did babysitting for them when Jesse H. and Mrs Jesse went out on the town (which for Nice People in G-boro means walking around the mall wishing there was something to do and then taking a piss in the public john). They had two regular teenage girls who usually came over and ignored their children for a fee, but when these darlettes were otherwise engaged, which meant they had a contract to get squeezed and poked by some half-zipped boy in exchange for a humbuger and a vid, they called upon Mother Hubbard's Homecare Hotline. So I most carefully assinuated myself into Mother Hubbard's estimable organization by passing myself off as a lamentably prepubic fourteen-year-old, specializing in the northwest section of town and on into the county. All this took a week, but Walker was in no hurry. Take the time to do it right, he said, if we hurry somebody's going to notice the blur of motion and look our way and just by looking at us they'll undo us. A horizontal mind that boy had.

Came a most delicious night when the Hunts went

335

out to play, and both their diddle-girls were busy being squeezed most delectably (and didn't we have a lovely time persuading two toddle-boys to do the squeezing that very night). This news came to Mr. and Mrs. Jesse at the very last minute, and they had no choice but to call Mother Hubbard's, and isn't it lovely that just a half hour before, sweet little Stevie Queen, being *moi*, called in and said that he was available for baby-stomping after all. Ein and ein made zwei, and there I was being dropped off by a Mother Hubbard driver at the door of the Jesse Hunt house, whereupon I not only got to look upon the beatific face of Mr. Fed himself, I also got to have my dear head patted by Mrs. Fed, and then had the privilege of preparing little snacks for fussy Fed Jr. and foul-mouthed Fedene, the five-year-old and the three-year-old, while Microfed, the one-year-old (not yet human and, if I am any judge of character, not likely to live long enough to become such) sprayed uric acid in my face while I was diapering him. A good time was had by all.

Because of my heroic efforts, the small creatures were in their truckle beds quite early, and being a most fastidious baby-tucker, I browsed the house looking for burglars and stumbling, quite by chance, upon the most useful information about the beak-rat whose secret self-chosen name I was trying to learn. For one thing, he had set a watchful hair upon each of his bureau drawers, so that if I had been inclined to steal, he would know that unlawful access of his drawers had been attempted. I learned that he and his wife had separate containers of everything in the bathroom, even when they used the same brand of toothpaste, and it was he, not she, who took care of all their prophylactic activities (and not

336

a moment too soon, thought I, for I had come to know their children). He was not the sort to use lubrificants or little pleasure-giving ribs, either. Only the regulation government-issue hard-as-concrete rubber rafts for him, which suggested to my most pernicious mind that he had almost as much fun between the sheets as me.

I learned all kinds of joyful information, all of it trivial, all of it vital. I never know which of the threads I grasp are going to make connections deep within the lumens of my brightest caves. But I never before had the chance to wander unmolested through a person's own house when searching for his P-word. I saw the notes his children brought home from school, the magazines his family received, and more and more I began to see that Jesse H. Hunt barely touched his family at any point. He stood like a waterbug on the surface of life, without ever getting his feet wet. He could die, and if nobody tripped over the corpse it would be weeks before they noticed. And yet this was not because he did not care. It was because he was so very very careful. He examined everything, but through the wrong end of the microscope, so that it all became very small and far away. I was a sad little boy by the end of that night, and I whispered to Microfed that he should practice pissing in male faces, because that's the only way he would ever sink a hook into his daddy's face.

"What if he wants to take you home?" Dogwalker asked me, and I said, "No way he would, nobody does that," but Dogwalker made sure I had a place to go all the same, and sure enough, it was Doggy who got voltage and me who went limp. I ended up riding in a beak-rat buggy, a genuine made-in-

America rattletrap station wagon, and he took me to the for-sale house where Mama Pimple was waiting crossly for me and made Mr. Hunt go away because he kept me out too late. Then when the door was closed Mama Pimple giggled her gig and chuckled her chuck, and Walker himself wandered out of the back room and said, "That's one less favor you owe me, Mama Pimple," and she said, "No, my dear boyoh, that's one more favor *you* owe *me*," and then they kissed a deep passionate kiss if you can believe it. Did you imagine anybody ever kissed Mama Pimple that way? Dogwalker is a boyful of shocks.

"Did you get all you needed?" he asks me.

"I have P-words dancing upward," says I, "and I'll have a name for you tomorrow in my sleep."

"Hold onto it and don't tell me," says Dogwalker. "I don't want to hear a name until after we have his finger."

That magical day was only hours away, because the girl—whose name I never knew and whose face I never saw—was to cast her spell over Mr. Fed the very next day. As Dogwalker said, this was no job for lingeree. The girl did not dress pretty and pretended to be lacking in the social graces, but she was a good little clerical who was going through a most distressing period in her private life, because she had undergone a premature hysterectomy, poor lass, or so she told Mr. Fed, and here she was losing her womanhood and she had never really felt like a woman at all. But he was so kind to her, for weeks he had been so kind, and Dogwalker told me afterward how he locked the door of his office for just a few minutes, and held her and kissed her to make her feel womanly, and once his fingers had all made

338

their little impressions on the thin electrified plastic microcoating all over her lovely naked back and breasts, she began to cry and most gratefully informed him that she did not want him to be unfaithful to his wife for her sake, that he had already given her such a much of a lovely gift by being so kind and understanding, and she felt better thinking that a man like him could bear to touch her knowing she was defemmed inside, and now she thought she had the confidence to go on. A very convincing act, and one calculated to get his hot naked handprints without giving him a crisis of conscience that might change his face and give him a whole new set of possible Ps.

The microsheet got all his fingers from several angles, and so Walker was able to dummy out a finger mask for our inside man within a single night. Right index. I looked at it most skeptically, I fear, because I had my doubts already dancing in the little lightpoints of my inmost mind. "Just one finger?"

"All we get is one shot," said Dogwalker. "One single try."

"But if he makes a mistake, if my first password isn't right, then he could use the middle finger on the second try."

"Tell me, my vertical pricket, whether you think Jesse H. Hunt is the sort of burr-oak rat who makes mistakes?"

To which I had to answer that he was not, and yet I had my misgivings and my misgivings all had to do with needing a second finger, and yet I am vertical, not horizontal, which means that I can see the present as deep as you please but the future's not mine to see, que sera, sera.

From what Doggy told me, I tried to imagine Mr.

339

Fed's reaction to this nubile flesh that he had pressed. If he had poked as well as peeked, I think it would have changed his P-word, but when she told him that she would not want to compromise his uncompromising virtue, it reinforced him as a most regular or even regulation fellow and his name remained pronouncedly the same, and his P-word also did not change. "InvictusXYZrwr," quoth I to Dogwalker, for that was his veritable password, I knew it with more certainty than I had ever had before.

"Where in hell did you come up with that?" says he.

"If I knew how I did it, Walker, I'd never miss at all," says I. "I don't even know if it's in the goo or in the zoo. All the facts go down, and it all gets mixed around, and up come all these dancing P-words, little pieces of P."

"Yeah but you don't just make it up, what does it mean?"

"Invictus is an old poem in a frame stuck in his bureau drawer, which his mama gave him when he was still a little fed-to-be. XYZ is his idea of randomizing, and rwr is the first U.S. President that he admired. I don't know why he chose these words now. Six weeks ago he was using a different P-word with a lot of numbers in it, and six weeks from now he'll change again, but right now—"

"Sixty percent sure?" asked Doggy.

"I give no percents this time," says I. "I've never roamed through the bathroom of my subject before. But this or give me an assectomy, I've never been more sure."

Now that he had the P-word, the inside guy began to wear his magic finger every day, looking for a chance to be alone in Mr. Fed's office. He had already created the preliminary files, like any routine green card requests, and buried them within his work area. All he needed was to go in, sign on as Mr. Fed, and then if the system accepted his name and P-word and finger, he could call up the files, approve them, and be gone within a minute. But he had to have that minute.

And on that wonderful magical day he had it. Mr. Fed had a meeting and his secretary sprung a leak a day early, and in went Inside Man with a perfectly legitimate note to leave for Hunt. He sat before the terminal, typed name and P-word and laid down his phony finger, and the machine spread wide its lovely legs and bid him enter. He had the files processed in forty seconds, laying down his finger for each green, then signed off and went on out. No sign, no sound that anything was wrong. As sweet as summertime, as smooth as ice, and all we had to do was sit and wait for green cards to come in the mail.

'Who you going to sell them to?" says I.

"I offer them to no one till I have clean greens in my hand," says he. Because Dogwalker is careful. What happened was not because he was not careful.

Every day we walked to the ten places where the envelopes were supposed to come. We knew they wouldn't be there for a week—the wheels of government grind exceeding slow, for good or ill. Every day we checked with Inside Man, whose name and face I have already given you, much good it will do, since both are no doubt different by now. He told us every time that all was the same, nothing was changed, and he was telling the truth, for the fed was most lugubrious and palatial and gave no leaks

341

that anything was wrong. Even Mr. Hunt himself did not know that aught was amiss in his little kingdom.

Yet even with no sign that I could name, I was jumpy every morning and sleepless every night. "You walk like you got to use the toilet," says Walker to me, and it is verily so. Something is wrong, I say to myself, something is most deeply wrong, but I cannot find the name for it even though I know, and so I say nothing, or lie to myself and try to invent a reason for my fear. "It's my big chance," says I. "To be twenty percent of rich."

"Rich," says he, "not just a fifth."

"Then you'll be double rich."

And he just grins at me, being the strong and silent type.

"But then why don't you sell nine," says I, "and keep the other green? Then you'll have the money to pay for it, and the green to go where you want in all the world."

But he just laughs at me and says, "Silly boy, my dear sweet pinheaded lightbrained little friend. If someone sees a pimp like me passing a green, he'll tell a fed, because he'll know there's been a mistake. Greens don't go to boys like me."

"But you won't be dressed like a pimp," says I, "and you won't stay in pimp hotels."

"I'm a low-class pimp," he says again, "and so however I dress that day, that's just the way pimps dress. And whatever hotel I go to, that's a low-class pimp hotel until I leave."

"Pimping isn't some disease," says I. "It isn't in your gonads and it isn't in your genes. If your daddy was a Kroc and your mama an Iacocca, you wouldn't be a pimp."

"The hell I wouldn't," says he. "I'd just be a high-

342

class pimp, like my mama and my daddy. Who do you think gets green cards? You can't sell no virgins on the street."

I thought that he was wrong and I still do. If anybody could go from low to high in a week, it's Dogwalker. He could be anything and do anything, and that's the truth. Or almost anything. If he could do *anything* then his story would have a different ending. But it not his fault. Unless you blame pigs because they can't fly. *I* was the vertical one, wasn't I? I should have named my suspicions and we wouldn't have passed those greens.

I held them in my hands, there in his little room, all ten of them when he spilled them out on the bed. To celebrate he jumped up so high he smacked his head on the ceiling again and again, which made them ceiling tiles dance and flip over and spill dust all over the room. "I flashed just one, a single one," says he, "and a cool million was what he said, and then I said what if ten? And he laughs and says fill in the check yourself."

"We should test them," says I.

"We can't test them," he says. "The only way to test it is to use it, and if you use it then your print and face are in its memory forever and so we could never sell it."

"Then sell one, and make sure it's clean."

"A package deal," he says. "If I sell one, and they think I got more by I'm holding out to raise the price, then I may not live to collect for the other nine, because I might have an accident and lose these little babies. I sell all ten tonight at once, and then I'm out of the green card business for life."

But more than ever that night I am afraid, he's out selling those greens to those sweet gentlebodies

343

who are commonly referred to as Organic Crime, and there I am on his bed, shivering and dreaming because I know that something will go most deeply wrong but I still don't know what and I still don't know why. I keep telling myself, you're only afraid because nothing could ever go so right for you, you can't believe that anything could ever make you rich and safe. I say this stuff so much that I believe that I believe it, but I don't really, not down deep, so I shiver again and finally I cry, because after all my body still believes I'm nine, and nine-year-olds have tear ducts very easy of access, no password required. Well he comes in late that night, and I'm asleep he thinks, and so he walks quiet instead of dancing, but I can hear the dancing in his little sounds, I know he has the money all safely in the bank, and so when he leans over to make sure if I'm asleep, I say, "Could I borrow a hundred thou?"

So he slaps me and he laughs and dances and sings, and I try to go along, you bet I do, I know I should be happy, but then at the end he says, "You just can't take it, can you? You just can't handle it," and then I cry all over again, and he just puts his arm around me like a movie dad and gives me play-punches on the head and says, "I'm gonna marry me a wife, I am, maybe even Mama Pimple herself, and we'll adopt you and have a little spielberg family in Summerfield, with a riding mower on a real grass lawn."

"I'm older than you *or* Mama Pimple," says I, but he just laughs. Laughs and hugs me until he thinks that I'm all right. Don't go home, he says to me that night, but home I got to go, because I know I'll cry again, from fear or something, anyway, and I don't want him to think his cure wasn't permanent. "No

344

thanks," says I, but he just laughs at me. "Stay here and cry all you want to, Goo Boy, but don't go home tonight. I don't want to be alone tonight, and sure as hell you don't either." And so I slept between his sheets, like a brother, him punching and tickling and pinching and telling dirty jokes about his whores, the most good and natural night I spent in all my life, with a true friend, which I know you don't believe, snickering and nickering and ickering your filthy little thoughts, there was no holes plugged that night because nobody was out to take pleasure from nobody else, just Dogwalker being happy and wanting me not to be so sad.

And after he was asleep, I wanted so bad to know who it was he sold them to, so I could call them up and say, "Don't use those greens, cause they aren't clean. I don't know how, I don't know why, but the feds are onto this, I know they are, and if you use those cards they'll nail your fingers to your face." But if I called would they believe me? They were careful too. Why else did it take a week? They had one of their nothing goons use a card to make sure it had no squeaks or leaks, and it came up clean. Only then did they give the cards to seven big boys, with two held in reserve. Even Organic Crime, the All-seeing Eye, passed those cards same as we did.

I think maybe Dogwalker was a little bit vertical too. I think he knew same as me that something was wrong with this. That's why he kept checking back with the inside man, cause he didn't trust how good it was. That's why he didn't spend any of his share. We'd sit there eating the same old schlock, out of his cut from some leg job or my piece from a data wipe, and every now and then he'd say, "Rich man's food sure tastes good." Or maybe even though he wasn't vertical he still thought maybe I was right when I thought something was wrong. Whatever he thought, though, it just kept getting worse and worse for me, until the morning when we went to see the inside man and the inside man was gone.

Gone clean. Gone like he never existed. His apartment for rent, cleaned out floor to ceiling. A phone call to the fed, and he was on vacation, which meant they had him, he wasn't just moved to another house with his newfound wealth. We stood there in his empty place, his shabby empty hovel that was ten times better than anywhere we ever lived, and Doggy says to me, real quiet, he says, "What was it? What did I do wrong? I thought I was like Hunt, I thought I never made a single mistake in this job, in this one job."

And that was it, right then I knew. Not a week before, not when it would do any good. Right then I finally knew it all, knew what Hunt had done. Jesse Hunt never made *mistakes*. But he was also so paranoid that he haired his bureau to see if the babysitter stole from him. So even though he would never *accidentally* enter the wrong P-word, he was just the kind who would do it *on purpose*. "He doublefingered every time," I says to Dog. "He's so damn careful he does his password wrong the first time every time, and then comes in on his second finger."

"So one time he comes in on the first try, so what?" He says this because he doesn't know computers like I do, being half-glass myself.

"The system knew the pattern, that's what. Jesse H. is so precise he never changed a bit, so when *we* came in on the first try, that set off alarms. It's my fault, Dog, I knew how crazy paranoidical he is, I

346

knew that something was wrong, but not till this minute I didn't know what it was. I should have known, I'm sorry, you never should have gotten me into this, I'm sorry, you should have listened to me when I told you something was wrong, I should have known, I'm sorry."

What I done to Doggy that I never meant to do. What I done to him! Anytime, I could have thought of it, it was all there inside my glassy little head, but no, I didn't think of it till after it was way too late. And maybe it's because I didn't want to think of it, maybe it's because I really wanted to be wrong about the green cards, but however it flew, I did what I do, which is to say I'm not the pontiff in his fancy chair, by which I mean I can't be smarter than myself.

Right away he called the gentlebens of Ossified Crime to warn them, but I was already plugged into the library sucking news as fast as I could and so I knew it wouldn't do no good, cause they got all seven of the big boys and their nitwit taster, too, locked up good and tight for card fraud.

And what they said on the phone to Dogwalker made things real clear. "We're dead," says Doggy.

"Give them time to cool," says I.

"They'll never cool," says he. "There's no chance, they'll never forgive this even if they know the whole truth, because look at the names they gave the cards to, it's like they got them for their biggest boys on the borderline, the habibs who bribe presidents of little countries and rake off cash from octopods like Shell and ITT and every now and then kill somebody and walk away clean. Now they're sitting there in jail with the whole life story of the organization in their brains, so they don't care if we meant to do it

347

or not. They're hurting, and the only way they know to make the hurt go away is to pass it on to somebody else. And that's us. They want to make us hurt, and hurt real bad, and for a long long time."

I never saw Dog so scared. That's the only reason we went to the feds ourselves. We didn't ever want to stool, but we needed their protection plan, it was our only hope. So we offered to testify how we did it, not even for immunity, just so they'd change our faces and put us in a safe jail somewhere to work off the sentence and come out alive, you know? That's all we wanted.

But the feds, they laughed at us. They had the inside guy, see, and he was going to get immunity for testifying. "We don't need you," they says to us, "and we don't care if you go to jail or not. It was the big guys we wanted."

"If you let us walk," says Doggy, "then they'll think we set them up."

"Make us laugh," says the feds. "Us work with street poots like you? They know that we don't stoop so low."

"They bought from us," says Doggy. "If we're big enough for them, we're big enough for the dongs."

"Do you believe this?" says one fed to his identical junior officer. "These jollies are begging us to take them into jail. Well listen tight, my jolly boys, maybe we don't want to add you to the taxpayers' expense account, did you think of that? Besides, all we'd give you is time, but on the street, those boys will give you time and a half, and it won't cost us a dime."

So what could we do? Doggy just looks like somebody sucked out six pints, he's so white. On the way out of the fedhouse, he says, "Now we're going to find out what it's like to die."

And I says to him, "Walker, they stuck no gun in your mouth yet, they shove no shiv in your eye. We still breathing, we got legs, so let's *walk* out of here."

"Walk!" he says. "You walk out of G-boro, glass-head, and you bump into trees."

"So what?" says I. "I can plug in and pull out all the data we want about how to live in the woods. Lots of empty land out there. Where do you think the marijuana grows?"

"I'm a city boy," he says. "I'm a city boy." Now we're standing out in front, and he's looking around. "In the city I got a chance, I know the city."

"Maybe in New York or Dallas," says I, "but G-boro's just too small, not even half a million people, you can't lose yourself deep enough here."

"Yeah well," he says, still looking around. "It's none of your business now anyway, Goo Boy. They aren't blaming *you*, they're blaming *me*."

"But it's my fault," says I, "and I'm staying with you to tell them so."

"You think they're going to stop and listen?" says he.

"I'll let them shoot me up with speakeasy so they know I'm telling the truth."

"It's nobody's fault," says he. "And I don't give a twelve-inch poker whose fault it is anyway. You're clean, but if you stay with me you'll get all muddy, too. I don't need you around, and you sure as hell don't need me. Job's over. Done. Get lost."

But I couldn't do that. The same way he couldn't go on walking dogs, I couldn't just run off and leave him to eat my mistake. "They know I was your P-word man," says I. "They'll be after me too."

"Maybe for a while, Goo Boy. But you transfer your twenty percent into Bobby Joe's Face Shop, so they aren't looking for you to get a refund, and then stay quiet for a week and they'll forget all about you."

He's right but I don't care. "I was in for twenty percent of rich," says I. "So I'm in for fifty percent of trouble."

All of a sudden he sees what he's looking for. "There they are, Goo Boy, the dorks they sent to hit me. In that Mercedes." I look but all I see are electrics. Then his hand is on my back and he gives me a shove that takes me right off the portico and into the bushes, and by the time I crawl out, Doggy's nowhere in sight. For about a minute I'm pissed about getting scratched up in the plants, until I realize he was getting me out of the way, so I wouldn't get shot down or hacked up or lased out, whatever it is they planned to do to him to get even.

I was safe enough, right? I should've walked away, I should've ducked right out of the city. I didn't even have to refund the money. I had enough to go clear out of the country and live the rest of my life where even Occipital Crime couldn't find me.

And I thought about it. I stayed the night in Mama Pimple's flophouse because I knew somebody would be watching my own place. All that night I thought about places I could go. Australia. New Zealand. Or even a foreign place; I could afford a good vocabulary crystal so picking up a new language would be easy.

But in the morning I couldn't do it. Mama Pimple didn't exactly ask me but she looked so worried and all I could say was, "He pushed me into the bushes and I don't know where he is."

350

And she just nods at me and goes back to fixing breakfast. Her hands are shaking she's so upset. Because she knows that Dogwalker doesn't stand a chance against Orphan Crime.

"I'm sorry," says I.

"What can you do?" she says. "When they want you, they get you. If the feds don't give you a new face, you can't hide."

"What if they didn't want him?" says I.

She laughs at me. "The story's all over the street. The arrests were in the news, and now everybody knows the big boys are looking for Walker. They want him so bad the whole street can smell it."

"What if they knew it wasn't his fault?" says I. "What if they knew it was an accident? A mistake?"

Then Mama Pimple squints at me—not many people can tell when she's squinting, but I can—and she says, "Only one boy can tell them that so they'll believe it."

"Sure, I know," says I.

"And if that boy walks in and says, Let me tell you why you don't want to hurt my friend Dogwalker—"

"Nobody said life was safe," I says. "Besides, what could they do to me that's worse than what already happened to me when I was nine?"

She comes over and just puts her hand on my head, just lets her hand lie there for a few minutes, and I know what I've got to do.

So I did it. Went to Fat Jack's and told him I wanted to talk to Junior Mint about Dogwalker, and it wasn't thirty seconds before I was hustled on out into the alley and driven somewhere with my face mashed into the floor of the car so I couldn't tell where it was. Idiots didn't know that somebody as vertical as me can tell the number of wheel revolutions and the exact trajectory of every curve. I could've drawn a freehand map of where they took me. But if I let them know that, I'd never come home, and since there was a good chance I'd end up dosed with speakeasy, I went ahead and erased the memory. Good thing I did—that was the first thing they asked me as soon as they had the drug in me.

Gave me a grown-up dose, they did, so I practically told them my whole life story and my opinion of them and everybody and everything else, so the whole session took hours, felt like forever, but at the end they knew, they absolutely knew that Dogwalker was straight with them, and when it was over and I was coming up so I had some control over what I said, I asked them, I begged them, Let Dogwalker live. Just let him go. He'll give back the money, and I'll give back mine, just let him go.

"OK," says the guy.

I didn't believe it.

"No, you can believe me, we'll let him go."

"You got him?"

"Picked him up before you even came in. It wasn't hard."

"And you didn't kill him?"

"Kill him? We had to get the money back first, didn't we, so we needed him alive till morning, and then you came in, and your little story changed our minds, it really did, you made us feel all sloppy and sorry for that poor old pimp."

For a few seconds there I actually believed that it was going to be all right. But then I knew from the way they looked, from the way they acted, I knew the same way I know about passwords.

They brought in Dogwalker and handed me a book. Dogwalker was very quiet and stiff and he

352

didn't look like he recognized me at all. I didn't even have to look at the book to know what it was. They scooped out his brain and replaced it with glass, like me only way over the line, way way over, there was nothing of Dogwalker left inside his head, just glass pipe and goo. The book was a User's Manual, with all the instructions about how to program him and control him.

I looked at him and he was Dogwalker, the same face, the same hair, everything. Then he moved or talked and he was dead, he was somebody else living in Dogwalker's body. And I says to them, "Why? Why didn't you just kill him, if you were going to do this?"

"This one was too big," says the guy. "Everybody in G-boro knew what happened, everybody in the whole country, everybody in the world. Even if it was a mistake, we couldn't let it go. No hard feelings, Goo Boy. He *is* alive. And so are you. And you both stay that way, as long as you follow a few simple rules. Since he's over the line, he has to have an owner, and you're it. You can use him however you want—rent out data storage, pimp him as a jig or a jaw—but he stays with you always. Every day, he's on the street here in G-boro, so we can bring people here and show them what happens to boys who make mistakes. You can even keep your cut from the job, so you don't have to scramble at all if you don't want to. That's how much we like you, Goo Boy. But if he leaves this town or doesn't come out, even one single solitary day, you'll be very sorry for the last six hours of your life. Do you understand?"

I understood. I took him with me. I bought this place, these clothes, and that's how it's been ever

353

since. That's why we go out on the street every day. I read the whole manual, and I figure there's maybe ten percent of Dogwalker left inside. The part that's Dogwalker can't ever get to the surface, can't even talk or move or anything like that, can't ever remember or even consciously think. But maybe he can still wander around inside what used to be his head, maybe he can sample the data stored in all that goo. Maybe someday he'll even run across this story and he'll know what happened to him, and he'll know that I tried to save him.

In the meantime this is my last will and testament. See, I have us doing all kinds of research on Orgasmic Crime, so that someday I'll know enough to reach inside the system and unplug it. Unplug it all, and make those bastards lose everything, the way they took everything away from Dogwalker. Trouble is, some places there ain't no way to look without leaving tracks. Goo is as goo do, I always say. I'll find out I'm not as good as I think I am when somebody comes along and puts a hot steel putz in my face. Knock my brains out when it comes. But there's this, lying in a few hundred places in the system. Three days after I don't lay down my code in a certain program in a certain place, this story pops into view. The fact you're reading this means I'm dead.

Or it means I paid them back, and so I quit suppressing this because I don't care anymore. So maybe this is my swan song, and maybe this is my victory song. You'll never know, will you, mate?

But you'll wonder. I like that. You wondering about us, whoever you are, you thinking about old Goo Boy and Dogwalker, you guessing whether the fangs who scooped Doggy's skull and turned him into self-propelled property paid for it down to the very last delicious little drop.

And in the meantime, I've got this goo machine to take care of. Only ten percent a man, he is, but then I'm only forty percent myself. All added up together we make only half a human. But that's the half that counts. That's the half that still wants things. The goo in me and the goo in him is all just light pipes and electricity. Data without desire. Lightspeed trash. But I have some desires left, just a few, and maybe so does Dogwalker, even fewer. And we'll get what we want. Every speck. Every sparkle. Believe it.

BUT WE TRY NOT TO
ACT LIKE IT

There was no line. Hiram Cloward commented on it to the pointy-faced man behind the counter. "There's no line."

"This is the complaint department. We pride ourselves on having few complaints." The pointy-faced man had a prim little smile that irritated Hiram. "What's the matter with your television?"

"It shows nothing but soaps, that's what's the matter. And asinine gothics."

"Well—that's programming, sir, not mechanical at all."

"It's mechanical. I can't turn the damn set off."

"What's your name and social security number?"

"Hiram Cloward. 528–80–693883–7."

"Address?"

"ARF-487-U7b."

"That's singles, sir. Of course you can't turn off your set."

"You mean because I'm not married I can't turn off my television?"

"According to congressionally authorized scientific studies carried out over a three-year period from 1989 to 1991, it is imperative that persons living

356

alone have the constant companionship of their television sets."

"I like solitude. I also like silence."

"But the Congress passed a *law*, sir, and we can't disobey the *law*—"

"Can't I talk to somebody intelligent?"

The pointy-faced man flared a moment, his eyes burning. But he instantly regained his composure, and said in measured tones, "As a matter of fact, as soon as any complainant becomes offensive or hostile, we immediately refer them to section A-6."

"What's that, the hit squad?"

"It's behind that door."

And Hiram followed the pointing finger to the glass door at the far end of the waiting room. Inside was an office, which was filled with comfortable, homey knickknacks, several chairs, a desk, and a man so offensively nordic that even Hitler would have resented him. "Hello," the Aryan said, warmly.

"Hi."

"Please, sit down." Hiram sat, the courtesy and warmth making him feel even more resentful—did they think they could fool him into believing he was not being grossly imposed upon?

"So you don't like something about your programming,' said the Aryan.

"*Your* programming, you mean. It sure as hell isn't mine. I don't know why Bell Television thinks it has the right to impose its idea of fun and entertainment on me twenty-four hours a day, but I'm fed up with it. It was bad enough when there was some variety, but for the last two months I've been getting nothing but soaps and gothics."

"It took you two months to notice?"

357

"I try to ignore the set. I like to *read*. You can bet that if I had more than my stinking little pension from our loving government, I could pay to have a room where there wasn't a TV so I could have some *peace*."

"I really can't help your financial situation. And the law's the law."

"Is that all I'm going to hear from you? The law? I could have heard that from the pointy-faced jerk out there."

"Mr. Cloward, looking at your records, I can certainly see that soaps and gothics are not appropriate for you."

"They aren't appropriate," Hiram said, "for anyone with an IQ over eight."

The Aryan nodded. "You feel that people who enjoy soaps and gothics aren't the intellectual equals of people who don't."

"Damn right. I have a Ph.D. in *literature*, for heaven's sake!"

The Aryan was all sympathy. "Of *course* you don't like soaps! I'm sure it's a mistake. We try not to make mistakes, but we're only human—except the computers, of course." It was a joke, but Hiram didn't laugh. The Aryan kept up the small talk as he looked at the computer terminal that he could see and Hiram could not. "We may be the only television company in town, you know, but—"

"But you try not to act like it."

"Yes. Ha. Well, you must have heard our advertising."

"Constantly."

"Well, let's see now. Hiram Cloward, Ph.D. Nebraska 1981. English literature, twentieth century, with a minor in Russian literature. Dissertation

358

on Dostoevski's influence on English-language novelists. A near-perfect class attendance record, and a reputation for arrogance and competence."

"How much do you *know* about me?"

"Only the standard consumer research data. But we do have a bit of a problem."

Hiram waited, but the Aryan merely punched a button, leaned back, and looked at Hiram. His eyes were kindly and warm and intense. It made Hiram uncomfortable.

"Mr. Cloward."

"Yes?"

"You are unemployed."

"Not willingly."

"Few people are willingly unemployed, Mr. Cloward. But you have no job. You also have no family. You also have no friends."

"That's consumer research? What, only people with friends buy Rice Krispies?"

"As a matter of fact, Rice Krispies are favored by solitary people. We have to know who is more likely to be receptive to advertising, and we direct our programming accordingly."

Hiram remembered that he ate Rice Krispies for breakfast almost every morning. He vowed on the spot to switch to something else. Quaker Oats, for instance. Surely they were more gregarious.

"You understand the importance of the Selective Programming Broadcast Act of 1985, yes?"

"Yes."

"It was deemed unfair by the Supreme Court for all programming to be geared to the majority. Minorities were being slighted. And so Bell Television was given the assignment of preparing an individually selected broadcast system so that each individual, in his own home, would have the programming perfect for him."

"I know all this."

"I must go over it again anyway, Mr. Cloward, because I'm going to have to help you understand why there can be no change in your programming."

Hiram stiffened in his chair, his hands flexing. "I knew you bastards wouldn't change."

"Mr. Cloward, we bastards would be delighted to change. But we are very closely regulated by the government to provide the most healthful programming for every American citizen. Now, I will continue my review."

"I'll just go home, if you don't mind."

"Mr. Cloward, we are directed to prepare programming for minorities as small as ten thousand people—but no smaller. Even for minorities of ten thousand the programming is ridiculously expensive—a program seen by so few costs far more per watching-minute to produce than one seen by thirty or forty million. However, you belong to a minority even smaller than ten thousand."

"That makes me feel so special."

"Furthermore, the Consumer Protection Broadcast Act of 1989 and the regulations of the Consumer Broadcast Agency since then have given us very strict guidelines. Mr. Cloward, we cannot show you any program with overt acts of violence."

"Why not?"

"Because you have tendencies toward hostility that are only exacerbated by viewing violence. Similarly, we cannot show you any programs with sex."

Cloward's face turned red.

"You have no sex life whatsoever, Mr. Cloward. Do you realize how dangerous that is? You don't even masturbate. The tension and hostility inside you must be tremendous."

Cloward leapt to his feet. There were limits to what a man had to put up with. He headed for the door.

"Mr. Cloward, I'm sorry." The Aryan followed him to the door. "I don't make these things up. Wouldn't you rather know *why* these decisions are reached?"

Hiram stopped at the door, his hand on the knob. The Aryan was right. Better to know why than to hate them for it.

"How?" Hiram asked. "How do they know what I do and do not do within the walls of my home?"

"We don't *know*, of course, but we're pretty sure. We've studied people for years. We know that people who have certain buying patterns and certain living patterns behave in certain ways. And, unfortunately, you have strong destructive tendencies. Repression and denial are your primary means of adaptation to stress, that and, unfortunately, occasional acting out."

"What the hell does all that mean?"

"It means that you lie to yourself until you can't anymore, and then you attack somebody."

Hiram's face was packed with hot blood, throbbing. I must look like a tomato, he told himself, and deliberately calmed himself. I don't care, he thought. They're wrong anyway. Damn scientific tests.

"Aren't there any movies you could program for me?"

"I am sorry, no."

"Not all movies have sex and violence."

The Aryan smiled soothingly. "The movies that don't wouldn't interest you anyway."

"Then turn the damn thing off and let me read!"

"We can't do that."

"Can't you turn it *down*?"

"No."

"I am so sick of hearing all about Sarah Wynn and her damn love life!"

"But isn't Sarah Wynn attractive?" asked the Aryan.

That stopped Hiram cold. He dreamed about Sarah Wynn at night. He said nothing. He had no attraction to Sarah Wynn.

"Isn't she?" the Aryan insisted.

"Isn't who what?"

"Sarah Wynn."

"Who was talking about Sarah Wynn? What about documentaries?"

"Mr. Cloward, you would become extremely hostile if the news programs were broadcast to you. You know that."

"Walter Cronkite's dead. Maybe I'd like them better now."

"You don't care about the news of the real world, Mr. Cloward, do you?"

"No."

"Then you see where we are. Not one iota of our programming is really appropriate for you. But ninety percent of it is downright harmful to you. And we can't turn the television off, because of the Solitude Act. Do you see our dilemma?"

"Do you see mine?"

"Of course, Mr. Cloward. And I sympathize completely. Make some friends, Mr. Cloward, and we'll turn off your television."

362

And so the interview was over.

For two days Cloward brooded. All the time he did, Sarah Wynn was grieving over her three-days' husband who had just been killed in a car wreck on Wiltshire Boulevard, wherever the hell that was. But now the body was scarcely cold and already her old suitors were back, trying to help her, trying to push their love on her. "Can't you let yourself depend on me, just a little?" asked Teddy, the handsome one with lots of money.

"I don't like depending on people," Sarah answered.

"You depended on George." George was the husband's name. The dead one.

"I know," she said, and cried for a moment. Sarah Wynne was good at crying. Hiram Cloward turned another page in *The Brothers Karamazov*.

"You need friends," Teddy insisted.

"Oh, Teddy, I know it," she said, weeping. "Will you be my friend?"

"Who writes this stuff?" Hiram Cloward asked aloud. Maybe the Aryan in the television company offices had been right. Make some friends. Get the damn set turned off whatever the cost.

He got up from his chair and went out into the corridor in the apartment building. Clearly posted on the walls were several announcements:

Chess club 5–9 Wed
Encounter groups nightly at 7
Learn to knit 6:30 bring yarn and needles
Games games games in game room (basement)
Just want to chat? Friends of the Family 7:30 to 10:30 nightly

Friends of the Family? Hiram snorted. Family was his maudlin mother and her constant weeping about how hard life was and how no one in her right mind would ever be born a woman if anybody had any choice but there was no choice and marriage was a trap men sprung on women, giving them a few minutes of pleasure for a lifetime of drudgery, and I swear to God if it wasn't for my little baby Hiram I'd ditch that bastard for good, it's for your sake I don't leave, my little baby, because if I leave you'll grow up into a macho bastard like your beerbelly father.

And friends? What friends ever come around when good old Dad is boozing and belting the living crap out of everybody he can get his hands on?

I read. That's what I do. *The Prince and the Pauper. Connecticut Yankee. Pride and Prejudice.* Worlds within worlds within worlds, all so pretty and polite and funny as hell.

Friends of the Family. Worth a shot, anyway.

Hiram went to the elevator and descended eighteen floors to the Fun Floor. Friends of the Family were in quite a large room with alcohol at one end and soda pop at the other. Hiram was surprised to discover that the term *soda pop* had been revived. He walked to the cola sign and asked the woman for a Coke.

"How many cups of coffee have you had today?" she asked.

"Three."

"Then I'm so sorry, but I can't give you a soda pop with caffeine in it. May I suggest Sprite?"

"You may not," Hiram said, clenching his teeth. "We're too damn overprotected."

"Exactly how I feel," said a woman standing beside him, Sprite in hand. "They protect and protect and protect, and what good does it do? People still die, you know."

"I suspected as much," Hiram said, struggling for a smile, wondering if his humor sounded funny or merely sarcastic. Apparently funny. The woman laughed.

"Oh, you're a gem, you are," she said. "What do you do?"

"I'm a detached professor of literature at Princeton."

"But how can you live *here* and work *there*?"

He shrugged. "I don't work there. I said detached. When the new television teaching came in, my PQ was too low. I'm not a screen personality."

"So few of us are," she said sagely, nodding and smiling. "Oh, how I long for the good old days. When ugly men like David Brinkley could deliver the news."

"You remember Brinkley?"

"Actually, no," she said, laughing. "I just remember my mother talking about him." Hiram looked at her appreciatively. Nose not very straight, of course—but that seemed to be the only thing keeping her off TV. Nice voice. Nice nice face. Body.

She put her hand on his thigh.

"What are you doing tonight?" she asked.

"Watching television," he grimaced.

"Really? What do you have?"

"Sarah Wynn."

She squealed in delight. "Oh, how wonderful! We must be kindred spirits then! I have Sarah Wynn, too!"

Hiram tried to smile.

"Can I come up to your apartment?"

Danger signal. Hand moving up thigh. Invitation to apartment. Sex.

"No."

"Why not?"

And Hiram remembered that the only way he could ever get rid of the television was to prove that he wasn't solitary. And fixing up his sex life—i.e., having one—would go a long way toward changing their damn profiles. "Come on," he said, and they left the Friends of the Family without further ado.

Inside the apartment she immediately took off her shoes and blouse and sat down on the old-fashioned sofa in front of the TV. "Oh," she said, "so many books. You really are a professor, aren't you?"

"Yeah," he said, vaguely sensing that the next move was up to him, and not having the faintest idea of what the next move was. He thought back to his only fumbling attempt at sex when he was (what?) thirteen? (no) fourteen and the girl was fifteen and was doing it on a lark. She had walked with him up the creekbed (back when there were creeks and open country) and suddenly she had stopped and unzipped his pants (back when there were zippers) but he was finished before she had hardly started and gave up in disgust and took his pants and ran away. Her name was Diana. He went home without his pants and had no rational explanation and his mother had treated him with loathing and brought it up again and again for years afterward, how a man is a man no matter how you treat him and he'll still get it when he can, who cares about the poor girl. But Hiram was used to that kind of talk. It rolled off him. What haunted him was the uncontrolled shivering of his body, the ecstasy of it, and then the look of disgust on the girl's face. He

366

had thought it was because—well, never mind. Never mind, he thought. I don't think of this anymore.

"Come *on*," said the woman.

"What's your name?" Hiram asked.

She looked at the ceiling. "Agnes, for heaven's sake, come *on*."

He decided that taking off his shirt might be a good idea. She watched, then decided to help.

"No," he said.

"What?"

"Don't touch me."

"Oh, for pete's sake. What's wrong? Impotent?"

Not at all. Not at all. Just uninterested. Is that all right?

"Look, I don't want to play around with a psycho case, all right? I've got better things to do. I make a hundred a whack, that's what I charge, that's standard, right?"

Standard what? Hiram nodded because he didn't dare ask what she was talking about.

"But you obviously, heaven knows how, buddy, you sure as hell obviously don't know what's going on in the world. Twenty bucks. Enough for the ten minutes you've screwed up for me. Right?"

"I don't have twenty," Hiram said.

Her eyes got tight. "A fairy *and* a deadbeat. What a pick. Look, buddy, next time you try a pickup, figure out what you want to do with her first, right?"

She picked up her shoes and blouse and left. Hiram stood there.

"Teddy, no," said Sarah Wynn.

"But I need you. I need you so desperately," said Teddy on the screen.

"It's only been a few days. How can I sleep with

367

another man only a few days after George was killed? Only four days ago we—oh, no, Teddy. Please."

"Then when? How soon? I love you so much."

Drivel, George thought in his analytical mind. But nevertheless obviously based on the Penelope story. No doubt her George, her Odysseus, would return, miraculously alive, ready to sweep her back into wedded bliss. But in the meantime, the suitors: enough suitors to sell fifteen thousand cars and a hundred thousand boxes of tampax and four hundred thousand packages of Cap'n Crunch.

The nonanalytical part of his mind, however, was not the least bit concerned with Penelope. For some reason he was clasping and unclasping his hands in front of him. For some reason he was shaking. For some reason he fell to his knees at the couch, his hands clasping and unclasping around *Crime and Punishment*, as his eyes strained to cry but could not.

Sarah Wynn wept.

But she can cry easily, Hiram thought. It's not fair, that she should cry so easily. Spin flax, Penelope.

The alarm went off, but Hiram was already awake. In front of him the television was singing about Dove with lanolin. The products haven't changed, Hiram thought. Never change. They were advertising Dove with lanolin in the little market carts around the base of the cross while Jesus bled to death, no doubt. For softer skin.

He got up, got dressed, tried to read, couldn't, tried to remember what had happened last night to leave him so upset and nervous, but couldn't, and at last he decided to go back to the Aryan at the Bell Television offices.

"Mr. Cloward," said the Aryan.

"You're a psychiatrist, aren't you?" Hiram asked.

"Why, Mr. Cloward, I'm an A-6 complaint representative from Bell Television. What can I do for you?"

"I can't stand Sarah Wynn anymore," Hiram said.

"That's a shame. Things are finally going to work out for her starting in about two weeks."

And in spite of himself, Hiram wanted to ask what was going to happen. It isn't fair for this nordic uberman to know what sweet little Sarah is going to be doing weeks before I do. But he fought down the feeling, ashamed that he was getting caught up in the damn soap.

"Help me," Hiram said.

"How can I help you?"

"You can change my life. You can get the television out of my apartment."

"Why, Mr. Cloward?" the Aryan asked. "It's the one thing in life that's absolutely free. Except that you get to watch commercials. And you know as well as I do that the commercials are downright entertaining. Why, there are people who actually choose to have double the commercials in their personal programming. We get a thousand requests a day for the latest McDonald's ad. You have no idea."

"I have a very good idea. I want to read. I want to be alone."

"On the contrary, Mr. Cloward, you long not to be alone. You desperately need a friend."

Anger. "And what makes you so damn sure of that?"

369

"Because, Mr. Cloward, your response is completely typical of your group. It's a group we're very concerned about. We don't have a budget to program for you—there are only about two thousand of you in the country—but a budget wouldn't do us much good because we really don't know what kind of programming you *want*."

"I am not part of any group."

"Oh, you're so much a part of it that you could be called typical. Dominant mother, absent and/or hostile father, no long-term relationships with anybody. No sex life."

"I have a sex life."

"If you have in fact attempted any sexual activity it was undoubtedly with a prostitute and she expected too high a level of sophistication from you. You are easily ashamed, you couldn't cope, and so you have not had intercourse. Correct?"

"What are you! What are you trying to do to me!"

"I *am* a psychoanalyst, of course. Anybody whose complaints can't be handled by our bureaucratic authority figure out in front obviously needs help, not another bureaucrat. I want to help you. I'm your friend."

And suddenly the anger was replaced by the utter incongruity of this nordic masterman wanting to help little Hiram Cloward. The unemployed professor laughed.

"Humor! Very healthy!" said the Aryan.

"What is this? I thought shrinks were supposed to be subtle."

"With some people—notably paranoids, which you are not, and schizoids, which you are not either."

"And what am I?"

370

"I told you. Denial and repression strategies. Very unhealthy. Acting out—less healthy yet. But you're extremely intelligent, able to do many things. I personally think it's a damn shame you can't teach."

"I'm an excellent teacher."

"Tests with randomly selected students showed that you had an extremely heavy emphasis on esoterica. Only people like you would really enjoy a class from a person like you. There aren't many people like you. You don't fit into many of the normal categories."

"And so I'm being persecuted."

"Don't try to pretend to be paranoid." The Aryan smiled. Hiram smiled back. This is insane. Lewis Carroll, where are you now that we really need you?

"If you're a shrink, then I should talk freely to you."

"If you like."

"I don't like."

"And why not?"

"Because you're so godutterlydamn Aryan, that's why."

The Aryan leaned forward with interest. "Does that bother you?"

"It makes me want to throw up."

"And why is that?"

The look of interest was too keen, too delightful. Hiram couldn't resist. "You don't know about my experiences in the war, then, is that it?"

"What war? There hasn't been a war recently enough—"

"I was very, very young. It was in Germany. My parents aren't really my parents, you know. They were in Germany with the American embassy. In Berlin in 1938, before the war broke out. My real

parents were there, too—German Jews, or half
Jews, anyway. My real father—but let that pass, you
don't need my whole genealogy. Let's just say that
when I was only eleven days old, totally unregis-
tered, my real Jewish father took me to his friend,
Mr. Cloward in the American embassy, whose wife
had just had a miscarriage. 'Take my child,' he said.

'Why?' Cloward asked.

" 'Because my wife and I have a perfect, utterly
foolproof plan to kill Hitler. But there is no way for
us to survive it.' And so Cloward, my adopted
father, took me in.

"And then, the next day, he read in the papers
about how my real parents had been killed in an
'accident' in the street. He investigated—and discovered that just by chance, while my parents were
on their way to carry out their foolproof plan, some
brown shirts in the street had seen them. Someone
pointed them out as Jews. They were bored—so
they attacked them. Had no idea they were saving
Hitler's life, of course. These nordic mastermen
started beating my mother, forcing my father to
watch as they stripped her and raped her and then
disemboweled her. My father was then subjected to
experimental use of the latest model testicle-crusher
until he bit off his own tongue in agony and bled to
death. I don't like nordic types." Hiram sat back,
his eyes full of tears and emotion, and realized that
he had actually been able to cry—not much, but it
was hopeful.

"Mr. Cloward," said the Aryan, "you were born
in Missouri in 1951. Your parents of record are your
natural parents."

Hiram smiled. "But it was one hell of a Freudian
fantasy, wasn't it? My mother raped, my father

emasculated to death, myself divorced from my true heritage, etc., etc."

The Aryan smiled. "You should be a writer, Mr. Cloward."

"I'd rather read. Please, let me read."

"I can't stop you from reading."

"Turn off Sarah Wynn. Turn off the mansions from which young girls flee from the menace of a man who turns out to be friendly and loving. Turn off the commercials for cars and condoms."

"And leave you alone to wallow in cataleptic fantasies among your depressing Russian novels?"

Hiram shook his head. Am I begging? he wondered. Yes, he decided. "I'm begging. My Russian novels aren't depressing. They're exalting, uplifting, overwhelming."

"It's part of your sickness, Mr. Cloward, that you long to be overwhelmed."

"Every time I read Dostoevski, I feel fulfilled."

"You have read everything by Dostoevski twenty times over. And everything by Tolstoy a dozen times."

"Every time I read Dostoevski is the first time!"

"We can't leave you alone."

"I'll kill myself!" Hiram shouted. "I can't live like this much longer!"

"Then make friends," the Aryan said simply. Hiram gasped and panted, gathering his rage back under control. This is not happening. I am not angry. Put it away, put it back, get control, smile. Smile at the Aryan.

"You're my friend, right?" Hiram asked.

"If you'll let me," the Aryan answered.

"I'll let you," Hiram said. Then he got up and left the office.

373

On the way home he passed a church. He had often seen the church before. He had little interest in religion—it had been too thoroughly dissected for him in the novels. What Twain had left alive, Dostoevski had withered and Pasternak had killed. But his mother was a passionate Presbyterian. He went into the church.

At the front of the building was a huge television screen. On it a very charismatic young man was speaking. The tones were subdued—only those in the front could hear it. Those in the back seemed to be meditating. Cloward knelt at a bench to meditate, too.

But he couldn't take his eyes off the screen. The young man stepped aside, and an older man took his place, intoning something about Christ. Hiram could hear the word *Christ*, but no others.

The walls were decorated with crosses. Row on row of crosses. This was a Protestant church—none of the crosses contained a figure of Jesus bleeding. But Hiram's imagination supplied him nonetheless. Jesus, his hands and wrists nailed to the cross, his feet pegged to the cross, his throat at the intersection of the beams.

Why the cross, after all? The intersection of two utterly opposite lines, perpendiculars that can only touch at one point. The epitome of the life of man, passing through eternity without a backward glance at those encountered along the way, each in his own, endlessly divergent direction. The cross. But not at all the symbol of today, Hiram decided. Today we are in spheres. Today we are curves, not lines, bending back on ourselves, touching everybody again and again, wrapped up inside little balls, none of us daring to be at the outside. Pull me in, we cry, pull me and keep me safe, don't let me fall out, don't let me fall off the edge of the world.

But the world has an edge now, and we can all see it, Hiram decided. We know where it is, and we can't bear to let anyone find his own way of staying on top.

Or do I want to stay on top?

The age of crosses is over. Now the age of spheres. Balls.

"We are your friends," said the old man on the screen. "We can help you."

There is a grandeur, Hiram answered silently, about muddling through alone.

"Why be alone when Jesus can take your burden?" said the man on the screen.

If I were alone, Hiram answered, there would be no burden to bear.

"Pick up your cross, fight the good fight," said the man on the screen.

If only, Hiram answered, I could find my cross to pick it up.

Then Hiram realized that he still could not hear the voice from the television. Instead, he had been supplying his own sermon, out loud. Three people near him in the back of the church were watching him. He smiled sheepishly, ducked his head in apology and left. He walked home whistling.

Sarah Wynne's voice greeted him. "Teddy. Teddy! What have we done? Look what we've done."

"It was beautiful," Teddy said. "I'm glad of it."

"Oh, Teddy! How can I ever forgive myself?" And Sarah wept.

Hiram stood transfixed, watching the screen. Penelope had given in. Penelope had left her flax and fornicated with a suitor! This is wrong, he thought.

"This is wrong," he said.

"I love you, Sarah," Teddy said.

"I can't bear it, Teddy," she answered. "I feel that in my heart I have murdered George! I have betrayed him!"

Penelope, is there no virtue in the world? Is there no Artemis, hunting? Just Aphrodite, bedding down every hour on the hour with every man, god, or sheep that promised forever and delivered a moment. The bargains are never fulfilled, never, Hiram thought.

At that moment on the screen, George walked in. "My dear," he exclaimed. "My dear Sarah! I've been wandering with amnesia for days! It was a hitchhiker who was burned to death in my car! I'm home!"

And Hiram screamed and screamed and screamed.

The Aryan found out about it quickly, at the same time that he got an alarming report from the research teams analyzing the soaps. He shook his head, a sick feeling in the pit of his stomach. Poor Mr. Cloward. Ah, what agony we do in the name of protecting people, the Aryan thought.

"I'm sorry," he said to Hiram. But Hiram paid him no attention. He just sat on the floor, watching the television set. As soon as the report had come in, of course, all the soaps—especially Sarah Wynn's—had gone off the air. Now the game shows were on, a temporary replacement until errors could be corrected.

"I'm so sorry," the Aryan said, but Hiram tried

to shrug him away. A black woman had just traded the box for the money in the envelope. It was what Hiram would have done, and it paid off. Five thousand dollars instead of a donkey pulling a cart with a monkey in it. She had just avoided being zonked.

"Mr. Cloward, I thought the problem was with you. But it wasn't at all. I mean, you were marginal, all right. But we didn't realize what Sarah Wynn was doing to people."

Sarah schmarah, Hiram said silently, watching the screen. The black woman was bounding up and down in delight.

"It was entirely our fault. There are thousands of marginals just like you who were seriously damaged by Sarah Wynn. We had no idea how powerful the identification was. We had no idea."

Of course not, thought Hiram. You didn't read enough. You didn't know what the myths do to people. But now was the Big Deal of the Day, and Hiram shook his head to make the Aryan go away.

"Of course the Consumer Protection Agency will pay you a lifetime compensation. Three times your present salary and whatever treatment is possible."

At last Hiram's patience ended. "Go away!" he said. "I have to see if the black woman there is going to get the car!"

"I just can't decide," the black woman said.

"Door number three!" Hiram shouted. "Please, God, door number three!"

The Aryan watched Hiram silently.

"Door number two!" the black woman finally decided. Hiram groaned. The announcer smiled.

"Well," said the announcer. "Is the car behind door number *two*? Let's just see!"

The curtain opened, and behind it was a man in a

377

hillbilly costume strumming a beat-up looking banjo. The audience moaned. The man with the banjo sang "Home on the Range." The black woman sighed.

They opened the curtains, and there was the car behind door number three. "I knew it," Hiram said, bitterly. "They never listen to me. Door number three, I say, and they never do it."

The Aryan turned to leave.

"I told you, didn't I?" Hiram asked, weeping.

"Yes," the Aryan said.

"I knew it. I knew it all along. I was *right*." Hiram sobbed into his hands.

"Yeah," the Aryan answered, and then he left to sign all the necessary papers for the commitment. Now Cloward fit into a category. No one can exist outside one for long, the Aryan realized. We are creating a new man. *Homo categoricus*. The classified man.

But the papers didn't have to be signed after all. Instead Hiram went into the bathroom, filled the tub, and joined the largest category of all.

"Damn," the Aryan said, when he heard about it.

I PUT MY BLUE GENES
ON

It had taken three weeks to get there—longer than any man in living memory had been in space, and there were four of us crammed into the little Hunter III skipship. It gave us a hearty appreciation for the pioneers, who had had to crawl across space at a tenth of the speed of light. No wonder only three colonies ever got founded. Everybody else must have eaten each other alive after the first month in space.

Harold had taken a swing at Amauri the last day, and if we hadn't hit the homing signal I would have ordered the ship turned around to go home to Núncamais, which was mother and apple pie to everybody but me—I'm from Pennsylvania. But we got the homing signal and set the computer to scanning the old maps, and after a few hours found ourselves in stationary orbit over Prescott, Arizona.

At least that's what the geologer said, and computers can't lie. It didn't look like what the old books *said* Arizona should look like.

But there was the homing signal, broadcasting in Old English: "God bless America, come in, safe landing guaranteed." The computer assured us that in Old English the word *guarantee* was *not* obscene, but rather had something to do with a statement being particularly trustworthy—we had a chuckle over that one.

But we were excited, too. When great-great-great-great to the umpteenth power grandpa and grandma upped their balloons from old Terra Firma eight hundred years ago, it had been to escape the ravages of microbiological warfare that was just beginning (a few germs in a sneak attack on Madagascar, quickly spreading to epidemic proportions, and South Africa holding the world ransom for the antidote; quick retaliation with virulent cancer; you guess the rest). And even from a couple of miles out in space, it was pretty obvious that the war hadn't stopped there. And yet there was this homing signal.

"Obviamente automática," Amauri observed.

'*Que* máquina, que ñão pofa em tantos anos, bichinha! Não acredito!" retorted Harold, and I was afraid I might have a rerun of the day before.

"English," I said. "Might as well get used to it. We'll have to speak it for a few days, at least."

Vladimir sighed. "Merda."

I laughed. "All right, you can keep your scatological comments in lingua deporto."

"Are you so sure there's anybody alive down there?" Vladimir asked.

What could I say? That I felt it in my bones? So I just threw a sponge at him, which scattered drinking water all over the cabin, and for a few minutes we had a waterfight. I know, discipline, discipline. But we're not a land army up here, and what the hell. I'd rather have my crew acting like crazy children than like crazy grown-ups.

Actually, I didn't believe that at the level of technology our ancestors had reached in 1992 they could build a machine that would keep running until 2810. Somebody had to be alive down there—or else they'd gotten smart. Again, the surface of old Terra didn't give many signs that anybody had gotten smart.

So somebody was alive down there. And that was exactly what we had been sent to find out.

They complained when I ordered monkeysuits.

"That's old Mother *Earth* down there!" Harold argued. For a halibut with an ike of 150 he sure could act like a baiano sometimes.

"Show me the cities," I answered. "Show me the millions of people running around taking the sun in their rawhide summer outfits."

"And there may be germs," Amauri added, in his snottiest voice, and immediately I had another argument going between two men brown enough to know better.

"We will follow," I said in my nasty captain's voice, "standard planetary procedure, whether it's Mother Earth or mother—"

And at that moment the monotonous homing signal changed.

"Please respond, please identify, please respond, or we'll blast your asses out of the sky."

We responded. And soon afterward found ourselves in monkeysuits wandering around in thick pea soup up to our navels (if we could have located our navels without a map, surrounded as they were with lifesaving devices) waiting for somebody to open a door.

A door opened and we picked ourselves up off a very hard floor. Some of the pea soup had fallen down the hatch with us. A gas came into the sterile chamber where we waited, and pretty soon the pea soup settled down and turned into mud.

"Mariajoseijesus!" Amauri muttered. "Aquela merdi *vivia*!"

"English," I muttered into the monkey mouth, "and clean up your language."

"That crap was alive," Amauri said, rephrasing and cleaning up his language.

"And now it isn't, but we are." It was hard to be patient.

For all we knew, what passed for humanity here liked eating spacemen. Or sacrificing them to some local deity. We passed a nervous four hours in that cubicle. And I had already laid about five hopeless escape plans—when a door opened, and a person appeared.

He was dressed in a white farmersuit, or at least close to it. He was very short, but smiled pleasantly and beckoned. Proof positive. Living human beings. Mission successful. *Now* we know there was no cause for rejoicing, but at that moment we rejoiced. Backslapping, embracing our little host (afraid of crushing him for a moment), and then into the labyrinth of U.S. MB Warfare Post 004.

They were all very small—not more than 140 centimeters tall—and the first thought that struck me was how much humanity had grown since then. The stars must agree with us, I thought.

Till quiet, methodical Vladimir, looking, as always, white as a ghost, pointedly turned a doorknob and touched a lightswitch (it actually was *mechanical*). They were both above eye level for our little friends. So it wasn't us colonists who had grown—it was our cousins from old Gaea who had shrunk.

We tried to catch them up on history, but all they cared about was their own politics. "Are you American?" they kept asking.

"I'm from Pennsylvania," I said, "but these humble-butts are from Núncamais."

They didn't understand.

"Núncamais. It means 'never again.' In lingua deporto."

Again puzzled. But they asked another question.

"Where did your colony *come from*?" One-track minds.

"Pennsylvania was settled by Americans from Hawaii. We lay no bets as to why they named the damned planet Pennsylvania."

One of the little people piped up, "That's obvious. Cradle of liberty. And *them*?"

"From Brazil," I said.

They conferred quietly on that one, and then apparently decided that while Brazilian ancestry wasn't a capital offense, it didn't exactly confer human status. From then on, they made no attempt to talk to my crew. Just watched them carefully, and talked to me.

Me they loved.

"God bless America," they said.

I felt agreeable. "God bless America," I answered.

Then, again, in unison, they made an obscene suggestion as to what I should do with the Russians. I glanced at my compatriots and fellow travelers and shrugged. I repeated the little folks' wish for the Russian's sexual bliss.

Fact time. I won't bore by repeating all the clever questioning and probing that elicited the following information. Partly because it didn't take any questioning. They seemed to have been rehearsing for years what they would say to any visitors from outer space, particularly the descendants of the long-lost colonists. It went this way:

Germ warfare had begun in earnest about three years after we left. Three very cleverly designed cancer viruses had been loosed on the world, apparently by no one at all, since both the Russians and the Americans denied it and the Chinese were all dead. That was when the scientists knuckled down and set to work.

Recombinant DNA had been a rough enough science when my ancestors took off for the stars—and we hadn't developed it much since then. When you're developing raw planets you have better things to do with your time. But under the pressure of warfare, the science of do-it-yourself genetics had a field day on planet Earth.

"We are constantly developing new strains of viruses and bacteria," they said. "And constantly we are bombarded by the Russians' latest weapons." They were hard-pressed. There weren't many of them in that particular MB Warfare Post, and the enemy's assaults were clever.

And finally the picture became clear. To all of us at once. It was Harold who said, "Fossa-me, mãe! You mean for eight hundred *years* you bunnies've been down here?"

They didn't answer until I asked the question—more politely, too, since I had noticed a certain set to those inscrutable jaws when Harold called them bunnies. Well, they *were* bunnies, white as white could be, but it was tasteless for Harold to call them that, particularly in front of Vladimir, who had more than a slight tendency toward white skin himself.

"Have you Americans been trapped down here ever since the war began?" I asked, trying to put awe into my voice, and succeeding. Horror isn't that far removed from awe, anyway.

They beamed with what I took for pride. And I was beginning to be able to interpret some of their facial expressions. As long as I had good words for America, I was all right.

"Yes, Captain Kane Kanea, we and our ancestors have been here from the beginning."

"Doesn't it get a little cramped?"

"Not for American soldiers, Captain. For the right to life, liberty, and the pursuit of happiness we would sacrifice anything." I didn't ask how much liberty and happiness-pursuing were possible in a hole in the rock. Our hero went on: "We fight on that millions may live, free, able to breathe the clean air of America unoppressed by the lashes of Communism."

And then they broke into a few choice hymns about purple mountains and yellow waves with a rousing chorus of God blessing America. It all ended with a mighty shout: "Better dead than red." When it was over we asked them if we could sleep, since according to our ship's time it was well past bedding-down hour.

They put us in a rather small room with three cots in it that were far too short for us. Didn't matter. We couldn't possibly be comfortable in our monkeysuits anyway.

Harold wanted to talk in lingua deporto as soon as we were alone, but I managed to convince him without even using my monkeysuit's discipliner button that we didn't want them to think we were trying to keep any secrets. We all took it for granted that they were monitoring us.

And so our conversation was the sort of conversation that one doesn't mind having overheard by a bunch of crazy patriots.

Amauri: "I am amazed at their great love for America, persisting so many centuries." Translation: "What the hell got these guys so nuts about something as dead as the ancient U.S. empire?"

Me: "Perhaps it is due to such unwavering loyalty to the flag, God, country, and liberty" (I admit I was laying it on thick, but better to be safe, etc.) "that they have been able to survive so long." Translation: "Maybe being crazy fanatics is all that's kept them alive in this hole."

Harold: "I wonder how long we can stay in this bastion of democracy before we must reluctantly go back to our colony of the glorious American dream." Translation: "What are the odds they don't let us go? After all, they're so loony they might think we're spies or something."

Vladimir: "I only hope we can learn from them. Their science is infinitely beyond anything we have hitherto developed with our poor resources." Translation: "We're not going anywhere until I have a chance to do *my* job and check out the local flora and fauna. Eight hundred years of recombining DNA has got to have something we can take back home to Núncamais."

And so the conversation went until we were sick of the flowers and perfume that kept dropping out of our mouths. Then we went to sleep.

The next day was guided tour day, Russian attack day, and damn near good-bye to the crew of the good ship Pollywog.

The guided tour kept us up hill and down dale for most of the morning. Vladimir was running the tracking computer from his monkeysuit. Mine was too busy analyzing the implications of all their comments while Amauri was absorbing the science and Harold was trying to figure out how to pick his nose with mittens on. Harold was along for the ride—a weapons expert, just in case. Thank God.

We began to be able to tell one little person from another. George Washington Steiner was our usual guide. The big boss, who had talked to us through most of the history lesson the day before, was Andrew Jackson Wallichinsky. And the guy who led the singing was Richard Nixon Dixon. The computer told us those were names of beloved American presidents, with surnames added.

And my monkeysuit's analysis also told us that the music leader was the *real* big boss, while Andy Jack Wallichinsky was merely the director of scientific research. Seems that the politicians ran the brains, instead of vice versa.

Our guide, G. W. Steiner, was very proud of his assignment. He showed us everything. I mean, even with the monkeysuit keeping three-fourths of the gravity away from me, my feet were sore by lunchtime (a quick sip of recycled xixi and cocó). And it was impressive. Again, I give it unto you in abbreviated form:

Even though the installation was technically airtight, in fact the enemy viruses and bacteria could get in quite readily. It seems that early in the twenty-first century the Russians had stopped making any kind of radio broadcasts. (I know, that sounds like a non sequitur. Patience, patience.) At first the Americans in 004 had thought they had won. And

387

then, suddenly, a new onslaught of another disease. At this time the 004 researchers had never been *personally* hit by any diseases—the airtight system was working fine. But their commander at that time, Rodney Fletcher, had been very suspicious.

"He thought it was a commie trick," said George Washington Steiner. I began to see the roots of superpatriotism in 004's history.

So Rodney Fletcher set the scientists to working on strengthening the base personnel's antibody system. They plugged away at it for two weeks and came up with three new strains of bacteria that selectively devoured practically anything that wasn't supposed to be in the human body. Just in time, too, because then that new disease hit. It wasn't stopped by the airtight system, because instead of being a virus, it was just two little amino acids and a molecule of lactose, put together *just so*. It fit right through the filters. It sailed right through the antibiotics. It entered right into the lungs of every man, woman, and child in 004. And if Rodney Fletcher hadn't been a paranoid, they all would have died. As it was, only about half lived.

Those two amino acids and the lactose molecule had the ability to fit right into *that* spot on a human DNA and then make the DNA replicate that way. Just one little change—and pretty soon nerves just stopped working.

Those two amino acids and the lactose molecule system worked just well enough to slow down the disease's progress until a plug could be found that fit even better into that spot on the DNA, keeping the Russians' little devices out. (Can they be called viruses? Can they be called alive? I'll leave it to the godcallers and the philosophers to decide that.)

Trouble was, the plugs also caused all the soldiers' babies to grow up to be very short with a propensity for having their teeth fall out and their eyes go blind at the age of thirty. G. W. Steiner was very proud of the fact that they had managed to correct for the eyes after four generations. He smiled and for the first time we really noticed that his teeth weren't like ours.

"We make them out of certain bacteria that gets very hard when a particular virus is exposed to it. My own great-great-grandmother invented it," Steiner said. "We're always coming up with new and useful tools."

I asked to see how they did this trick, which brings us full circle to what we saw on the guided tour that day. We saw the laboratories where eleven researchers were playing clever little games with DNA. I didn't understand any of it, but my monkey-suit assured me that the computer was getting it all.

We also saw the weapons delivery system. It was very clever. It consisted of setting a culture dish full of a particular nasty weapon in a little box, closing the door to the box, and then pressing a button that opened another door to the box that led outside.

"We let the wind take it from there," said Steiner. "We figure it takes about a year for a new weapon to reach Russia. But by then it's grown to a point that it's irresistible."

I asked him what the bacteria lived on. He laughed. "Anything," he said. It turns out that their basic breeding stock is a bacterium that can photosynthesize and dissolve any form of iron, both at the same time. "Whatever else we change about a particular weapon, we don't change that," Steiner said. "Our weapons can travel anywhere without hosts. Quarantines don't do any good."

Harold had an idea. I was proud of him. "If these little germs can dissolve steel, George, why the hell aren't they in here dissolving this whole installation?"

Steiner looked like he had just been hoping we'd ask that question.

"When we developed our basic breeder stock, we also developed a mold that inhibits the bacteria from reproducing and eating. The mold only grows on metal and the spores die if they're away from both mold and metal for more than one-seventy-seventh of a second. That means that the mold grows all the way around this installation—and nowhere else. My fourteenth great-uncle William Westmoreland Hannamaker developed the mold."

"Why," I asked, "do you keep mentioning your blood relationship to these inventors? Surely after eight hundred years here everybody's related?"

I thought I was asking a simple question. But G. W. Steiner looked at me coldly and turned away, leading us to the next room.

We found bacteria that processed other bacteria that processed still other bacteria that turned human excrement into very tasty, nutritious food. We took their word for the tasty. I know, we were still eating recycled us through the tubes in our suit. But at least we knew where *ours* had been.

They had bacteria that without benefit of sunlight processed carbon dioxide and water back into oxygen and starch. So much for photosynthesis.

And we got a list of what shelf after shelf of weapons could do to an unprepared human body. If somebody ever broke all those jars on Núncamais or Pennsylvania or Kiev, everybody would simply disappear, completely devoured and incorporated into the life-systems of bacteria and viruses and trained amino-acid sets.

No sooner did I think of that, than I said it. Only I didn't get any farther than the word *Kiev*.

"Kiev? One of the colonies is named Kiev?"

I shrugged. "There are only three planets colonized. Kiev, Pennsylvania, and Núncamais."

"*Russian* ancestry?"

Oops, I thought. Oops is an all-purpose word standing for every bit of profanity, blasphemy, and pornographic and scatological exculpation I could think of.

The guided tour ended right then.

Back in our bedroom, we became aware that we had somehow dissolved our hospitality. After a while, Harold realized that it was my fault.

"Captain, by damn, if you hadn't told them about Kiev we wouldn't be locked in here like this!"

I agreed, hoping to pacify him, but he didn't calm down until I used the discipliner button in my monkeysuit.

Then we consulted the computers.

Mine reported that in all we had been told, two areas had been completely left out: While it was obvious that in the past the little people had done extensive work on human DNA, there had been no hint of any work going on in that field today. And though we had been told of all kinds of weapons that had been flung among the Russians on the other side of the word, there had been no hint of any kind of limited effect antipersonnel weapon *here*.

"Oh," Harold said. "There's nothing to stop us from walking out of here anytime we can knock the

391

door down. And I can knock the door down anytime I want to," he said, playing with the buttons on his monkeysuit. I urged him to wait until all the reports were done.

Amauri informed us that he had gleaned enough information from their talk and his monkeyeyes that we could go home with the entire science of DNA recombination hidden away in our computer.

And then Vladimir's suit played out a holomap of Post 004.

The bright green, infinitesimally thin lines marked walls, doors, passages. We immediately recognized the corridors we had walked in throughout the morning, located the laboratories, found where we were imprisoned. And then we noticed a rather larger area in the middle of the holomap that seemed empty.

"Did you see a room like that?" I asked. The others shook their heads. Vladimir asked the holomap if we had been in it. The suit answered in its whispery monkeyvoice: "No. I have only delineated the unpenetrated perimeter and noted apertures that perhaps give entry."

"So they didn't let us in there," Harold said. "I knew the bastards were hiding something."

"And let's make a guess," I said. "That room either has something to do with antipersonnel weapons, or it has something to do with human DNA research."

We sat and pondered the revelations we had just had, and realized they didn't add up to much. Finally Vladimir spoke up. Trust a half-bunny to come up with the idea where three browns couldn't. Just goes to show you that a racial theory is a bunch of waggy-woggle.

"Antipersonnel hell," Vladimir said. "They don't need antipersonnel. All they have to do is open a little hole in our suits and let the germs come through."

"Our suits close immediately," Amauri said, but then corrected himself. "I guess it doesn't take long for a virus to get through, does it?"

Harold didn't get it. "Let one of those bunnies try to lay a knife on me, and I'll split him from ass to armpit."

We ignored him.

"What makes you think there are germs in here? Our suits don't measure that," I pointed out.

Vladimir had already thought of that. "Remember what they said. About the Russians getting those little amino-acid monsters in here."

Amauri snorted. "Russians."

"Yeah, right," Vladimir said, "but keep the voice down, viado."

Amauri turned red, started to say, "Quem é que cê chama de viado!"—but I pushed the discipliner button. No time for any of that crap.

"Watch your language, Vladimir. We got enough problems."

"Sorry, Amauri, Captain," Vladimir said. "I'm a little wispy, you know?"

"So's everybody."

Vladimir took a breath and went on. "Once those bugs got in here, 004 must have been pretty thoroughly permeable. The, uh, Russians must've kept pumping more variations on the same into Post 004."

"So why aren't they all dead?"

"What I think is that a lot of these people *have* been killed—but the survivors are ones whose bodies

393

took readily to those plugs they came up with. The plugs are regular parts of their body chemistry now. They'd have to be, wouldn't they? They told us they were passed on in the DNA transmitted to the next generation."

I got it. So did Amauri, who said, "So they've had seven or eight centuries to select for adaptability."

"Why not?" Vladimir asked. "Didn't you notice? Eleven researchers on developing new weapons. And only two on developing new defenses. They can't be *too* worried."

Amauri shook his head. "Oh, Mother Earth. Whatever got into you?"

"Just caught a cold," Vladimir said, and then laughed. "A virus. Called humanity."

We sat around looking at the holomap for a while. I found four different routes from where we were to the secret area—if we wanted to get there. I also found three routes to the exit. I pointed them out to the others.

"Yeah," Harold said. "Trouble is, who knows if those doors really lead into that unknown area? I mean, what the hell, three of the four doors might lead to the broom closets or service stations."

A good point.

We just sat there, wondering whether we should head for the Pollywog or try to find out what was in the hidden area, when the Russian attack made up our minds for us. There was a tremendous bang. The floor shook, as if some immense dog had just picked up Post 004 and given it a good shaking. When it stopped the lights flickered and went out.

"Golden opportunity," I said into the monkey-mouth. The others agreed. So we flashed on the lights from our suits and pointed them at the door.

Harold suddenly felt very important. He went to the door and ran his magic flipper finger all the way around the door. Then he stepped back and flicked a lever on his suit.

"Better turn your backs," he said. "This can flash pretty bright."

Even looking at the back wall the explosion blinded me for a few seconds. The world looked a little green when I turned around. The door was in shreds on the floor, and the doorjamb didn't look too healthy.

"Nice job, Harold," I said.

"Graças a deus," he answered, and I had to laugh. Odd how little religious phrases refused to die, even with an irreverent filho de punta like Harold.

Then I remembered that I was in charge of order-giving. So I gave.

The second door we tried led into the rooms we wanted to see. But just as we got in, the lights came on.

"Damn. They've got the station back in order," Amauri said. But Vladimir just pointed down the corridor.

The pea soup had gotten in. It was oozing sluggishly toward us.

"Whatever the Russians did, it must have opened up a big hole in the station." Vladimir pointed his laser finger at the mess. Even on full power, it only made a little spot steam. The rest just kept coming.

"Anyone for swimming?" I asked. No one was. So I hustled them all into the not-so-hidden room.

There were some little people in there, cowering in the darkness. Harold wrapped them in cocoons and stuck them in a corner. So we had time to look around.

There wasn't that much to see, really. Standard lab equipment, and then thirty-two boxes, about a meter square. They were under sunlamps. We looked inside.

The animals were semisolid looking. I didn't touch one right then, but the sluggish way it sent out pseudopodia, I concluded that the one I was watching, at least, had a rather crusty skin—with jelly inside. They were all a light brown—even lighter than Vladimir's skin. But there were little green spots here and there. I wondered if they photosynthesized.

"Look what they're floating in," Amauri said, and I realized that it was pea soup.

"They've developed a giant amoeba that lives on all other microorganisms, I guess," Vladimir said. "Maybe they've trained it to carry bombs. Against the Russians."

At that moment Harold began firing his arsenal, and I noticed that the little people were gathered at the door to the lab, looking agitated. A few at the front were looking dead.

Harold probably would have killed all of them, except that we were still standing next to a box with a giant amoeba in it. When he screamed, we looked and saw the creature fastened against his leg. Even as we watched, Harold fell, the bottom half of his leg dropping away as the amoeba continued eating up his thigh.

We watched just long enough for the little people to grab hold of us in sufficient numbers that resistance would have been ridiculous. Besides, we couldn't take our eyes off Harold.

At about the groin, the amoeba stopped eating. it didn't matter. Harold was dead anyway—we didn't know what disease got him, but as soon as his suit had cracked he started vomiting into his suit. There were pustules all over his face. In short, Vladimir's guess about the virus content of Post 004 had been pretty accurate.

And now the amoeba formed itself into a pentagon. Five very smooth sides, the creature sitting in a clump on the gaping wound that had once been a pelvis. Suddenly, with a brief convulsion, all the sides bisected, forming sharp angles, so that now there were ten sides to the creature. A hairline crack appeared down the middle. And then, like jelly sliced in the middle and finally deciding to split, the two halves slumped away on either side. They quickly formed into two new pentagons, and then they relaxed into pseudopodia again, and continued devouring Harold.

"Well," Amauri said. "They *do* have an anti-personnel weapon."

When he spoke, the spell of stillness was broken, and the little people had us spread on tables with sharp-pointed objects pointed at us. If any one of those punctured a suit even for a moment, we would be dead. We held very still.

Richard Nixon Dixon, the top halibut, interrogated us himself. It all started with a lot of questions about the Russians, when we had visited them, why we had decided to serve them instead of the Americans, etc. We kept insisting that they were full of crap.

But when they threatened to open a window into Vladimir's suit, I decided enough was enough.

"Tell 'em!" I shouted into the monkeymouth, and Vladimir said, "All right," and the little people leaned back to listen.

"There *are* no Russians," Vladimir said.

The little people got ready to carve holes.

"No, wait, it's true! After we got your homing signal, before we landed, we made seven orbital passes over the entire planet. There is absolutely no human life anywhere but here!"

"Commie lies," Richard Nixon Dixon said.

"God's own truth!" I shouted. "Don't touch him, man! He's telling the truth! The only thing out there over this whole damn planet is that pea soup! It covers every inch of land and every inch of water, except a few holes at the poles."

Dixon began to feel a little confused, and the little people murmured. I guess I sounded sincere.

"If there aren't any people,' Dixon said, "where do the Russian attacks come from?"

Vladimir answered that one. For a bunny, he was quick on the uptake. "Spontaneous recombination! You and the Russians got new strains of every microbe developing like crazy. All the people, all the animals, all the *plants* were killed. And only the microbes lived. But you've been introducing new strains constantly, tough competitors for all those beasts out there. The ones that couldn't adapt died. And now that's all that's left—the ones who adapt. Constantly."

Andrew Jackson Wallichinsky, the head researcher, nodded. "It sounds plausible."

"If there's anything we've learned about commies in the last thousand years," Richard Nixon Dixon said, "it's that you can't trust 'em any farther than you can spit."

"Well," Andy Jack said, "it's easy enough to test them."

Dixon nodded. "Go ahead."

So three of the little people went to the boxes and each came back with an amoeba. In a minute it was clear that they planned to set them on us. Amauri screamed. Vladimir turned white. I would have screamed but I was busy trying to swallow my tongue.

"Relax," Andy Jack said. "They won't hurt you."

"Acre*dito*!" I shouted. "Like it didn't hurt Harold!"

"Harold was killing people. These won't harm you. Unless you were lying."

Great, I thought. Like the ancient test for witches. Throw them in the water, if they drown they're innocent, if they float they're guilty so kill 'em.

But *maybe* Andy Jack was telling the truth and they wouldn't hurt us. And if we refused to let them put those buggers on us they'd "know" we had been lying and punch holes in our monkeysuits.

So I told the little people to put one on me only. They didn't need to test us all.

And then I put my tongue between my teeth, ready to bite down hard and inhale the blood when the damn thing started eating me. Somehow I thought I'd feel better about going honeyduck if I helped myself along.

They set the thing on my shoulder. It didn't penetrate my monkeysuit. Instead it just oozed up toward my head.

It slid over my faceplate and the world went dark.

"Kane Kanea," said a faint vibration in the faceplate.

"Meu deus," I muttered.

The amoeba could talk. But I didn't have to speak to answer it. A question would come through the vibration of the faceplate. And then I would lie there

399

and—it knew my answer. Easy as pie. I was so scared I urinated twice during the interview. But my imperturbable monkeysuit cleaned it all up and got it ready for breakfast, just like normal.

And at last the interview was over. The amoeba slithered off my faceplate and returned to the waiting arms of one of the little people, who carried it back to Andy Jack and Ricky Nick. The two men put their hands on the thing, and then looked at us in surprise.

"You're telling the truth. There are no Russians."

Vladimir shrugged. "Why would we lie?"

Andy Jack started toward me, carrying the writhing monster that had interviewed me.

"I'll kill myself before I let that thing touch me again."

Andy Jack stopped in surprise. "You're still afraid of that?"

"It's intelligent," I said. "It read my mind."

Vladimir looked startled, and Amauri muttered something. But Andy Jack only smiled. "Nothing mysterious about that. It can read and interpret the electromagnetic fields of your brain, coupled with the amitron flux in your thyroid gland."

"What *is* it?" Vladimir asked.

Andy Jack looked very proud. "This one is my son."

We waited for the punch line. It didn't come. And suddenly we realized that we had found what we had been looking for—the result of the little people's research into recombinant human DNA.

"We've been working on these for years. Finally we got it right about four years ago," Andy Jack said. "They were our last line of defense. But now that we know the Russians are dead—well, well, there's no reason for them to stay in their nests."

And the man reached down and laid the amoeba into the pea soup that was now about sixty centimeters deep on the floor. Immediately it flattened out on the surface until it was about a meter in diameter. I remembered the whispering voice through my faceplate.

"It's too flexible to have a brain," Vladimir said.

"It doesn't have one," Andy Jack answered. "The brain functions are distributed throughout the body. If it were cut in forty pieces, each piece would have enough memory and enough mindfunction to continue to live. It's indestructible. And when several of them get together, they set up a sympathetic field. They become very bright, then."

"Head of the class and everything, I'm sure," Vladimir said. He couldn't hide the loathing in his voice. Me, I was trying not to be sick.

So this is the next stage of evolution, I thought. Man screws up the planet till it's fit for nothing but microbes—and then changes himself so that he can live on a diet of bacteria and viruses.

"It's really the perfect step in evolution," Andy Jack said. "This fellow can adapt to new species of parasitic bacteria and viruses almost by reflex. Control the makeup of his own DNA consciously. Manipulate the DNA of other organisms by absorbing them through the semipermeable membranes of specialized cells, altering them, and setting them free again."

"Somehow it doesn't make me want to feed it or change its diapers."

Andy Jack laughed lightly. "Since they reproduce by fission, they're never infant. Oh, if the piece were

401

too small, it would take a while to get back to adult competence again. But otherwise, in the normal run of things, it's always an adult."

Then Andy Jack reached down, let his son wrap itself around his arm, and then walked back to where Richard Nixon Dixon stood watching. Andy Jack put the arm that held the amoeba around Dixon's shoulder.

"By the way, sir," Andy Jack said. "With the Russians dead, the damned war is over, sir."

Dixon looked startled. "And?"

"We don't need a commander anymore."

Before Dixon could answer, the amoeba had eaten through his neck and he was quite dead. Rather an abrupt coup, I thought, and looked at the other little people for a reaction. No one seemed to mind. Apparently their superpatriotic militarism was only skin deep. I felt vaguely relieved. Maybe they had something in common with me after all.

They decided to let us go, and we were glad enough to take them up on the offer. On the way out, they showed us what had caused the explosion in the last "Russian" attack. The mold that protected the steel surface of the installation had mutated slightly in one place, allowing the steel-eating bacteria to enter into a symbiotic relationship. It just happened that the mutation occurred at the place where the hydrogen storage tanks rested against the wall. When a hole opened, one of the first amino-acid sets that came through with the pea soup was one that combines radically with raw hydrogen. The effect was a three-second population explosion. It knocked out a huge chunk of Post 004.

We were glad, when we got back to our skipship, that we had left dear old Pollywog floating some

402

forty meters off the ground. Even so, there had been some damage. One of the airborne microbes had a penchant for lodging in hairline cracks and reproducing rapidly, widening microscopic gaps in the structure of the ship. Nevertheless, Amauri judged us fit for takeoff.

We didn't kiss anybody good-bye.

So now I've let you in on the true story of our visit to Mother Earth back in 2810. The parallel with our current situation should be obvious. If we let Pennsylvania get soaked into this spongy little war between Kiev and Núncamais, we'll deserve what we get. Because those damned antimatter convertors will do things that make germ warfare look as pleasant as sniffing pinkweeds.

And if anything human survives the war, it sure as hell won't look like anything we call human now.

And maybe that doesn't matter to anybody these days. But it matters to me. I don't like the idea of amoebas for grandchildren, and having an antimatter great-nephew thrills me less. I've been human all my life, and I like it.

So I say, turn on our repressors and sit out the damned war. Wait until they've disappeared each other, and then go about the business of keeping humanity alive—and human.

So much for the political tract. If you vote for war, though, I can promise you there'll be more than one skipship heading for the wild black yonder. We've colonized before, and we can do it again. In case no one gets the hint, that's a call for volunteers, if, as, and when. Over.

Not over. On the first printing of this program, I got a lot of inquiries as to why we didn't report all this

403

when we got back home. The answer's simple. On Núncamais it's a capital crime to alter a ship's log. But we had to.

As soon as we got into space from Mother Earth, Vladimir had the computer present all its findings, all its data, and all its conclusions about recombinant DNA. And then he erased it all.

I probably would have stopped him if I'd known what he was doing in advance. But once it was done, Amauri and I realized that he was right. That kind of merda didn't belong in the universe. And then we systematically covered our tracks. We erased all reference to Post 004, eradicated any hint of a homing signal. All we left in the computer was the recording of our overflight, showing nothing but pea soup from sea to soupy sea. It was tricky, but we also added a serious malfunction of the EVA life-support gear on the way home—which cost us the life of our dear friend and comrade, Harold.

And then we recorded in the ship's log, "Planet unfit for human occupancy. No human life found."

Hell. It wasn't even a lie.

In the Doghouse

(with Jay A. Parry)

As Mklikluln awoke, he felt the same depression that he had felt as he went to sleep ninety-seven years ago. And though he knew it would only make his depression worse, he immediately scanned backward as his ship decelerated, hunting for the star that had been the sun. He couldn't find it. Which meant that even with acceleration and deceleration time, the light from the nova—or supernova—had not yet reached the system he was heading for.

Sentimentality be dammed, he thought savagely as he turned his attention to the readouts on the upcoming system. So the ice cliffs will melt, and the sourland will turn to huge, planet-spanning lakes. So the atmosphere will fly away in the intense heat. Who cares? Humanity was safe.

As safe as bodiless minds can be, resting in their own supporting mindfields somewhere in space, waiting for the instantaneous message that *here* is a planet with bodies available, *here* is a home for the millions for whom there had been no spaceships, *here* we can once again—

Once again what?

No matter how far we search, Mklikluln reminded himself, we have no hope of finding those graceful, symmetrical, hexagonally delicate bodies we left behind to burn.

Of course, Mklikluln still had his, but only for a while.

Thirteen true planetary bodies, two of which co-orbited as binaries in the third position. Ignoring the gas giants and the crusty pebbles outside the habitable range, Mklikluln got increasingly more complex readouts on the binary and the single in the fourth orbit, a red midget.

The red was dead, the smaller binary even worse, but the blue-green larger binary was ideal. Not because it matched the conditions on Mklikluln's home world—that would be impossible. But because it had life. And not only life—intelligent life.

Or at least fairly bright life. Energy output in the sub- and supravisible spectra exceeded reflection from the star (No, I must try to think of it as the *sun*) by a significant degree. Energy clearly came from a breakdown of carbon compounds, just what current theory (current? ninety-seven-year-old) had assumed would be the logical energy base of a developing world in this temperature range. The professors would be most gratified.

And after several months of maneuvering his craft, he was in stationary orbit around the larger binary. He began monitoring communications on the supravisible wavelengths. He learned the language quickly, though of course he couldn't have produced it with his own body, and sighed a little when he realized that the aliens, like his own people, called their little star "the sun," their minor binary "the moon," and their own humble, overhot planet "earth" (terra, mund, etc.). The array of languages was impressive—to think that people would go to all the trouble of thinking out hundreds of completely different ways of communicating for the sheer love of the logical exercise was amazing—what minds they must have!

For a moment he fleetingly thought of taking over for his people's use the bipedal bodies of the dominant intelligent race; but law was law, and his people would commit mass suicide if they realized—as they would surely realize—that they had gained their bodies at the expense of another intelligent race. One could think of such bipedals as being almost human, right down to the whimsical sense of humor that so reminded Mklikluln of his wife (Ah, Glundnindn, and you the pilot who volunteered to plunge into the sun, scooping out the sample that killed you, but saved us!); but he refused to mourn.

The dominant race was out. Similar bipedals were too small in population, too feared or misunderstood by the dominant race. Other animals with appropriate populations didn't have body functions that could easily support intelligence without major revisions—and many were too weak to survive unaided, too short of lifespan to allow civilization.

And so he narrowed down the choices to two quadrupeds, of very different sorts, of course, but well within the limits of choice: both had full access to the domiciles of the dominant race; both had adequate body structure to support intellect; both had potential means of communicating; both had sufficient population to hold all the encapsulated minds waiting in the space between the stars.

Mklikluln did the mental equivalent of flipping a coin—would have flipped a coin, in fact, except that he had neither hand nor coin nor adequate gravity for flipping.

407

The choice made—for the noisy one of greater intelligence that already had the love of most members of the master race—he set about making plans on how to introduce the transceivers that would call his people. (The dominant race must not know what is happening; and it can't be done without the cooperation of the dominant race.)

Mklikluln's six points vibrated just a little as he thought.

Abu was underpaid, underfed, underweight, and within about twelve minutes of the end of his lifespan. He was concentrating on the first problem, however, as the fourth developed.

"Why am I being paid less than Faisel, who sits on his duff by the gate while I walk back and forth in front of the cells all day?" he righteously said—under his breath, of course, in case his supervisor should overhear him. "Am I not as good a Muslim? Am I not as smart? Am I not as loyal to the Party?"

And as he was immersed in righteous indignation at man's inhumanity, not so much to mankind as to Abu ibn Assur, a great roaring sound tore through the desert prison, followed by a terrible, hot, dry, sand-stabbing wind. Abu screamed and covered his eyes—too late, however, and the sand ripped them open, and the hot air dried them out.

That was why he didn't see the hole in the outside wall of cell 23, which held a political prisoner condemned to die the next morning for having murdered his wife—normally not a political crime, except when the wife was also the daughter of somebody who could make phone calls and get people put in prison.

That was why he didn't see his supervisor come

in, discover cell 23 empty, and then aim his sub-machine gun at Abu as the first step to setting up the hapless guard as the official scapegoat for this fiasco. Abu did, however, hear and feel the discharge of the gun, and wondered vaguely what had happened as he died.

Mklikluln stretched the new arms and legs (the four-ness of the body, the two-sidedness, the overwhelming sexuality of it—all were amazing, all were delightful) and walked around his little spacecraft. And the fiveness and tenness of the fingers and toes! (What we could have done with fingers and toes! except that we might not have developed thought-talk, then, and would have been tied to the vibration of air as are these people.) Inside the ship he could see his own body melting as the hot air of the Kansas farmland raised the temperature above the melting point of ice.

He had broken the law himself, but could see no way around it. Necessary as his act had been, and careful as he had been to steal the body of a man doomed anyway to die, he knew that his own people would try him, convict him, and execute him for depriving an intelligent being of life.

But in the meantime, it was a new body and a whole range of sensations. He moved the tongue over the teeth. He made the buzzing in his throat that was used for communication. He tried to speak.

It was impossible. Or so it seemed, as the tongue and lips and jaw tried to make the Arabic sounds the reflex pathways were accustomed to, while Mklikluln tried to speak in the language that had dominated the airwaves.

He kept practicing as he carefully melted down

his ship (though it was transparent to most electro-magnetic spectra, it might still cause comment if found) and by the time he made his way into the nearby city, he was able to communicate fairly well. Well enough, anyway, to contract with the Kansas City Development Corporation for the manufacture of the machine he had devised; with Farber, Farber, and Maynard to secure patents on every detail of the machinery; and with Sidney's carpentry shop to manufacture the doghouses.

He sold enough diamonds to pay for the first 2,000 finished models. And then he hit the road, humming the language he had learned from the radio. "It's the real thing, Coke is," he sang to himself. "Mr. Transmission will put in commission the worst trans-missions in town."

The sun set as he checked into a motel outside Manhattan, Kansas. "How many?" asked the clerk.

"One," said Mklikluln.

"Name?"

"Robert," he said, using a name he had randomly chosen from among the many thousands mentioned on the airwaves. "Robert Redford."

"Ha-ha," said the clerk. "I bet you get teased about that a lot."

"Yeah. But I get in to see a lot of important people."

The clerk laughed. Mklikluln smiled. Speaking was fun. For one thing, you could lie. An art his people had never learned to cultivate.

"Profession?"

"Salesman."

"Really, Mr. Redford? What do you sell?"

Mklikluln shrugged, practicing looking mildly embarrassed. "Doghouses," he said.

410

Royce Jacobsen pulled open the front door of his sweltering hot house and sighed. A salesman.

"We don't want any," he said.

"Yes you do," said the man, smiling.

Royce was a little startled. Salesmen usually didn't argue with potential customers—they usually whined. And those that did argue rarely did it with such calm self-assurance. The man was an ass, Royce decided. He looked at the sample case. On the side were the letters spelling out: "Doghouses Unlimited."

"We don't got a dog," Royce said.

"But you *do* have a very warm house, I believe," the salesman said.

"Yeah. Hotter'n Hades, as the preachers say. Ha." The laugh would have been bigger than one *Ha*, but Royce was hot and tired and it was only a salesman.

"But you have an air conditioner."

"Yeah," Royce said. "What I don't have is a permit for more than a hundred bucks worth of power from the damnpowercompany. So if I run the air conditioner more than one day a month, I get the refrigerator shut down, or the stove, or some other such thing."

The salesman looked sympathetic.

"It's guys like me,' Royce went on, "who always get the short end of the stick. You can bet your boots that the mayor gets all the air conditioning he wants. You can bet your boots *and* your overalls, as the farmers say, ha ha, that the president of the damnpowercompany takes three hot showers a day and three cold showers a night and leave his windows open in the winter, too, you can bet on it."

"Right," said the salesman. "The power companies own this whole country. They own the whole world, you know? Think it's any different in England? In Japan? They got the gas, and so they get the gold."

"Yeah," Royce agreed. "You're my kind of guy. You come right in. House is hot as Hades, as the preachers say, ha ha ha, but it sure beats standing in the sun."

They sat on a beat-up-looking couch and Royce explained exactly what was wrong with the damnpowercompany and what he thought of the damnpowercompany's executives and in what part of their anatomy they should shove their quotas, bills, rates, and periods of maximum and minimum use. "I'm sick to death of having to take a shower at 2:00 A.M.!" Royce shouted.

"Then do something about it!" the salesman rejoindered.

"Sure. Like what?"

"Like buy a doghouse from me."

Royce thought that was funny. He laughed for a good long while.

But then the salesman started talking very quietly, showing him pictures and diagrams and cost analysis papers that proved—what?

"That the solar energy utilizer built into this doghouse can power your entire house, all day every day, with four times as much power as you could use if you turned on all your home appliances all day every day, for exactly zero once you pay me this simple one-time fee."

Royce shook his head, though he coveted the doghouse. "Can't. Illegal. I think they passed a law against solar energy thingies back in '85 or '86, to protect the power companies."

The salesman laughed. "How much protection do the power companies need?"

"Sure," Royce answered, "it's me that needs protection. But the meter reader—if I stop using power, he'll report me, they'll investigate—"

"That's why we don't put your whole house on it. We just put the big power users on it, and gradually take more off the regular current until you're paying what, maybe fifteen dollars a month. Right? Only instead of fifteen dollars a month and cooking over a fire and sweating to death in a hot house, you've got the air conditioner running all day, the heater running all day in the winter, showers whenever you want them, and you can open the refrigerator as often as you like."

Royce still wasn't sure.

"What've you got to lose?" the salesman asked.

"My seat," Royce answered. "You hear that? My seat. Ha ha ha ha."

"That's why we build them into doghouses—so that nobody'll suspect anything."

"Sure, why not?" Royce asked. "Do it. I'm game. I didn't vote for the damncongressman who voted in that stupid law anyway."

The air conditioner hummed as the guests came in. Royce and his wife, Junie, ushered them into the living room. The television was on in the family room and the osterizer was running in the kitchen. Royce carelessly flipped on a light. One of the women gasped. A man whispered to his wife. Royce and Junie carelessly began their conversation—as Royce *left the door open*.

A guest noticed it—Mr. Detweiler from the bowl-

413

ing team. He said, "Hey!" and leaped from the chair toward the door.

Royce stopped him, saying, "Never mind, never mind, I'll get it in a minute. Here, have some peanuts." And the guests all watched the door in agony as Royce passed the peanuts around, then (finally!) went to the door to close it.

"Beautiful day outside," Royce said, holding the door open a few minutes longer.

Somebody in the living room mentioned a name of the deity. Somebody else countered with a one-word discussion of defecation. Royce was satisfied that the point had been made. He shut the door.

"Oh, by the way," he said. "I'd like you to meet a friend of mine. His name is Robert Redford."

Gasp, gasp, of course you're joking, Robert Redford, what a laugh, sure.

"Actually, his name *is* Robert Redford, but he isn't, of course, the all-time greatest star of stage, screen, and the Friday Night Movie, as the disc jockeys say, ha ha. He is, in short, my friends, a doghouse salesman."

Mklikluln came in then, and shook hands all around.

"He looks like an Arab," a woman whispered.

"Or a Jew," her husband whispered back. "Who can tell?"

Royce beamed at Mklikluln and patted him on the back. "Redford here is the best salesman I ever met."

"Must be, if he sold you a doghouse, and you not even got a dog," said Mr. Detweiler of the bowling league, who could sound patronizing because he was the only one in the bowling league who had ever had a perfect game.

414

"Neverthemore, as the raven said, ha ha ha, I want you all to see my doghouse." And so Royce led the way past a kitchen where all the lights were on, where the refrigerator was standing open ("Royce, the fridge is open!" "Oh, I guess one of the kids left it that way." "I'd kill one of my kids that did something like that!"), where the stove *and* microwave *and* osterizer *and* hot water were all running at once. Some of the women looked faint.

And as the guests tried to rush through the back door all at once, to conserve energy, Royce said, "Slow down, slow down, what's the panic, the house on fire? Ha ha ha." But the guests still hurried through.

On the way out to the doghouse, which was located in the dead center of the backyard, Detweiler took Royce aside.

"Hey, Royce, old buddy. Who's your touch with the damnpowercompany? How'd you get your quota upped?"

Royce only smiled, shaking his head. "Quota's the same as ever, Detweiler." And then, raising his voice just a bit so that everybody in the backyard could hear, he said, "I only pay fifteen bucks a month for power as it is."

"Woof woof," said a small dog chained to the hook on the doghouse.

"Where'd the dog come from?" Royce whispered to Mklikluln.

"Neighbor was going to drown 'im," Mklikluln answered. "Besides, if you don't have a dog the power company's going to get suspicious. It's cover."

Royce nodded wisely. "Good idea, Redford. I just

hope this party's a good idea. What if somebody talks?"

"Nobody will," Mklikluln said confidently.

And then Mklikluln began showing the guests the finer points of the doghouse.

When they finally left, Mklikluln had twenty-three appointments during the next two weeks, checks made out to Doghouses Unlimited for $221.23, including taxes, and many new friends. Even Mr. Detweiler left smiling, his check in Mklikluln's hand, even though the puppy had pooped on his shoe.

"Here's your commission," Mklikluln said as he wrote out a check for three hundred dollars to Royce Jacobsen. "It's more than we agreed, but you earned it," he said.

"I feel a little funny about this," Royce said. "Like I'm conspiring to break the law or something."

"Nonsense," Mklikluln said. "Think of it as a Tupperware party."

"Sure," Royce said after a moment's thought. "It's not as if I actually did any selling myself, right?"

Within a week, however, Detweiler, Royce, and four other citizens of Manhattan, Kansas, were on their way to various distant cities of the United States, Doghouses Unlimited briefcases in their hands.

And within a month, Mklikluln had a staff of three hundred in seven cities, building doghouses and installing them. And into every doghouse went a frisky little puppy. Mklikluln did some figuring. In about a year, he decided. One year and I can call my people.

"What's happened to power consumption in Manhattan, Kansas?" asked Bill Wilson, up-and-coming young executive in the statistical analysis section of Central Kansas Power, otherwise known as the damnpowercompany.

"It's gotten lower," answered Kay Block, relic of outdated affirmative action programs in Central Kansas Power, who had reached the level of records examiner before the ERA was repealed to make our bathrooms safe for mankind.

Bill Wilson sneered, as if to say, "That much I knew, woman." And Kay Block simpered, as if to say, "Ah, the boy has an IQ after all, eh?"

But they got along well enough, and within an hour they had the alarming statistic that power consumption in the city of Manhattan, Kansas, was down by forty percent.

"What was consumption in the previous trimester?"

Normal. Everything normal.

"Forty percent is ridiculous," Bill fulminated.

"Don't fulminate at me," Kay said, irritated at her boss for raising his voice. "Go yell at the people who unplugged their refrigerators!"

"No," Bill said. "*You* go yell at people who unplugged their refrigerators. Something's gone wrong there, and if it isn't crooked meter readers, it's people who've figured out a way to jimmy the billing system."

After two weeks of investigation, Kay Block sat in the administration building of Kansas State University (9–2 last football season, coming *that* close to copping the Plains Conference pennant for '98) refusing to admit that her investigation had turned up a big fat zero. A random inspection of thirty-eight meters showed no tampering at all. A complete audit of the local branch office's books showed no doctoring at all. And a complete examination of KSU's power consumption figures showed absolutely nothing. No change in consumption—no change in billing system—and yet a sharp drop in electricity use.

"The drop in power use may be localized," Kay suggested to the white-haired woman from the school who was babysitting her through the process. "The stadium surely uses as much light as ever—so the drop must be somewhere else, like in the science labs."

The white-haired woman shook her head. "That may be so, but the figures you see are the figures we've got."

Kay sighed and looked out the window. Down from the window was the roof of the new Plant Science Building. She looked at it as her mind struggled vainly to find something meaningful in the data she had. Somebody was cheating—but how?

There was a doghouse on the roof of the Plant Science Building.

"What's a doghouse doing on the roof of that building?" asked Kay.

"I would assume," said the white-haired woman, "for a dog to live in."

"On the roof?"

The white-haired woman smiled. "Fresh air, perhaps," she said.

Kay looked at the doghouse awhile longer, telling herself that the only reason she was suspicious was because she was hunting for *anything* unusual that could explain the anomalies in the Manhattan, Kansas, power usage pattern.

"I want to see that doghouse," she said.

"Why?" asked the white-haired lady. "Surely you don't think a generator could hide in a doghouse! Or solar-power equipment! Why, those things take whole buildings!"

Kay looked carefully at the white-haired woman and decided that she protested a bit too much. "I insist on seeing the doghouse," she said again.

The white-haired woman smiled again. "Whatever you want, Miss Block. Let me call the custodian so he can unlock the door to the roof."

After the phone call they went down the stairs to the main floor of the administration building, across the lawns, and then up the stairs to the roof of the Plant Science Building. "What's the matter, no elevators?" Kay asked sourly as she panted from the exertion of climbing the stairs.

"Sorry," the white-haired woman said. "We don't build elevators into buildings anymore. They use too much power. Only the power company can afford elevators these days."

The custodian was at the door of the roof, looking very apologetic.

"Sorry if old Rover's been causin' trouble, ladies. I keep him up on the roof nowadays, ever since the break-in attempt through the roof door last spring. Nobody's tried to jimmy the door since."

"Arf," said a frisky, cheerful-looking mix between an elephant and a Labrador retriever (just a quick guess, of course) that bounded up to them.

"Howdy, Rover old boy," said the custodian. "Don't bite nobody."

"Arf," the dog answered, trying to wiggle out of

419

his skin and looking as if he might succeed. "Gur-rarf."

Kay examined the roof door from the outside. "I don't see any signs of anyone jimmying at the door," she said.

"Course not," said the custodian. "The burglars was seen from the administration building before they could get to the door."

"Oh," said Kay. "Then why did you need to put a dog up here?"

"Cause what if the burglars hadn't been seen?" the custodian said, his tone implying that only a moron would have asked such a question.

Kay looked at the doghouse. It looked like every other doghouse in the world. It looked like cartoons of doghouses, in fact, it was so ordinary. Simple arched door. Pitched roof with gables and eaves. All it lacked was a water dish and piles of doggy-do and old bones. No doggy-do?

"What a talented dog," Kay commented. "He doesn't even go to the bathroom."

"Uh," answered the custodian, "he's really house-broken. He just won't go until I take him down from here to the lawns, will ya Rover?"

Kay surveyed the wall of the roof-access building they had come through. "Odd. He doesn't even mark the walls."

"I told you. He's really housebroken. He wouldn't think of mucking up the roof here."

"Arf," said the dog as it urinated on the door and then defecated in a neat pile at Kay's feet. "Woof woof woof," he said proudly.

"All that training," Kay said, "and it's all gone to waste."

Whether the custodian's answer was merely

420

describing what the dog had done or had a more emphatic purpose was irrelevant. Obviously the doghouse was not normally used for a dog. And if that was true, what was a doghouse doing on the roof of the Plant Science Building?

The damnpowercompany brought civil actions against the city of Manhattan, Kansas, and a court injunction insisted that all doghouses be disconnected from all electric wiring systems. The city promptly brought countersuit against the damnpowercompany (a very popular move) and appealed the court injunction.

The damnpowercompany shut off all the power in Manhattan, Kansas.

Nobody in Manhattan, Kansas, noticed, except the branch office of the damnpowercompany, which now found itself the only building in the city without electricity.

The "Doghouse War" got quite a bit of notoriety. Feature articles appeared in magazines about Doghouses Unlimited and its elusive founder, Robert Redford, who refused to be interviewed and in fact could not be found. All five networks did specials on the cheap energy source. Statistics were gathered showing that not only did seven percent of the American public *have* doghouses, but also that 99.8 percent of the American public *wanted* to have doghouses. The 0.2 percent represented, presumably, power company stockholders and executives. Most politicians could add, or had aides who could, and the prospect of elections coming up in less than a year made the result clear.

The antisolar power law was repealed.

The power companies' stock plummeted on the stock market.

The world's most unnoticed depression began.

With alarming rapidity an economy based on expensive energy fell apart. The OPEC monolith immediately broke up, and within five months petroleum had fallen to 38¢ a barrel. Its only value was in plastics and as a lubricant, and the oil-producing nations had been overproducing for those needs.

The reason the depression wasn't much noticed was because Doghouses Unlimited easily met the demand for their product. Scenting a chance for profit, the government slapped a huge export tax on the doghouses. Doghouses Unlimited retaliated by publishing the complete plans for the doghouse and declaring that foreign companies would not be used for manufacturing it.

The U.S. government just as quickly removed the huge tax, whereupon Doghouses Unlimited announced that the plans it had published were not complete, and continued to corner the market around the world.

As government after government, through subterfuge, bribery, or, in a few cases, popular revolt, were forced to allow Doghouses Unlimited into their countries, Robert Redford (the doghouse one) became even more of a household word than Robert Redford (the old-time actor). Folk legends which had formerly been ascribed to Kuan Yu, Paul Bunyan, or Gautama Buddha became, gradually, attached to Robert Doghouse Redford.

And, at last, every family in the world that wanted one had a cheap energy source, an unlimited energy source, and everybody was happy. So happy that they shared their newfound plenty with all God's creatures, feeding birds in the winter, leaving bowls of milk for stray cats, and putting dogs in the doghouses.

Mklikluln rested his chin in his hands and reflected on the irony that he had, quite inadvertently, saved the world for the bipedal dominant race, solely as a byproduct of his campaign to get a good home for every dog. But good results are good results, and humanity—either his own or the bipedals—couldn't condemn him completely for his murder of an Arab political prisoner the year before.

"What will happen when you come?" he asked his people, though of course none of them could hear him. "I've saved the world—but when these creatures, bright as they are, come in contact with our infinitely superior intelligence, won't it destroy them? Won't they suffer in humiliation to realize that we are so much more powerful than they; that we can span galactic distances at the speed of light, communicate telepathically, separate our minds and allow our bodies to die while we float in space unscathed, and then, at the beck of a simple machine, come instantaneously and inhabit the bodies of animals completely different from our former bodies?"

He worried—but his responsibility to his own people was clear. If this bipedal race was so proud they could not cope with inferiority, that was not Mklikluln's problem.

He opened the top drawer of his desk in the San Diego headquarters of Doghouses Unlimited, his latest refuge from the interview seekers, and pushed a button on a small box.

From the box, a powerful burst of electromagnetic

423

energy went out to the eighty million doghouses in southern California. Each doghouse relayed the same signal in an unending chain that gradually spread all over the world—wherever doghouses could be found.

When the last doghouse was linked to the network, all the doghouses simultaneously transmitted something else entirely. A signal that only sneered at lightspeed and that crossed light-years almost instantaneously. A signal that called millions of encapsulated minds that slept in their mindfields until they heard the call, woke, and followed the signal back to its source, again at speeds far faster than poor pedestrian light.

They gathered around the larger binary in the third orbit from their new sun, and listened as Mklikluln gave a full report. They were delighted with his work, and commended him highly, before convicting him of murder of an Arabian political prisoner and ordering him to commit suicide. He felt very proud, for the commendation they had given him was rarely awarded, and he smiled as he shot himself.

And then the minds slipped downward toward the doghouses that still called to them.

"Argworfgyardworfl," said Royce's dog as it bounded excitedly through the backyard.

"Dog's gone crazy," Royce said, but his two sons laughed and ran around with the dog as it looped the yard a dozen times, only to fall exhausted in front of the doghouse.

"Griffwigrofrf," the dog said again, panting happily. It trotted up to Royce and nuzzled him.

"Cute little bugger," Royce said.

The dog walked over to a pile of newspapers waiting for a paper drive, pulled the top newspaper off the stack, and began staring at the page.

"I'll be humdingered," said Royce to Junie, who was bringing out the food for their backyard picnic supper. "Dog looks like he's readin' the paper."

"Here, Robby!" shouted Royce's oldest son, Jim. "Here, Robby! Chase a stick."

The dog, having learned how to read and write from the newspaper, chased the stick, brought it back, and instead of surrendering it to Jim's outstretched hand, began to write with it in the dirt.

"Hello, man,' wrote the dog. "Perhaps you are surprised to see me writing."

"Well," said Royce, looking at what the dog had written. "Here, Junie, will you look at that. This is some dog, eh?" And he patted the dog's head and sat down to eat. "Now I wonder, is there anybody who'd pay to see a dog do that?"

"We mean no harm to your planet," wrote the dog.

"Jim," said Junie, slapping spoonfuls of potato salad onto paper plates, "you make sure that dog doesn't start scratching around in the petunias."

"C'mere, Robby," said Jim. "Time to tie you up."

"Wrowrf," the dog answered, looking a bit perturbed and backing away from the chain.

"Daddy," said Jim, "the dog won't come when I call anymore."

Impatiently, Royce got up from his chair, his mouth full of chicken salad sandwich. "Doggonit, Jim, if you don't control the dog we'll just have to get rid of it. We only got it for you kids anyway!" And Royce grabbed the dog by the collar and dragged it to where Jimmy held the other end of the chain.

Clip.

"Now you learn to obey, dog, cause if you don't I don't care what tricks you can do, I'll sell ya."

"Owrf."

"Right. Now you remember that."

The dog watched them with sad, almost frightened eyes all through dinner. Royce began to feel a little guilty, and gave the dog a leftover ham.

That night Royce and Junie seriously discussed whether to show off the dog's ability to write, and decided against it, since the kids loved the dog and it was cruel to use animals to perform tricks. They were, after all, very enlightened people.

And the next morning they discovered that it was a good thing they'd decided that way—because all anyone could talk about was their dog's newfound ability to write, or unscrew garden hoses, or lay and start an entire fire from a cold empty fireplace to a bonfire. "I got the most talented dog in the world," crowed Detweiler, only to retire into grim silence as everyone else in the bowling team bragged about his own dog.

"Mine goes to the bathroom in the toilet now, and flushes it, too!" one boasted.

"And mine can fold an entire laundry, after washing her little paws so nothing gets dirty."

The newspapers were full of the story, too, and it became clear that the sudden intelligence of dogs was a nationwide—a world-wide—phenomenon. Aside from a few superstitious New Guineans, who burned their dogs to death as witches, and some Chinese who didn't let their dogs' strange behavior stop them from their scheduled appointment with the dinnerpot, most people were pleased and proud of the change in their pets.

426

"Worth twice as much to me now," boasted Bill Wilson, formerly an up-and-coming executive with the damnpowercompany. "Not only fetches the birds, but plucks 'em and cleans 'em and puts 'em in the oven."

And Kay Block smiled and went home to her mastiff, which kept her good company and which she loved very, very much.

"In the five years since the sudden rise in dog intelligence," said Dr. Wheelwright to his class of graduate students in animal intelligence, "we have learned a tremendous amount about how intelligence arises in animals. They very suddenness of it has caused us to take a second look at evolution. Apparently mutations can be much more complete than we had supposed, at least in the higher functions. Naturally, we will spend much of this semester studying the research on dog intelligence, but for a brief overview:

"At the present time it is believed that dog intelligence surpasses that of the dolphin, though it still falls far short of man's. However, while the dolphin's intelligence is nearly useless to us, the dog can be trained as a valuable, simple household servant, and at last it seems that man is no longer alone on his planet. To which animal such a rise in intelligence will happen next, we cannot say, any more than we can be certain that such a change *will* happen to any other animal."

Question from the class.

"Oh, well, I'm afraid it's like the big bang theory. We can guess and guess at the cause of certain phenomena, but since we can't repeat the event in a laboratory, we will never be quite sure. However, the best guess at present is that some critical mass of total dog population in a certain ratio to the total mass of dog brain was reached that pushed the entire species over the edge into a higher order of intelligence. This change, however, did not affect *all* dogs equally—primarily it affected dogs in civilized areas, leading many to speculate on the possibility that continued exposure to man was a contributing factor. However, the very fact that many dogs, mostly in uncivilized parts of the world, were *not* affected destroys completely the idea that cosmic radiation or some other influence from outer space was responsible for the change. In the first place, any such influence would have been detected by the astronomers constantly watching every wavelength of the night sky, and in the second place, such an influence would have affected all dogs equally."

Another question from a student.

"Who knows? But I doubt it. Dogs, being incapable of speech, though many have learned to write simple sentences in an apparently mnemonic fashion somewhere between the blind repetition of parrots and the more calculating repetition at high speeds by dolphins—um, how did I get into this sentence? I can't get out!"

Student laughter.

"Dogs, I was saying, are incapable of another advance in intelligence, particularly an advance bringing them to equal intellect with man, because they cannot communicate verbally and because they lack hands. They are undoubtedly at their evolutionary peak. It is only fortunate that so many circumstances combined to place man in the situation he has reached. And we can only suppose that somewhere, on some other planet, some other species might have an even more fortunate combination leading to even higher intelligence. But let us hope not!" said the professor, scratching the ears of his dog, B. F. Skinner. "Right, B. F.? Because man may not be able to cope with the presence of a more intelligent race!"

Student laughter.

"Owrowrf," said B. F. Skinner, who had once been called Hihiwnkn on a planet where white hexagons had telepathic\ally conquered time and space; hexagons who had only been brought to this pass by a solar process they had not quite learned how to control. What he wished he could say was, "Don't worry, professor. Humanity will never be fazed by a higher intelligence. It's too damn proud to notice."

But instead he growled a little, lapped some water from a bowl, and lay down in a corner of the lecture room as the professor droned on.

It snowed in September in Kansas in the autumn of the year 2000, and Jim (Don't call me Jimmy anymore, I'm grown up) was out playing with his dog Robby as the first flakes fell.

Robby had been uprooting crabgrass with his teeth and paws, a habit much encouraged by Royce and Junie, when Jim yelled, "Snow!" and a flake landed on the grass in front of the dog. The flake melted immediately, but Robby watched for another, and another, and another. And he saw the whiteness of the flakes, and the delicate six-sided figures so spare and strange and familiar and beautiful, and he wept.

"Mommy!" Jim called out. "It looks like Robby's crying!"

"It's just water in his eyes," Junie called back

429

from the kitchen, where she stood washing radishes in front of an open window. "Dogs don't cry."

But the show fell deep all over the city that night, and many dogs stood in the snow watching it fall, sharing an unspoken reverie.

"Can't we?" again and again the thought came from a hundred, a thousand minds.

"No, no, no," came the despairing answer. For without fingers of *some* kind, how could they ever build the machines that would let them encapsulate again and leave this planet?

And in their despair, they cursed for the millionth time that fool Mklikluln, who had got them into this.

"Death was too good for the bastard," they agreed, and in a worldwide vote they removed the commendation they had voted him. And then they all went back to having puppies and teaching them everything they knew.

The puppies had it easier. They had never known their ancestral home, and to them snowflakes were merely fun, and winter was merely cold. And instead of standing out in the snow, they curled up in the warmth of their doghouses and slept.

The Originist

Leyel Forska sat before his lector display, reading through an array of recently published scholarly papers. A holograph of two pages of text hovered in the air before him. The display was rather larger than most people needed their pages to be, since Leyel's eyes were no younger than the rest of him. When he came to the end he did not press the PAGE key to continue the article. Instead he pressed NEXT.

The two pages he had been reading slid backward about a centimeter, joining a dozen previously discarded articles, all standing in the air over the lector. With a soft beep, a new pair of pages appeared in front of the old ones.

Deet spoke up from where she sat eating breakfast. "You're only giving the poor soul *two pages* before you consign him to the wastebin?"

"I'm consigning him to oblivion," Leyel answered cheerfully. "No, I'm consigning him to hell."

"What? Have you rediscovered religion in your old age?"

"I'm creating one. It has no heaven, but it has a terrible everlasting hell for young scholars who think they can make their reputation by attacking my work."

"Ah, you have a theology," said Deet. "Your work is holy writ, and to attack it is blasphemy."

"I welcome *intelligence* attacks. But this young tube-headed professor from—yes, of course, Minus University—"

"Old Minus U?"

"He thinks he can refute me, destroy me, lay me in the dust, and all he has bothered to cite are studies published within the last thousand years."

"The principle of millennial depth is still widely used—"

"The principle of millennial depth is the confession of modern scholars that they are not willing to spend as much effort on research as they do on academic politics. I shattered the principle of millennial depth thirty years ago. I proved that it was—"

"Stupid and outmoded. But my dearest darling sweetheart Leyel, you did it by spending part of the immeasurably vast Forska fortune to search for inaccessible and forgotten archives in every section of the Empire."

"Neglected and decaying. I had to reconstruct half of them."

"It would take a thousand universities' library budgets to match what you spent on research for 'Human Origin on the Null Planet.'"

"But once I spent the money, all those archives were open. They *have* been open for three decades. The *serious* scholars all use them, since millenial depth yields nothing but predigested, preexcreted muck. They search among the turds of rats who have devoured elephants, hoping to find ivory."

"So colorful an image. My breakfast tastes much better now." She slid her tray into the cleaning slot and glared at him. "Why are you so snappish? You used to read me sections from their silly little papers and we'd laugh. Lately you're just nasty."

Leyel sighed. "Maybe it's because I once dreamed of changing the galaxy, and every day's mail brings more evidence that the galaxy refuses to change."

"Nonsense. Hari Seldon has promised that the Empire will fall any day now."

There. She had said Hari's name. Even though she had too much tact to speak openly of what bothered him, she was hinting that Leyel's bad humor was because he was still waiting for Hari Seldon's answer. Maybe so—Leyel wouldn't deny it. It *was* annoying that it had taken Hari so long to respond. Leyel had expected a call the day Hari got his application. At least within the week. But he wasn't going to give her the satisfaction of admitting that the waiting bothered him. "The Empire will be killed by its own refusal to change. I rest my case."

"Well, I hope you have a wonderful morning, growling and grumbling about the stupidity of everyone in origin studies—except your esteemed self."

"Why are you teasing me about my vanity today? I've always been vain."

"I consider it one of your most endearing traits."

"At least I make an effort to live up to my own opinion of myself."

"That's nothing. You even live up to *my* opinion of you." She kissed the bald spot on the top of his head as she breezed by, heading for the bathroom.

Leyel turned his attention to the new essay at the front of the lector display. It was a name he didn't recognize. Fully prepared to find pretentious writing and puerile thought, he was surprised to find himself becoming quite absorbed. This woman had been following a trail of primate studies—a field so long neglected that there simply *were* no papers within the range of millennial depth. Already he knew she was his kind of scholar. She even mentioned the fact that she was using archives opened by the Forska Research Foundation. Leyel was not above being pleased at this tacit expression of gratitude.

It seemed that the woman—a Dr. Thoren Magolissian—had been following Leyel's lead, searching for the *principles* of human origin rather than wasting time on the irrelevant search for one particular planet. She had uncovered a trove of primate research from three millennia ago, which was based on chimpanzee and gorilla studies dating back to seven thousand years ago. The earliest of these had referred to original research so old it may have been conducted before the founding of the Empire—but those most ancient reports had not yet been located. They probably didn't exist anymore. Texts abandoned for more than five thousand years were very hard to restore; texts older than eight thousand years were simply unreadable. It was tragic, how many texts had been "stored" by librarians who never checked them, never refreshed or recopied them. Presiding over vast archives that had lost every scrap of readable information. All neatly catalogued, of course, so you knew *exactly* what it was that humanity had lost forever.

Never mind.

Magolissian's article. What startled Leyel was her conclusion that primitive language capability seemed to be inherent in the primate mind. Even in primates incapable of speech, other symbols could easily be learned—at least for simple nouns and verbs—and the nonhuman primates could come up with sentences and ideas that had never been spoken to them. This meant that mere production of language, *per se*, was prehuman, or at least not the determining factor of humanness.

It was a dazzling thought. It meant that the difference between humans and nonhumans—the real origin of humans in recognizably human form—was postlinguistic. Of course this came as a direct contradiction of one of Leyel's own assertions in an early paper—he had said that "since language is what separates human from beast, historical linguistics may provide the key to human origins"—but this was the sort of contradiction he welcomed. He wished he could shout at the other fellow, make him look at Magolissian's article. See? This is how to do it! Challenge my assumption, not my conclusion, and do it with new evidence instead of trying to twist the old stuff. Cast a light in the darkness, don't just churn up the same old sediment at the bottom of the river.

Before he could get into the main body of the article, however, the house computer informed him that someone was at the door of the apartment. It was a message that crawled along the bottom of the lector display. Leyel pressed the key that brought the message to the front, in letters large enough to read. For the thousandth time he wished that sometime in the decamillennia of human history, somebody had invented a computer capable of *speech*.

"Who is it?" Leyel typed.

A moment's wait, while the house computer interrogated the visitor.

The answer appeared on the lector: "Secure courier with a message for Leyel Forska."

The very fact that the courier had got past house

435

security meant that it was genuine—and important. Leyel typed again. "From?"

Another pause. "Hari Seldon of the Encyclopedia Galactica Foundation."

Leyel was out of his chair in a moment. He got to the door even before the house computer could open it, and without a word took the message in his hands. Fumbling a bit, he pressed the top and bottom of the black glass lozenge to prove by fingerprint that it was he, by body temperature and pulse that he was alive to receive it. Then, when the courier and her bodyguards were gone, he dropped the message into the chamber of his lector and watched the page appear in the air before him.

At the top was a three-dimensional version of the logo of Hari's Encyclopedia Foundation. Soon to be my insignia as well, thought Leyel. Hari Seldon and I, the two greatest scholars of our time, joined together in a project whose scope surpasses anything ever attempted by any man or group of men. The gathering together of all the knowledge of the Empire in a systematic, easily accessible way, to preserve it through the coming time of anarchy so that a new civilization can quickly rise out of the ashes of the old. Hari had the vision to foresee the need. And I, Leyel Forska, have the understanding of all the old archives that will make the Encyclopedia Galactica possible.

Leyel started reading with a confidence born of experience; had he ever really desired anything and been denied?

My dear friend:

I was surprised and honored to see an application from you and insisted on writing your answer personally. It is gratifying beyond measure that you believe in the Foundation enough to apply to take part. I can truthfully tell you that we have received no application from any other scholar of your distinction and accomplishment.

Of course, thought Leyel. There *is* no other scholar of my stature, except Hari himself, and perhaps Deet, once her current work is published. At least we have no equals by the standards that Hari and I have always recognized as valid. Hari created the science of psychohistory. I transformed and revitalized the field of originism.

And yet the tone of Hari's letter was wrong. It sounded like—flattery. That was it. Hari was softening the coming blow. Leyel knew before reading it what the next paragraph would say.

Nevertheless, Leyel, I must reply in the negative. The Foundation on Terminus is designed to collect and preserve knowledge. Your life's work has been devoted to expanding it. You are the opposite of the sort of researcher we need. Far better for you to remain on Trantor and continue your inestimably valuable studies, while lesser men and women exile themselves on Terminus.

Your servant,
Hari

Did Hari imagine Leyel to be so vain he would read these flattering words and preen himself contentedly? Did he think Leyel would believe that this

437

was the real reason his application was being denied? Could Hari Seldon misknow a man so badly?

Impossible. Hari Seldon, of all people in the Empire, knew how to know other people. True, his great work in psychohistory dealt with large masses of people, with populations and probabilities. But Hari's fascination with populations had grown out of his interest in and understanding of individuals. Besides, he and Hari had been friends since Hari first arrived on Trantor. Hadn't a grant from Leyel's own research fund financed most of Hari's original research? Hadn't they held long conversations in the early days, tossing ideas back and forth, each helping the other hone his thoughts? They may not have seen each other much in the last—what, five years? Six?—but they were adults, not children. They didn't need constant visits in order to remain friends. And this was not the letter a true friend would send to Leyel Forska. Even if, doubtful as it might seem, Hari Seldon really meant to turn him down, he would not suppose for a moment that Leyel would be content with a letter like *this*.

Surely Hari would have known that it would be like a taunt to Leyel Forska. "Lesser men and women," indeed! The Foundation on Terminus was so valuable to Hari Seldon that he had been willing to risk death on charges of treason in order to launch the project. It was unlikely in the extreme that he would populate Terminus with second-raters. No, this was the form letter sent to placate prominent scholars who were judged unfit for the Foundation. Hari would have known Leyel would immediately recognize it as such.

There was only one possible conclusion. "Hari could not have written this letter," Leyel said.

"Of course he could," Deet told him, blunt as always. She had come out of the bathroom in her dressing gown and read the letter over his shoulder.

"If *you* think so then I truly *am* hurt," said Leyel. He got up, poured a cup of peshat, and began to sip it. He studiously avoided looking at Deet.

"Don't pout, Leyel. Think of the problems Hari is facing. He has so little time, so much to do. A hundred thousand people to transport to Terminus, most of the resources of the Imperial Library to duplicate—"

"He already *had* those people—"

"All in six months since his trial ended. No wonder we haven't seen him, socially or professionally, in—years. A decade!"

"You're saying that he no longer knows me? Unthinkable."

"I'm saying that he knows you very well. He knew you would recognize his message as a form letter. He also knew that you would understand at once what this meant."

"Well, then, my dear, he overestimated me. I do *not* understand what it means, unless it means he did not send it himself."

"Then you're getting old, and I'm ashamed of you. I shall deny we are married and pretend you are my idiot uncle whom I allow to live with me out of charity. I'll tell the children they were illegitimate. They'll be very sad to learn they won't inherit a bit of the Forksa estate."

He threw a crumb of toast at her. "You are a cruel and disloyal wench, and I regret raising you out of poverty and obscurity. I only did it for pity, you know."

This was an old tease of theirs. She had commanded a decent fortune in her own right, though of course Leyel's dwarfed it. And, technically, he *was* her uncle, since her stepmother was Leyel's older half sister Zenna. It was all very complicated. Zenna had been born to Leyel's mother when she was married to someone else—before she married Leyel's father. So while Zenna was well dowered, she had no part in the Forska fortune. Leyel's father, amused at the situation, once remarked, "Poor Zenna. Lucky you. My semen flows with gold." Such are the ironies that come with great fortune. Poor people don't have to make such terrible distinctions between their children.

Deet's father, however, assumed that a Forska was a Forska, and so, several years after Deet had married Leyel, he decided that it wasn't enough for his daughter to be married to uncountable wealth, he ought to do the same favor for himself. He *said*, of course, that he loved Zenna to distraction, and cared nothing for fortune, but only Zenna believed him. Therefore she married him. Thus Leyel's half sister became Deet's stepmother, which made Leyel his wife's stepuncle—and his own stepuncle-in-law. A dynastic tangle that greatly amused Leyel and Deet.

Leyel of course compensated for Zenna's lack of inheritance with a lifetime stipend that amounted to ten times her husband's income each year. It had the happy effect of keeping Deet's old father in love with Zenna.

Today, though, Leyel was only half teasing Deet. There were times when he needed her to confirm him, to uphold him. As often as not she contradicted him instead. Sometimes this led him to rethink his position and emerge with a better understanding—

thesis, antithesis, synthesis, the dialectic of marriage, the result of being espoused to one's intellectual equal. But sometimes her challenge was painful, unsatisfying, infuriating.

Oblivious to his underlying anger, she went on. "Hari assumed that you would take his form letter for what it is—a definite, final no. He isn't hedging, he's not engaging in some bureaucratic deviousness, he isn't playing politics with you. He isn't stringing you along in hopes of getting more financial support from you—if that were it you know he'd simply ask."

"I already know what he *isn't* doing."

"What he *is* doing is turning you down with finality. An answer from which there is no appeal. He gave you credit for having the wit to understand that."

"How convenient for you if I believe that."

Now, at last, she realized he was angry. "What's that supposed to mean?"

"You can stay here on Trantor and continue your work with all your bureaucratic friends."

Her face went cold and hard. "I told you. I am quite happy to go to Terminus with you."

"Am I supposed to believe that, even now? Your research in community formation with the Imperial bureaucracy cannot possibly continue on Terminus."

"I've already done the most important research. What I'm doing with the Imperial Library staff is a test."

"Not even a scientific one, since there's no control group."

She looked annoyed. "I'm the one who told *you* that."

It was true. Leyel had never even heard of control groups until she taught him the whole concept of experimentation. She had found it in some very old child-development studies from the 3100s G.E. "Yes, I was just agreeing with you," he said lamely.

"The point is, I can write my book as well on Terminus as anywhere else. And yes, Leyel, you *are* supposed to believe that I'm happy to go with you, because I said it, and therefore it's so."

"I believe that you believe it. I also believe that in your heart you are very glad that I was turned down, and you don't want me to pursue this matter any further so there'll be no chance of your having to go to the godforsaken end of the universe."

Those had been her words, months ago, when he first proposed applying to join the Seldon Foundation. "We'd have to go to the godforsaken end of the universe!" She remembered now as well as he did. "You'll hold that against me forever, won't you! I think I deserve to be forgiven my first reaction. I did consent to go, didn't I?"

"Consent, yes. But you never wanted to."

"Well, Leyel, that's true enough. I never *wanted* to. Is that your idea of what our marriage means? That I'm to subsume myself in you so deeply that even your desires become my own? I thought it was enough that from time to time we consent to sacrifice for each other. I never expected you to *want* to leave the Forska estates and come to Trantor when I needed to do my research here. I only asked you to *do* it—whether you wanted to or not—because *I* wanted it. I recognized and respected your sacrifice. I am very angry to discover that *my* sacrifice is despised."

"*Your* sacrifice remains unmade. We are still on Trantor."

"Then by all means, go to Hari Seldon, plead with

442

him, humiliate yourself, and then realize that what I told you is true. He doesn't want you to join his Foundation and he will not allow you to go to Terminus."

"Are you so certain of that?"

"No, I'm not *certain*. It merely seems likely."

"I *will* go to Terminus, if he'll have me. I hope I don't have to go alone."

He regretted the words as soon as he said them. She froze as if she had been slapped, a look of horror on her face. Then she turned and ran from the room. A few moments later, he heard the chime announcing that the door of their apartment had opened. She was gone.

No doubt to talk things over with one of her friends. Women have no sense of discretion. They cannot keep domestic squabbles to themselves. She will tell them all the awful things I said, and they'll cluck and tell her it's what she must expect from a husband, husbands demand that their wives make all the sacrifices, you poor thing, poor poor Deet. Well, Leyel didn't begrudge her this barnyard of sympathetic hens. It was part of human nature, he knew, for women to form a perpetual conspiracy against the men in their lives. That was why women have always been so certain that men also formed a conspiracy against *them*.

How ironic, he thought. Men have no such solace. Men do not bind themselves so easily into communities. A man is always aware of the possibility of betrayal, of conflicting loyalties. Therefore when a man *does* commit himself truly, it is a rare and sacred bond, not to be cheapened by discussing it with others. Even a marriage, even a *good* marriage like theirs—*his* commitment might be absolute, but he could never trust hers so completely.

Leyel had buried himself within the marriage, helping and serving and loving Deet with all his heart. She was wrong, completely wrong about his coming to Trantor. He hadn't come as a sacrifice, against his will, solely because she wanted to come. On the contrary: because she wanted so much to come, he *also* wanted to come, changing even his desires to coincide with hers. She commanded his very heart, because it was impossible for him not to desire anything that would bring her happiness.

But she, no, she could not do that for him. If *she* went to Terminus, it would be as a noble sacrifice. She would never let him forget that she hadn't wanted to. To him, their marriage was his very soul. To Deet, their marriage was just a friendship with sex. Her soul belonged as much to these other women as to him. By dividing her loyalties, she fragmented them; none were strong enough to sway her deepest desires. Thus he discovered what he supposed all faithful men eventually discover—that no human relationship is ever anything but tentative. There is no such thing as an unbreakable bond between people. Like the particles in the nucleus of the atom. They are bound by the strongest forces in the universe, and yet they can be shattered, they can break.

Nothing can last. Nothing is, finally, what it once seemed to be. Deet and he had had a perfect marriage until there came a stress that exposed its imperfection. Anyone who thinks he has a perfect marriage, a perfect friendship, a perfect trust of any kind, he only believes this because the stress that will break it has not yet come. He might die with the illusion of happiness, but all he has proven is that sometimes death comes before betrayal. If you live long enough, betrayal will inevitably come.

Such were the dark thoughts that filled Leyel's mind as he made his way through the maze of the city of Trantor. Leyel did not seal himself inside a private car when he went about in the planet-wide city. He refused the trappings of wealth; he insisted on experiencing the life of Trantor as an ordinary man. Thus his bodyguards were under strict instructions to remain discreet, interfering with no pedestrians except those carrying weapons, as revealed by a subtle and instantaneous scan.

It was much more expensive to travel through the city this way, of course—every time he stepped out the door of his simple apartment, nearly a hundred high-paid bribeproof employees went into action. A weaponproof car would have been much cheaper. But Leyel was determined not to be imprisoned by his wealth.

So he walked through the corridors of the city, riding cabs and tubes, standing in lines like anyone else. He felt the great city throbbing with life around him. Yet such was his dark and melancholy mood today that the very life of the city filled him with a sense of betrayal and loss. Even you, great Trantor, the Imperial City, even you will be betrayed by the people who made you. Your empire will desert you, and you will become a pathetic remnant of yourself, plated with the metal of a thousand worlds and asteroids as a reminder that once the whole galaxy promised to serve you forever, and now you are abandoned. Hari Seldon had seen it. Hari Seldon understood the changeability of humankind. He knew that the great empire would fall, and so—

unlike the government, which depended on things remaining the same forever—Hari Seldon could actually take steps to ameliorate the Empire's fall, to prepare on Terminus a womb for the rebirth of human greatness. Hari was creating the future. It was unthinkable that he could mean to cut Leyel Forska out of it.

The Foundation, now that it had legal existence and Imperial funding, had quickly grown into a busy complex of offices in the four-thousand-year-old Putassuran Building. Because the Putassuran was originally built to house the Admiralty shortly after the great victory whose name it bore, it had an air of triumph, of monumental optimism about it—rows of soaring arches, a vaulted atrium with floating bubbles of light rising and dancing in channeled columns of air. In recent centuries the building had served as a site for informal public concerts and lectures, with the offices used to house the Museum Authority. It had come empty only a year before Hari Seldon was granted the right to form his Foundation, but it seemed as though it had been built for this very purpose. Everyone was hurrying this way and that, always seeming to be on urgent business, and yet also happy to be part of a noble cause. There had been no noble causes in the Empire for a long, long time.

Leyel quickly threaded his way through the maze that protected the Foundation's director from casual interruption. Other men and women, no doubt, had tried to see Hari Seldon and failed, put off by this functionary or that. Hari Seldon is a very busy man. Perhaps if you make an appointment for later. Seeing him today is out of the question. He's in meetings all afternoon and evening. Do call before coming next time.

But none of this happened to Leyel Forska. All he had to do was say, "Tell Mr. Seldon that Mr. Forska wishes to continue a conversation." However much awe they might have of Hari Seldon, however they might intend to obey his orders not to be disturbed, they all knew that Leyel Forska was the universal exception. Even Linge Chen would be called out of a meeting of the Commission of Public Safety to speak with Forska, especially if Leyel went to the trouble of coming in person.

The ease with which he gained entry to see Hari, the excitement and optimism of the people, of the building itself, had encouraged Leyel so much that he was not at all prepared for Hari's first words.

"Leyel, I'm surprised to see you. I thought you would understand that my message was final."

It was the worst thing that Hari could possibly have said. Had Deet been right after all? Leyel studied Hari's face for a moment, trying to see some sign of change. Was all that had passed between them through the years forgotten now? Had Hari's friendship never been real? No. Looking at Hari's face, a bit more lined and wrinkled now, Leyel saw still the same earnestness, the same plain honesty that had always been there. So instead of expressing the rage and disappointment that he felt, Leyel answered carefully, leaving the way open for Hari to change his mind. "I understood that your message was deceptive, and therefore could not be final."

Hari looked a little angry. "Deceptive?"

"I know which men and women you've been taking into your Foundation. They are not second-raters."

447

"Compared to you they are," said Hari. "They're academics, which means they're clerks. Sorters and interpreters of information."

"So am I. So are all scholars today. Even *your* inestimable theories arose from sorting through a trillion bytes of data and interpreting it."

Hari shook his head. "I didn't just sort through data. I had an idea in my head. So did you. Few others do. You and I are expanding human knowledge. Most of the rest are only digging it up in one place and piling it in another. That's what the Encyclopedia Galactica *is*. A new pile."

"Nevertheless, Hari, you know and I know that this is not the real reason you turned me down. And don't tell me that it's because Leyel Forska's presence on Terminus would call undue attention to the project. You already have so much attention from the government that you can hardly breathe."

"You are unpleasantly persistent, Leyel. I don't like even having this conversation."

"That's too bad, Hari. I want to be part of your project. I would contribute to it more than any other person who might join it. I'm the one who plunged back into the oldest and most valuable archives and exposed the shameful amount of data loss that had arisen from neglect. I'm the one who launched the computerized extrapolation of shattered documents that your Encyclopedia—"

"Absolutely depends on. Our work would be impossible without your accomplishments."

"And yet you turned me down, and with a crudely flattering note."

"I didn't mean to give offense, Leyel."

"You also didn't mean to tell the truth. But you

448

will tell me, Hari, or I'll simply go to Terminus anyway."

"The Commission of Public Safety has given my Foundation absolute control over who may or may not come to Terminus."

"Hari. You know perfectly well that all I have to do is hint to some lower-level functionary that I want to go to Terminus. Chen will hear of it within minutes, and within an hour he'll grant me an exception to your charter. If I did that, and if you fought it, you'd lose your charter. You *know* that. If you want me not to go to Terminus, it isn't enough to forbid me. You must persuade me that I ought not to be there."

Hari closed his eyes and sighed. "I don't think you're willing to be persuaded, Leyel. Go if you must."

For a moment Leyel wondered if Hari was giving in. But no, that was impossible, not so easily. "Oh, yes, Hari, but then I'd find myself cut off from everybody else on Terminus except my own serving people. Fobbed off with useless assignments. Cut out of the real meetings."

"That goes without saying," said Hari. "You are not part of the Foundation, you will not be, you cannot be. And if you try to use your wealth and influence to force your way in, you will succeed only in annoying the Foundation, not on joining it. Do you understand me?"

Only too well, thought Leyel in shame. Leyel knew perfectly well the limitations of power, and it was beneath him to have tried to bluster his way into getting something that could only be given freely. "Forgive me, Hari. I wouldn't have tried to force you. You know I don't do that sort of thing."

449

"I know you've never done it since we've been friends, Leyel. I was afraid that I was learning something new about you." Hari sighed. He turned away for a long moment, then turned back with a different look on his face, a different kind of energy in his voice. Leyel knew that look, that vigor. It meant Hari was taking him more deeply into his confidence. "Leyel, you have to understand, I'm not just creating an encyclopedia on Terminus."

Immediately Leyel grew worried. It had taken a great deal of Leyel's influence to persuade the government not to have Hari Seldon summarily exiled when he first started disseminating copies of his treatises about the impending fall of the Empire. They were sure Seldon was plotting treason, and had even put him on trial, where Seldon finally persuaded them that all he wanted to do was create the Encyclopedia Galactica, the repository of all the wisdom of the Empire. Even now, if Seldon confessed some ulterior motive, the government would move against him. It was to be assumed that the Pubs—Public Safety Office—were recording this entire conversation. Even Leyel's influence couldn't stop them if they had a confession from Hari's own mouth.

'No, Leyel, don't be nervous. My meaning is plain enough. For the Encyclopedia Galactica to succeed, I have to create a thriving city of scholars on Terminus. A colony full of men and women with fragile egos and unstemmable ambition, all of them trained in vicious political infighting at the most dangerous and terrible schools of bureaucratic combat in the Empire—the universities."

"Are you actually telling me you won't let me join your Foundation because I never attended one of those pathetic universities? My self-education is worth ten times their lockstep force-fed pseudo-learning."

"Don't make your antiuniversity speech to me, Leyel. I'm saying that one of my most important concerns in staffing the Foundation is compatibility. I won't bring anyone to Terminus unless I believe he—or *she*—would be happy there."

The emphasis Hari put on the word *she* suddenly made everything clearer. "This isn't about me at all, is it?" Leyel said. "It's about Deet."

Hari said nothing.

"You know she doesn't want to go. You know she prefers to remain on Trantor. And that's why you aren't taking me! Is that it?"

Reluctantly, Hari conceded the point. "It does have something to do with Deet, yes."

"Don't you know how much the Foundation means to me?" demanded Leyel. "Don't you know how much I'd give up to be part of your work?"

Hari sat there in silence for a moment. Then he murmured, "Even Deet?"

Leyel almost blurted out an answer. Yes, of course, even Deet, anything for this great work.

But Hari's measured gaze stopped him. One thing Leyel had known since they first met at a conference back in their youth was that Hari would not stand for another man's self-deception. They had sat next to each other at a presentation by a demographer who had a considerable reputation at the time. Leyel watched as Hari destroyed the poor man's thesis with a few well-aimed questions. The demographer was furious. Obviously he had not seen the flaws in his own argument—but now that they had been shown to him, he refused to admit that they were flaws at all.

Afterward, Hari had said to Leyel, "I've done him a favor."

"How, by giving him someone to hate?" said Leyel.

"No. Before, he believed his own unwarranted conclusions. He had deceived himself. No he doesn't believe them."

"But he still propounds them."

"So—now he's more of a liar and less of a fool. I have improved his private integrity. His public morality I leave up to him."

Leyel remembered this and knew that if he told Hari he could give up Deet for any reason, even to join the Foundation, it would be worse than a lie. It would be foolishness.

"It's a terrible thing you've done," said Leyel. "You know that Deet is part of myself. I can't give her up to join your Foundation. But now for the rest of our lives together I'll know that I could have gone, if not for her. You've given me wormwood and gall to drink, Hari."

Hari nodded slowly. "I hoped that when you read my note you'd realize I didn't want to tell you more. I hoped you wouldn't come to me and ask. I can't lie to you, Leyel. I wouldn't if I could. But I did withhold information, as much as possible. To spare us both problems."

"It didn't work."

"It isn't Deet's fault, Leyel. It's who she is. She belongs on Trantor, not on Terminus. And you belong with her. It's a fact, not a decision. We'll never discuss this again."

"No," said Leyel.

452

They sat there for a long minute, gazing steadily at each other. Leyel wondered if he and Hari would ever speak again. No. Never again. I don't ever want to see you again, Hari Seldon. You've made me regret the one unregrettable decision of my life — Deet. You've made me wish, somewhere in my heart, that I'd never married her. Which is like making me wish I'd never been born.

Leyel got up up from his chair and left the room without a word. When he got outside, he turned to the reception room in general, where several people were waiting to see Seldon. "Which of you are mine?" he asked.

Two women and one man stood up immediately.

"Fetch me a secure car and a driver."

Without a glance at each other, one of them left on the errand. The others fell in step beside Leyel. Subtlety and discretion were over for the moment. Leyel had no wish to mingle with the people of Trantor now. He only wanted to go home.

Hari Seldon left his office by the back way and soon found his way to Chandrakar Matt's cubicle in the Department of Library Relations. Chanda looked up and waved, then effortlessly slid her chair back until it was in the exact position required. Hari picked up a chair from the neighboring cubicle and, again without showing any particular case, set it exactly where it had to be.

Immediately the computer installed inside Chanda's lector recognized the configuration. It recorded Hari's costume of the day from three angles and superimposed the information on a long-stored holoimage of Chanda and Hari conversing pleasantly. Then, once Hari was seated, it began displaying the hologram. The hologram exactly matched the positions of the real Hari and Chanda, so that infrared sensors would show no discrepancy between image and fact. The only thing different was the faces—the movement of lips, blinking of eyes, the expressions. Instead of matching the words Hari and Chanda were actually saying, they matched the words being pushed into the air outside the cubicle— a harmless, randomly chosen series of remarks that took into account recent events so that no one would suspect that it was a canned conversation.

It was one of Hari's few opportunities for candid conversation that the Pubs would not overhear, and he and Chanda protected it carefully. They never spoke long enough or often enough that the Pubs would wonder at their devotion to such empty conversations. Much of their communication was subliminal—a sentence would stand for a paragraph, a word for a sentence, a gesture for a word. But when the conversation was done, Chanda knew where to go from there, what to do next; and Hari was reassured that his most important work was going on behind the smokescreen of the Foundation.

"For a moment I thought he might actually leave her."

"Don't underestimate the lure of the Encyclopedia."

"I fear I've wrought too well, Chanda. Do you think someday the Encyclopedia Galactica might actually exist?"

"It's a good idea. Good people are inspired by it. It wouldn't serve its purpose if they weren't. What should I tell Deet?"

"Nothing, Chanda. The fact that Leyel is staying, that's enough for her."

"If he changes his mind, will you actually let him go to Terminus?"

"If he changes his mind, then he *must* go, because if he would leave Deet, he's not the man for us."

"Why not just tell him? Invite him?"

"He must become part of the Second Foundation without realizing it. He must do it by natural inclination, not by a summons from me, and above all not by his own ambition."

"Your standards are so high, Hari, it's no wonder so few measure up. Most people in the Second Foundation don't even know that's what it is. They think they're librarians. Bureaucrats. They think Deet is an anthropologist who works among them in order to study them."

"No so. They once thought that, but now they think of Deet as one of them. As one of the *best* of them. She's defining what it means to be a librarian. She's making them proud of the name."

"Aren't you ever troubled, Hari, by the fact that in the practice of your art—"

"My *science*."

"Your meddlesome magical *craft*, you old wizard, you don't fool *me* with all your talk of science. I've seen the scripts of the holographs you're preparing for the vault on Terminus."

"That's all a pose."

"I can just imagine you saying those words. Looking perfectly satisfied with yourself. 'If you care to smoke, I wouldn't mind . . . Pause for chuckle . . . Why should I? I'm not really here.' Pure showmanship."

Hari waved off the idea. The computer quickly found a bit of dialogue to fit his gesture, so the false scene would not seem false. "No, I'm *not* troubled

455

by the fact that in the practice of my *science* I change the lives of human beings. Knowledge has always changed people's lives. The only difference is that I *know* I'm changing them—and the changes I introduce are planned, they're under control. Did the man who invented the first artificial light—what was it, animal fat with a wick? A light-emitting diode?— did he realize what it would do to humankind, to be given power over night?"

As always, Chanda deflated him the moment he started congratulating himself. "In the first place, it was almost certainly a woman, and in the second place, she knew exactly what she was doing. It allowed her to find her way through the house at night. Now she could put her nursing baby in another bed, in another room, so she could get some sleep at night without fear of rolling over and smothering the child."

Hari smiled. "If artificial light was invented by a woman, it was certainly a prostitute, to extend her hours of work."

Chanda grinned. He did not laugh—it was too hard for the computer to come up with jokes to explain laughter. "We'll watch Leyel carefully, Hari. How will we know when he's ready, so we can begin to count on him for protection and leadership?"

"When you already count on him, then he's ready. When his commitment and loyalty are firm, when the goals of the Second Foundation are already in his heart, when he acts them out in his life, then he's ready."

There was a finality in Hari's tone. The conversation was nearly over.

"By the way, Hari, you were right. No one has even questioned the omission of any important psychohistorical data from the Foundation library on Terminus."

"Of course not. Academics never look outside their own discipline. That's another reason why I'm glad Leyel isn't going. *He* would notice that the only psychologist we're sending is Bor Alurin. Then I'd have to explain more to him than I want. Give my love to Deet, Chanda. Tell her that her test case is going very well. She'll end up with a husband *and* a community of scientists of the mind."

"Artists. Wizards. Demigods."

"Stubborn misguided women who don't know science when they're doing it. All in the Imperial Library. Till next time, Chanda."

If Deet had asked him about his interview with Hari, if she had commiserated with him about Hari's refusal, his resentment of her might have been uncontainable, he might have lashed out at her and said something that could never be forgiven. Instead, she was perfectly herself, so excited about her work and so beautiful, even with her face showing all the sag and wrinkling of her sixty years, that all Leyel could do was fall in love with her again, as he had so many times in their years together.

"It's working beyond anything I hoped for, Leyel. I'm beginning to hear stories that I created months and years ago, coming back as epic legends. You remember the time I retrieved and extrapolated the accounts of the uprising at Misercordia only three days before the Admiralty needed them?"

"Your finest hour. Admiral Divart still talks about how they used the old battle plots as a strategic guideline and put down the Tellekers' strike in a single three-day operation without loss of a ship."

"You have a mind like a trap, even if you *are* old."

"Sadly, all I can remember is the past."

"Dunce, that's all *anyone* can remember."

He prompted her to go on with her account of today's triumph. "It's an epic legend now?"

"It came back to me without my name on it, and bigger than life. As a reference. Rinjy was talking with some young librarians from one of the inner provinces who were on the standard interlibrary tour, and one of them said something about how you could stay in the Imperial Library on Trantor all your life and never see the real world at all."

Leyel hooted. "Just the thing to say to Rinjy!"

"Exactly. Got her dander up, of course, but the important thing is, she immediately told them the story of how a librarian, *all on her own*, saw the similarity between the Misercordia uprising and the Tellekers' strike. She knew no one at the Admiralty would listen to her unless she brought them all the information at once. So she delved back into the ancient records and found them in deplorable shape—the original data had been stored in glass, but that was forty-two centuries ago, and no one had refreshed the data. None of the secondary sources actually showed the battle plots or ship courses—Misercordia had mostly been written about by biographers, not military historians—"

"Of course. It was Pol Yuensau's first battle, but he was just a pilot, not a commander—"

"I know *you* remember, my intrusive pet. The point is what Rinjy *said* about this mythical librarian."

"You."

"I was standing right there. I don't think Rinjy

knew it was me, or she would have said something—
she wasn't even in the same division with me then,
you know. What matters is that Rinjy heard a version of the story and by the time she told it, it was
transformed into a magic hero tale. The prophetic
librarian of Trantor."

"What does *that* prove? You *are* a magic hero."

"The way she told it, I did it all on my own
initiative—"

"You did. You were assigned to do document
extrapolation, and you just happened to start with
Misercordia."

"But in Rinjy's version, I had *already* seen its
usefulness with the Tellekers' strike. She said the
librarian sent it to the Admiralty and only then did
they realize it was the key to bloodless victory."

"Librarian saves the Empire."

"Exactly."

"But you did."

"But I didn't *mean* to. And Admiralty requested
the information—the only really extraordinary thing
was that I had already finished two weeks of document restoration—"

"Which you did brilliantly."

"Using programs you had helped design, thank
you very much, O Wise One, as you indirectly praise
yourself. It was sheer coincidence that I could give
them exactly what they wanted within five minutes
of their asking. But now it's a hero story within the
community of librarians. In the Imperial Library
itself, and now spreading outward to all the other
libraries."

"This is so anecdotal, Deet. I don't see how you
can publish this."

"Oh, I don't intend to. Except perhaps in the

introduction. What matters to me is that it proves my theory."

"It has no statistical validity."

"It proves it to *me*. I know that my theories of community formation are true. That the vigor of a community depends on the allegiance of its members, and the allegiance can be created and enhanced by the dissemination of epic stories."

"She speaks the language of academia. I should be writing this down, so you don't have to think up all those words again."

"Stories that make the community seem more important, more central to human life. Because Rinjy could tell this story, it made her more proud to be a librarian, which increased her allegiance to the community and gave the community more power within her."

"You are possessing their souls."

"And they've got mine. Together our souls are possessing each other."

There was the rub. Deet's role in the library had begun as applied research—joining the library staff in order to confirm her theory of community formation. But that task was impossible to accomplish without in fact becoming a committed part of the library community. It was Deet's dedication to serious science that had brought them together. Now that very dedication was stealing her away. It would hurt her more to leave the library than it would to lose Leyel.

Not true. Not true at all, he told himself sternly. Self-pity leads to self-deception. Exactly the opposite is true—it would hurt her more to lose Leyel than to leave her community of librarians. That's why she consented to go to Terminus in the first place. But could he blame her for being glad that she didn't have to choose? Glad that she could have both?

Yet even as he beat down the worst of the thoughts arising from his disappointment, he couldn't keep some of the nastiness from coming out in his conversation. "How will you know when your experiment is over?"

She frowned. "It'll never be *over*, Leyel. They're all really librarians—I don't pick them up by the tails like mice and put them back in their cages when the experiment's done. At some point I'll simply stop, that's all, and write my book."

"Will you?"

"Write the book? I've written books before, I think I can do it again."

"I meant, will you stop?"

"When, now? Is this some test of my love for you, Leyel? Are you jealous of my friendships with Rinjy and Animet and Fin and Urik?"

No! Don't accuse me of such childish, selfish feelings!

But before he could snap back his denial, he knew that his denial would be false.

"Sometimes I am, yes, Deet. Sometimes I think you're happier with them."

And because he had spoken honestly, what could have become a bitter quarrel remained a conversation. "But I *am*, Leyel," she answered, just as frankly. "It's because when I'm with them, I'm creating something new, I'm creating something *with them*. It's exciting, invigorating, I'm discovering new things every day, in every word they say, every smile, every tear someone sheds, every sign that

461

being one of *us* is the most important thing in their lives."

"I can't compete with that."

"No, you can't, Leyel. But you complete it. Because it would all mean nothing, it would be more frustrating than exhilarating if I couldn't come back to you every day and tell you what happened. You always understand what it means, you're always excited for me, you validate my experience."

"I'm your audience. Like a parent."

"Yes, old man. Like a husband. Like a child. Like the person I love most in all the world. You are my root. I make a brave show out there, all branches and bright leaves in the sunlight, but I come here to suck the water of life from your soil."

"Leyel Forska, the font of capillarity. You are the tree, and I am the dirt."

"Which happens to be full of fertilizer." She kissed him. A kiss reminiscent of younger days. An invitation, which he gladly accepted.

A softened section of floor served them as an impromptu bed. At the end, he lay beside her, his arm across her waist, his head on her shoulder, his lips brushing the skin of her breast. He remembered when her breasts were small and firm, perched on her chest like small monuments to her potential. Now when she lay on her back they were a ruin, eroded by age so they flowed off her chest to either side, resting wearily on her arms.

"You are a magnificent woman," he whispered, his lips tickling her skin.

Their slack and flabby bodies were now capable of greater passion than when they were taut and strong. Before, they were all potential. That's what we love in youthful bodies, the teasing potential.

462

Now hers is a body of accomplishment. Three fine children were the blossoms, then the fruit of this tree, gone off and taken root somewhere else. The tension of youth could now give way to a relaxation of the flesh. There were no more promises in their lovemaking. Only fulfillment.

She murmured softly in his ear, "That was a ritual, by the way. Community maintenance."

"So I'm just another experiment?"

"A fairly successful one. I'm testing to see if this little community can last until one of us drops."

"What if you drop first? Who'll write the paper then?"

"You will. But you'll sign my name to it. I want the Imperial medal for it. Posthumously. Glue it to my memorial stone."

"I'll wear it myself. If you're selfish enough to leave all the real work to me, you don't deserve anything better than a cheap replica."

She slapped his back. "You are a nasty selfish old man, then. The real thing or nothing."

He felt the sting of her slap as if he deserved it. A nasty selfish old man. If she only knew how right she was. There had been a moment in Hari's office when he'd almost said the words that would deny all that there was between them. The words that would cut her out of his life. Go to Terminus without her! I would be more myself if they took my heart, my liver, my brain.

How could I have thought I wanted to go to Terminus, anyway? To be surrounded by academics of the sort I most despise, struggling with them to get the encyclopedia properly designed. They'd each fight for their petty little province, never catching the vision of the whole, never understanding that

the encyclopedia would be valueless if it were com-
partmentalized. It would be life in hell, and in the
end he'd lose, because the academic mind was
incapable of growth or change.

It was here on Trantor that he could still accomplish something. Perhaps even solve the question of human origin, at least to his own satisfaction—and perhaps he could do it soon enough that
he could get his discovery included in the Encyclopedia Galactica before the Empire began to break
down at the edges, cutting Terminus off from the
rest of the Galaxy.

It was like a shock of static electricity passing
through his brain; he even saw an afterglow of light
around the edges of his vision, as if a spark had
jumped some synaptic gap.

"What a sham," he said.

"Who, you? Me?"

"Hari Seldon. All this talk about his Foundation
to create the Encyclopedia Galactica."

"Careful, Leyel." It was almost impossible that
the Pubs could have found a way to listen to what
went on in Leyel Forska's own apartments. Almost.

"He told me twenty years ago. It was one of his
first psychohistorical projections. The Empire will
crumble at the edges first. He projected it would
happen within the next generation. The figures were
crude then. He must have it down to the year now.
Maybe even the month. Of course he put his Foundation on Terminus. A place so remote that when
the edges of the Empire fray, it will be among the
first threads lost. Cut off from Trantor. Forgotten at
once!"

"What good would *that* do, Leyel? They'd never
hear of any new discoveries then."

"What you said about us. A tree. Our children like the fruit of that tree."

"I never said that."

"I thought it, then. He is dropping his Foundation out on Terminus like the fruit of Empire. To grow into a new Empire by and by."

"You frighten me, Leyel. If the Pubs ever heard you say that—"

"That crafty old fox. That sly, deceptive—he never actually lied to me, but of course he couldn't send me there. If the Forska fortune was tied up with Terminus, the Empire would never lose track of the place. The edges might fray elsewhere, but never there. Putting me on Terminus would be the undoing of the *real* project." It was such a relief. Of course Hari couldn't tell him, not with the Pubs listening, but it had nothing to do with him or Deet. It wouldn't have to be a barrier between them after all. It was just one of the penalties of being the keeper of the Forska fortune.

"Do you really think so?" asked Deet.

"I was a fool not to see it before. But Hari was a fool too if he thought I wouldn't guess it."

"Maybe he expects you to guess everything."

"Oh, nobody could ever come up with *everything* Hari's doing. He has more twists and turns in his brain than a hyperpath through core space. No matter how you labor to pick your way through, you'll always find Hari at the end of it, nodding happily and congratulating you on coming this far. He's ahead of us all. He's already planned everything, and the rest of us are doomed to follow in his footsteps."

"Is it doom?"

"Once I thought Hari Seldon was God. Now I

465

know he's much less powerful than that. He's merely Fate."

"No, Leyel. Don't say that."

"Not even Fate. Just our guide through it. He sees the future, and points the way."

"Rubbish." She slid out from under him, got up, pulled her robe from its hook on the wall. "My old bones get cold when I lie about naked."

Leyel's legs were trembling, but not with cold. "The future is his, and the present is yours, but the past belongs to me. I don't know how far into the future his probability curves have taken him, but I can match him, step for step, century for century into the past."

"Don't tell me you're going to solve the question of origin. You're the one who proved it wasn't worth solving."

"I proved that it wasn't important or even possible to find the planet of origin. But I also said that we could still discover the natural laws that accounted for the origin of man. Whatever forces created us as human beings must still be present in the universe."

"I did read what you wrote, you know. You said it would be the labor of the next millennium to find the answer."

"Just now. Lying here, just now, I saw it, just out of reach. Something about your work and Hari's work, and the tree."

"The tree was about me needing you, Leyel. It wasn't about the origin of humanity."

"It's gone. Whatever I saw for a moment there, it's gone. But I can find it again. It's there in your work, and Hari's Foundation, and the fall of the Empire, and the damned pear tree."

"I never said it was a pear tree."

"I used to play in the pear orchard on the grounds of the estate in Holdwater. To me the word 'tree' always means a pear tree. One of the deep-worn ruts in my brain."

"I'm relieved. I was afraid you were reminded of pears by the shape of these ancient breasts when I bend over."

"Open your robe again. Let me see if I think of pears."

Leyel paid for Hari Seldon's funeral. It was not lavish. Leyel had meant it to be. The moment he heard of Hari's death—not a surprise, since Hari's first brutal stroke had let him half-paralyzed in a wheelchair—he set his staff to work on a memorial service appropriate to honor the greatest scientific mind of the millennium. But word arrived, in the form of a visit from Commissioner Rom Divart, that any sort of public services would be . . .

"Shall we say, inappropriate?"

"The man was the greatest genius I've ever heard of! He virtually invented a branch of science that clarified things that—he made a science out of the sort of thing that soothsayers and—and—*economists* used to do!"

Rom laughed at Leyel's little joke, of course, because he and Leyel had been friends forever. Rom was the only friend of Leyel's childhood who had never sucked up to him or resented him or stayed cool toward him because of the Forska fortune. This way, of course, because the Divart holdings were, if anything, slightly greater. They had played together unencumbered by strangeness or jealousy or awe.

They even shared a tutor for two terrible, glorious years, from the time Rom's father was murdered until the execution of Rom's grandfather, which caused so much outrage among the nobility that the mad Emperor was stripped of power and the Imperium put under the control of the Commission of Public Safety. Then, as the youthful head of one of the great families, Rom had embarked on his long and fruitful career in politics.

Rom said later that for those two years it was Leyel who taught him that there was still some good in the world; that Leyel's friendship was the only reason Rom hadn't killed himself. Leyel always thought this was pure theatrics. Rom was a born actor. That's why he so excelled at making stunning entrances and playing unforgettable scenes on the grandest stage of all—the politics of the Imperium. Someday he would no doubt exit as dramatically as his father and grandfather had.

But he was not all show. Rom never forgot the friend of his childhood. Leyel knew it, and knew also that Rom's coming to deliver this message from the Commission of Public Safety probably meant that Rom had fought to make the message as mild as it was. So Leyel blustered a bit, then made his little joke. It was his way of surrendering gracefully.

What Leyel didn't realize, right up until the day of the funeral, was exactly *how* dangerous his friendship with Hari Seldon had been, and how stupid it was for him to associate himself with Hari's name now that the old man was dead. Linge Chen, the Chief Commissioner, had not risen to the position of greatest power in the Empire without being fiercely suspicious of potential rivals and brutally efficient about eliminating them. Hari had maneuvered Chen into a position such that it was more dangerous to kill the old man than to give him his Foundation on

Terminus. But now Hari was dead, and apparently Chen was watching to see who mourned.

Leyel did—Leyel and the few members of Hari's staff who had stayed behind on Trantor to maintain contact with Terminus up to the moment of Hari's death. Leyel should have known better. Even alive, Hari wouldn't have cared who came to his funeral. And now, dead, he cared even less. Leyel didn't believe his friend lived on in some ethereal plane, watching carefully and taking attendance at the services. No, Leyel simply felt he had to be there, felt he had to speak. Not for Hari, really. For himself. To continue to be himself, Leyel had to make some kind of public gesture toward Hari Seldon and all he had stood for.

Who heard? Not many. Deet, who thought his eulogy was too mild by half. Hari's staff, who were quite aware of the danger and winced at each of Leyel's list of Hari's accomplishments. Naming them—and emphasizing that only Seldon had the vision to do these great works—was inherently a criticism of the level of intelligence and integrity in the Empire. The Pubs were listening, too. They noted that Leyel clearly agreed with Hari Seldon about the certainty of the Empire's fall—that in fact as a galactic empire it had probably already fallen, since its authority was no longer coextensive with the Galaxy.

If almost anyone else had said such things, to such a small audience, it would have been ignored, except to keep him from getting any job requiring a security clearance. But when the head of the Forska family came out openly to affirm the correctness of the views of a man who had been tried before the Commission of Public Safety—that posed a greater danger to the Commission than Hari Seldon.

For, as head of the Forska family, if Leyel Forska wanted, he could be one of the great players on the political stage, could have a seat on the Commission along with Rom Divart and Linge Chen. Of course, that would also have meant constantly watching for assassins—either to avoid them or to hire them— and trying to win the allegiance of various military strongmen in the farflung reaches of the Galaxy. Leyel's grandfather had spent his life in such pursuits, but Leyel's father had declined, and Leyel himself had thoroughly immersed himself in science and never so much as inquired about politics.

Until now. Until he made the profoundly political act of paying for Hari Seldon's funeral and then *speaking* at it. What would he do next? There were a thousand would-be warlords who would spring to revolt if a Forska promised what would-be emperors so desperately needed: a noble sponsor, a mask of legitimacy, and *money*.

Did Linge Chen really believe that Leyel meant to enter politics at his advanced age? Did he really think Leyel posed a threat?

Probably not. If he *had* believed it, he would surely have had Leyel killed, and no doubt all his children as well, leaving only one of his minor grandchildren, whom Chen would carefully control through the guardians he would appoint, thereby acquiring control of the Forska fortune as well as his own.

Instead, Chen only believed that Leyel *might* cause trouble. So he took what were, for him, mild steps.

That was why Rom came to visit Leyel again, a week after the funeral.

Leyel was delighted to see him. "Not on somber business this time, I hope," he said. "But such bad luck—Deet's at the library again, she practically lives there now, but she'd want to—"

"Leyel." Rom touched Leyel's lips with his fingers.

So it *was* somber business after all. Worse than somber. Rom recited what had to be a memorized speech.

"The Commission of Public Safety has become concerned that in your declining years—"

Leyel opened his mouth to protest, but again Rom touched his lips to silence him.

"That in your declining years, the burdens of the Forska estates are distracting you from your exceptionally important scientific work. So great is the Empire's need for the new discoveries and understanding your work will surely bring us, that the Commission of Public Safety has created the office of Forska Trustee to oversee all the Forska estates and holdings. You will, of course, have unlimited access to these funds for your scientific work here on Trantor, and funding will continue for all the archives and libraries you have endowed. Naturally, the Commission has no desire for you to thank us for what is, after all, our duty to one of our noblest citizens, but if your well-known courtesy required you to make a brief public statement of gratitude it would not be inappropriate."

Leyel was no fool. He knew how things worked. He was being stripped of his fortune and being placed under arrest on Trantor. There was no point in protest or remonstrance, no point even in trying

471

to make Rom feel guilty for having brought him such a bitter message. Indeed, Rom himself might be in great danger—if Leyel so much as hinted that he expected Rom to come to his support, his dear friend might also fall. So Leyel nodded gravely, and then carefully framed his words of reply.

"Please tell the Commissioners how grateful I am for their concern on my behalf. It has been a long, long time since anyone went to the trouble of easing my burdens. I accept their kind offer. I am especially glad because this means that now I can pursue my studies unencumbered."

Rom visibly relaxed. Leyel wasn't going to cause trouble. "My dear friend, I will sleep better knowing that you are always here on Trantor, working freely in the library or taking your leisure in the parks."

So at least they weren't going to confine him to his apartment. No doubt they would never let him off-planet, but it wouldn't hurt to ask. "Perhaps I'll even have time now to visit my grandchildren now and then."

"Oh, Leyel, you and I are both too old to enjoy hyperspace any more. Leave that for the youngsters—they can come visit you whenever they want. And sometimes they can stay home, while their parents come to see you."

Thus Leyel learned that if any of his children came to visit him, *their* children would be held hostage, and vice versa. Leyel himself would never leave Trantor again.

"So much the better," said Leyel. "I'll have time to write several books I've been meaning to publish."

"The Empire waits eagerly for every scientific treatise you publish." There was a slight emphasis

472

on the word "scientific." "But I hope you won't bore us with one of those tedious autobiographies."

Leyel agreed to the restriction easily enough. "I *promise*, Rom. You know better than anyone else exactly how boring my life has always been."

"Come now. *My* life's the boring one, Leyel, all this government claptrap and bureaucratic bushwa. You've been at the forefront of scholarship and learning. Indeed, my friend, the Commission hopes you'll honor us by giving us first look at every word that comes out of your scriptor."

"Only if you promise to read it carefully and point out any mistakes I might make." No doubt the Commission intended only to censor his work to remove political material—which Leyel had never included anyway. But Leyel had already resolved never to publish anything again, at least as long as Linge Chen was Chief Commissioner. The safest thing Leyel could do now was to disappear, to let Chen forget him entirely—it would be egregiously stupid to send occasional articles to Chen, thus reminding him that Leyel was still around.

But Rom wasn't through yet. "I must extend that request to Deet's work as well. We really want first look at it—do tell her so."

"Deet?" For the first time Leyel almost let his fury show. Why should Deet be punished because of Leyel's indiscretion? "Oh, she'll be too shy for that, Rom—she doesn't think her work is *important* enough to deserve any attention from men as busy as the Commissioners. They'll think you only want to see her work because she's my wife—she's always annoyed when people patronize her."

"You must insist, then, Leyel," said Rom. "I assure you, her studies of the functions of the

473

Imperial bureaucracy have long been interesting to the Commission for their own sake."

Ah. Of course. Chen would never have allowed a report on the workings of government to appear without making sure it wasn't dangerous. Censorship of Deet's writings wouldn't be Leyel's fault after all. Or at least not entirely.

"I'll tell her that, Rom. She'll be flattered. But won't you stay and tell her yourself? I can bring you a cup of peshat, we can talk about old times—"

Leyel would have been surprised if Rom had stayed. No, this interview had been at least as hard on Rom as it had been on him. The very fact that Rom had been forced into being the Commission's messenger to his childhood friend was a humiliating reminder that the Chens were in the ascendant over the Divarts. But as Rom bowed and left, it occurred to Leyel that Chen might have made a mistake. Humiliating Rom this way, forcing him to place his dearest friend under arrest like this—it might be the straw to break the camel's back. After all, though no one had ever been able to find out who hired the assassin who killed Rom's father, and no one had ever learned who denounced Rom's grandfather, leading to his execution by the paranoid Emperor Wassiniwak, it didn't take a genius to realize that the House of Chen had profited most from both events.

"I wish I could stay," said Rom. "But duty calls. Still, you can be sure I'll think of you often. Of course, I doubt I'll think of you as you are *now*, you old wreck. I'll remember you as a boy, when we used to tweak our tutor—remember the time we recoded his lector, so that for a whole week explicit

474

pornography kept coming up on the display whenever the door of his room opened?"

Leyel couldn't help laughing. "You never forget anything, do you!"

"The poor fool. He never figured out that it was us! Old times. Why couldn't we have stayed young forever?" He embraced Leyel and then swiftly left.

Linge Chen, you fool, you have reached too far. Your days are numbered. None of the Pubs who were listening in on their conversation could possibly know that Rom and Leyel had never teased their tutor—and that they had never done anything to his lector. It was just Rom's way of letting Leyel know that they were still allies, still keeping secrets together—and that someone who had authority over both of them was going to be in for a few nasty surprises.

It gave Leyel chills, thinking about what might come of all this. He loved Rom Divart with all his heart, but he also knew that Rom was capable of biding his time and then killing swiftly, efficiently, coldly. Linge Chen had just started his latest six-year term of office, but Leyel knew he'd never finish it. And the next Chief Commissioner would not be a Chen.

Soon, though, the enormity of what had been done to him began to sink in. He had always thought that his fortune meant little to him—that he would be the same man with or without the Forska estates. But now he began to realize that it wasn't true, that he'd been lying to himself all along. He had known since childhood how despicable rich and powerful men could be—his father had made sure he saw and understood how cruel men became when their money persuaded them they had a right to use others

475

however they wished. So Leyel had learned to despise his own birthright, and, starting with his father, had pretended to others that he could make his way through the world solely by wit and diligence, that he would have been exactly the same man if he had grown up in a common family, with a common education. He had done such a good job of acting as if he didn't care about his wealth that he came to believe it himself.

Now he realized that Forska estates had been an invisible part of himself all along, as if they were extensions of his body, as if he could flex a muscle and cargo ships would fly, he could blink and mines would be sunk deep into the earth, he could sigh and all over the Galaxy there would be a wind of change that would keep blowing until everything was exactly as he wanted it. Now all those invisible limbs and senses had been amputated. Now he was crippled—he had only as many arms and legs and eyes as any other human being.

At last he was what he had always pretended to be. An ordinary, powerless man. He hated it.

For the first hours after Rom left, Leyel pretended he could take all this in stride. He sat at the lector and spun through the pages smoothly—without anything on the pages registering in his memory. He kept wishing Deet were there so he could laugh with her about how little this hurt him; then he would be glad that Deet was not there, because one sympathetic touch of her hand would push him over the edge, make it impossible to contain his emotion.

Finally he could not help himself. Thinking of Deet, of their children and grandchildren, of all that had been lost to them because he had made an empty gesture to a dead friend, he threw himself to the softened floor and wept bitterly. Let Chen listen to recordings of what the spy beam shows of this! Let him savor his victory! I'll destroy him somehow, my staff is still loyal to me, I'll put together an army, I'll hire assassins of my own, I'll make contact with Admiral Sipp, and then Chen will be the one to sob, crying out for mercy as I disfigure him the way he has mutilated me—

Fool.

Leyel rolled over onto his back, dried his face on his sleeve, then lay there, eyes closed, calming himself. No vengeance. No politics. That was Rom's business, not Leyel's. Too late for him to enter the game now—and who would help him, anyway, now that he had already lost his power? There was nothing to be done.

Leyel didn't really want to do anything, anyway. Hadn't they guaranteed that his archives and libraries would continue to be funded? Hadn't they guaranteed him unlimited research funds? And wasn't that all he had cared about anyway? He had long since turned over all the Forska operations to his subordinates—Chen's trustee would simply do the same job. And Leyel's children wouldn't suffer much—he had raised them with the same values that he had grown up with, and so they all pursued careers unrelated to the Forska holdings. They were true children of their father and mother—they wouldn't have any self-respect if they didn't earn their own way in the world. No doubt they'd be disappointed by having their inheritance snatched away. But they wouldn't be destroyed.

I am not ruined. All the lies that Rom told are really true, only they didn't realize it. All that matters in my life, I still have. I really *don't* care about

477

my fortune. It's just the *way* I lost it that made me so furious. I can go on and be the same person I always was. This will even give me an opportunity to see who my true friends are—to see who still honors me for my scientific achievements, and who despises me for my poverty.

By the time Deet got home from the library— late, as was usual these days—Leyel was hard at work, reading back through all the research and speculation on protohuman behavior, trying to see if there was anything other than half-assed guess-work and pompous babble. He was so engrossed in his reading that he spent the first fifteen minutes after she got home telling her of the hilarious stupidities he had found in the day's reading, and then sharing a wonderful, impossible thought he had had.

"What if the human species isn't the only branch to evolve on our family tree? What if there's some other primate species that looks exactly like us, but can't interbreed with us, that functions in a completely different way, and we don't even know it, we all think everybody's just like us, but here and there all over the Empire there are whole towns, cities, maybe even worlds of people who secretly aren't human at all."

"But Leyel, my overwrought husband, if they look just like us and act just like us, then they *are* human."

"But they *don't* act exactly like us. There's a difference. A completely different set of rules and assumptions. Only they don't know that we're different, and we don't know that *they're* different. Or even if we suspect it, we're never sure. Just two different species, living side by side and never guessing it."

478

She kissed him. "You poor fool, that isn't speculation, it already exists. You have just described the relationship between males and females. Two completely different species, completely unintelligible to each other, living side by side and thinking they're really the same. The fascinating thing, Leyel, is that the two species persist in marrying each other and having babies, sometimes of one species, sometimes of the other, and the whole time they can't understand why they can't understand each other."

He laughed and embraced her. "You're right, as always, Deet. If I could once understand women, then perhaps I'd know what it is that makes men human."

"Nothing could possibly make men human," she answered. "Every time they're just about to get it right, they end up tripping over the damned Y chromosome and turning back into beasts." She nuzzled his neck.

It was then, with Deet in his arms, that he whispered to her what had happened when Rom visited that day. She said nothing, but held him tightly for the longest time. Then they had a very late supper and went about their nightly routines as if nothing had changed.

Not until they were in bed, not until Deet was softly snoring beside him, did it finally occur to Leyel that Deet was facing a test of her own. Would she still love him, now that he was merely Leyel Forska, scientist on a pension, and not Lord Forska, master of worlds? Of course she would *intend* to. But just as Leyel had never been aware of how much he depended on his wealth to define himself, so also she might not have realized how much of what she loved about him was his vast power; for even though he didn't flaunt it, it had always been there, like a solid platform underfoot, hardly noticed except now, when it was gone, when their footing was unsure.

Even before this, she had been slipping away into the community of women in the library. She would drift away even faster now, not even noticing it as Leyel became less and less important to her. No need for anything as dramatic as divorce. Just a little gap between them, an empty space that might as well be a chasm, might as well be the abyss. My fortune was a part of me, and now that it's gone, I'm no longer the same man she loved. She won't even know that she doesn't love me anymore. She'll just get busier and busier in her work, and in five or ten years when I die of old age, she'll grieve—and then suddenly she'll realize that she isn't half as devastated as she thought she'd be. In fact, she won't be devastated at all. And she'll get on with her life and won't even remember what it was like to be married to me. I'll disappear from all human memory then, except perhaps for a few scientific papers and the libraries.

I'm like the information that was lost in all those neglected archives. Disappearing bit by bit, unnoticed, until all that's left is just a little bit of noise in people's memories. Then, finally, nothing. Blank.

Self-pitying fool. That's what happens to everyone, in the long run. Even Hari Seldon—someday he'll be forgotten, sooner rather than later, if Chen has his way. We all die. We're all lost in the passage of time. The only thing that lives on after us is the new shape we've given to the communities we lived in. There are things that are known because I said them, and even though people have forgotten who said it, they'll go on knowing. Like the story Rinjy was telling—she had forgotten, if she ever knew it, that Deet was the librarian in the original tale. But still she remembered the tale. The community of librarians was different because Deet had been among them. They would be a little different, a little braver, a little stronger, because of Deet. She had left traces of herself in the world.

And then, again, there came that flash of insight, that sudden understanding of the answer to a question that had long been troubling him.

But in the moment that Leyel realized that he held the answer, the answer slipped away. He couldn't remember it. You're asleep, he said silently. You only dreamed that you understood the origin of humanity. That's the way it is in dreams—the truth is always so beautiful, but you can never hold on to it.

"How is he taking it, Deet?"

"Hard to say. Well, I think. He was never much of a wanderer anyway."

"Come now, it can't be that simple."

"No. No, it isn't."

"Tell me.'

"The social things—those were easy. We rarely went anyway, but now people don't invite us. We're politically dangerous. And the few things we had scheduled got canceled or, um, postponed. You know—we'll call you as soon as we have a new date."

"He doesn't mind this?"

"He *likes* that part. He always hated those things. But they've canceled his speeches. And the lecture series on human ecology."

"A blow."

"He pretends not to mind. But he's brooding."

"Tell me."

"Works all day, but he doesn't read it to me any-more, doesn't make me sit down at the lector the minute I get home. I think he isn't writing anything."

"Doing nothing?"

"No. Reading. That's all."

"Maybe he just needs to do research."

"You don't know Leyel. He *thinks* by writing. Or talking. He isn't doing either."

"Doesn't talk to you?"

"He answers. I try to talk about things here at the library, his answers are—what? Glum. Sullen."

"He resents your work?"

"That's not possible. Leyel has always been as enthusiastic about my work as about his own. And he won't talk about his own work, either. I ask him, and he says nothing."

"Not surprising."

"So it's all right?"

"No. It's just not surprising."

"What is it? Can't you tell me?"

"What good is telling you? It's what we call ILS—Identity Loss Syndrome. It's identical to the passive strategy for dealing with loss of body parts."

"ILS. What happens in ILS?"

"Deet, come on, you're a scientist. What do you expect? You've just described Leyel's behavior, I tell you that it's called ILS, you want to know what ILS is, and what am I going to do?"

"Describe Leyel's behavior back to me. What an idiot I am."

"Good, at least you can laugh."

"Can't you tell me what to expect?"

"Complete withdrawal from you, from everybody.

482

Eventually he becomes completely antisocial and starts to strike out. Does something self-destructive—like making public statements against Chen, that'd do it."

"No!"

"Or else he severs his old connections, gets away from you, and reconstructs himself in a different set of communities."

"This would make him happy?"

"Sure. Useless to the Second Foundation, but happy. It would also turn you into a nasty-tempered old crone, not that you aren't already, mind you."

"Oh, you think Leyel's the only thing keeping me human?"

"Pretty much, yes. He's your safety valve."

"Not lately."

"I know."

"Have I been so awful?"

"Nothing that we can't bear. Deet, if we're going to be fit to govern the human race someday, shouldn't we first learn to be good to each other?"

"Well, I'm glad to provide you all with an opportunity to test your patience."

"You should be glad. We're doing a fine job so far, wouldn't you say?"

"Please. You were teasing me about the prognosis, weren't you?"

"Partly. Everything I said was true, but you know as well as I do that there are as many different ways out of a B-B syndrome as there are people who have them."

"Behavioral cause, behavioral effect. No little hormone shot, then?"

"Deet. He doesn't know who he is."

"Can't I help him?"

"Yes."

"What? What can I do?"

"This is only a guess, since I haven't talked to him."

"Of course."

"You aren't home much."

"I can't *stand* it there, with him brooding all the time."

"Fine. Get him out with you."

"He won't go."

"Push him."

"We barely talk. I don't know if I even have any leverage over him."

"Deet. You're the one who wrote, 'Communities that make few or no demands on their members cannot command allegiance. All else being equal, members who feel most needed have the strongest allegiance.'"

"You memorized that?"

"Psychohistory *is* the psychology of populations, but populations can only be quantified as communities. Seldon's work on statistical probabilities only worked to predict the future within a generation or two until you first published your community theories. That's because statistics *can't* deal with cause and effect. Stats tell you what's happening, never why, never the result. Within a generation or two, the present statistics evaporate, they're meaningless, you have whole new populations with new configurations. Your community theory gave us a way of predicting which communities would survive, which would grow, which would fade. A way of looking across long stretches of time and space."

"Hari never told me he was using community theory in any important way."

"How could he tell you that? He had to walk a tightrope—publishing enough to get psychohistory taken seriously, but not so much that anybody outside the Second Foundation could ever duplicate or continue his work. Your work was a key—but he couldn't say so."

"Are you just saying this to make me feel better?"

"Sure. That's why I'm saying it. But it's also true—since lying to you wouldn't make you feel better, would it? Statistics are like taking cross sections of the trunk of a tree. It can tell you a lot about its history. You can figure how healthy it is, how much volume the whole tree has, how much is root and how much is branch. But what it *can't* tell you is where the tree will branch, and which branches will become major, which minor, and which will rot and fall off and die."

"But you can't *quantify* communities, can you? They're just stories and rituals that bind people together—"

"You'd be surprised what we can quantify. We're very good at what we do, Deet. Just as you are. Just as Leyel is."

"*Is* his work important? After all, human origin is only a historical question."

"Nonsense, and you know it. Leyel has stripped away the historical issues and he's searching for the scientific ones. The principles by which human life, as we understand it, is differentiated from non-human. If he finds that—don't you see, Deet? The human race is re-creating itself all the time, on every world, in every family, in every individual. We're born animals, and we teach each other how to be human. Somehow. It matters that we find out how.

485

It matters to psychohistory. It matters to the Second Foundation. It matters to the human race."

"So—you aren't just being kind to Leyel."

"Yes, we are. You are, too. Good people are kind."

"Is that all? Leyel is just one man who's having trouble?"

"We need him. He isn't important just to you. He's important to *us*."

"Oh. Oh."

"Why are you crying?"

"I was so afraid—that I was being selfish—being so worried about him. Taking up your time like this."

"Well, if that doesn't—I thought you were beyond surprising me."

"Our problems were just—our problems. But now they're not."

"Is that so important to you? Tell me, Deet—do you really value this community so much?"

"Yes."

"More than Leyel?"

"No! But enough—that I felt *guilty* for caring so much about him."

"Go home, Deet. Just go home."

"What?"

"That's where you'd rather be. It's been showing up in your behavior for two months, ever since Hari's death. You've been nasty and snappish, and now I know why. You *resent* us for keeping you away from Leyel."

"No, it was my choice, I—"

"Of course it was your choice! It was your *sacrifice* for the good of the Second Foundation. So now I'm telling you—healing Leyel is more important to

Hari's plan than keeping up with your day-to-day responsibilities here."

"You're not removing me from my position, are you?"

"No. I'm just telling you to ease up. And get Leyel out of the apartment. Do you understand me? Demand it! Reengage him with *you*, or we've all lost him."

"Take him *where*?"

"I don't know. Theater. Athletic events. Dancing."

"We don't *do* those things."

"Well, what *do* you do?"

"Research. And then talk about it."

"Fine. Bring him here to the library. Do research with him. Talk about it."

"But he'll meet people here. He'd certainly meet *you*."

"Good. Good. I like that. Yes, let him come here."

"But I thought we had to keep the Second Foundation a secret from him until he's ready to take part."

"I didn't say you should introduce me as First Speaker."

"No, no, of course you didn't. What am I thinking of? Of course he can meet you, he can meet everybody."

"Deet, listen to me."

"Yes, I'm listening."

"It's all right to love him, Deet."

"I know that."

"I mean, it's all right to love him more than you love us. More than you love any of us. More than you love all of us. There you are, crying again."

"I'm so—".

"Relieved."

"How do you understand me so well?"

"I only know what you show me and what you tell me. It's all we ever know about each other. The only thing that helps is that nobody can ever lie for long about who they really are. Not even to themselves."

For two months Leyel followed up on Magolissian's paper by trying to find some connection between language studies and human origins. Of course this meant weeks of wading through old, useless point-of-origin studies, which kept indicating that Trantor was the focal point of language throughout the history of the Empire, even though *nobody* seriously put forth Trantor as the planet of origin. Once again, though, Leyel rejected the search for a particular planet; he wanted to find out regularities, not unique events.

Leyel hoped for a clue in the fairly recent work—only two thousand years old—of Dagawell Kispitorian. Kispitorian came from the most isolated area of a planet called Artashat, where there were traditions that the original settlers came from an earlier world named Armenia, now uncharted. Kispitorian grew up among mountain people who claimed that long ago, they spoke a completely different language. In fact, the title of Kispitorian's most interesting book was *No Man Understood Us*; many of the folk tales of these people began with the formula "Back in the days when no man understood us . . ."

Kispitorian had never been able to shake off this tradition of his upbringing, and as he pursued the field of dialect formation and evolution, he kept coming across evidence that at one time the human species spoke not one but many languages. It had always been taken for granted that Galactic Standard was the up-to-date version of the language of the planet of origin—that while a few human groups might have developed dialects, civilization was impossible without mutually intelligible speech. But Kispitorian had begun to suspect that Galactic Standard did not become the universal human language until *after* the formation of the Empire—that, in fact, one of the first labors of the Imperium was to stamp out all other competing languages. The mountain people of Artashat believed that their language had been stolen from them. Kispitorian eventually devoted his life to proving they were right.

He worked first with names, long recognized as the most conservative aspect of language. He found that there were many separate naming traditions, and it was not until about the year 6000 GE that all were finally amalgamated into one Empire-wide stream. What was interesting was that the farther back he went, the *more* complexity he found.

Because certain worlds tended to have unified traditions, and so the simplest explanation of this was the one he first put forth—that humans left their home world with a unified language, but the normal forces of language separation caused each new planet to develop its own offshoot, until many dialects became mutually unintelligible. Thus, different languages would not have developed until humanity moved out into space; this was one of the reasons why the Galactic Empire was necessary to restore the primeval unity of the species.

Kispitorian called his first and most influential

book *Tower of Confusion*, using the widespread legend of the Tower of Babble as an illustration. He supposed that this story might have originated in that pre-Empire period, probably among the rootless traders roaming from planet to planet, who had to deal on a practical level with the fact that no two worlds spoke the same language. These traders had preserved a tradition that when humanity lived on one planet, they all spoke the same language. They explained the linguistic confusion of their own by recounting the tale of a great leader who built the first "tower," or starship, to raise mankind up into heaven. According to the story, "God" punished these upstart people by confusing their tongues, which forced them to disperse among the different worlds. The story presented the confusion of tongues as the *cause* of the dispersal instead of its result, but cause-reversal was a commonly recognized feature of myth. Clearly this legend preserved a historical fact.

So far, Kispitorian's work was perfectly acceptable to most scientists. But in his forties he began to go off on wild tangents. Using controversial algorithms—on calculators with a suspiciously high level of processing power—he began to tear apart Galactic Standard itself, showing that many words revealed completely separated phonetic traditions, incompatible with the mainstream of the language. They could not comfortably have evolved within a population that regularly spoke either Standard or its primary ancestor language. Furthermore, there were many words with clearly related meanings that showed they had once diverged according to standard linguistic patterns and then were brought together later, with different meanings or implications. But the time scale implied by the degree of change was far too great to be accounted for in the period between humanity's first settlement of space and the formation of the Empire. Obviously, claimed Kispitorian, there had been many different languages *on the planet of origin*; Galactic Standard was the *first* universal human language. Throughout all human history, separation of languages had been a fact of life; only the Empire had had the pervasive power to unify speech.

After that, Kispitorian was written off as a fool, of course—his own Tower of Babble interpretation was now used against him as if an interesting illustration had now become a central argument. He very narrowly escaped execution as a separatist, in fact, since there was an unmistakable tone of regret in his writing about the loss of linguistic diversity. The Imperium did succeed in cutting off all his funding and jailing him for a while because he had been using a calculator with an illegal level of memory and processing power. Leyel suspected that Kispitorian got off easy at that—working with language as he did, getting the results he got, he might well have developed a calculator so intelligent that it could understand and produce human speech, which, if discovered, would have meant either the death penalty or a lynching.

No matter now. Kispitorian insisted to the end that his work was pure science, making no value judgments on whether the Empire's linguistic unity was a Good Thing or not. He was merely reporting that the natural condition of humanity was to speak many different languages. And Leyel believed that he was right.

Leyel could not help but feel that by combining

491

Kispitorian's language studies with Magolissian's work with language-using primates he could come up with something important. But what was the connection? The primates had never developed their *own* languages—they only learned nouns and verbs presented to them by humans. So they could hardly have developed diversity of language. What connection could there be? Why would diversity ever have developed? Could it have something to do with why humans became human?

The primates used only a tiny subset of Standard. For that matter, so did most people—most of the two million words in Standard were used only by a few professionals who actually needed them, while the common vocabulary of humans throughout the Galaxy consisted of a few thousand words.

Oddly, though, it was that small subset of Standard that was the *most* susceptible to change. Highly esoteric scientific or technical papers written in 2000 GE were still easily readable. Slangy, colloquial passages in fiction, especially in dialogue, became almost unintelligible within five hundred years. The language shared by the most different communities was the language that changed the most. But over time, that mainstream language always changed *together*. It made no sense, then, for there ever to be linguistic diversity. Language changed most when it was most unified. Therefore when people were most divided, their language should remain most similar.

Never mind, Leyel. You're out of your discipline. Any competent linguist would know the answer to that.

But Leyel knew that wasn't likely to be true. People immersed in one discipline rarely questioned

492

the axioms of their profession. Linguists all took for granted the fact that the language of an isolated population is invariably more archaic, less susceptible to change. Did they understand why?

Leyel got up from his chair. His eyes were tired from staring into the lector. His knees and back ached from staying so long in the same position. He wanted to lie down, but knew that if he did, he'd fall asleep. The curse of getting old—he could fall asleep so easily, yet could never stay asleep long enough to feel well rested. He didn't *want* to sleep now, though. He wanted to think.

No, that wasn't it. He wanted to *talk*. That's how his best and clearest ideas always came, under the pressure of conversation, when someone else's questions and arguments forced him to think sharply. To make connections, invent explanations. In a contest with another person, his adrenaline flowed, his brain made connections that would never otherwise be made.

Where was Deet? In years past, he would have been talking this through with Deet all day. All week. She would know as much about his research as he did, and would constantly say "Have you thought of this?" or "How can you possibly think that!" And he would have been making the same challenges to *her* work. In the old days.

But these weren't the old days. She didn't need him anymore—she had her friends on the library staff. Nothing wrong with that, probably. After all, she wasn't *thinking* now, she was putting old thoughts into practice. She needed *them*, not *him*. But he still needed *her*. Did she ever think of that? I might as well have gone to Terminus—damn Hari for refusing to let me go. I stayed for Deet's sake,

493

and yet I don't have her after all, not when I need her. How *dare* Hari decide what was right for Leyel Forska!

Only Hari hadn't decided, had he? He would have let Leyel go—without Deet. And Leyel hadn't stayed with Deet so she could help him with his research. He had stayed with her because . . . because . . .

He couldn't remember why. Love, of course. But he couldn't think why that had been so important to him. It wasn't important to *her*. Her idea of love these days was to urge him to come to the library. "You can do your research there. We could be together more during the days."

The message was clear. The only way Leyel could remain part of Deet's life was if he became part of her new "family" at the library. Well, she could forget that idea. If she chose to get swallowed up in that place, fine. If she chose to leave him for a bunch of—*indexers* and *cataloguers*—fine. Fine.

No. It wasn't fine. He wanted to *talk* to her. Right now, at this moment, he wanted to tell her what he was thinking, wanted her to question him and argue with him until she made him come up with an answer, or lots of answers. He needed her to see what he wasn't seeing. He needed her a lot more than *they* needed her.

He was out amid the thick pedestrian traffic of Maslo Boulevard before he realized that this was the first time since Hari's funeral that he'd ventured beyond the immediate neighborhood of his apartment. It was the first time in months that he'd had anyplace to go. That's what I'm doing here, he thought. I just need a change of scenery, a sense of destination. That's the only reason I'm heading to

494

the library. All that emotional nonsense back in the apartment, that was just my unconscious strategy for making myself get out among people again.

Leyel was almost cheerful when he got to the Imperial Library. He had been there many times over the years, but always for receptions or other public events—having his own high-capacity lector meant that he could get access to all the library's records by cable. Other people—students, professors from poorer schools, lay readers—they actually *had* to come here to read. But that meant that they knew their way around the building. Except for finding the major lecture halls and reception rooms, Leyel hadn't the faintest idea where anything was.

For the first time it dawned on him how very large the Imperial Library was. Deet had mentioned the numbers many times—a staff of more than five thousand, including machinists, carpenters, cooks, security, a virtual city in itself—but only now did Leyel realize that this meant that many people here had never met each other. Who could possibly know *five thousand* people by name? He couldn't just walk up and ask for Deet by name. What was the department Deet worked in? She had changed so often, moving through the bureaucracy.

Everyone he saw was a patron—people at lectors, people at catalogues, even people reading books and magazines printed on paper. Where were the librarians? The few staff members moving through the aisles turned out not to be librarians at all—they were volunteer docents, helping newcomers learn how to use the lectors and catalogues. They knew as little about library staff as he did.

He finally found a room full of real librarians, sitting at calculators preparing the daily access and circulation reports. When he tried to speak to one, she merely waved a hand at him. He thought she was telling him to go away until he realized that her hand remained in the air, a finger pointing to the front of the room. Leyel moved toward the elevated desk where a fat, sleepy-looking middle-aged woman was lazily paging through long columns of figures, which stood in the air before her in military formation.

"Sorry to interrupt you," he said softly.

She was resting her cheek on her hand. She didn't even look at him when he spoke. But she answered. "I pray for interruptions."

Only then did he notice that her eyes were framed with laugh lines, that her mouth even in repose turned upward into a faint smile.

"I'm looking for someone. My wife, in fact. Deet Forska."

Her smile widened. She sat up. "You're the beloved Leyel."

It was an absurd thing for a stranger to say, but it pleased him nonetheless to realize that Deet must have spoken of him. Of course everyone would have known that Deet's husband was *the* Leyel Forska. But this woman hadn't said it that way, had she? Not as *the* Leyel Forska, the celebrity. No, here he was known as "the beloved Leyel." Even if this woman meant to tease him, Deet must have let it be known that she had some affection for him. He couldn't help but smile. With relief. He hadn't known that he feared the loss of her love so much, but now he wanted to laugh aloud, to move, to dance with pleasure.

"I imagine I am," said Leyel.

496

"I'm Zay Wax. Deet must have mentioned me, we have lunch every day."

No, she hadn't. She hardly mentioned anybody at the library, come to think of it. These two had lunch every day, and Leyel had never heard of her. "Yes, of course," said Leyel. "I'm glad to meet you."

"And I'm relieved to see that your feet actually touch the ground."

"Now and then."

"She works up in Indexing these days." Zay cleared her display.

"Is that on Trantor?"

Zay laughed. She typed in a few instructions and her display now filled with a map of the library complex. It was a complex pile of rooms and corridors, almost impossible to grasp. "This shows only this wing of the main building. Indexing is these four floors."

Four layers near the middle of the display turned to a brighter color.

"And here's where you are right now."

A small room on the first floor turned white. Looking at the labyrinth between the two lighted sections, Leyel had to laugh aloud. "Can't you just give me a ticket to guide me?"

"Our tickets only lead you to places where patrons are allowed. But this isn't really hard, Lord Forska. After all, you're a genius, aren't you?"

"Not at the interior geography of buildings, whatever lies Deet might have told you."

"You just go out this door and straight down the corridor to the elevators—can't miss them. Go up to fifteen. When you get out, turn as if you were continuing down the same corridor, and after a while you go through an archway that says 'Indexing.'

497

Then you lean back your head and bellow 'Deet' as loud as you can. Do that a few times and either she'll come or security will arrest you."

"That's what I was going to do if I *didn't* find somebody to guide me."

"I was hoping you'd ask me." Zay stood up and spoke loudly to the busy librarians. "The cat's going away. The mice can play."

"About time," one of them said. They all laughed. But they kept working.

"Follow me, Lord Forska."

"Leyel, please."

"Oh, you're such a flirt." When she stood, she was even shorter and fatter than she had looked sitting down. "Follow me."

They conversed cheerfully about nothing much on the way down the corridor. Inside the elevator, they hooked their feet under the rail as the gravitic repulsion kicked in. Leyel was so used to weightlessness after all these years of using elevators on Trantor that he never noticed. But Zay let her arms float in the air and sighed noisily. "I *love* riding the elevator," she said. For the first time Leyel realized that weightlessness must be a great relief to someone carrying as many extra kilograms as Zay Wax. When the elevator stopped, Zay made a great show of staggering out as if under a great burden. "My idea of heaven is to live forever in gravitic repulsion."

"You can get gravitic repulsion for your apartment, if you live on the top floor."

"Maybe *you* can," say Zay. "But *I* have to live on a librarian's salary."

Leyel was mortified. He had always been careful not to flaunt his wealth, but then, he had rarely talked at any length with people who couldn't afford

498

gravitic repulsion. "Sorry," he said. "I don't think I could either, these days."

"Yes, I heard you squandered your fortune on a real bang-up funeral."

Startled that she would speak so openly of it, he tried to answer in the same joking tone. "I suppose you could look at it that way."

"I say it was worth it," she said. She looked slyly up at him. "I knew Hari, you know. Losing him cost humanity more than if Trantor's sun went nova."

"Maybe," said Leyel. The conversation was getting out of hand. Time to be cautious.

"Oh, don't worry. I'm not a snitch for the Pubs. Here's the Golden Archway into Indexing. The Land of Subtle Conceptual Connections."

Through the arch, it was as though they had passed into a completely different building. The style and trim were the same as before, with deeply lustrous fabrics on the walls and ceiling and floor made of the same smooth sound-absorbing plastic, glowing faintly with white light. But now all pretense at symmetry was gone. The ceiling was at different heights, almost at random; on the left and right there might be doors or archways, stairs or ramps, an alcove or a huge hall filled with columns, shelves of books and works of art surrounding tables where indexers worked with a half-dozen scriptors and lectors at once.

"The form fits the function," said Zay.

"I'm afraid I'm rubbernecking like a first-time visitors to Trantor."

"It's a strange place. But the architect was the daughter of an indexer, so she knew that standard, orderly, symmetrical interior maps are the enemy of freely connective thought. The finest touch — and the

499

most expensive too, I'm afraid—is the fact that from day to day the layout is rearranged."

"Rearranged! The rooms move?"

"A series of random routines in the master calculator. There are rules, but the program isn't afraid to waste space, either. Some days only one room is changed, moved off to some completely different place in the Indexing area. Other days, everything is changed. The only constant is the archway leading in. I really wasn't joking when I said you should come here and bellow."

"But—the indexers must spend the whole morning just finding their stations."

"Not at all. Any indexer can work from any station."

"Ah. So they just call up the job they were working on the day before."

"No. They merely pick up on the job that is already in progress on the station they happen to choose that day."

"Chaos!" said Leyel.

"Exactly. How do you think a good hyperindex is made? If one person alone indexes a book, then the only connections that book will make are the ones that person knows about. Instead, each indexer is forced to skim through what his predecessor did the day before. Inevitably he'll add some new connections that the other indexer didn't think of. The environment, the work pattern, everything is designed to break down habits of thought, to make everything surprising, everything *new*."

"To keep everybody off balance."

"Exactly. Your mind works quickly when you're running along the edge of the precipice."

"By that reckoning, acrobats should all be geniuses."

"Nonsense. The whole labor of acrobats is to learn their routines so perfectly they *never* lose balance. An acrobat who improvises is soon dead. But indexers, when they lose their balance, they fall into wonderful discoveries. That's why the indexes of the Imperial Library are the only ones worth having. They startle and challenge as you read. All the others are just—clerical lists."

"Deet never mentioned this."

"Indexers rarely discuss what they're doing. You can't really explain it anyway."

"How long has Deet been an indexer?"

"Not long, really. She's still a novice. But I hear she's very, very good."

"Where *is* she?"

Zay grinned. Then she tipped her head back and bellowed. "Deet!"

The sound seemed to be swallowed up at once in the labyrinth. There was no answer.

"Not nearby, I guess," said Zay. "We'll have to probe a little deeper."

"Couldn't we just *ask* somebody where she is?"

"Who would know?"

It took two more floors and three more shouts before they heard a faint answering cry. "Over here!"

They followed the sound. Deet kept calling out, so they could find her.

"I got the flower room today, Zay! Violets!"

The indexers they passed along the way all looked up—some smiled, some frowned.

"Doesn't it interfere with things?" asked Leyel. "All this shouting?"

501

"Indexers *need* interruption. It breaks up the chain of thought. When they look back down, they have to rethink what they were doing."

Deet, not so far away now, called again. "The smell is so intoxicating. Imagine—the same room twice in a month!"

"Are indexers often hospitalized?" Leyel asked quietly.

"For what?"

"Stress."

"There's no stress on this job," said Zay. "Just play. We come up here as a *reward* for working in other parts of the library."

"I see. This is the time when librarians actually get to *read* the books in the library."

"We all chose this career because we love books for their own sake. Even the old inefficient corruptible paper ones. Indexing is like—writing in the margins."

The notion was startling. "Writing in someone *else's* book?"

"It used to be done all the time, Leyel. How can you possibly engage in dialogue with the author without writing your answers and arguments in the margins? Here she is." Zay preceded him under a low arch and down a few steps.

"I heard a man's voice with you, Zay," said Deet.

"Mine," said Leyel. He turned a corner and saw her there. After such a long journey to reach her, he thought for a dizzying moment that he didn't recognize her. That the library had randomized the librarians as well as the rooms, and he had happened upon a woman who merely resembled his long-familiar wife; he would have to reacquaint himself with her from the beginning.

502

"I thought so," said Deet. She got up from her station and embraced him. Even this startled him, though she usually embraced him upon meeting. It's only the setting that's different, he told himself. I'm only surprised because usually she greets me like this at home, in familiar surroundings. And usually it's Deet arriving, not me.

Or was there, after all, a greater warmth in her greeting here? As if she loved him more in this place than at home? Or, perhaps, as if the new Deet were simply a warmer, more comfortable person?

I thought that she was comfortable with me.

Leyel felt uneasy, shy with her. "If I'd known my coming would cause so much trouble," he began. Why did he need so badly to apologize?

"What trouble?" asked Zay.

"Shouting. Interrupting."

"Listen to him, Deet. He thinks the world has stopped because of a couple of shouts."

In the distance they could hear a man bellowing someone's name.

"Happens all the time," said Zay. "I'd better get back. Some lordling from Mahagonny is probably fuming because I haven't granted his request for access to the Imperial account books."

"Nice to meet you," said Leyel.

"Good luck finding your way back," said Deet.

"Easy this time," said Zay. She paused only once on her way through the door, not to speak, but to slide a metallic wafer along an almost unnoticeable slot in the doorframe, above eye level. She turned back and winked at Deet. Then she was gone.

Leyel didn't ask what she had done—if it were his business, something would have been said. But he suspected that Zay had either turned on or turned

503

off a recording system. Unsure of whether they had privacy here from the library staff, Leyel merely stood for a moment, looking around. Deet's room really was filled with violets, real ones, growing out of cracks and apertures in the floor and walls. The smell was clear but not overpowering. "What is this room *for*?"

"For *me*. Today, anyway. I'm so glad you came."

"You never told me about this place."

"I didn't know about it until I was assigned to this section. Nobody talks about Indexing. We never tell outsiders. The architect died three thousand years ago. Only our own machinists understand how it works. It's like—"

"Fairyland."

"Exactly."

"A place where all the rules of the universe are suspended."

"Not all. We still stick with good old gravity. Inertia. That sort of thing."

"This place is right for you, Deet. This room."

"Most people go years without getting the flower room. It isn't always violets, you know. Sometimes climbing roses. Sometimes periwinkle. They say there's really a dozen flower rooms, but never more than one at a time is accessible. It's been violets for me both times, though."

Leyel couldn't help himself. He laughed. It was funny. It was delightful. What did this have to do with a library? And yet what a marvelous thing to have hidden away in the heart of this somber place. He sat down on a chair. Violets grew out of the top of the chairback, so that flowers brushed his shoulders.

"You finally got tired of staying in the apartment all day?" asked Deet.

Of course she would wonder why he finally came out, after all her invitations had been so long ignored. Yet he wasn't sure if he could speak frankly. "I needed to talk with you." He glanced back at the slot Zay had used in the doorframe. "Alone," he said.

Was that a look of dread that crossed her face?

"We're alone," Deet said quietly. "Zay saw to that. Truly alone, as we can't be even in the apartment."

It took Leyel a moment to realize what she was asserting. He dared not even speak the word. So he mouthed his question: Pubs?

"They never bother with the library in their normal spying. Even if they set up something special for you, there's now an interference field blocking out our conversation. Chances are, though, that they won't bother to monitor you again until you leave here."

She seemed edgy. Impatient. As if she didn't like having this conversation. As if she wanted him to get on with it, or maybe just get it over with.

"If you don't mind," he said. "I haven't interrupted you here before, I thought that just this once—"

"Of course," she said. But she was still tense. As if she feared what he might say.

So he explained to her all his thoughts about language. All that he had gleaned from Kispitorian's and Magolissian's work. She seemed to relax almost as soon as it became clear he was talking about his research. What did she dread, he wondered. Was she afraid I came to talk about our relationship? She hardly needed to fear *that*. He had no intention of making things more difficult by whining about things that could not be helped.

When he was through explaining the ideas that had come to him, she nodded carefully—as she had done a thousand times before, after he explained an idea or argument. "I don't know," she finally said. As so many times before, she was reluctant to commit herself to an immediate response.

And, as he had often done, he insisted. "But what do you *think*?"

She pursed her lips. "Just offhand—I've never tried a serious linguistic application of community theory, beyond jargon formation, so this is just my first thought—but try this. Maybe small isolated populations *guard* their language—jealously, because it's part of who they are. Maybe language is the most powerful ritual of all, so that people who have the same language are one in a way that people who can't understand each other's speech never are. We'd never know, would we, since everybody for ten thousand years has spoken Standard."

"So it isn't the size of the population, then, so much as—"

"How much they *care* about their language. How much it defines them as a community. A large population starts to think that everybody talks like them. They want to *distinguish* themselves, form a separate identity. Then they start developing jargons and slangs to separate themselves from others. Isn't that what happens to common speech? Children try to find ways of talking that their parents don't use. Professionals talk in private vocabularies so laymen won't know the passwords. All rituals for community definition."

506

Leyel nodded gravely, but he had one obvious doubt.

Obvious enough that Deet knew it, too. "Yes, yes, I know, Leyel. I immediately interpreted your question in terms of my own discipline. Like physicists who think that everything can be explained by physics."

Leyel laughed. "I thought of that, but what you said makes sense. And it would explain why the natural tendency of communities is to diversify language. We want a common tongue, a language of open discourse. But we also want private languages. Except a *completely* private language would be useless—whom would we talk to? So wherever a community forms, it creates at least a few linguistic barriers to outsiders, a few shibboleths that only insiders will know."

"And the more allegiance a person has to a community, the more fluent he'll become in that language, and the more he'll speak it."

"Yes, it makes sense,' said Leyel. "So easy. You see how much I need you?"

He knew that his words were a mild rebuke—why weren't you home when I needed you—but he couldn't resist saying it. Sitting here with Deet, even in this strange and redolent place, felt right and comfortable. How could she have withdrawn from him? To him, her presence was what made a place home. To her, this place was home whether he was there or not.

He tried to put it in words—in abstract words, so it wouldn't sting. "I think the greatest tragedy is when one person has more allegiance to his community than any of the other members."

507

Deet only half smiled and raised her eyebrows. She didn't know what he was getting at.

"He speaks the community language all the time," said Leyel. "Only nobody else ever speaks it to him, or not enough anyway. And the more he speaks it, the more he alienates the others and drives them away, until he's alone. Can you imagine anything more sad? Somebody who's filled up with a language, hungry to speak, to hear it spoken, and yet there's no one left who understands a word of it."

She nodded, her eyes searching him. Does she understand what I'm saying? He waited for her to speak. He had said all he dared to say.

"But imagine this," she finally said. "What if he left that little place where no one understood him, and went over a hill to a new place, and all of a sudden he heard a hundred voices, a thousand, speaking the words he had treasured all those lonely years. And then he realized that he had never really known the language at all. The words had hundreds of meanings and nuances he had never guessed. Because each speaker changed the language a little just by speaking it. And when he spoke at last, his own voice sounded like music in his ears, and the others listened with delight, with rapture, his music was like the water of life pouring from a fountain, and he knew that he had never been home before."

Leyel couldn't remember hearing Deet sound so — rhapsodic, that was it, she herself was singing. She is the person she was talking about. In this place, her voice is different, that's what she meant. At home with me, she's been alone. Here in the library she's found others who speak her secret language. It isn't that she didn't want our marriage to succeed. She hoped for it, but I never understood her. These

508

people did. Do. She's home here, that's what she's telling me.

"I understand," he said.

"Do you?" She looked searchingly into his face.

"I think so. It's all right."

She gave him a quizzical look.

"I mean, it's fine. It's good. This place. It's fine."

She looked relieved, but not completely. "You shouldn't be so *sad* about it, Leyel. This is a happy place. And you could do everything here that you ever did at home."

Except love you as the other part of me, and have you love me as the other part of you. "Yes, I'm sure."

"No, I mean it. What you're working on—I can see that you're getting close to something. Why not work on it *here*, where we can talk about it?"

Leyel shrugged.

"You *are* getting close, aren't you?"

"How do I know? I'm thrashing around like a drowning man in the ocean at night. Maybe I'm close to shore, and maybe I'm just swimming farther out to sea."

"Well, what do you have? Didn't we get closer just now?"

"No. This language thing—if it's just an aspect of community theory, it can't be the answer to human origin."

"Why not?"

"Because many primates have communities. A lot of other animals. Herding animals, for instance. Even schools of *fish*. Bees. Ants. Every multicelled organism is a community, for that matter. So if linguistic diversion grows out of community, then

509

it's inherent in prehuman animals and therefore isn't part of the definition of humanity."

"Oh. I guess not."

"Right."

She looked disappointed. As if she had really hoped they would find the answer to the origin question right there, that very day.

Leyel stood up. "Oh well. Thanks for your help."

"I don't think I helped."

"Oh, you did. You showed me I was going up a dead-end road. You saved me a lot of wasted—thought. That's progress, in science, to know which answers aren't true."

His words had a double meaning, of course. She had also shown him that their marriage was a dead-end road. Maybe she understood him. Maybe not. It didn't matter—he had understood *her*. That little story about a lonely person finally discovering a place where she could be at home—how could he miss the point of that?

"Leyel," she said. "Why not put your question to the indexers?"

"Do you think the library researchers could find answers where *I* haven't?"

"Not the research department. *Indexing.*"

"What do you mean?"

"Write down your questions. All the avenues you've pursued. Linguistic diversity. Primate language. And the other questions, the old ones. Archaeological, historical approaches. Biological. Kinship patterns. Customs. Everything you can think of. Just put it together as questions. And then we'll have them index it."

"Index my *questions*?"

"It's what we do—we read things and think of

other things that might be related somehow, and we connect them. We don't say what the connection means, but we know that it means something, that the connection is real. We won't give you answers, Leyel, but if you follow the index, it might help you to think of connections. Do you see what I mean?"

"I never thought of that. Do you think a couple of indexers might have the time to work on it?"

"Not a couple of us. *All* of us."

"Oh, that's absurd, Deet. I wouldn't even ask it."

"*I* would. We aren't supervised up here, Leyel. We don't meet quotas. Our job is to read and think. Usually we have a few hundred projects going, but for a day we could easily work on the same document."

"It would be a waste. I can't publish anything, Deet."

"It doesn't have to be published. Don't you understand? Nobody but us knows what we do here. We can take it as an unpublished document and work on it just the same. It won't ever have to go online for the library as a whole."

Leyel shook his head. "And then if they lead me to the answer—what, will we publish it with two hundred bylines?"

"It'll be *your* paper, Leyel. We're just indexers, not authors. You'll still have to make the connections. Let us try. Let us be *part* of this."

Suddenly Leyel understood why she was so insistent on this. Getting him involved with the library was her way of pretending she was still part of his life. She could believe she hadn't left him, if he became part of her new community.

Didn't she know how unbearable that would be? To see her here, so happy without him? To come here as just one friend among many, when once they had been—or he had thought they were—one indivisible soul? How could he possibly do such a thing?

And yet she wanted it, he could see it in the way she was looking at him, so girlish, so pleading that it made him think of when they were first in love, on another world—she would look at him like that whenever he insisted that he had to leave. Whenever she thought she might be losing him.

Doesn't she know who has lost whom?

Never mind. What did it matter if she didn't understand? If it would make her happy to have him pretend to be part of her new home, part of these librarians—if she wanted him to submit his life's work to the ministrations of these absurd indexers, then why not? What would it cost him? Maybe the process of writing down all his questions in some coherent order would help him. And maybe she was right—maybe a Trantorian index would help him solve the origin question.

Maybe if he came here, he could still be a small part of her life. It wouldn't be like marriage. But since that was impossible, then at least he could have enough of her here that he could remain himself, remain the person that he had become because of loving her for all these years.

"Fine," he said. "I'll write it up and bring it in."

"I really think we can help."

"Yes," he said, pretending to more certainty than he felt. "Maybe.' He started for the door.

"Do you have to leave already?"

He nodded.

"Are you sure you can find your way out?"

"Unless the rooms have moved."

512

"No, only at night."

"Then I'll find my way out just fine." He took a few steps toward her, then stopped.

"What?" she asked.

"Nothing."

"Oh." She sounded disappointed. "I thought you were going to kiss me good-bye." Then she puckered up like a three-year-old child.

He laughed. He kissed her—like a three-year-old—and then he left.

For two days he brooded. Saw her off in the morning, then tried to read, to watch the vids, anything. Nothing held his attention. He took walks. He even went topside once, to see the sky overhead—it was night, thick with stars. None of it engaged him. Nothing *held*. One of the vid programs had a moment, just briefly, a scene on a semiarid world, where a strange plant grew that dried out at maturity, broke off at the root, and then let the wind blow it around, scattering seeds. For a moment he felt a dizzying empathy with the plant as it tumbled by—am I as dry as that, hurtling through dead land? But no, he knew even that wasn't true, because the tumbleweed had life enough left in it to scatter seeds. Leyel had no seed left. That was scattered years ago.

On the third morning he looked at himself in the mirror and laughed grimly. "Is this how people feel before they kill themselves?" he asked. Of course not—he knew that he was being melodramatic. He felt no desire to die.

But then it occurred to him that if this feeling of uselessness kept on, if he never found anything to engage himself, then he might as well be dead, mightn't he, because his being alive wouldn't accomplish much more than keeping his clothes warm.

He sat down at the scriptor and began writing down questions. Then, under each question, he would explain how he had already pursued that particular avenue and why it didn't yield the answer to the origin question. More questions would come up then—and he was right, the mere process of summarizing his own fruitless research made answers seem tantalizingly close. It was a good exercise. And even if he never found an answer, this list of questions might be of help to someone with a clearer intellect—or better information—decades or centuries or millennia from now.

Deet came home and went to bed with Leyel still typing away. She knew the look he had when he was fully engaged in writing—she did nothing to disturb him. He noticed her enough to realize that she was carefully leaving him alone. Then he settled back into writing.

The next morning she awoke to find him lying in bed beside her, still dressed. A personal message capsule lay on the floor in the doorway from the bedroom. He had finished his questions. She bent over, picked it up, took it with her to the library.

"His questions aren't academic after all, Deet."

"I told you they weren't."

"Hari was right. For all that he seemed to be a dilettante, with his money and his rejection of the universities, he's a man of substance."

"Will the Second Foundation benefit, then, if he comes up with an answer to his question?"

"I don't know, Deet. Hari was the fortune-teller.

514

Presumably mankind is already human, so it isn't as if we have to start the process over."

"Do you think not?"

"What, should we find some uninhabited planet and put some newborns on it and let them grow up feral, and then come back in a thousand years and try to turn them human?"

"I have a better idea. Let's take ten thousand worlds filled with people who live their lives like animals, always hungry, always quick with their teeth and their claws, and let's strip away the veneer of civilization to expose to them what they really are. And then, when they see themselves clearly, let's come back and teach them how to be *really* human this time, instead of only having bits and flashes of humanity."

"All right. Let's do that."

"I knew you'd see it my way."

"Just make sure your husband finds out *how* the trick is done. Then we have all the time in the world to set it up and pull it off."

When the index was done, Deet brought Leyel with her to the library when she went to work in the morning. She did not take him to Indexing, but rather installed him in a private research room lined with vids—only instead of giving the illusion of windows looking out into an outside scene, the screens filled all the walls from floor to ceiling, so it seemed that he was on a pinnacle high above the scene, without walls or even a railing to keep him from falling off. It gave him flashes of vertigo when he looked around—only the door broke the illusion. For a moment he thought of asking for a different room. But then he remembered Indexing, and realized that maybe he'd do better work if he too felt a bit off balance all the time.

At first the indexing seemed obvious. He brought the first page of his questions to the lector display and began to read. The lector would track his pupils, so that whenever he paused to gaze at a word, other references would begin to pop up in the space beside the page he was reading. Then he'd glance at one of the references. When it was uninteresting or obvious, he'd skip to the next reference, and the first one would slide back on the display, out of the way, but still there if he changed his mind and wanted it.

If a reference engaged him, then when he reached the last line of the part of it on display, it would expand to full-page size and slide over to stand in front of the main text. Then, if this new material had been indexed, it would trigger new references— and so on, leading him farther and farther away from the original document until he finally decided to go back and pick up where he left off.

So far, this was what any index could be expected to do. It was only as he moved farther into reading his own questions that he began to realize the quirkiness of this index. Usually, index references were tied to important words, so that if you just wanted to stop and think without bringing up a bunch of references you didn't want, all you had to do was keep your gaze focused in an area of placeholder words, empty phrases like "If this were all that could be . . ." Anyone who made it a habit to read indexed works soon learned this trick and used it till it became reflex.

But when Leyel stopped on such empty phrases, references came up anyway. And instead of having a clear relationship to the text, sometimes the refer-

516

ences were perverse or comic or argumentative. For instance, he paused in the middle of reading his argument that archaeological searches for "primitiveness" were useless in the search for origins because all "primitive" cultures represented a decline from a star-going culture. He had written the phrase "All this primitivism is useful only because it predicts what we might become if we're careless and don't preserve our fragile links with civilization." By habit his eyes focused on the empty words "what we might become if." Nobody could index a phrase like that.

Yet they had. Several references appeared. And so instead of staying within his reveries, he was distracted, drawn to what the indexers had tied to such an absurd phrase.

One of the references was a nursery rhyme that he had forgotten he knew:

> *Wrinkly Grandma Posey*
> *Rockets all are rosy.*
> *Lift off, drift off,*
> *All fall down.*

Why in the world had the indexer put *that* in? The first thought that came to Leyel's mind was himself and some of the servants' children, holding hands and walking in a circle, round and round till they came to the last words, whereupon they threw themselves to the ground and laughed insanely. The sort of game that only little children could possibly think was fun.

Since his eyes lingered on the poem, it moved to the main document display and new references appeared. One was a scholarly article on the evolu-

517

tion of the poem, speculating that it might have arisen during the early days of starflight on the planet of origin, when rockets may have been used to escape from a planet's gravity well. Was that why this poem had been indexed to his article? Because it was tied to the planet of origin?

No, that was too obvious. Another article about the poem was more helpful. It rejected the early-days-of-rockets idea, because the earliest versions of the poem never used the word "rocket." The oldest extant version went like this:

> *Wrinkle down a rosy,*
> *Pock-a fock-a posy,*
> *Lash us, dash us,*
> *All fall down.*

Obviously, said the commentator, these were mostly nonsense words—the later versions had arisen because children had insisted on trying to make sense of them.

And it occurred to Leyel that perhaps this was why the indexer had linked this poem to his phrase—because the poem had once been nonsense, but we insisted on making sense out of it.

Was this a comment on Leyel's whole search for origins? Did the indexer think it was useless?

No—the poem had been tied to the empty phrase "what we might become if." Maybe the indexer was saying that human beings are like this poem—our lives make no sense, but we insist on making sense out of them. Didn't Deet say something like that once, when she was talking about the role of story-telling in community formation? The universe resists causality, she said. But human intelligence demands it. So we tell stories to impose causal relationships among the unconnected events of the world around us.

That includes ourselves, doesn't it? Our own lives are nonsense, but we impose a story on them, we sort our memories into cause-and-effect chains, forcing them to make sense even though they don't. Then we take the sum of our stories and call it our "self." This poem shows us the process—from randomness to meaning—and then we think our meanings are "true."

But somehow all the children had come to agree on the new version of the poem. By the year 2000 G.E., only the final and current version existed in all the worlds, and it had remained constant ever since. How was it that all the children on every world came to agree on the same version? How did the change spread? Did ten thousand kids on ten thousand worlds happen to make up the same changes?

It had to be word of mouth. Some kid somewhere made a few changes, and his version spread. A few years, and all the children in his neighborhood use the new version, and then all the kids in his city, on his planet. It could happen very quickly, in fact, because each generation of children lasts only a few years—seven-year-olds might take the new version as a joke, but repeat it often enough that five-year-olds think it's the true version of the poem, and within a few years there's nobody left among the children who remembers the old way.

A thousand years is long enough for the new version of the poem to spread. Or for five or a dozen new versions to collide and get absorbed into each other and then spread back, changed to worlds that had revised the poem once or twice already.

And as Leyel sat there, thinking these thoughts, he conjured up an image in his mind of a network of children, bound to each other by the threads of this poem, extending from planet to planet throughout the Empire, and then back through time, from one generation of children to the previous one, a three-dimensional fabric that bound all children together from the beginning.

And yet as each child grew up, he cut himself free from the fabric of that poem. No longer would he hear the words "Wrinkly Grandma Posey" and immediately join hands with the child next to him. He wasn't part of the song anymore.

But his own children were. And then his grandchildren. All joining hands with each other, changing from circle to circle, in a never-ending human chain reaching back to some long-forgotten ritual on one of the worlds of mankind—maybe, maybe on the planet of origin itself.

The vision was so clear, so overpowering, that when he finally noticed the lector display it was as sudden and startling as waking up. He had to sit there, breathing shallowly, until he calmed himself, until his heart stopped beating so fast.

He had found some part of his answer, though he didn't understand it yet. That fabric connecting all the children, that was part of what made us human, though he didn't know why. This strange and perverse indexing of a meaningless phrase had brought him a new way of looking at the problem. Not that the universal culture of children was a new idea. Just that he had never thought of it as having anything to do with the origin question.

Was this what the indexer meant by including this poem? Had the indexer also seen this vision?

Maybe, but probably not. It might have been nothing more than the idea of becoming something that made the indexer think of transformation — becoming old, like wrinkly Grandma Posey? Or it might have been a general thought about the spread of humanity through the stars, away from the planet of origin, that made the indexer remember how the poem seemed to tell of rockets that rise up from a planet, drift for a while, then come down to settle on a planet. Who knows what the poem meant to the indexer? Who knows why it occurred to her to link it with his document on that particular phrase?

Then Leyel realized that in his imagination, he was thinking of Deet making that particular connection. There was no reason to think it was her work, except that in his mind she was all the indexers. She had joined them, become one of them, and so when indexing work was being done, she was part of it. That's what it meant to be part of a community — all its works became, to a degree, your works. All that the indexers did, Deet was a part of it, and therefore Deet had done it.

Again the image of a fabric came to mind, only this time it was a topologically impossible fabric, twisted into itself so that no matter what part of the edge of it you held, you held the entire edge, and the middle, too. It was all one thing, and each part held the whole within it.

But if it was true, then when Deet came to join the library, so did Leyel, because she contained Leyel within her. So in coming here, she had not left him at all. Instead, she had woven him into a new fabric, so that instead of losing something he was gaining. He was part of all this, because *she* was, and so if he lost her it would only be because he rejected her.

Leyel covered his eyes with his hands. How did his meandering thoughts about the origin question lead him to thinking about his marriage? Here he thought he was on the verge of profound understanding, and then he fell back into self-absorption.

He cleared away all the references to "Wrinkly Grandma Posey" or "Wrinkle Down a Rosy" or whatever it was, then returned to reading his original document, trying to confine his thoughts to the subject at hand.

Yet it was a losing battle. He could not escape from the seductive distraction of the index. He'd be reading about tool use and technology, and how it could not be the dividing line between human and animal because there were animals that made tools and taught their use to others.

Then, suddenly, the index would have him reading an ancient terror tale about a man who wanted to be the greatest genius of all time, and he believed that the only thing preventing him from achieving greatness was the hours he lost in sleep. So he invented a machine to sleep for him, and it worked very well until he realized that the machine was having all his dreams. Then he demanded that his machine tell him what it was dreaming.

The machine poured forth the most astonishing, brilliant thoughts ever imagined by any man—far wiser than anything this man had ever written during his waking hours. The man took a hammer and smashed the machine, so that he could have his dreams back. But even when he started sleeping again, he was never able to come close to the clarity of thought that the machine had had.

Of course he could never publish what the machine had written—it would be unthinkable to put forth the product of a machine as if it were the work of a man. After the man died—in despair—people found the printed text of what the machine had written, and thought the man had written it and hidden it away. They published it, and he was widely acclaimed as the greatest genius who had ever lived.

This was universally regarded as an obscenely horrifying tale because it had a machine stealing part of a man's mind and using it to destroy him, a common theme. But why did the indexer refer to it in the midst of a discussion of tool-making?

Wondering about that led Leyel to think that this story itself was a kind of tool. Just like the machine the man in the story had made. The storyteller gave his dreams to the story, and then when people heard it or read it, his dreams—his nightmares—came out to live in their memories. Clear and sharp and terrible and true, those dreams they received. And yet if he tried to *tell* them the same truths, directly, not in the form of a story, people would think his ideas were silly and small.

And then Leyel remembered what Deet had said about how people absorb stories from their communities and take them into themselves and use these stories to form their own spiritual autobiography. They remember doing what the heroes of the stories did, and so they continue to act out each hero's character in their own lives, or, failing that, they measure themselves against the standard the story set for them. Stories become the human conscience, the human mirror.

Again, as so many other times, he ended these ruminations with his hands pressed over his eyes, trying to shut out—or lock in?—images of fabrics and mirrors, worlds and atoms, until finally, finally, he opened his eyes and saw Deet and Zay sitting in front of him.

No, leaning over him. He was on a low bed, and they knelt beside him.

"Am I ill?" he asked.

"I hope not,' said Deet. "We found you on the floor. You're exhausted, Leyel. I've been telling you—you have to eat, you have to get a normal amount of sleep. You're not young enough to keep up this work schedule."

"I've barely started."

Zay laughed lightly. "Listen to him, Deet. I told you he was so caught up in this that he didn't even know what day it was."

"You've been doing this for three weeks, Leyel. For the last week you haven't even come home. I bring you food, and you won't eat. People talk to you, and you forget that you're in a conversation, you just drift off into some sort of—trance. Leyel, I wish I'd never brought you here, I wish I'd never suggested indexing—"

"No!" Leyel cried. He struggled to sit up.

At first Deet tried to push him back down, insisting he should rest. It was Zay who helped him sit. "Let the man talk," she said. "Just because you're his wife doesn't mean you can stop him from talking."

"The index is wonderful," said Leyel. "Like a tunnel opened up into my own mind. I keep seeing light just *that* far out of reach, and then I wake up and it's just me alone on a pinnacle except for the pages up on the lector. I keep losing it—"

"No, Leyel, we keep losing *you*. The index is poisoning you, it's taking over your mind—"

"Don't be absurd, Deet. You're the one who suggested this, and you're right. The index keeps surprising me, making me think in new ways. There are some answers already."

"Answers?" asked Zay.

"I don't know how well I can explain it. What makes us human. It has to do with communities and stories and tools and—it has to do with you and me, Deet."

"I should hope we're human,' she said. Teasing him, but also urging him on.

"We lived together all those years, and we formed a community—with our children, till they left, and then just us. But we were like animals."

"Only sometimes," she said.

"I mean like herding animals, or primate tribes, or any community that's bound together only by the rituals and patterns of the present moment. We had our customs, our habits. Our private language of words and gestures, our dances, all the things that flocks of geese and hives of bees can do."

"Very primitive."

"Yes, that's right, don't you see? That's a community that dies with each generation. When we die, Deet, it will be all gone with us. Other people will marry, but none of them will know our dances and songs and language and—"

"Our children will."

"No, that's my point. They knew us, they even think they *know* us, but they were never part of the community of our marriage. Nobody is. Nobody *can* be. That's why, when I thought you were leaving me for this—"

"When did you think that I—"

"Hush, Deet," said Zay. "Let the man babble."

"When I thought you were leaving me, I felt like I was dead, like I was losing everything, because if you weren't part of our marriage, then there was nothing left. You see?"

"I don't see what that has to do with human origins, Leyel. I only know that I would never leave you, and I can't believe that you could think—"

"Don't distract him, Deet."

"It's the children. All the children. They play Wrinkly Grandma Posey, and then they grow up and don't play anymore, so the actual community of these particular five or six children doesn't exist anymore—but other kids are still doing the dance. Chanting the poem. For ten thousand years!"

"This makes us human? Nursery rhymes?"

"They're all part of the same community! Across all the empty space between the stars, there are still connections, they're still somehow the *same kids*. Ten thousand years, ten thousand worlds, quintillions of children, and they all knew the poem, they all did the dance. Story and ritual—it doesn't die with the tribe, it doesn't stop at the border. Children who never met face-to-face, who lived so far apart that the light from one star still hasn't reached the other, they belonged to the same community. We're human because we conquered time and space. We conquered the barrier of perpetual ignorance between one person and another. We found a way to slip my memories into your head, and yours into mine."

"But these are the ideas you already rejected, Leyel. Language and community and—"

"No! No, not just language, not just tribes of chimpanzees chattering at each other. *Stories*, epic tales that define a community, mythic tales that teach us how the world works, we use them to create each other. We became a different species, we became *human*, because we found a way to extend gestation beyond the womb, a way to give each child ten thousand parents that he'll never meet face-to-face."

Then, at last, Leyel fell silent, trapped by the inadequacy of his words. They couldn't tell what he had seen in his mind. If they didn't already understand, they never would.

"Yes," said Zay. "I think indexing your paper was a very good idea."

Leyel sighed and lay back down on the bed. "I shouldn't have tried."

"On the contrary, you've succeeded," said Zay.

Deet shook her head. Leyel knew why—Deet was trying to signal Zay that she shouldn't attempt to soothe Leyel with false praise.

"Don't hush me, Deet. I know what I'm saying. I may not know Leyel as well as you do, but I know truth when I hear it. In a way, I think Hari knew it instinctively. That's why he insisted on all his silly holodisplays, forcing the poor citizens of Terminus to put up with his pontificating every few years. It was his way of continuing to create them, of remaining alive within them. Making them feel like their lives had purpose behind them. Mythic and epic story, both at once. They'll all carry a bit of Hari Seldon within them just the way that children carry their parents with them to the grave."

At first Leyel could only hear the idea that Hari would have approved of his ideas of human origin. Then he began to realize that there was much more to what Zay had said than simple affirmation.

"You knew Hari Seldon?"

"A little," said Zay.

"Either tell him or don't," said Deet. "You can't take him this far in, and not bring him the rest of the way."

"I knew Hari the way you know Deet," said Zay.

"No," said Leyel. "He would have mentioned you."

"Would he? He never mentioned his students."

"He had thousands of students."

"I know, Leyel. I saw them come and fill his lecture halls and listen to the half-baked fragments of psychohistory that he taught them. But then he'd come away, here to the library, into a room where the Pubs never go, where he could speak words that the Pubs would never hear, and there he'd teach his real students. Here is the only place where the science of psychohistory lives on, where Deet's ideas about the formation of community actually have application, where your own vision of the origin of humanity will shape our calculations for the next thousand years."

Leyel was dumbfounded. "In the Imperial Library? Hari had his own college here in the library?"

"Where else? He had to leave us at the end, when it was time to go public with his predictions of the Empire's fall. Then the Pubs started watching him in earnest, and in order to keep them from finding us, he couldn't ever come back here again. It was the most terrible thing that ever happened to us. As if he died, for us, years before his body died. He was part of us, Leyel, the way that you and Deet are part of each other. She knows. She joined us before he left."

It stung. To have had such a great secret, and not to have been included. "Why Deet, and not me?"

"Don't you know, Leyel? Our little community's

528

survival was the most important thing. As long as you were Leyel Forska, master of one of the greatest fortunes in history, you couldn't possibly be part of this—it would have provoked too much comment, too much attention. Deet could come, because Commissioner Chen wouldn't care that much what she did—he never takes spouses seriously, just one of the ways he proves himself to be a fool."

"But Hari always meant for you to be one of us," said Deet. "His worst fear was that you'd go off half-cocked and force your way into the First Foundation, when all along he wanted you in this one. The Second Foundation."

Leyel remembered his last interview with Hari. He tried to remember—did Hari ever lie to him? He told him that Deet couldn't go to Terminus—but now that took on a completely different meaning. The old fox! He never lied at all, but he never told the truth, either.

Zay went on. "It was tricky, striking the right balance, encouraging you to provoke Chen just enough that he'd strip away your fortune and then forget you, but not so much that he'd have you imprisoned or killed."

"You were making that happen?"

"No, no, Leyel. It was going to happen anyway, because you're who you are and Chen is who he is. But there was a range of possibility, somewhere between having you and Deet tortured to death on the one hand, and on the other hand having you and Rom conspire to assassinate Chen and take control of the Empire. Either of those extremes would have made it impossible for you to be part of the Second Foundation. Hari was convinced—and so is Deet, and so am I—that you belong with us. Not dead. Not in politics. Here."

It was outrageous, that they should make such choices for him, without telling him. How could Deet have kept it secret all this time? And yet they were so obviously correct. If Hari had told him about this Second Foundation, Leyel would have been eager, proud to join it. Yet Leyel couldn't have been told, couldn't have joined them until Chen no longer perceived him as a threat.

"What makes you think Chen will ever forget me?"

"Oh, he's forgotten you, all right. In fact, I'd guess that by tonight he'll have forgotten everything he ever knew."

"What do you mean?"

"How do you think we've dared to speak so openly today, after keeping silence for so long? After all, we aren't in Indexing now."

Leyel felt a thrill of fear run through him. "They can hear us?"

"If they were listening. At the moment, though, the Pubs are very busy helping Rom Divart solidify his control of the Commission of Public Safety. And if Chen hasn't been taken to the radiation chamber, he soon will be."

Leyel couldn't help himself. The news was too glorious—he sprang up from his bed, almost danced at the news. "Rom's doing it! After all these years—overthrowing the old spider!"

"It's more important than mere justice or revenge," said Zay. "We're absolutely certain that a significant number of governors and prefects and military commanders will refuse to recognize the overlordship of the Commission of Public Safety. It will take Rom Divart the rest of his life just to put

530

down the most dangerous of the rebels. In order to concentrate his forces on the great rebels and pretenders close to Trantor, he'll grant an unprecedented degree of independence to many, many worlds on the periphery. To all intents and purposes, those outer worlds will no longer be part of the Empire. Imperial authority will not touch them, and their taxes will no longer flow inward to Trantor. The Empire is no longer Galactic. The death of Commissioner Chen—today—will mark the beginning of the fall of the Galactic Empire, though no one but us will notice what it means for decades, even centuries to come."

"So soon after Hari's death. Already his predictions are coming true."

"Oh, it isn't just coincidence," said Zay. "One of our agents was able to influence Chen just enough to ensure that he sent Rom Divart in person to strip you of your fortune. That was what pushed Rom over the edge and made him carry out this coup. Chen would have fallen—or died—sometime in the next year and a half no matter what we did. But I'll admit we took a certain pleasure in using Hari's death as a trigger to bring him down a little early, and under circumstances that allowed us to bring you into the library."

"We also used it as a test," said Deet. "We're trying to find ways of influencing individuals without their knowing it. It's still very crude and haphazard, but in this case we were able to influence Chen with great success. We had to do it—your life was at stake, and so was the chance of your joining us."

"I feel like a puppet," said Leyel.

"Chen was the puppet," said Zay. "You were the prize."

"That's all nonsense," said Deet. "Hari loved you,

531

I love you. You're a great man. The Second Foundation had to have you. And everything you've said and stood for all your life made it clear that you were hungry to be part of our work. Aren't you?"

"Yes," said Leyel. Then he laughed. "The index!"

"What's so funny?" asked Zay, looking a little miffed. "We worked very hard on it."

"And it was wonderful, transforming, hypnotic. To take all these people and put them together as if they were a single mind, far wiser in its intuition than anyone could ever be alone. The most intensely unified, the most powerful human community that's ever existed. If it's our capacity for storytelling that makes us human, then perhaps our capacity for indexing will make us something better than human."

Deet patted Zay's hand. "Pay no attention to him, Zay. This is clearly the mad enthusiasm of a proselyte."

Zay raised an eyebrow. "*I'm* still waiting for him to explain why the index made him *laugh*."

Leyel obliged her. "Because all the time, I kept thinking—how could librarians have done this? Mere librarians! And now I discover that these librarians are all of Hari Seldon's prize students. My questions were indexed by psychohistorians!"

"Not exclusively. Most of us *are* librarians. Or machinists, or custodians, or whatever—the psychologists and psychohistorians are rather a thin current in the stream of the library. At first they were seen as outsiders. Researchers. *Users* of the library, not members of it. That's what Deet's work has been for these last few years—trying to bind us all together into one community. She came here as a researcher too, remember? Yet now she has made everyone's allegiance to the library more important than any other loyalty. It's working beautifully too, Leyel, you'll see. Deet is a marvel."

"We're *all* creating it together," said Deet. "It helps that the couple of hundred people I'm trying to bring in are so knowledgeable and understanding of the human mind. They understand exactly what I'm doing and then try to help me make it work. And it *isn't* fully successful yet. As years go by, we have to see the psychology group teaching and accepting the children of librarians and machinists and medical officers, in full equality with their own, so that the psychologists don't become a ruling caste. And then intermarriage between the groups. Maybe in a hundred years we'll have a truly cohesive community. This is a democratic city-state we're building, not an academic department or a social club."

Leyel was off on his own tangent. It was almost unbearable for him to realize that there were hundreds of people who knew Hari's work, while Leyel didn't. "You have to teach me!" Leyel said. "Everything that Hari taught you, all the things that have been kept from me—"

"Oh, eventually, Leyel," said Zay. "At present, though, we're much more interested in what you have to teach *us*. Already, I'm sure, a transcription of the things you said when you first woke up is being spread through the library."

"It was recorded?" asked Leyel.

"We didn't know if you were going to go catatonic on us at any moment, Leyel. You have no idea how you've been worrying us. Of course we recorded it— they might have been your last words."

"They won't be. I don't feel tired at all."

"Then you're not as bright as we thought. Your body is dangerously weak. You've been abusing yourself terribly. You're not a young man, and we insist that you stay away from your lector for a couple of days."

"What, are you now my doctor?"

"Leyel," Deet said, touching him on his shoulder the way she always did when he needed calming. "You *have* been examined by doctors. And you've got to realize—Zay is First Speaker."

"Does that mean she's commander?"

"This isn't the Empire," said Zay, "and I'm not Chen. All that it means to be First Speaker is that I speak first when we meet together. And then, at the end, I bring together all that has been said and express the consensus of the group."

"That's right," said Deet. "*Everybody* thinks you ought to rest."

"*Everybody* knows about me?" asked Leyel.

"Of course," said Zay. "With Hari dead you're the most original thinker we have. Our work needs you. Naturally we care about you. Besides, Deet loves you so much, and we love *Deet* so much, we feel like we're all a little bit in love with you ourselves."

She laughed, and so did Leyel, and so did Deet. Leyel noticed, though, that when he asked whether they all *knew* of him, she had answered that they cared about him and loved him. Only when Zay said this did he realize that she had answered the question he really meant to ask.

"And while you're recuperating," Zay continued, "Indexing will have a go at your new theory—"

"Not a theory, just a proposal, just a *thought*—"

"—and a few psychohistorians will see whether it can be quantified, perhaps by some variation on the formulas we've been using with Deet's laws of com-

534

munity development. Maybe we can turn origin studies into a real science yet."

"Maybe," Leyel said.

"Feel all right about this?" asked Zay.

"I'm not sure. Mostly. I'm very excited, but I'm also a little angry at how I've been left out, but mostly I'm—I'm so relieved."

"Good. You're in a hopeless muddle. You'll do your best work if we can keep you off balance forever." With that, Zay led him back to the bed, helped him lie down, and then left the room.

Alone with Deet, Leyel had nothing to say. He just held her hand and looked up into her face, his heart too full to say anything with words. All the news about Hari's byzantine plans and a Second Foundation full of psychohistorians and Rom Divart taking over the government—that receded into the background. What mattered was this: Deet's hand in his, her eyes looking into his, and her heart, her self, her soul so closely bound to his that he couldn't tell and didn't care where he left off and she began.

How could he ever have imagined that she was leaving him? They had created each other through all these years of marriage. Deet was the most splendid accomplishment of his life, and he was the most valued creation of hers. We are each other's parent, each other's child. We might accomplish great works that will live on in this other community, the library, the Second Foundation. But the greatest work of all is the one that will die with us, the one that no one else will ever know of, because they remain perpetually outside. We can't even explain it to them. They don't have the language to understand us. We can only speak it to each other.

Afterword

"A THOUSAND DEATHS"

My early fiction won me a reputation for cruelty. The most memorable line was from a review in *Locus*: "Reading Card is like playing pattycake with Baby Huey." This sort of comment, however well-phrased, worried me more than a little. Clearly my fiction was giving the impression of being bloodier than most writers' stories, and yet that was never my intent. I'm an innately nonviolent person. I have almost never struck another person in anger; my custom in school when the subject of fighting came up was to talk my way out when I couldn't simply run. I never tortured animals. I don't enjoy pain. So why was I writing fiction that made grown men gag?

This story, "A Thousand Deaths," was one of a pair (the other is "Kingsmeat") that did most to earn me that reputation. It is the one story I've written that was so sickening that my wife couldn't finish reading it—she never has, as far as I know. And yet I couldn't see at the time—and still can't—how it could be written any other way.

The story is about noncompliance. It was triggered in part by a line in Robert Bolt's *A Man for All*

Seasons, which dwells in my memory in this form: "I do none harm, I think none harm, and if this be not enough to keep a man alive, then in faith I long not to live." There are times when a government, to stay in power, requires that certain people be broken, publicly. Their noncompliance with the will of the government is a constant refreshment to the enemies of the state. One thinks of Nelson Mandela, who, to be set free, has only to sign a statement renouncing violence as a means of obtaining the rights of his people. One thinks of the wonderful line from the movie *Gandhi* (which had not been made when I wrote this story, though the line expresses the theme of this story almost perfectly): "They can even kill me. What will they have then? My dead body. Not my obedience." It is the power of passive resistance, even in the face of a government that has the power to inflict the ultimate penalty, that eventually breaks the power of that government.

With "A Thousand Deaths" I simply did what satiric science fiction always does—I set up a society that exaggerates the point in question. In this case, it was the power of the state to inflict punishment in order to control the behavior of others, and my *what-if* was, "What if a government could, not just threaten to kill you, but actually kill you over and over until it finally got the confession it needed?" The mechanism was easy enough—I had already developed the drug somec and had stolen the idea of brain-taping from many other writers years before, for my *Worthing Chronicle* series. What mattered to me, though, was to focus on the point where coercion ultimately breaks down, and that is on the rock of truth. The government kills the story's hero, trying to break him to the point where he will confess his wrong, and confess the rightness of the government. The trouble is that the government will only measure his confession against a standard too high for him to meet. It isn't enough that his confession be passionate. It must also be *believed*. And that is the one thing that the hero cannot deliver—a believable confession. He can't believe it himself; neither can anyone else. That is what coercion cannot do. It can win compliance from fearful people. But it cannot win belief. The heart is an unstormable citadel.

How, tell me please, could I possibly have told this story without making you, the reader, believe absolutely in the hero's deaths? You have to experience some shadow of the suffering in order to understand the impossibility of his confession. If you find the story unbearable, remember that there have been far more deaths than this, and more terrible ones as well, in the same struggle in the real world.

A footnote: In the late seventies, I set this story in a United States ruled by a Soviet government. In this I was not seriously predicting something I believed likely to happen. But I was trying to place the story of a totalitarian state within the United States if only to bring home the idea to American readers, who, outside of the experience of American blacks in many a Southern town, are ignorant of the suffering and terror of totalitarianism. Once the decision to set the story here was made, I had two choices: to show an America ruled by a homegrown demagogue, or to show an America ruled by a foreign conqueror. I rejected the former, in part because at that time it had lately become a cliché of American literateurs to pretend that the only danger to the U.S. was from conservative extremists. I preferred to show America ruled by the most cruel and efficient totalitarian system ever to exist on the face of the Earth: the Stalinist version of the Communist Party.

The events of 1989 in eastern Europe do not change this; it was the very unwillingness of Gorbachev to play Stalin that led to the unshackling of the captive nations. Had he been willing to resort to the machine gun and the tank, as his predecessors did, there would be no more Solidarity, no second Prague Spring, no holes in the Berlin Wall, no bullet-riddled body of Ceausescu, no Hungarian border open to Austria. Or would there? Gorbachev was the man who brought Russia over that moral cusp—but I think it would have had to come eventually, with him or someone else. "A Thousand Deaths" is a true story, and I used the Soviets in it because they are the most recent world power to prove that it is true.

"CLAP HANDS AND SING"

Once, back in the mid–1970s, I had a conversation with a young woman I had once thought myself to be in love with. "I had such a crush on you before you went on your mission," she said. "And the poems you wrote me while you were gone . . . I thought something would come of it when you got home. But when you returned from Brazil, I waited and waited and you never even called."

"I thought of calling," I said. "Often."

"But you never did. And on the rebound from you I fell in love with someone else."

Here's the funny thing: I never guessed how *she*

felt. One reason I never called her was because I thought she might think I was weird to try to convert a friendship to something more. Thus do adolescents manage to work at cross-purposes often enough to make romantic tragedies possible.

In the years since, I have found a much deeper love and stronger commitment than anything I ever imagined in those days. But when I was exploring the idea of time travel, and thought of an ironic story in which two people, unknown to each other, both journey back in time to have a perfect night together, my mind naturally turned to that moment of impotent frustration when I realized that this young lady and I, had I but acted a bit differently, might have ended up together. Since it's much easier to use real events than to make up phony ones, I stole from my own life to find, I hoped, that sense of bittersweet memory that is the stuff of movie romances.

"DOGWALKER"

Cyberpunk was all the rage, and I was driving home from ArmadilloCon, the science fiction convention held in Austin, the see of the bishop of cyberpunk, Bruce Sterling. I had long had an ambivalent feeling toward cyberpunk. Bruce Sterling's ideas about science fiction fascinated me greatly, if only because he was the one person I could hear talking about science fiction in terms that weren't either warmed-over James Blish and Damon Knight or stolen from the moldering corpse of Modernism that still stinks to high heaven in the English departments of American universities. In short, Sterling actually had Ideas instead of Echoes.

540

At the same time, I could not help but be a bit disgusted at what was being done in the name of cyberpunk. William Gibson, though quite talented, seemed to be writing the same story over and over again. Furthermore, it was the same self-serving story that was being churned out in every creative writing course in America and published in every little literary magazine at least once an issue: the suffering artist who is alienated from his society and is struggling to find out a reason to live. My answer is easy enough: An artist who is alienated from his society *has* no reason to live—as an artist, anyway. You can only live as an artist when you're firmly connected to the community to whom you offer your art.

But the worst thing about cyberpunk was the shallowness of those who imitated it. Splash some drugs onto brain-and-microchip interface, mix it up with some vague sixties-style counterculture, and then use really self-conscious, affected language, and you've got cyberpunk. Never mind that the actual stories being told were generally clichés that were every bit as stupid and derivative as the worst of the stuff Bruce Sterling had initially rebelled against. Even if the underlying stories had been highly original, stylistic imitation and affectation are crimes enough to make a literary movement worthy of the death sentence.

So, being the perverse and obnoxious child that I am, I challenged myself: Is the derivativeness of cyberpunk the source or a symptom of its emptiness? Is it possible to write a good story that uses all the clichés of cyberpunk? The brain-microchip interface, the faked-up slang, the drugs, the counterculture . . . Could I, a good Mormon boy who watched the

541

sixties through the wrong end of the binoculars, write a convincing story in that mode—and also tell a tale that would satisfy *me* as good fiction?

One thing was certain—I couldn't imitate anybody else's *story*. It was the language, the *style* that I was imitating. So I had to violate my own custom and start, not with the story, but with the voice. With a monologue. The first two paragraphs of *Dogwalker* were the first two I wrote, pretty much as they stand now. The plot came only after I had the voice and the character of the narrator pretty well established.

I got the thing done soon after returning home, and sent it off to Gardner Dozois at *Asimov's*. I expected the story to get bounced. I had a mental picture of Gardner staggering out into the hall at Davis Publications, gagging and choking, holding out the manuscript as if it were a bag of burning dog dung. "Look at this. *Card* is trying to write cyberpunk now." Instead, Gardner sent me a contract. It rather spoiled my plans—I expected to use the story as my entry at Sycamore Hill that summer, but since it had sold I couldn't do that. The result was that I ended up writing my novella "Pageant Wagon" during that workshop, so it wasn't a total loss.

In the meantime, however, Gardner never published "Dogwalker." He held it two-and-a-half years before I finally sent a note pointing out that our contract had expired and if they didn't have immediate plans to publish it, I wanted it back to sell it elsewhere. At that point they seemed to have suddenly remembered that they had it, and it was scheduled and published barely in time to be included in this book.

In a way, though, Gardner did me a favor—per-

542

haps on purpose. By holding the story so long, he had seen to it that "Dogwalker" appeared in print *after* the spate of cyperpunk imitations was over. The story was not so clearly pegged as derivative. And though it was clearly not like a "typical Card story" on its surface, it could more easily be received as my work than as pale-imitation Gibson. Thus was I spared the fate of appearing as pathetic as, say, Barbra Streisand singing disco with the Bee Gees.

"BUT WE TRY NOT TO ACT LIKE IT"

For a short time, Kristine's and my favorite restaurant in Salt Lake City was the Savoy, a purportedly English restaurant that nevertheless had wonderful food. We brought friends, we went alone—we did everything we could to make that restaurant succeed. Furthermore it was always crowded. And six months later, it was out of business.

It happens over and over. TV shows I like are doomed to cancellation. Authors I fall in love with stop writing the kind of book I loved. (Come on, Mortimer and Rendell! Rumpole and Wexford are the reason you were born! As for you, Gregory McDonald, write Fletch or die!) Trends in science fiction and fantasy that I applaud quickly vanish; the ones that make me faintly sick seem to linger like herpes. For one reason or another, my tastes are just not reflected in the real world.

That's what gave rise to this story. Unfortunately, I never let the story rise above its origin. I have learned since then that I shouldn't write a story from a single idea, but rather should wait for a second, unrelated idea, so that out of their confluence can

543

come something truly alive. The result is that this story bears the curse of most of science fiction—it is idea-driven rather than character-driven, which means that it is ultimately forgettable. That doesn't mean it's valueless—I hope it's kind of fun to read it once. But you'll certainly not be rewarded for reading it again. You already received everything it had to offer on the first reading.

"I PUT MY BLUE GENES ON"

Jim Baen wrote an editorial in *Galaxy* magazine in which he called on science fiction writers to stop writing the same old "futures" and take a look at what science was doing *now*. Where, for example, were the stories extrapolating on current research in recombinant DNA?

I was still working at *The Ensign* magazine then, and Jay and Lane and I took this as a personal challenge. Naturally, in the tradition of young sci-fi writers, I mechanically took the idea of gene-splicing (I'd been reading *Scientific American* like a good boy, so I could fake it up pretty well), carried it to an extreme, and served it up in a stereotypical plot about two nations in a life-and-death struggle—only one of the nations doesn't realize that the other one was wiped out long ago and that its struggle is now against the very world they have destroyed. As a let's-stop-messing-up-the-world polemic, I think the story still holds up pretty well. As an artful story, it's definitely a work of my youth. Recombining DNA has been treated far better since then, both in my own stories (*Wyrms, Speaker for the Dead*) and in the works of writers who've done the subject more justice. (I think particularly of the magnificent work

Octavia Butler has done with *Dawn, Adulthood Rites*, and *Imago*.) If you want proof that I was but an adolescent playing at fiction-writing, you have only to look at the title, a bad pun on a fun-but-dumb popular song that was, I believe, written as the theme music for a jeans ad.

I notice now, however, that some later interests of mine were already cropping up in "I Put My Blue Genes On." For one thing, I actually put Brazilians in space. I was not the first to do it, but it was the beginning of my deliberate effort to try to get American sci-fi writers to realize that the future probably does *not* belong to America. Science fiction of the pre-World War I era always seemed to put Englishmen and Frenchmen into space; now, in this post-imperialist world, we think of that as a rather quaint idea. I firmly believe that in fifty years the idea of Americans leading the world anywhere will be just as anachronistic, and only those of us who put Brazilians, Thais, Chinese, and Mexicans into space will look at all prescient.

Of course, maybe I'm wrong about the specific prediction I'm making. But there's another reason to open up science fiction to other cultures, and that is that science fiction is the one lasting American contribution to prose literature. In every other area, we're derivative to the—well, not to the core, because in those areas we *have* no core. Nobody in other countries aspires to write Westerns, and nobody in Russia or Germany or Japan looks to Updike or Bellow to teach them how to write "serious" fiction. They already have literary traditions older and better than our so-called best. But in science fiction, they *all* look to us. They want to write science fiction, too, because those who read it in every nation see it as the fiction of possibility, the fiction of strangeness. It's the one genre now that allows the writer to do satire that isn't recognized as satire, to do metaphysical fiction that isn't seen as philosophical or religious proselytizing. In short, it is the freest, most open literature in the world today, and it is the one literature that foreign writers are learning first and foremost from Americans.

Why, then, do science fiction writers persist in imagining only American futures? Our audience is much broader than these shores. And there are countries where our words are taken far more seriously than they are here. If we actually aspire to change the world with our fiction—and I can't think of any other reason for ever setting pen to paper— then we ought to be talking to the world. And one sure way to let the world know we are talking to them is to put them—citizens of other countries, children of other cultures—into our futures. To do otherwise is to slap them in the face and say, "I have seen the future, and you aren't there." Well, I *have* seen the future, and they *are* there—in great numbers, with great power. I want my voice to have been one of the voices they listened to on their way up to be king of the hill. And, in "I Put My Blue Genes On," I took my first step along that road.

"IN THE DOGHOUSE" (with Jay A. Parry)

What if the aliens don't come to us in alien form? What if they come in a form we already recognize, that we already think we understand? Jay Parry and I toyed with the idea of telling this story differently— with the aliens coming in the form of an oppressed minority. American Indians or blacks, we thought.

But the problems at the time seemed insurmountable—particularly the political problems. It's a very tricky business, for a white writer to try to express the black point of view without being politically incorrect. It seemed to me then that there were things that black writers could say about and on behalf of blacks that white writers couldn't, not without the message being taken wrong. In the years since then, I've learned that a writer of any race or sex or religion or nation can write about any other race or sex or religion or nation; he only needs to:

1. Do enough research that he doesn't make an ass of himself.
2. Tell the truth as he sees it without pandering or condescending to any group.
3. Have a thick enough skin to accept the fact that he'll be impaled with a thousand darts no matter how well he does at 1 and 2.

Being timid, Jay and I worked out the plot using animals that have been as firmly pegged in our human prejudices as any human group. Faithful, beloved dogs. Man's best friend. All the same possibilities were there—the White Man's Burden, the condescending affection (some of my best friends are dogs), and, above all, the rigid determination to keep them in their place.

"THE ORIGINIST"

In my review column in *The Magazine of Fantasy and Science Fiction*, I wrote a diatribe deploring the 1980s trend of trying to turn sci-fi authors' private worlds into generic brand name universes where

547

other writers can romp. It began with *Star Trek*, and it was not part of anybody's grand design. There were these *Star Trek* fans, you see, who got impatient with Paramount's neglect of their heroes and began to write their *own* stories about the crew of the starship Enterprise. (In a way this was singularly appropriate: The original series was written and performed like somebody's garage production anyway, so why not continue the tradition?) Legend has it that Paramount at first intended to sue, until it dawned on them that there might be *money* in publishing never-filmed stories about Kirk, Spock, and the other crew members of *Wagon Train among the Cheap Interplanetary Sets*. They were right, to the tune of many readers and many dollars. A new industry was born: Science fiction written in somebody else's poorly imagined but passionately studied universe.

I suppose it was inevitable that publishers who weren't getting any of those *Star Trek* bucks would try to turn other successful imagined futures into equally lucrative backdrops where one writer's work would be as good as any others'. There ensued in the late 1980s a spate of novels set "in the world of____," in which journeyman writers who often didn't have a clue about the inner truth that led the Old Pro to create his or her world tried to set their own stories in it. The result was stories that nobody was proud of and nobody cared about.

What was unspoken (I hope) was the true premise of all these worlds-as-brand-names books: The readers won't be able to tell the difference. Here's what they found out: Unlike the *Star Trek* audience, the readers of most science fiction *can* tell the difference and they care very much. Written science fiction has

548

an author-driven audience. The *real* science fiction audience doesn't want to read John Varley's Dune novel or Lisa Goldstein's Lensman novel or Howard Waldrop's Dragonworld novel. (Well, actually, I would *love* to read Howard Waldrop's Dragonworld novel, but not for any reason I'm proud of.)

So I laid down the law in my column. Writers should not waste their time or talent trying to tell stories in someone else's universe. Furthermore, established writers should not cooperate in the wasting of younger writers' talent by allowing their worlds to be franchised.

As soon as that column hit print, Martin Harry Greenberg mentioned to me that he was preparing a festschrift anthology commemorating Isaac Asimov's fiftieth year in publishing, a book called *Foundation's Friends*. And for this one anthology, Dr. Asimov was allowing the participants to set stories within his own closely-held fictional universes, using his own established characters. We could actually write robot stories using the three laws and positronic brains and Susan Calvin. We could actually write Foundation stories using Hari Seldon and Trantor and Terminus and the Mule.

Suddenly I was sixteen years old again and I remembered the one story I wanted so badly to read, the one that Asimov had never written—the story of how the Second Foundation actually got started in the library at Trantor.

Did I forget that I had just gotten through banning the franchising of universes for all time? No. I simply have a perverse streak in me that says that whenever somebody lays down a law, that law is meant to be broken—even when I was the lawgiver. So I wrote

549

"The Originist" as both a tribute to and, perhaps, a sidelight on Asimov's masterwork.

This doesn't mean that I think the law I stated isn't true. In fact, I stand by it as firmly as ever. It's just that, like all laws, this one *can* be circumvented if you work hard enough. The reason why franchised worlds generally don't work is because the junior writers don't understand the original world well enough, don't know what it is about the original writer's work that made his stories work, and don't feel enough personal responsibility to do their best work under these circumstances. Well, in my arrogance, I thought I *did* know the Foundation universe well enough—not in the trivial details, but in the overall sweep of the story, in what it *means*. (Yes, I've read *Decline and Fall*, too, but that isn't the foundation of Foundation, either.) Also, I thought I understood something of how the stories worked—the delight of discovering that no matter how many curtains you peel back, you never find the *real* curtain or the *real* man behind it in Asimov's Oz. There are always plans underlying plans, causes hidden behind plausible causes.

And, finally, I had a compelling story of my own to tel!. I had already made a stab at it, with a fragment of a novel that was to be called *Genesis*—a book I may still write someday. In it I was trying to show the borderline between human and animal, the exact comma in the punctuational model of evolution that marked the transition between non-human and human. For me, that borderline is the human universal of storytelling; that is what joins a community together across time; that is what preserved a human identity after death and defines it in life. Without stories, we aren't human; with them, we are. But *Genesis* became impossible to write, in part because to do it properly I had to visit Kashmir and Ethiopia, two places where it is not terribly safe to travel these days.

But I *could* develop many of the same themes, though at a greater distance, in my story of "The Originist." Moreover, Asimov himself had broached a related question in *Foundation*, when he presented a character who was searching through libraries in order to find the planet of origin of the human species. I was able to take a purely Asimovian point— the futility of secondary research—and interlayer it with my own point—the fundamental role of storytelling in shaping human individuals and communities. I went further in my effort to make "The Originist" a true Foundation story. I also used a form that Asimov has perfected, but I had never tried before: the story in which almost nothing happens except dialogue. Asimov can make this work because of the piercing clarity of his writing and the sublime intelligence of his ideas—it is never boring listening to his characters discuss ideas, because you are never lost and the ideas are always worth hearing. The challenge was to come as close as I could to matching that clarity; I had to trust that others would find my ideas as interesting as I had always found Asmimov's.

So it was that, even though I knew "The Originist" would never be received as standing on its own, I poured a novel's worth of love and labor into it. In the long run, I proved my own law—I wrote this story at the expense of a purely Orson Scott Card novel that will probably never be written. Yet I think it was worth doing—once—partly to prove it could be done well (if in fact I did it well), and partly

because I'm proud of the story itself: because of the
achievement of it, because of what the story says,
and because it is a tribute to the writer that I firmly
believe is the finest writer of American prose in our
time, bar none.